Beneath the
Cypress Tree

Margaret Pemberton is the bestselling author of over thirty novels in many different genres, some of which are contemporary in setting and some historical.

She has served as Chairman of the Romantic Novelists' Association and has three times served as a committee member of the Crime Writers' Association. Born in Bradford, she is married to a Londoner, has five children and two dogs, and lives in Whitstable, Kent. Apart from writing, her passions are tango, travel, English history and the English countryside.

Beneath the Cypress Tree

MARGARET PEMBERTON

PAN BOOKS

First published 2017 by Pan Books
an imprint of Pan Macmillan
20 New Wharf Road, London N1 9RR
Associated companies throughout the world
www.panmacmillan.com

ISBN 978-1-4472-4867-5

1 3 5 7 9 8 6 4 2

A CIP catalogue record for this book is available from the British Library.

Typeset in Ehrhardt MT Std by Palimpsest Book Production Ltd, Falkirk, Stirlingshire
Printed and bound by CPI Group (UK) Ltd, Croydon, CR0 4YY

To Cheryl Warren

Without friends, no one would choose to live,
though he had all other goods.

ARISTOTLE

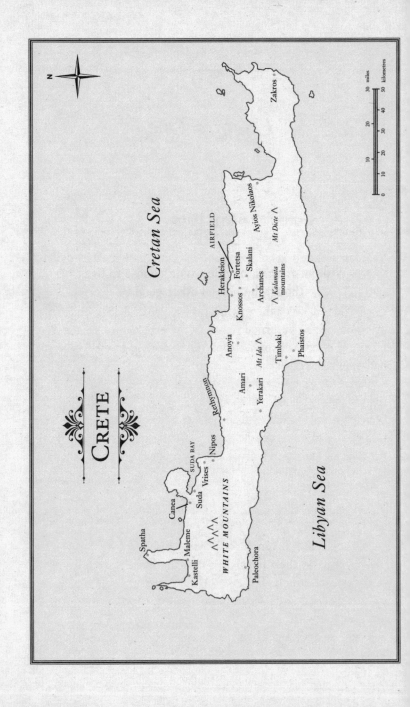

Chapter One

APRIL 1936

'It'll be a grand jaunt, lass, seeing your college friends and Oxford again.'

The pride Ella Tetley's father always took in saying the word 'Oxford' was there in full measure, and Ella knew that by the time she returned home in the early hours of the next morning, the whole of Wilsden village would know where she had spent the day.

Because she understood the reason for her being such a talking point – no one else in the village had ever had the benefit of an Oxford education, far less received a first-class honours in classical archaeology – she was always patient about the interest shown in her. Her embarrassment at such attention was, however, often acute.

'I've made you a packed lunch,' her mother said, fussing around her. 'You've got a long day ahead of you. I don't want you going hungry.'

As her reunion lunch with Kate and Daphne was taking place in one of their favourite Oxford pubs, Ella had no need of the packed lunch. To have said so, though, would have been to hurt her mother's feelings, so she put the sandwiches into her shoulder-bag.

From a rocking chair in a corner of the kitchen her

grandfather said, 'Did yer give 'er drip and bread, Alice? I allus liked drip and bread fer me snap.'

'Of course I haven't given Ella drip and bread!' Alice Tetley's outrage was profound.

Aware that he'd scored a bullseye, Jos Tetley, once the village rag-and-bone man, cackled with laughter and then said, grinning toothlessly across at Ella, 'Is your young man tecking thee to t'station?'

'If you mean Sam Jowett, he's a friend, Granddad, not my young man; and yes, he is taking me to the station.'

Alice exchanged a meaningful glance with her husband. If Sam Jowett wasn't Ella's 'young man', it wasn't for the want of his trying. And as he was the son of a doctor and he, too, would soon be a qualified doctor, nothing would have pleased her and Alfred more than that Sam's efforts should meet with success.

The clock above the kitchen table struck seven and Alfred Tetley slid his packed lunch into a pocket of his donkey jacket. 'I'll 'appen see you as I come off my shift and as you start yours,' he said to Alice, and then, to Ella, 'You'd be better off waiting for t'Jowett lad out on t'doorstep than in t'kitchen.'

Recognizing the truth of this, Ella buttoned up her coat, slid the strap of her bag over her shoulder, gave her mother a goodbye kiss and followed her father out of the house.

Once on the doorstep with the door closed behind her, she watched her father stride off in the direction of the local mill. Their house was one of a small row of terraced cottages on the outskirts of the village and there were no houses on the other side of the road, only rising open land and, at the foot of the rise, a field – the retirement home of Bessie, the piebald mare that had once pulled her granddad's rag-and-bone cart.

As she waited for Sam to turn into the road on his motorbike and sidecar, she thought of the past year and of how different it had been from Kate's year, or Daphne's. With a degree in archaeology under her belt and funded by middle-class parents, Kate had enrolled for postgraduate study in prehistoric, Greek and Roman pottery at the world-renowned British School at Athens. Daphne, the daughter of an earl, had left university with a first in Classics and had put further study or job-hunting on the back-burner. Instead she had been presented at Court and had thrown herself wholeheartedly into the glamorous social life of a debutante.

The rarefied options open to Kate and Daphne had not been open to Ella. She'd had to find work straight away and had done so on a Roman dig in Somerset. What she really wanted, though, was a position on a dig abroad. There was a huge dig presently taking place at Amarna, in Egypt, and a dig on the Greek island of Ithaca that, though far smaller than the Amarna dig, had the potential of becoming just as big, if the suspected existence of a Bronze Age temple there was confirmed.

The sound of Sam's motorbike and sidecar trundling up the road broke into her thoughts. He came to a halt a few feet away from her. Keeping the engine ticking over, he said in amusement, 'You're looking preoccupied. What is it this time? Roman coins? Roman votive offerings?'

'Neither,' she said amiably. Ignoring the sidecar, she straddled the pillion and covered her flame-red hair with a scarf to stop it blowing in her eyes. 'I was wondering how I could get a position on a dig abroad. Egypt at a pinch, but Greece for preference.'

'Do you have to work on a dig? Why not try for a position at a museum?'

She knew what he really meant was why couldn't she get a permanent job near to home? A job that would keep her in Yorkshire, so that he would be able to see more of her.

As he revved the engine, she held on to his waist, shouting above the engine noise, 'Museum work is boring, compared to working on a dig. Being on a dig is where all the exciting things happen. Can you imagine how Howard Carter felt breaking through into Pharaoh Tutankhamun's tomb? Or Sir Arthur Evans when he realized he'd unearthed the palace of a Bronze Age Cretan king?'

Sam couldn't and, knowing it was useless to try, put the bike into gear.

Seconds later they were rounding the corner by the Ling Bob public house and roaring up the short hill that led away from Wilsden's outskirts. From the top of the hill there was a magnificent view of the moors and then, for the next five miles, it was all downhill, gently at first and then, as they neared Bradford's soot-blackened city centre, far more steeply.

They halted outside the Exchange station with fifteen minutes to spare before her train left.

'Have you time for a quick cup of tea?' Sam took off his motorcycle goggles and ran a hand over straw-coloured hair.

'I don't think so. If the train is already in the station I'd like to get straight on it, if you don't mind, Sam.'

He said, hiding his disappointment, 'Then let's get your ticket and maybe tomorrow night we could go to the cinema? *The Scarlet Pimpernel* is showing at the Rialto.'

'That would be lovely.' She meant it. The film starred Leslie Howard and he was one of her favourite actors.

Once she had her ticket, Sam found her an empty carriage on the train. 'Because I know you like reading when you're travelling,' he said as she stepped into the carriage and he closed the door after her, 'and, with luck, there'll be no one to disturb you all the way to Oxford.'

The carriage window was down and she rested her arms on its sill. 'Where are you going from here, Sam? Straight back to Wilsden?'

'No. I'm going to head to Ilkley and blow the cobwebs away by riding over the moor.'

'Then take my picnic lunch, because I have no need of it.' Opening her shoulder-bag, she took out the packet of sandwiches her mother had given her and handed them to him. 'Mum made them, and I don't know what's in them. Probably potted meat.'

All down the length of the train, carriage doors were closing. The whistle blew. Hasty goodbyes were shouted. Sam wished he'd had the nerve to kiss her goodbye before she'd stepped into the carriage, but as Ella didn't regard him in a romantic light, a busy station platform hadn't seemed the best place to try, yet again, to get her to think differently about him.

A much better time and place would be when they went to see *The Scarlet Pimpernel*.

''Bye,' he shouted as, amid great billows of steam, the train began moving away. 'I'll be here tonight to meet you off the last train!'

'Thank you,' she shouted back at him. The last train from Oxford didn't get in to Bradford until midnight, well after buses to Wilsden had stopped running. Without Sam meeting her and giving her a lift home, she would have had to get a taxi, and a taxi to Wilsden would have been expensive. Gratefully she blew him a kiss.

Her gesture transformed the expression on Sam's good-natured face. Smiling broadly, he blew a kiss back.

Ella, busy closing the window, saw neither his reaction nor his response.

As the train steamed out of the station she made herself comfortable in a corner seat and, with Sam already far from her thoughts, took a copy of *The Palace of Minos* out of her shoulder-bag. Written by Sir Arthur Evans, it was his own account of his discovery of the Bronze Age palace that he had spent more than thirty years excavating at Knossos, in Crete.

Ever since she had been a child, Ella had been enchanted by the legends of ancient Greece. Her favourite story had been

5

that of Theseus slaying the Minotaur, the half-man, half-bull monster that lived in the centre of a labyrinth at the palace of King Minos.

As he had excavated at Knossos, Sir Arthur had found hundreds and hundreds of artefacts linking history to legend: coins showing images of a labyrinth, and others bearing the features of a Minotaur; a wall painting depicting a young man somersaulting over the back of a bull; drinking vessels shaped like the head of a bull; ivory figurines of bull-leapers in mid-air. As the Knossos dig had continued, it had become obvious that Sir Arthur had unearthed not only a palace, but a previously unknown civilization – a civilization that he had named Minoan.

Though all the major work of excavation was now complete, excavations of tomb sites near to the palace were still taking place, and Kate's older brother, Kit, was field director at one of them.

When Kate had casually mentioned this to Ella and Daphne, even Daphne had been impressed. They had been walking down a busy corridor towards the quad and, moving the pile of books she was carrying from one arm to the other, Kate had said, 'What really pleases Kit is that his accommodation is at the villa Evans built for himself and his fellow archaeologists when the excavation of the palace was taking place. Evans is rarely there now, but as study at the site is ongoing, the Villa Ariadne still serves as home to archaeologists and scholars working there.'

Such a close link with the most famous archaeological site of the century had seemed incredible to Ella, but Kate never made a big thing of Kit's connection to Knossos. Like Daphne, who carried the title Lady Daphne St Maur, she was completely without side.

Despite her innate self-confidence, coming from the background she did, Ella had found her first few weeks at Oxford daunting. Her years at Bradford Girls' Grammar School had, with no effort on her part, smoothed out her broad Yorkshire accent to such an extent that her grandfather was always accusing her of having become 'posh'.

She hadn't sounded posh at St Hugh's. Though the stated aim of the college was to admit students regardless of their educational or social background, no one in her year came from her kind of working–class family. For the first time in her life Ella had found it hard to fit in; or she had until she'd made friends with Kate and Daphne.

It was her parents who'd had difficulty in taking in their stride her friendship with Kate and Daphne.

'A lass whose father is a magistrate is one thing,' Alfred Tetley had said, speaking of Kate, 'but a lass whose father is an earl is quite another. I'd leave 'er to 'er own kind if I was you, love. They're a rum lot, the aristocracy, and best avoided.'

Knowing her father would think differently about Daphne if he was ever to meet her, it was advice Ella hadn't taken.

During the long vacation in their second year at St Hugh's the three of them had spent several weeks as volunteers on a Roman dig in Northumberland. Kate, whose family home was in Canterbury, had met up with Daphne in London and then the two of them had travelled in Daphne's nifty open-topped car to Yorkshire in order to pick up Ella.

It was such a golden opportunity for her parents to meet Kate and Daphne that Ella had suggested they stay overnight at the Ling Bob.

A visit that on so many levels could have been awkward had, instead, gone without a hitch.

On the evening of their arrival Kate and Daphne had joined the Tetley family for a fish-and-chip supper and later, when Ella had walked Kate and Daphne up the street to the pub, her father and granddad, taking it as an ideal opportunity for a pint of bitter each, had walked with them. Once in the pub,

Jos had insisted on teaching Kate and Daphne how to play darts. By the end of the evening there was no question of Alfred holding to his belief that, as a member of the aristocracy, Daphne was best avoided. Instead, as he'd walked back home in the moonlit darkness with Jos and Ella, he'd said, 'What a grand couple o' lassies yon two are. It's a shame for 'em they aren't Yorkshire-born.'

Ella's thoughts had now strayed so far from the book she was reading that she laid it down, surprised to see, as she looked out of the window, that they were leaving Coventry and would soon be in Oxford. Happy anticipation flooded through her. It was going to be great seeing Kate and Daphne again and she couldn't wait to be in The High, walking past buildings, pubs and shops that were as familiar to her as any in the centre of Bradford.

Though Kate hadn't said so in her letters, Ella was certain Kate couldn't have spent a year in Athens without having travelled to Crete to spend time with Kit at Knossos, and the prospect of Kate having first-hand gossip from such a famous site was thrilling. Now that Kate had finished her postgraduate studies she would be looking for a job, and as the train flashed past fields and woods, Ella wondered if Kit might help her find one; that perhaps he might even find her one at the dig of which he was field director. If he didn't, then perhaps she and Kate could find work together somewhere; perhaps on the second season of the Somerset dig? Or perhaps on one of many Roman excavation sites in Northumberland?

She slid *The Palace of Minos* into her shoulder-bag. The best thing of all would be if Daphne decided she'd had enough of being a debutante and was finally going to put her first-class degree to good use.

That would be the ultimate: the three of them working together on the same site – especially if the site was Bronze Age and somewhere in Greece.

Chapter Two

Kate Shelton settled herself in the front passenger seat of her father's dark-green Riley and said, with loving exasperation, 'There's really no need for you to take me to the station, Daddy. I've got plenty of time and I could walk it in five minutes.'

'That's not the point, Katherine.' There was equal loving exasperation in her father's voice.

'Then what is?'

Giles Shelton put the car into gear and pulled away from the front of his eighteenth-century home. 'The Capuchins' lay in the shade of Canterbury Cathedral and was one of the finest detached houses within the city walls, its only drawback being that its Georgian splendour looked out on to an ancient cobbled street barely wider than his car.

'First of all, it's my pleasure to chauffeur you around whenever I have the opportunity to do so,' he said, carefully navigating into another street only a little wider, 'and secondly, in my day, no young woman would set off for a railway station unaccompanied.'

Kate laughed. 'It's 1936, Daddy. Not 1906. And I've just come back from a year in Greece, somewhere I travelled to and returned from unaccompanied.'

'And *you* may remember,' Giles said, 'that I was very opposed to you doing so.'

Kate did remember and knew she had been very fortunate that he had, after much persuasion, sanctioned her year of study in Athens. It had been the long journey – rail to Italy, then down the length of Italy to Brindisi, followed by an overnight steamer to Piraeus – that had caused him most concern, and she shuddered to think what he would have thought of some of the solo trips she had made from Athens to other parts of Greece.

To get to Mycenae, a major archaeological site only fifty-six miles from Athens, she'd sat in a stuffy bus for two days, her travelling companions black-skirted, headscarfed peasant women with baskets of fruit and vegetables on their knees, which they had either just bought at a local market or were about to sell at one. On the last leg of her journey the woman next to her had been nursing a cockerel in a wicker cage.

Suddenly suspicious that Kate wasn't listening to him, Giles Shelton cleared his throat and said, as they drove beneath the arch of a medieval gatehouse, 'And so what do you think, Kate? Are you in agreement with your mother and I that a position at the museum would be an ideal first job choice for you?'

Kate dragged herself back into the present. 'What museum? The British Museum? I should be so lucky. Permanent jobs like that are terrifically hard to come by, and are impossible for someone fresh from postgraduate study with no job experience behind them.'

Her father made a right turn towards the station car park.

'Then not the British Museum,' he said, bringing the Riley to a halt and switching off the engine, 'but what about the museum here in Canterbury? Or a museum somewhere else locally?'

'I wouldn't stand a chance and even if, in another dozen years or so I did, curatorship doesn't interest me.'

He looked so disappointed that she kissed him on the cheek.

'Darling Daddy,' she said gently, 'it's very sweet of you to try and be so helpful, but there's absolutely no need for you to worry about me – my plans are already made.'

He drew breath to make a concerned response and, before he could do so, she stepped out of the car, saying firmly before closing the car door, 'I want to specialize in Bronze Age Greek pottery, and with Kit's help I'm going to do so, and I'm going to do so in Crete.'

With her bombshell dropped, she waved him goodbye and strode swiftly into the station, knowing guiltily that she had made it sound as if Kit securing her a place on his team in Crete was a done deal, when all he had actually said was: 'I'll give it some thought, Sis, but it's a bit too much like nepotism for comfort and I'm not promising anything.'

Kate hadn't cared about the nepotism. On his retirement Sir Arthur Evans had handed the Knossos site over to the British School of Archaeology. As a postgraduate of the school, she was a legitimate candidate for a place on one of the tomb digs and her hopes were high.

It was early April and a new season of excavation work wasn't due to start until mid-May. She had dug her nails into the palms of her hands. She had to be on one of the digs. She *had* to be.

Even before her year in Athens she'd set her sights on working in Greece, and preferably in Crete. It would have been hard not to have had Crete at the forefront of her mind, when Kit was there and he had such wonderful contacts. It was her year in Athens, though, that had turned Greece from being a rational choice of country in which to look for work into being the *only* country in which she wanted to work, for from the moment she had arrived in Greece, she had fallen in love with it.

The British School was on the city's outskirts. Trams ran

down the steep streets into the centre of Athens, but as they were always uncomfortably crowded she had got into the habit of walking everywhere. Walking was never boring. In Greece, life took place in the open air and there had always been something interesting to see. Women did household tasks in the doorways of their homes: peeling potatoes, shelling peas, sewing and darning. Closer to the city centre, shop frontages opened on to the street, so that in barber shops it seemed as if men were being shaved and having their hair cut on the pavement. At outdoor cafes men sat over glasses of ouzo, watching her with curious eyes.

Kate understood the curiosity. Long years of political chaos in Greece meant there were fewer tourists in Athens than at other classical sites in Europe; and her clothes, and the fact that she was taller than most Greek women, meant that she stood out distinctively.

In the heart of the city the hustle and bustle was incredible, and she had loved feeling a part of it. At the end of almost every turning there was a view of the Acropolis and whenever she wasn't in class, or working on an essay, she had climbed up to it, spending hour after hour making notes and taking photographs and then, totally exhausted, sitting on the steps of the Parthenon, looking out in blissful contentment over the sun-glazed city towards the sea.

During the long midsummer vacation she hadn't returned home. Instead she had made the seven-hour crossing from Piraeus to Crete and spent the hottest weeks of the summer at Knossos with Kit. She had arrived at the end of one excavating season and before the beginning of the next one; and Kit, who was taking advantage of the break between seasons to work on a book, had not had much time to give her.

It hadn't mattered. The curator at Knossos, Mr Hutchinson – known to everyone as the Squire – had made her very welcome, as had his elderly mother, who acted as his house-keeper. Also in residence at the Villa Ariadne were a handful of students and she'd joined them under the supervision of their professor in sorting excavated pottery sherds. Other days she'd visited the remains of two smaller Minoan palaces at Phaistos and Mallia, and she'd spent hours and hours in the museum at Heraklion.

An archaeologist who didn't stay at the Villa Ariadne, but who occasionally joined them for dinner, was Lewis Sinclair, a Scot from Sutherland. He was excavating on a site some twenty miles south-west of Knossos where, eight years earlier, a shepherd boy had unearthed a gold Minoan hair comb.

At the dining table Professor Cottingley had said bluntly that he thought Lewis Sinclair was wasting his time.

'The geographical position is all wrong,' he'd said, helping himself to moussaka. 'It has no strategic importance. It doesn't overlook a plain, as Phaistos does, nor does it look out to sea and have the convenience of a nearby harbour, as Mallia does. The hair-comb find was a fluke, nothing more.'

'I disagree.' Lewis Sinclair had been flatly dismissive.

Professor Cottingley hadn't allowed the subject to drop and had proceeded to list lots of other reasons why Lewis's excavation work would, in his opinion, yield nothing.

Lewis Sinclair had listened stony-faced, a nerve throbbing at the corner of his jaw indicating how unhappy he was at having his judgement publicly doubted, especially when the doubter was someone so eminent.

The Squire had turned the conversation to other things and although Kate had tried hard to concentrate on what was being said, her attention had kept straying in Lewis Sinclair's direction. Like Kit, he was in his late twenties, but unlike Kit he wasn't academic-looking, nor did he look remotely Scottish. His hair was dark and as thick and curly as a Greek's, and his skin was tanned from years of working outdoors beneath a hot sun.

There was always a nod towards formality at the Villa and the men were all wearing jackets, shirts and ties. Lewis Sinclair's jacket was of cream linen and he had long ago dragged his tie loose and opened his shirt at the throat. He was not very tall, an inch or two under six foot, but he was toughly built, and when he moved it was with the kind of easy strength more typical of a champion boxer than a classicist obsessed with Minoan history.

From the moment she had first been introduced to him, Kate had found him devastatingly attractive. His manner, though, had been off-putting.

After dinner when, with everyone else, they were seated outside on the terrace, she had asked him under whose authority and whose funding the dig that he was director of was being carried out.

'It's taking place under Greek government authority,' he had said, a glass of raki in one hand, a half-smoked cigarette in the other, 'and it's privately sponsored,' he had added, his voice unnecessarily curt.

She'd been about to ask what kind of a team he had assembled and if there was room on it for another member when, from the garden, there came the sound of a gate creaking. Abruptly he had put his glass down and risen to his feet.

'Excuse me,' he'd said, without looking towards her. Dropping his cigarette to the ground, he'd crushed it beneath his heel and, without saying a word to anyone else seated on the terrace, had walked swiftly across it and down the steps that led into the unlit garden.

Kate had stared after him, not knowing which emotion was uppermost: disbelief that he hadn't had the manners to continue their conversation, or exasperation that she hadn't had the chance to ask the question she'd been intending to ask.

As everyone around her continued laughing and talking, she had risen to her feet and walked across to the top of the steps.

'Careful, Kate,' Kit had called across to her. 'The paths down there are so uneven they're only safe at night when the lanterns are lit.'

She was appreciative of his warning, but it hadn't been necessary, for she hadn't had the slightest intention of following Lewis Sinclair into the garden. She had, though, been curious as to what had taken him there so abruptly.

A second later she'd found out.

The conversation on the terrace had fallen into a lull and from the garden had come the sound of a girl's hastily smothered laughter.

On the terrace one of the students had sniggered.

'I believe Sinclair has met up with a girl!' Professor Cottingley had spluttered, outraged. 'Surely the wall gate should be locked?'

'Locked?' the Squire had said vaguely, as if the concept of a locked gate was entirely new to him. 'Oh, I think not, Cottingley. There's absolutely no need, dear chap. And the girl will be Nikoleta, Christos Kourakis's sister.'

'Christos is Lewis's site supervisor,' Mrs Hutchinson had said helpfully. 'The family live nearby and when Lewis visits Knossos, Nikoleta, who is seventeen and has a young girl's crush on him, is never far away.' She had been knitting and she laid her work down, saying reminiscently, 'When I was her age I had a most desperate crush on the local vicar. Naturally he gave me no encouragement, just as Lewis gives Nikoleta no encouragement.'

Professor Cottingley hadn't looked convinced as to Lewis

Sinclair's lack of encouragement and, remembering the smothered laughter, Kate hadn't been convinced, either.

Comfortably seated on the London train now, and reflecting on her experiences of the last twelve months, she was more relieved than disappointed by Lewis Sinclair's lack of interest in her. If he'd been interested in her, he would have offered her a place on his team and then Kit would be making no effort to secure her a place on the dig on which he was field director. On her CV the name Knossos would be a thousand times more impressive than Lewis Sinclair's dig – especially if Professor Cottingley was right and that dig proved to be void, with nothing of Minoan value found there.

As the train sped through the Kentish countryside she couldn't help but think how wonderful the Cretan countryside would be looking. 'The wild flowers,' Mrs Hutchinson had said to her, 'are at their best in April. All over the island the air is full of the scent of lemon blossom and jasmine, and there are great swathes of achingly beautiful wild tulips.'

Determination flooded through her. Kit may not yet have secured her a place on one of the tomb digs, but she was going to return to Crete anyway. She was going to see the wild tulips before their flowering time was over, and if Kit didn't organize a place for her on one of the digs, then she was sure the kindly Mr Hutchinson would.

Chapter Three

Daphne St Maur was high above the English Channel in a two-seater plane being piloted by a man she had met only thirty-six hours earlier.

'This is spiffing!' she shouted from behind him, 'How long would it take me to get a pilot's licence?' Above the roar of the engine, Sholto Hertford shouted back, 'I've heard about your car-driving, Daphne! You don't stand a hope of ever getting a pilot's licence.'

Only the thought that if she jolted him he might lose control of the plane and send it into a spin prevented Daphne from punching him hard on the shoulder. Instead, she laughed, knowing she could achieve anything she wanted, if she set her mind to it. At the moment she rather thought she wanted Sholto Hertford.

They had met at a twenty-first birthday party that had taken place in Paris. Daphne had struck up a friendship with Miranda Seeley, whose birthday it was, when the two of them had been next to each other in line, on being presented to King George and Queen Mary. Sholto, twenty-eight and a diplomat at the Foreign Office, was a family friend of Miranda's French-born mother.

That he was older than her usual run of boyfriends was, for Daphne, a point in his favour. Other points in his favour were that his light-brown hair wasn't heavily brilliantined to

17

a glassy shine and that he wore it longer than was normal for men of his class and profession. To Daphne, it indicated a strong bohemian streak – and she liked people who weren't afraid of breaking a few of society's rules.

'Sholto Hertford,' he'd said, handing her a glass of champagne. 'I don't believe we've met.'

'Daphne St Maur,' she'd said, liking the fact that he was over six foot tall and looked like a man who could take care of himself in a crisis.

'I don't want to rush you,' he'd said, indicating the champagne he'd just given her, 'but would you like to dance?'

The band was playing Cole Porter's 'Anything Goes'. Unhesitatingly Daphne had put the glass of champagne down.

'I'd love to,' she had said, and hadn't been remotely surprised when, seconds later, she'd discovered that Sholto Hertford danced like a dream.

Not too much later she'd discovered that he kissed like a dream, too.

All in all, Daphne had counted the party a huge success and was glad she'd overcome her hesitation about attending it. The hesitation had been because of her long-standing arrangement to meet up in Oxford with Kate and Ella two days afterwards – which meant no enjoyable lingering in Paris, for she would need to cross the Channel again the next day, in order to drive from London to Oxford the following morning.

This also meant she couldn't now take Sholto Hertford up on his suggestion that they spend a few days together in Monte Carlo.

'I can't,' she'd said, her head leaning against his chest. 'I have to travel back to London to be at an engagement in Oxford the day after.'

'Cancel Oxford,' he'd said in a deep, rich voice that made her dizzy with desire.

18

She'd pulled away from him a little. 'I can't. Sorry, but there it is. I need to be on the boat train tomorrow evening at the very latest.'

'No, you don't.'

For a second she'd thought he was going to spoil everything by proving himself to be the kind of man who expected a woman to fall in with his every wish and always overrode any objections to the contrary. If he was, then despite the spine-tingling kisses, she was going to walk away from him very smartly.

'You don't,' he had continued, 'because we can spend all day together. It's four in the morning, in case you hadn't noticed, and tomorrow morning I can have you in Oxford for whatever the engagement is that is so important to you.'

'It's a lunch engagement, not a dinner engagement,' she had said, 'and I don't fancy a crack-of-dawn Channel crossing and then a rushed dash to Oxford, without having had the chance to change clothes.'

He'd quirked an eyebrow and for the first time she'd noticed that his grey eyes had flecks of gold in the iris. 'I flew myself here,' he'd said. 'And I can fly you back to Oxford tomorrow morning in time for lunch.'

'Wonderful.' She'd stepped back into the circle of his arms, saying in blissful contentment, 'I knew you were a man who could handle a crisis.'

The next morning at a late breakfast Miranda had said, 'You made a killing last night, Daphne. Sholto never left your side. He's scrumptious, isn't he? And he's a viscount. His father is the Marquess of Knotley. My mother once had an affair with Knotley.' She'd collapsed into giggles. 'Wouldn't it be hysterical if Sholto was my half-brother? D'you think I should suggest it to him? D'you think we look at all alike?'

'You're five foot two,' Daphne had said in response. 'Sholto is six foot – probably an inch or two over. Your eyes are brown. His are grey. All in all, it isn't very likely, is it? And no, I wouldn't suggest it to him, although if you did, I rather think he'd take it in his stride.'

As the white cliffs of Dover came into view, Sholto shouted over the wind and engine noise, 'Marvellous sight, aren't they? I never get tired of flying over them!'

Daphne thought the cliffs spellbinding, especially when seen from a two-seater Leopard Moth. It occurred to her to wonder where they would land. She couldn't think of an airport conveniently close to Oxford.

'Where are we going to put down?' she shouted. 'It's half-eleven. If you're going to land near London, I'm going to be late!'

'Don't fuss,' he shouted back. 'We're not going to land in London and you won't be late.'

Daphne looked out of the cockpit window. Below them were grassy fields with sheep grazing in them.

'You're not going to land in a field, are you? Because if you are, the farmer won't like it! And what about the sheep? They aren't going to be too happy.'

He hadn't answered, merely laughed, and twenty minutes later the plane banked, turning in a long, smooth curve as it began its descent. Below them, in the middle of a grand estate of rolling acres, Daphne saw what was perhaps the most magnificent stately home in England.

'That's Blenheim Palace!' she shrieked. 'You can't land in front of it. You'll be arrested. We'll *both* be arrested!'

He was too busy concentrating on what he was doing to answer her.

Several minutes later, as the Leopard Moth rolled to a halt on a makeshift runway out of sight of the palace, Sholto said reassuringly, 'A couple of farmers bought this land from the Blenheim estate a few months ago and they're turning it into an aerodrome to service Oxford.'

He opened the cockpit door, put a foot on one of the wing struts for balance and then jumped down on to grass.

'So far things are pretty rough-and-ready,' he continued, as she threw her weekend case down to him, 'but it's hellishly convenient when visiting Blenheim – which is what I shall be doing while you're at your thrash.'

As she jumped, he broke her fall by catching her in his arms, saying as he set her on her feet, 'The duke is a friend of mine.'

This came as no surprise to Daphne.

He looked down at his watch, a lock of hair falling low over his forehead. 'We're tight for time, but we'll be able to do it. Things are still pretty basic here, but there's a phone in the office,' he indicated a wooden building on the edge of the field, 'and I'll be able to ring for a cab.'

'*We'll* be able to do it?'

'I thought I'd drop you off at your function.'

'I'm not going to a function, Sholto. I'm meeting up with two college friends.'

'Then why the devil are we not now in the South of France? If it's only a lunch with friends you're going to, surely it wouldn't have mattered if you hadn't turned up?'

'It would have mattered to me.'

They'd reached the wooden building now and, not knowing whether her attitude amused or annoyed him, she saw him open the door.

'I'll stay out here,' she said. 'Will you please tell the cab company it's an emergency?'

The door swung shut behind him and she took a cigarette case and lighter from her shoulder-bag. Although Sholto hadn't said so specifically, he'd strongly indicated that he intended meeting up with her when her reunion with Kate and Ella was over, which was fine by her.

She lit her cigarette, wondering if the evening would then be spent at Blenheim. As the present duke was middle-aged and had a young family, she wasn't sure how she felt about that. It could make for a tedious evening. What would be preferable would be if they flew back across the Channel, and Sholto followed up with his first suggestion of flying down to Monte Carlo together.

A few minutes later the door opened and he rejoined her, saying, 'The cab will be ten minutes, maybe less.'

Knowing that he hadn't taken kindly to her preferring lunch with college friends to their spending time in the Mediterranean sun, Daphne shot him a conciliatory smile. 'Cigarette?' she asked, reaching into her bag.

She was smoking a Sobranie and he shook his head. 'Thanks, but no thanks.'

He took a cigarette case out of his inside jacket pocket. 'Who are your friends?' he asked, removing a cigarillo from it. 'Who are their people?'

Laughter rose in Daphne's throat.

'Kate's family home is Canterbury,' she said, enjoying herself hugely. 'Her surname is Shelton. Ella is a Tetley. Her family home is Wilsden, in Yorkshire.'

Sholto blew a plume of blue smoke into the air. 'Shelton? Are they a branch of the Fox-Strangways?'

'No.' With growing amusement, Daphne waited for him to move on to Ella's surname.

Aware that he was now taking part in some kind of quiz, Sholto obliged her by saying, 'You're right in thinking I'm not familiar with the Tetleys. I'm assuming the family is the northern brewing family? Does Wilsden have good shooting?'

'Wilsden isn't an estate. It's a village on the outskirts of Bradford. And Ella's family has no connection at all with the brewing family, although her father and grandfather enjoy a pint of Tetley's at the local pub, given the chance.'

He laughed. 'Okay. I walked straight into that one. I suppose you're going to tell me Ella's father and grandfather are coal-miners.'

'I'm not sure there is any mining in that part of Yorkshire. Alfred Tetley, Ella's father, is a mill worker. A weaver. As is Ella's mother. Her grandfather used to be Wilsden's rag-and-bone man.'

Sholto said, vastly amused, 'How did you fall in with such a colourful crew?'

'Ella is a grammar-school girl who won a scholarship to St Hugh's – and, before you think any differently, there's nothing of the social climber about Ella. She makes friends with people she likes, and not for any other reason.'

Looking at her cameo-like profile and fashionable bob of ivory-pale hair, Sholto experienced a sharp stab of danger. All he had intended was a few fun-filled days with a girl he found stunningly beautiful and who was, for such a young woman, remarkably sophisticated and worldly. She hadn't, for instance, made any protest at all when he had suggested they spend time in Monte Carlo getting to know each other better. How the devil she would have accounted for leaving Paris – where she'd been staying with the Seeleys – for Monte Carlo, he had no idea. He could only assume she was well practised in living a private life that her parents were oblivious of.

What he hadn't intended was embarking on a serious relationship. He was already in one of those with Francine, Miranda's mother, and had been for the last four years. Francine was eight years older than he was. She was very French, very elegant and, best of all, safely married to a man who, with a mistress of his own, had no intention of causing waves.

Daphne was eight years his junior, heart-stopping to look at and very clearly a loose cannon; and for a man in the diplomatic service, loose cannons were best avoided. Most disconcerting of all, she was single and – even for the daughter of an earl – he knew himself to be a very good catch, in the marriage stakes.

He chewed the corner of his lip. That was, of course, if he allowed himself to be caught.

Having decided that as he now knew all the dangers, there was no danger, he pulled her tightly against him.

'What explanation will you give for Monte Carlo?' he asked, knowing that when Francine heard of it, it would be payback for the way she'd so casually told him at the birthday party that she'd once had an affair with his father.

Uncaring that they could be seen from the windows of the building, Daphne pressed herself closer than ever against Sholto and slid her arms up and around his neck.

'I don't have to give any explanation. I'm twenty-two, not twelve, and I don't live at home. I share a flat in Kensington with Lord Crailsford's daughter.'

Her lips were only a tantalizing couple of inches away from his, but he resisted the temptation to kiss her in front of what he knew was an audience.

'Was Sandy Crailsford at St Hugh's with you?'

'Heavens, no. Sandy would think three years at Oxford a complete waste of her time. She went to a finishing school in Switzerland and was *Tatler* magazine's debutante of the year two years ago.'

It occurred to him to wonder what kind of a degree Daphne had left Oxford with. Out of the corner of his eye he could see a cab turning in, by the sign that declared visitors were entering what would one day be a municipal airport.

'What did you read at Oxford? Art history?'

It was a safe enough guess and his attention was elsewhere; specifically on how he was going to hide his erection, once Daphne stepped away from him to enter the cab.

'No,' she said, enjoying the surprise she was about to deal him. 'Classics.'

He forgot about the fast-approaching cab and his erection. His eyebrows shot nearly into his hair. 'But you have to be fully competent in Greek and Latin for a Classics degree!'

'Yes,' she said, her smile dazzling. 'And I am.'

Then, as she finally accepted that he wasn't going to kiss her in front of prurient eyes, and as the cab came to a halt beside them, she took the initiative and kissed him full on the mouth.

It was an action that did nothing at all to minimize his arousal.

The cab driver opened the rear passenger door of the cab and cleared his throat.

Daphne headed towards him.

Sholto, stunned at the realization that he'd met a woman whose educational achievements were equal to his own, followed her, carrying her Louis Vuitton weekend case at what was a useful, if awkward angle.

Chapter Four

The port of Piraeus was busy and chaotic as, in deepening dusk, Kate made her way down the dockside towards the *Theseus*, which was to take her on an overnight crossing to Heraklion. It was only five days since she had made the decision that she was going to Crete, with or without an invitation and a job waiting for her, and in those five days she'd scarcely had time to draw breath.

There had been rail tickets through France and the length of Italy to arrange; passage on the Brindisi–Piraeus steamer, and on the steamer she was about to board. Packing had been easy. Even though she intended her stay in Crete to be a long one, she was travelling light and the clothes she had packed were those suitable for working on a dig in a hot climate – shorts and cotton skirts and blouses and, for evening meals at the Villa Ariadne, a couple of pretty cotton dresses. What hadn't been easy was persuading her parents that she wasn't acting rashly.

'You're leaving for Crete on Thursday?' her mother had said, bewildered. 'But why, darling?'

'To see Kit and, hopefully, to be taken on as a member of his excavation team,' she'd said, avoiding her father's eye.

Her father had put his pipe down and had said in measured tones, 'I didn't realize you'd had confirmation from Kit about a place on his team.'

'I haven't had official confirmation, but that would simply be a formality,' she'd said, uncomfortably aware that Kit would view the matter rather differently. 'You know how long the mail takes, Daddy. I dare say there's a letter somewhere in the post urging me to leave immediately for Knossos. My arriving there in three days' time will be a nice surprise for him.'

'If it isn't, you are to come straight back to England,' her father had said. 'You are not to make a nuisance of yourself to Kit. It wouldn't be fair to him. Do I have your promise on that, Kate?'

'Of course!' she'd said indignantly, not promising that if there wasn't a job for her, she would come straight back to England, and hoping her father wouldn't notice the omission.

To her vast relief, he hadn't.

News of what she intended doing had been greeted with far more enthusiasm by Ella and Daphne.

'Go for it, Kate,' Daphne had said, raising a glass to her in The Chequers, a five-hundred-year-old pub in Oxford's High Street.

'That's wonderful news!' Ella's delicately boned face had shone with delight. 'It means you'll be at Knossos on the anniversary of the dedication of Sir Arthur Evans's bust, in the Palace of Minos's courtyard. I read in the Archaeological Society's magazine that he intends being there for it. Wouldn't it be marvellous if you were to be introduced to him?'

Thinking about the possibility, as she followed a steward down the companionway to a cabin, Kate's stomach muscles tightened. To be introduced to the great Sir Arthur Evans at the world-famous site he had excavated would be the experience of a lifetime. As she walked into a tiny cabin, which contained a bunk, a porthole, a cracked and stained washbasin and nothing else, another thought struck her. If Sir Arthur was expected at the Villa within the next week or so, then she might not be able to stay there. It was also possible that her arrival at such a time would exasperate Kit to such an extent that he would be in no mood to look kindly on her reason for being there.

Being negative wasn't in her nature, and deciding that any problems she met were problems she would overcome, she stowed her luggage away and hurried back on deck in order to be in a good position by the rails when, as they left port, mainland Greece began sliding from view.

Half an hour later and by the light of a rising moon, it did so magnificently. In the distance there was a romantic glimpse of the Parthenon, standing high above Athens in ghostly-white splendour.

She hugged her arms against the chill of the night breeze, wishing she had someone to share the romance of the moment with. Although she'd had boyfriends at Oxford and had indulged in a whole shoal of flirtations, she'd never yet been head-over-heels in love and had never indulged in the kind of full-blown relationship that Daphne had, yet again, seemingly embarked upon.

'Sholto is quite a dish,' Daphne had said, over the champagne they were celebrating their reunion with, 'and though he's a diplomat, he's not at all stuffy. Rather the reverse. I think the next few weeks are going to be fun.'

'A few weeks?' Ella had raised her eyebrows. 'That would mean him lasting longer than most. You were mad about Teddy Rowbotham-Smythe, and you were bored to death by him in less than a month.'

'Teddy thought a pottery sherd was something new by Royal Doulton. Sholto does at least have brains.'

'And an aeroplane,' Kate had added drily.

Their laughter had turned the heads of everyone seated near to them.

Thinking of that moment now, Kate smiled. It had been wonderful spending time with Daphne and Ella again. The only flaw had been that their enjoyment of each other's company had been so short. By the time they had finished lunch, caught up on each other's news, walked down the High Street to the bridge, hired a punt, spent a pleasurable couple of hours on the river and enjoyed an early evening glass of wine in The Boar, another of their favourite pubs, it had been time to take Ella to the train station.

'Are you being met at the other end?' Kate had asked her, aware that it was going to be midnight when the train arrived in Bradford.

'Yes.' Ella had hitched her shoulder-bag a little higher on her shoulder. 'Sam is meeting me.'

Kate had exchanged a quick glance with Daphne. Neither of them had met Sam, but Ella had spoken of him often enough for them to have formed the opinion that his and Ella's friendship was a romance in the making.

Before she had stepped on to the train, Ella had said to her, 'If you get taken on as a team member at a Knossos tomb dig, put in a word for me. I've a job waiting for me on a Roman dig in Somerset, but I'd far rather be part of a Cretan Bronze Age team.'

'I promise,' she had said and, wanting Ella's companionship on a dig just as much as Ella wanted hers, the promise was one she intended keeping.

With mainland Greece no longer discernible in the darkness and the chill breeze now ice-cold, Kate gave the heaving waves a last look and began making her way back to her cabin.

Twenty minutes later she was lying in her bunk, euphoric that she would be at Knossos in the morning and, with luck, would soon be a member of one of the outlying digs.

The crossing to Crete was nearly always turbulent, and as the *Theseus* pitched and rolled she closed her eyes in an effort to sleep through the unpleasantness. Her dreams, when they came, were not of retrieving precious artefacts buried for thousands of years. Instead, they were of a man with hair as thick and curly as a ram's fleece, and of a girl she had never met; a girl recognizable to her only because her hands were across her mouth, smothering her laughter – laughter that, for some indecipherable reason, Kate was sure had been at her expense.

'Taxi, *Kyria*! Taxi here! Taxi!'

The shouts by drivers trying to attract her attention came from all sides and, attempting to remember if *Kyria* meant 'Lady' or 'Miss', Kate good-naturedly ignored them and, having no need of help with her suitcase, crossed the road to where the buses left for Knossos. There were a cluster of tourists at the bus stop and she joined them, aware that as it was a Sunday the wait could possibly be a long one.

It wasn't.

Fifteen minutes later she was not only aboard a bus, but the vehicle was already rumbling through Heraklion's outskirts. Watching a grubby-faced urchin on a bicycle trying to keep up with them, she wondered if Kit would be at the Villa when she arrived. She hoped he would, because otherwise she would have to explain her arrival to Mrs Hutchinson or, trickier still, to the Squire.

Now they were clear of Heraklion, flat fields were giving way to arid hills hazed with lavender and dotted with Judas trees. Blue sage and pale-lilac mallow grew thickly at the roadside, and beyond the village of Fortetsa she had her first glimpse of wild tulips. Spectacular as the blaze of flowers was, Kate's mind wasn't on them. Now that she was almost at Knossos, she was belatedly wondering what kind of a reception she was going to get.

Initially, of course, Kit's reaction would be one of total surprise, but what would it be when she told him she wasn't in Crete for a few days' unexpected holiday? That she was there in the expectation of being employed as a member of his excavation team? The two of them had always had a good relationship, but he was five years her senior and those five years meant there had always been a certain constraint between them.

When she had been at junior school in Canterbury, Kit had been at Harrow. Even during vacations the five-year difference meant they had spent little time together. Kit hadn't wanted her trailing at his heels, and so Kate hadn't trailed. He'd had his friends, and she'd had hers. There were times when she'd even thought he would have preferred it if she had chosen a different subject at university, rather than following in his footsteps by studying archaeology, and though he could surely have arranged for her to come out to Crete as a member of his team the instant she'd asked it of him, he hadn't done so. That being the case, it wasn't very likely he was going to be over the moon at her unexpected arrival.

'Knossos!' the driver shouted, breaking into her thoughts. 'Knossos.'

The tourists picked up rucksacks and guidebooks and thronged to the front of the bus. Kate, hampered by her suit-case, brought up the rear. Once off the bus, she didn't follow everyone else towards the sandy path that led through trees to the ticket booth and the huge area of the excavated palace. Instead she walked fifty yards or so back down the road, until she came to the Villa Ariadne's lodge gates.

The lodge keeper nodded his head in recognition and Kate continued up the familiar path and through the gate leading into Sir Arthur Evans's stylized Greek-Edwardian garden. Large palm trees gave it shade. Pomegranate flowers gleamed a silky scarlet. Flanking a wrought-iron seat were terracotta pots massed with blue irises. Even though it was Sunday and she doubted if anyone would be working on the outlying sites, there was no one about, nor could she hear the distant sound of talking.

In the hot stillness she walked up the flight of wide stone steps leading to a door that she remembered always being open, and which was now ominously closed. Putting her suitcase down, she took a deep breath and, fiercely hoping for the best, dropped a bull-headed knocker against the door.

It was opened by a maid she had never seen before.

Whenever she had thought of this moment, she had always imagined herself speaking to someone who knew her, and knew of her relationship to Kit. Now, faced with someone who didn't, it suddenly felt bad manners to be asking for Kit before she had met up with Mrs Hutchinson or the Squire.

'Mrs Hutchinson, please,' she said, trying to sound certain of her welcome.

The girl smiled shyly and opened the door wide to let Kate step inside.

Brief minutes later, Mrs Hutchinson was leading her downstairs to where, for coolness in the heat of the summer, the bedrooms were located. 'This is such a lovely surprise, Kate,' she said, showing her into the same small room she had stayed in previously. 'Kit didn't tell us you were coming to see the spring wild flowers, but you are very welcome. You must take a trip out to the Omalos Plain. At this time of year it's simply carpeted with tulips. Kit is in Heraklion at the moment. It's the only place he can buy an English-language newspaper. The minute he arrives back, I'll tell him where to find you.'

When Mrs Hutchinson had hurried away, Kate sat down on the edge of the bed, relieved at Mrs Hutchinson's innocent assumption as to the reason for her being there. All she needed now was for Kit to greet her in an equally warm manner.

A little while later, when she heard her brother coming down the passageway at a run, she knew he wasn't going to do so.

The door burst open and she leapt to her feet.

'What the *blazes* are you playing at?' Kit was angrier than she had ever seen him. 'Does Dad know you're here? Does he know you're here uninvited?'

Aware that angry retaliation would be of no help, she said stiffly, 'Yes, Daddy does know I'm here. All he asked of me was that I wouldn't be a nuisance to you.'

Kit ran a hand through his untidy straight hair, struggling for composure. Still white-lipped, he said tautly, 'Well, now you're here, I suppose I'll have to make the best of it.' He took off his horn-rimmed glasses and pinched the bridge of his nose. 'How many days were you hoping to stay? If it's any longer than a week, you're out of luck. Sir Arthur is expected by then, and he may well be bringing family and guests with him.'

'That isn't a problem. I'll move into a hotel in Heraklion, and if Heraklion's hotels are full, I'll find somewhere to board in one of the nearby villages, Fortetsa or Archanes – and if necessary I'll do so long-term.'

'Long-term?' He stared at her. 'Why the devil would you need somewhere long-term?'

'I'm not here for a few days' holiday, Kit. I'm here to work. Hopefully as a member on a tomb dig-team.'

'As a member of . . . ? God in heaven, Kate, I'll say this for you! You win first prize for pig-headed persistence!'

She couldn't tell whether he was admiring or appalled.

'I'm more than suitably qualified, Kit.'

He stared at her for a long moment, then he put his glasses back on. 'I'll have a word with the Squire,' he said tersely. 'Just don't get your hopes up.'

When the sound of his footsteps had receded, she wondered how she was going to survive the tension until he returned. The small room suddenly seemed claustrophobic and she opened its narrow French window and stepped out into the dense greenery of the lower rear garden.

It was the garden where Lewis Sinclair had outraged

Professor Cottingley by, if the Squire's assumption was correct, meeting Nikoleta Kourakis. Remembering the unpleasant sensation that her dream of Nikoleta had left her with, Kate closed her mind to the memory, sitting on a garden seat that could easily be seen from her bedroom and hoping that when Kit stepped out into the garden, he would do so with a spring in his step signifying good news.

A half-hour passed, and then an hour.

The optimism she had been feeling began to fade.

When two hours had passed, deep pessimism set in. Convinced that Kit was simply delaying giving her bad news for as long as he could, she rose to her feet, intending to walk back up the road to where, by the bus stop and opposite the entrance to the Palace of Minos, there was a small cafe.

'Kate!'

She whirled round. 'You can relax,' he called out, striding towards her. 'The Squire's come up trumps.'

'That's marvellous.' She ran towards him. 'Am I really and truly on a Cretan dig-team?'

'Really and truly.'

'What will I do about lodgings? Will I be staying here, at the Villa? Or will I be living with a local family?'

'Probably with a local family. You certainly won't be staying here. It's miles too far from the dig.'

'But you stay here.'

'That's because the excavation site I'm working on is within easy distance.'

She frowned, puzzled. 'I don't understand. If I'm not to be working on one of the tomb digs, where am I to be working?'

'On Lewis's dig. He wasn't too happy with the idea at first, but the Squire talked him round. Go get your case. We're leaving now.'

Chapter Five

It was so unexpected that Kate was speechless.

Seeing her reaction, Kit said, 'It's far better that Lewis takes you on as a member of his team than that I do. You must see that, Kate? In the future, when you have a couple of major digs beneath your belt, then maybe it will be different. For now, I can't be seen to be giving my kid sister a place on a team somewhere as prestigious as Knossos, when she has nothing previous on her CV. There would be murmurings of nepotism, and you know how much I hate that word. If you want to work on a Bronze Age dig in Crete, the new dig Lewis is about to start at Kalamata is by far your best bet.'

'And what is he hoping to find?'

'A small palace. If his instinct is correct, you could well find yourself excavating a major Minoan site.'

'But if he's had to be pressured into taking me on? Isn't that going to make for an uncomfortable situation?'

Kit never laughed easily, but he laughed now. 'If you're going to survive in the cut-throat world of archaeology, you're going to have to develop a thicker skin, Kate.'

She grinned ruefully. 'Okay. Point taken. What kind of a team does Lewis Sinclair have?'

'A small one. I'll tell you more on the way there. Collect your suitcase and say goodbye to Mrs H. I'll meet you in the Sally at the lodge gates.'

'The Sally?

'One of the small trucks used by the excavating teams.'

'So tell me about the Kalamata team,' she said twenty minutes later as the small truck rattled up a dusty road in the direction of the mountains that ran almost unbroken down the backbone of the island. 'Is it mainly a British team?'

'It will be a little more so when you arrive.' Kit changed gear and swerved to avoid a boy herding a couple of sheep.

'Explain,' she said, tense once again.

'Like the last dig, this one is being privately sponsored and, until it's known whether it's going to be viable or not, only a handful of people are working on it. Apart from Lewis, and now you, they're from Kalamata or from villages in this part of Crete. All of them have worked on excavation sites before,' he added hastily. 'Christos's father worked on the Knossos site when the palace was being excavated, and Christos was brought up with Minoan excavation in his veins. Where practical work is concerned, his experience is second to none.'

He shot her an encouraging smile.

'You can see now what a chance this is for you, Sis. You're not going to be just another member of a team. You'll be on a dig where you can play a part of real importance.'

'But I'm also going to be a woman alone in an isolated village, with a Scotsman who is ill-mannered at the best of times and who isn't enthused at having me dumped on him. Add to that an unspecified number of Greeks – all male, and with presumably little English. It doesn't make for an ideal situation.'

She tried to visualize what their father would think of such an arrangement, but her imagination wouldn't stretch that far.

At the doubts in her voice, Kit said, irritated, 'The Greeks you will be working with will all have some English, and your classical Greek and your year in Greece have served you well, haven't they? Also there will be women at whatever lodging Lewis arranges for you. They'll find you a bit of a novelty at first, but they'll be welcoming. Greeks always are.'

Kate, aware that her doubts were out of place, considering how lucky she was to have been given a place on any dig in Crete, was immediately repentant. 'Sorry, Kit. I was just trying to get my head round being the only woman on the team. It's something I'll be able to take in my stride, so forget the mild panic attack. Does Lewis Sinclair have a truck at Kalamata? I've been driving Daddy's Riley for years, and driving a truck won't be a problem for me.'

'You'll have use of a truck. It's essential, in order to get in and out of Heraklion for stores and suchlike.'

He slowed down a little as they entered the small hill town of Archanes. It was where Kate had thought she might stay, if Sir Arthur's presence at the Villa Ariadne had made being a guest there impossible and, seeing it now for the first time, she thought it would have suited her very well. The houses in the narrow streets all had blazingly white walls, and balconies crammed with pots of scarlet geraniums and pale-yellow lilies. Cafes in the small central square had chequered-cloth tables set outside them, and beyond the square was a pretty church with a bell-tower. As they drove past it, Kit said, 'There are Byzantine frescoes in the church. You should try and find time to see them.'

'I will. Have we much further to go?'

'Quite a bit. Even for a Cretan village, Kalamata is well off the beaten track.'

It was so far off the beaten track that for the first time Kate wondered just how the Squire and Lewis Sinclair had been able to make contact with each other. Villa Ariadne was on the telephone, but a telephone in the area they were now in was as unthinkable as a red London bus.

'Is Lewis Sinclair at Kalamata now, waiting for me?' she asked as they turned off on to a steep, winding, perilously narrow mountain road.

'Nope, but he won't be far behind us. When the Squire tracked him down he was at the museum in Heraklion.'

Crete's mountainous landscape was laced with unexpected valleys and plateaus, and just when Kate thought it impossible for them to climb any higher, a plain of fertile fields and windmills opened up in front of them. At its heart lay a huddle of houses and a church.

'Kalamata,' Kit said, not driving into the village, but bringing the truck to a shuddering halt so that they could take in the view. 'It's very picturesque, don't you think?'

Kate drew in a slow, rapturous breath. It wasn't merely picturesque: it was beautiful. Far to the east were the snow-capped peaks of Mount Dicte, mythological birthplace of Zeus, king of the gods; to the west lay the great mountain range of Ida, where Zeus was said to have grown to manhood. On the northern side was a glittering glimpse of the distant sea.

'We'd best continue into the village,' Kit said at last. 'I'll stay with you until Lewis arrives, but then I'm going to head straight back.'

She felt a pang of alarm and quelled it. Although Kalamata was isolated, it wasn't as isolated as a dig in Persia or Arabia would have been. In a truck she could be in Heraklion in little over an hour. The very nature of archaeology meant long periods of time spent in places with few, if any, modern conveniences; and living and working alongside colleagues who could be difficult to get along with was something all archae-ologists had to put up with at times.

'How far is the site from the village?' she asked as Kit put the truck into gear again.

'About a fifteen-minute walk. I'd take you there now, only

I think Lewis will want to be the first to show you around. There's the usual *cafeneion* in the heart of the village. It's where he will expect to find us when he arrives.'

The instant the truck reached the outlying houses, children raced towards them, forcing Kit to a snail's pace as they shouted out questions and greetings.

Kate's Greek was good enough to understand what was being asked. The question the children most wanted answering was whether or not she was his wife; and, on Kit answering that she was not his wife, but his sister, if she was Kyrie Sinclair's wife.

'My sister is here to work,' Kit said, time and again. 'She is here to help Kyrie Sinclair with the village excavation.'

This last bit of news was met with incomprehension. How could the *Kyria* help with the village excavation? An excavation was man's work. Had the *Kyria* no house and husband to look after? No children to care for? No animals that needed tending?

When they at last drew to a halt on the bare earth of the village square they were saved from further bombardment by the cafe's owner rushing to greet them and shooing the children away as he did so.

The children, giggling, retreated several yards and then squatted down on the ground to wait and see whether Kyrie Sinclair's friend and his sister would have coffee inside the village *cafeneion* or outside it.

'It's always the same,' Kit said as they sat at a rickety iron table beneath a sun-bleached awning. 'Visitors in a village this isolated are rare events and always end up attracting this kind of attention. Would you like lemonade? It will be made with fresh lemons.'

When the cafe owner had served Kate with lemonade and Kit with a small cup of thick black Turkish coffee, he introduced himself. 'My name is Andre Stathopoulos,' he said, beaming at them from behind a thick, drooping crescent of a moustache. 'I am a man of Kalamata and it is a poor village, but when a great palace is excavated, it will be famous and my cafe will be full all day long with tourists.'

'Then let's hope a palace is found,' Kit said, trying to insert caution into his voice.

'Oh, it will be found! Kyrie Sinclair is sure of it.'

As if on cue, they heard the sound of a vehicle approaching the village. The children scrambled to their feet. Kate's tummy muscles tightened. Kit said, 'Here comes Lewis. Now we'll be able to find out where you'll be staying.'

Seconds later a small truck roared into the square and, as it slewed to a halt in front of the cafe, the children swarmed around it, shouting out to Lewis that the *Kyria* had come to work on the excavation team and that if she could work on the excavation team, why couldn't they?

To Kate's surprise, Lewis Sinclair's reaction wasn't irritation. Instead, with his mouth tugging into a smile, he took a handful of sweets from his pocket, throwing them for the children to scamper after.

When he joined them at their table she didn't receive a similar smile, only a courteous acknowledging nod.

Andre bustled up and, without being asked, set a glass of raki in front of Lewis. Kit said conversationally, 'That Kate is wanting the experience of working on a Minoan dig, and that you are on such an under-funded budget that you've no professionally qualified team members, is pretty fortuitous, don't you think, Lewis?'

'"Fortuitous" could be one word for it. What do you think of the arrangement, Kate?' For the first time he looked at her directly. 'Are you happy with it?'

'Yes,' she said with more composure than she felt. 'Very.'

Lewis turned his attention back to Kit. 'Then in that case

you're right, Kit. Your sister will be a big help. Tom Wilkinson from the British School was here until a month ago, but the political troubles in Spain have claimed him.'

Kate could see that the mention of Spain had caught Kit's attention, and before he could change the subject to Franco, she said, with a question mark in her voice, 'Kit tells me that the Kalamata site supervisor isn't a qualified archaeologist, but that he's very experienced?'

'Christos Kourakis's father, Kostas, worked on the Knossos dig from the first shovel-stroke. As a small child, Christos made himself useful in whatever way he could and Arthur Evans always took a great interest in him, and in the rest of Christos's family. When it comes to removing fragile objects without breaking them, Christos has the best pair of hands I've ever come across and he's an excellent site supervisor. He'll find it odd having a woman on the team, but as long you don't expect preferential treatment, you'll find him easy to get along with.'

'And other members of the team?' Kit said, as with the beaming smile that rarely left his face Andre set another cup of coffee down in front of him.

'Like Christos, they have all worked on previous Bronze Age digs – a couple of them at the Palace of Minos before the dig there came to an end. Dimitri and Angelos were at Olympia, which was a German excavation and is the reason their German is as good as their English. Pericles, Nico and Yanni have had experience on American digs, and Adonis has worked for a French excavation team at Corinth. It means that as they live in the village, or have relatives in the village with whom they can stay, there's no tented accommodation as yet, though there will be, once a palace is located and a bigger labour force is brought in.'

It was accommodation for herself that Kate wanted to know

about. Mrs Hutchinson had said the Kourakis family lived close to Knossos and she wondered what kind of accommodation had been found for Christos in Kalamata – and what kind of accommodation Lewis Sinclair enjoyed.

She was just drumming up the nerve to ask him where he slept at night when Kit said, 'And you, Lewis? Where do you stay? And where will Kate be staying?'

'Heraklion's deputy mayor has an unused family home here. I'm renting it from him. There are two bedrooms and at the moment Christos and I have a room each, but we can easily share. Christos won't mind.'

Kate waited for her brother to say that Christos might not mind, but that – on her behalf – he did. No such objection came and so she said reasonably, 'I'm not settling for sharing a house in the back of beyond with a man I barely know and a man I've not yet met. Sorry, but there's going to have to be a rethink.'

Lewis took a drink of his beer, put the glass down and rose to his feet. 'Give me five minutes,' he said, in the voice of a man whose patience was being strained to the upmost.

When he walked away, it wasn't in the direction of his truck, but into the cafe.

Kit said, 'Whatever arrangements are made, I think it would be best if you kept the Villa Ariadne as your address, where our parents are concerned.'

'Yes.' Kate had already imagined her father's alarm if he was to attempt the impossible and try to find a place as small as Kalamata on a map of Crete. 'I'll go along with that.'

Her glass of lemonade was now empty, but Andre didn't come rushing out of the cafe to take an order for another one. She knew why. It was because he and Lewis were in deep discussion about where she was to be lodged. She tapped a sandalled foot, hoping that when they came to a solution it would be one she could go along with.

Fifteen minutes later, when Lewis and Andre emerged, they were accompanied by a small-boned woman wearing a traditional bodice, a near ankle-length skirt kilted up to show a heavy underskirt, and with a black head-kerchief covering her hair. Her skin was sun-weathered and wrinkled, but her eyes were bright and full of interest and welcome.

'My wife, Agata,' Andre said as Kate rose to her feet. 'She has a room she wishes to show to you. It is a good room. The room of our daughters who work in Athens.'

From behind her, Kate heard Kit breathe a sigh of relief.

'Welcome.' Agata took Kate's hands in hers as if Kate was a child. 'Pleased I am to meet thee.'

'And I thee,' Kate said, responding in the Greek familiar, as if they were family or old friends.

While Kit and Lewis remained seated and Andre went back inside the *cafeneion* for another coffee for Kit, Agata led her around the side of the *cafeneion* to an outside staircase.

It led up to the Stathopoulos's living quarters. The interior was sparsely furnished, as Kate had expected it would be. It was also scrupulously clean.

'And this is the bedroom,' Agata said with pride, opening a door, after the stairs inside the house had been climbed.

The walls were whitewashed. The wooden floor was swept and scrubbed. There were two narrow beds with a small crucifix over each iron bedhead, two ancient sets of drawers and hooks in the wall for clothes to be hung on. From the window the mountain range of Mount Ida could be seen in the distance, and below the window hens roamed happily between rows of vines.

It was perfect, and Kate said so.

As they went back down the stairs, her thoughts were on Ella. It had always been her intention that once she had secured a place for herself on a dig, she would set about securing a place for Ella as well. She had imagined this would have had to wait a few weeks, until she had become settled. Now, having seen the two beds in the little room and knowing how short of professional help Lewis was, she saw no reason at all why she shouldn't immediately suggest Ella joining the team at Kalamata.

As she walked back across to Lewis and Kit's table, Kit said, 'Everything okay, Kate?'

'Absolutely.' She sat down and, without wasting a beat of time, said to Lewis, 'The bedroom has two beds in it. I have a friend who has a first-class honours in classical archaeology and who is as passionate as I am about Bronze Age Greece. She'd be a huge asset here. What d'you say to me writing to her?'

At her presumptuousness, his eyes narrowed.

'It would mean no local gossip about my being the only woman on the team,' she said swiftly, hoping to give him something to think about, before he refused out of hand, 'and although Ella hasn't already spent time in Greece, her classical Greek will be sufficient for there not to be any problems.'

'Is your friend an Oxford graduate?'

'Yes. St Hugh's.'

He hesitated, and then he said, 'You have to understand that if she doesn't work out, she'll be on the first plane back to Britain.'

'Oh, Ella will work out all right.' Kate felt as gleeful as the children had sounded when scooping up his shower of sweets. 'I'll write to her now. Kit can post the letter when he gets back to Knossos.'

Chapter Six

Ella was in Somerset when she received Kate's letter. The redirected address on the envelope was in her father's carefully laborious handwriting and, as the letter had been sent airmail from Greece, she knew the kind of anxiety it must have awoken in him. Until Kate's year in Athens, no airmail letters had ever arrived at their little home in Wilsden, and since they had begun doing so they had always aroused in her parents the kind of foreboding that a letter from a government department would have aroused.

The letter didn't arouse a similar sensation in Ella. She snatched it happily from the letter-rack above the reception desk of the bed-and-breakfast she was staying in and, instead of joining other members of the team for an end-of-day drink in the B&B's small bar, hurried off to her bedroom where she would be able to read it uninterrupted.

Dearest Ella,

Wonderful news! I have a place on a Bronze Age dig. In Crete! Accommodation for two is above the village cafe. I've spoken to the site director, who is short of professionals, and there is a place for you on the team. When you write back, address the letter c/o the Villa Ariadne, Knossos, Heraklion. Kit will act as postman. The village – Kala-mata – is too remote for dependable postal deliveries. Please,

*please, please ditch Somerset Romans and come out here as
fast as you can!*
Best love, Kate

Excitement spiralled through Ella until she felt almost sick
with it. The dig she was on was coming to a close and she
would have had to be looking for something else, with or
without Kate's letter. The prospect of addressing a letter to
the fabled Villa Ariadne, accepting the offer of work on Crete,
was so wonderful as to be almost unbelievable.

Shrugging herself out of her outdoor jacket and kicking off
her work boots, she scrabbled in the dressing-table drawer for
pen and paper.

Dear Kate,
  *My job comes to an end here at the end of the month.
Please tell the site director I will be joining the team the first
week of June. As for travel – is the cheapest way train
through France and Italy to Brindisi, and then steamer to
Piraeus and from there a steamer to Crete? I seem to
remember that was the route you took. Where do I go after
that? The site? (You haven't said just where it is.) Or the
Villa Ariadne?*
  Love, Ella

When she had finished the letter and written the magical words
'The Villa Ariadne' as part of the address, she ate a peppermint,
flicked through her diary, paused for thought and then began
another letter.

Dear Sam,
  *I've just been offered a position on an excavation in Crete.
The dig here is coming to an end and I will be beginning work*

*in Crete the first week in June. I'll be in Wilsden on the first
and second to say goodbye to Mum and Dad, and if you can
get time off from the Infirmary and can be in Wilsden, it
would be nice to see you. I expect it will be several months –
if not longer – before I'll be back in England again.*

She paused, not knowing quite how to continue. Since their
date at the Rialto to see *The Scarlet Pimpernel*, their relationship had changed. Although still not a full-blown romance, it
was no longer mere friendship. How could it be, after he had
kissed her long and deeply, and after she had surprised herself
by how willingly she had responded?

They hadn't met since then because there had been no
opportunity to do so. The next day Sam had been back on-duty
at Leeds Infirmary, where he was in the final stages of his
medical training, and she had travelled down to the Somerset
dig, only to discover that it was soon to be wound up. What
hadn't happened in the short time in between was either of
them writing to each other.

So how did she sign the letter? 'All best, Ella?' 'Love, Ella?'
'Affectionately, Ella?' In the end, she simply wrote 'Ella',
adding a little cross for a kiss next to it.

Five days later, when she returned back to the bed-and-
breakfast with the rest of the team, Sam was waiting for her
by the half-moon reception desk.

'I'm here until tomorrow,' he said. 'This B&B is full to the
rafters, but I've managed to get a room in a guest house not
too far away.'

'But why have you come?' Sheer shock made Ella clumsily
blunt. 'It isn't as if it's the weekend tomorrow. It's just an
ordinary day for me, and I'll be working.'

The reception area was small, and all the time they were

talking people were squeezing past them to get to the stairs, or to the door leading into the lounge.

'I need to talk with you, Ella. About Crete. About us.'

'Why don't you both come in the bar for a drink?' one of her male colleagues asked, dropping a friendly hand on Ella's shoulder.

'Perhaps later,' she said, knowing Sam wouldn't want to spend the time he had with her in a bar with other people.

Sam put a hand beneath her arm. 'Let's get some air.' He steered her in the direction of the door she had just come in by. 'Forget having your evening meal here. We'll find somewhere quiet to eat.'

As they stepped outside on to the pavement, he tucked her hand in the crook of his arm and shot her his easy smile. 'You are pleased to see me, aren't you?'

'Yes, of course I am.' It was true, although she'd had to get over her stunned surprise first, and wasn't looking forward to the conversation he'd come such a distance to have. 'There's a fish-and-chip shop nearby that has a restaurant attached to it,' she said, trying to behave as if the evening was just one of their normal evenings out together. 'The fish and chips aren't up to Yorkshire standards – they do their batter differently down here – but they'll come with peas, bread and butter and tea, just as they do up north.'

'It sounds just the ticket.' Taking his cue from her, until in the restaurant he could bring up the subject he so urgently wanted to speak to her about, Sam said, 'Somerset countryside is far different to Yorkshire's, isn't it? It's a lot gentler and the high-hedged lanes take a bit of getting used to.'

'Are you telling me you came down here from Leeds on your motorbike, Sam Jowett?'

'Every single mile – and there's two hundred and thirty-three of them. You didn't think I'd come by train, did you?'

'Of course I did! What if it had been raining? What if it's raining when you ride back? You'll get saturated.'

'I've got waterproofs,' he said, her concern for him giving him hope. 'Is this the fish-and-chip shop?'

They walked in and past the line of people queuing for takeaways and into the little room beyond, where there were a handful of tables with salt cellars and bottles of malt vinegar on them.

'What's it to be?' he asked as they sat opposite each other at one of the tables. 'Cod, as usual?'

She nodded, and when he'd ordered he reached across and took her hands in his. 'This Crete thing,' he said, not wasting any more time. 'Did your friend Kate arrange it?'

'Yes. It's a wonderful opportunity for me, Sam. The Minoan civilization discovered by Sir Arthur Evans on Crete pre-dates any other known Western civilization, and there are still sites and artefacts waiting to be discovered.'

'What's wrong with excavating British Roman sites?'

'Nothing – but right now the most exciting place for an archaeologist to be is on Crete.'

At the enthusiasm in her voice and the fervour in her eyes, he knew his journey was going to prove fruitless.

She squeezed hold of his hands. 'Please be happy for me, Sam. Kalamata is going to be a wonderful start to my career.'

'Kalamata?'

'The village closest to the dig.'

The waitress came, putting a plate of bread and butter on the table and two mugs of steaming tea. When she'd walked away from them, he said, 'How many months is the Kalamata dig likely to be?'

'I don't know, Sam. You may as well ask how long a piece of string is.'

'But you'll be back by the end of the summer?'

For the first time it occurred to Ella that he knew nothing whatsoever about archaeology, or of her feelings, where Greece was concerned.

In an effort to help him understand, she said, 'Hopefully the dig will prove to be a long one and, if it is, I doubt I'll be coming home between seasons. Once I'm in Greece I'm not going to want to leave it. And if the dig proves to be a short one, lasting only a few months, then I know what Kate's attitude will be. It will be that we find work on another dig in Crete and, if that isn't possible, that we look for work on another of the Greek islands, or on the mainland.'

Although she hadn't meant to do so, she couldn't have made it clearer that in the ranking of what was truly important to her, their romance had low priority.

Sam felt as if he'd been punched in the stomach, hardly able to believe that a girl who looked so feminine and fragile could be so single-minded and tough, where her career was concerned. Then he remembered how extraordinary it was that a girl from her background should have gained a place at Oxford and, on gaining it, had left with a first-class honours degree. Of course Ella was tough. She had to be, to have achieved all that she had.

Aware of the blow she'd dealt him, she said gently, 'If it was the other way around, Sam – if my place of work was in Yorkshire and never likely to be anywhere else, and if you were offered the chance of a position in a top-flight hospital in Boston, or New York – you would do the same thing, wouldn't you? It would surely be an opportunity you would leap at?'

'Perhaps. But I would have asked you to marry me first. I would only have gone if you were to come with me.'

Her throat closed with such emotion she couldn't speak. It didn't matter, for there was nothing she could say. Realizing it, Sam didn't say anything further, either.

The waitress came with their fish and chips: fish and chips they no longer had an appetite for. Sam pushed his plate away, saying, 'I don't think we need stay here any longer, need we, Ella? I wouldn't mind a bit of a walk, though.'

'I'd like a walk as well, Sam.'

He paid the bill, assuring the waitress there was nothing wrong with their fish and chips and that they were simply no longer hungry.

'Although, to tell the truth,' Sam said, as they stepped outside into a street hazed with the dusk of a summer evening, 'I probably wouldn't have cared for them if I had been hungry. My fish still had its skin on.'

'It's the way battered fish is served in the south.'

Sam grinned, determined to get things back on to some kind of an easy footing before they said goodbye. 'Then it's another good reason to be grateful for having been born in Yorkshire. Battered fish with skin on! What on earth would your granddad say?'

'He'd say, "Southerners know nowt",' she replied, laughter in her voice. 'And where fish and chips are concerned, he would be right.'

Companionably they walked along the street, hand-in-hand. By letting Ella know that where their future was concerned he had marriage on his mind, Sam had, he hoped, given her plenty to think about. He thought of her spending months, or even a year, in Greece; and he thought that, too, could work to his advantage. After all, Ella was a Yorkshire girl. By the time she returned home she wouldn't want to spend another night outside Yorkshire, and she wasn't likely to become romantically involved with anyone. How could she, when the only people she was likely to meet were Greek villagers?

The deep despair he had felt in the restaurant vanished. Ella's time in Crete would put things in perspective for her.

By the time she returned she would know what it was she wanted; and it would be him. When they said goodbye he was going to give her a kiss she wouldn't forget, no matter how long she was away; and he was going to tell her that even if she didn't yet love him, he loved her – that he would always love her.

'Ella! *Ella!*'

Ella had barely stepped foot on Heraklion's quay when she heard her name being shouted and saw Kate weaving a way towards her through the crowd of disembarking passengers.

With her suitcase banging against the side of her leg, she broke into a run.

Seconds later they were hugging each other tightly.

'Isn't this wonderful?' Kate's face was radiant. 'Isn't this just the best thing ever?'

'It's stupendous! All the way through France and Italy I've felt as if I were dreaming. I still can't quite believe I'm actually here, Kate. In Greece! On Crete!'

'And about to leave your suitcase at the Villa Ariadne's lodge and see the fabled Palace of Minos ruins and reconstructions for the first time.'

'Is that what we are about to do?'

They were crossing a busy road to a bus stop.

'It is. Unless we go to the Palace of Minos before Kit and the Squire know you have arrived, it's doubtful I'm going to have the chance to show you around it. They'll think it more important that we head off straight for Kalamata; and once we're at Kalamata it could be days, or weeks, till we'll be at Knossos again. And you are absolutely itching to see the palace, aren't you?'

'I'm desperate to see it. Ever since I was a little girl and first read of how the site was found, I've longed to see it for myself. Today is a fairy tale come true.'

As always, the bus to Knossos was crammed with tourists and they had to push and shove their way to the back of the bus to get a seat.

'What's new on the home front?' Kate asked as they finally found room in which to sit down. 'Have you heard from Daphne lately? Is she still seeing Sholto Hertford? Did you know he's a viscount? I don't think she told us, when we all had lunch together in Oxford. I only found out myself when I rang her to say I was leaving for Crete.'

'I had a postcard from her in the middle of May. She'd sent it from Cornwall and didn't mention Sholto, so whether or not they are still together I don't know.'

As the bus continued bumping and jolting its way through Heraklion's outskirts, Kate said, 'And you? How is Sam? Is he still the hopeful suitor?'

Ella was used to Daphne and Kate teasing her about Sam and usually she barely reacted. This time, though, her cheeks warmed. 'Things have changed slightly between Sam and me. Not hugely,' she added hurriedly, 'but we are on more romantic terms than we used to be.'

She wondered whether to tell Kate that Sam had let her know he'd never accept a job outside the country without first asking her to marry him; but, as it would raise questions she didn't yet know how to answer, she decided not to.

Instead she said, 'Did Sir Arthur visit Knossos on the anniversary of the dedication of his bust? Were you introduced to him?'

'No such luck. I'm not too sure he ever did make a definite arrangement to be at Knossos. I think everyone at the Villa Ariadne was just living in hope. He was eighty-five this year, and privately I rather think Sir Arthur's days of travelling to

Crete are over.' She looked out of the dusty window and rose to her feet. 'Come on. We're nearly at the lodge gates. The driver will drop us off at them, if we ask nicely, and it will save you carrying your suitcase fifty yards back down the road.'

Fifteen minutes later, and minus the suitcase, they were walking along the sandy tree-shaded path that led into the Palace of Minos's West Court.

There was no need for Kate to give any explanations as to the layout of the palace to Ella. Ella, she knew, already had a detailed plan of it in her head. All the same, she couldn't help saying, 'Reading that the full extent of the excavated site extends over six acres, and actually physically experiencing the size of it, is always a slam to the heart.'

The first slam to Ella's heart as, beneath a hot sun, they stepped on to the paving stones that had served the palace as a ceremonial entrance court was the sight of a head-high pillar mounted by a bronze bust of Sir Arthur Evans.

She stood before it, feeling something close to reverence, trying to imagine what it must have been like to have discovered not only the palace, but a civilization. Then, hardly able to breathe for the excitement of the moment, she turned and looked towards the vast, labyrinthine remains that he had, over a period of thirty years, excavated and, in parts, controversially reconstructed.

A maze of walls – some discernible only enough to show the outlines of rooms, chambers and hallways; others shoulder-high; and still others showing where the palace had originally been two and three storeys high – sprawled in a vast interconnected complex. Supporting scarlet pillars, banded in black, glittered in the sun. A raised walkway, its purpose to allow the ceremonial processions of more than three thousand years ago to be seen easily by throngs of spectators, led across the paved court they were standing on.

'Today you have less time here than even the most cursory visitor,' Kate said apologetically. 'An hour is the most we can hope to get away with, before starting for Kalamata. Don't panic about it. There's always some member of the team driving to and from Heraklion, and you won't have much problem getting here on your days off. For now, though, what is to be? What is your most urgent priority? The Throne Room? The bull fresco at the North Entrance? The Shrine of the Double Axes?'

'The Great Courtyard. I want to be able to imagine it as it was, when bulls thundered across it and young men with ringleted hair raced headlong towards them and then leapt high, somersaulting down the length of a bull's back. And don't tell me that Minoan bull-leaping may only be a myth. The palace frescoes tell a different story.'

In jewelled light they made their way into the shade of the court's porch, its plastered floor the same dull red as the room's supporting columns.

'You would think that from here there would be a direct route into the centre of the palace,' Kate said, as they left the porch from its eastern end and continued along what Sir Arthur had named the Corridor of the Procession, 'but nowhere in the palace is there a direct route to anywhere. Lewis Sinclair believes the labyrinth in the legend of Theseus and the Mino-taur is the palace itself.'

'In the legend, the Minotaur's labyrinth was underground.'

'He has an answer for that as well.'

They walked up shallow steps and past an altar base.

'Which is?' Ella was curious about the site director for whom she had come to work. So far, Kate had told her next to nothing about him.

'Many parts of the palace must have had very little light and could very well have seemed to be underground. And then there are the earthquakes Crete suffers from. Lewis thinks that, to the Minoans, the rumbling in the earth would sound like the bellowing of a bull.'

At the top of the steps was a low retaining wall and they sat down on it.

'Is Lewis easy to work for? You haven't said.'

'He's efficient and the Cretans like him.'

'And you?'

'We're politely civil to each other, but I suspect he thinks Kit was out of order asking him if he'd give me a place on the team, and I don't think he liked the fact that he was so short-handed he couldn't afford to turn the offer down.'

'He sounds difficult to get on with. Is he very old-school?'

'No. He's twenty-eight, the same age as Kit, only he doesn't look like Kit. He's dark-haired and dark-eyed enough to pass for a Greek.'

Though Kate's voice was studiedly neutral, Ella knew her too well to be fooled.

Her eyebrows nearly shot into her hair. 'You're smitten, Kate Shelton! Does he feel the same way about you?'

'Of course I'm not smitten! And he certainly isn't smitten with me. He's in a relationship with a Cretan girl.' She jumped to her feet, not wanting to think about Nikoleta Kourakis. 'Let's cut straight to the Great Courtyard before we run out of time. Three thousand years ago it was flagged with blue schist stone. There's no paving there now, just plain earth, but self-seeded flowers have made it just as colourful as it must have been originally.'

Ella, who was sensitive enough to know when a subject was best left alone, rose to her feet. Unlike Daphne, who was always falling in love, Kate had never, to her knowledge, ever done so. That she might have done so now – with the site director they were both working for, and with whom they would be living in unavoidable close proximity, and who apparently was already in a relationship – threatened all kinds of uncomfortable problems.

She gave herself a sharp mental shake. There was no need to anticipate problems that might never happen. Kate was far too level-headed and sensible to allow her private feelings to affect the close-knit spirit that was essential to a successful dig. The next few months weren't going to be full of problems; they were going to be amazing.

She hooked her arm into Kate's, knowing that if a Minoan palace *was* found at Kalamata, the next few months would be more than amazing. Where their careers were concerned, they would be the most important months of their lives.

Chapter Seven

Daphne was in Berlin. It was the first week of August and she wasn't there out of any particular liking for the city, but because the Olympic Games were being held there and her father had expressed the desire that she accompany him to them.

After a long day at the Reichssportfeld, where they had seen Jack Lovelock of New Zealand make a heroic dash to the tape to win the 1,500 metres event, she was walking with her father towards the Adlon Hotel, where they were staying.

'I must say that nothing is as grim here as some of our news chappies have been trying to make out,' her father said, waving an ebony-knobbed walking cane in a way that indicated he wasn't only talking about the street they were on, but the city as a whole. 'I don't see any signs forbidding Jews entry, or forbidding them from sitting on park seats, do you?'

'No, Daddy. And that's because all such signs have been removed for the duration of the Games.'

'And who told you that?'

'Sholto.'

The earl gave a rude snort. The trouble with Sholto Hertford was that he was a Foreign Office diplomat and so his opinions on foreign affairs couldn't easily be discounted. All the same, he didn't agree with Sholto, where Germany was concerned. The country had been in a shambles ten years ago. It wasn't in a shambles now. Thanks to Hitler, there were no more running battles in the streets between splinter-party groups and Communists, because Hitler had refused to tolerate them. The Communists had been rounded up and incarcerated in a new kind of prison on Berlin's outskirts and there were no longer any splinter-party groups, just one central party: Hitler's Nazi Party.

'And there's no unemployment,' he said stubbornly as they walked through one of the Brandenburg Gate's monolithic arches. 'That's a miracle that Britain and America are nowhere close to achieving.'

Daphne rolled her eyes to heaven, unable to summon up the energy to say that the reason for German employment was that jobless men were drafted to work on government projects for few or no wages. Her father, who harboured a passionate fear of Communism, saw Hitler's Germany through rose-coloured glasses. Sholto didn't and, thanks to Sholto, neither did she.

The instant they stepped into the Adlon's baroque reception area she saw Miranda Seeley.

'Excuse me, Daddy.' She slid her arm from his. 'There's a friend of mine at the reception desk. I must say hello to her.'

With a wide smile on her face, she ran across to Miranda.

At the sight of Daphne, Miranda's eyes widened: first with surprise at so unexpectedly meeting up with her in the middle of Berlin, and then with consternation. 'I'm here with my mother,' she said instantly, as if it should mean something.

Daphne, to whom it meant nothing, laughed. 'And I'm here with my father. Anyone would think we were still children. Have you only just arrived? We've been here two days already. Sholto is somewhere in the city as well, although as one of the official guests and he's not staying here, worst luck.'

'We arrived two hours ago.'

'Spiffing. I'd count it a huge favour if we were all to meet up for a drink before dinner. My father can be an awful drain when there's no one to share the load with, and half an hour in your mother's company is bound to perk him up.'

Taking Miranda's acquiescence for granted, Daphne gave her a hasty kiss on the cheek and darted back to her father, saying as she again hooked her arm in his, 'You're in luck, Daddy. We're having pre-dinner drinks with Miranda and her mamma this evening. Mrs Seeley is French and, by your standards, young. She is also elegant and very *chic*.'

Her father made another of those sounds in his throat that were never easy to interpret. As they moved towards the lift, he said, 'We have the opera tonight. *Tristan und Isolde*. I don't think social chit-chat with a Frenchwoman will put me in a good mood for it.'

'Of course it will.' A uniformed attendant rolled back the door of a caged lift for them. 'If you're not careful, you're going to turn into an old fuddy-duddy. All you need to put a spring in your step is a long, deep bath and a large whisky and soda.'

Stepping into the lift, the attendant closed the door and began operating it upwards.

Daphne looked across at her father. There was a mutinous look on his face and she knew that if she wanted a little light relief before enduring Wagner, she was going to have to give him more encouragement.

'Mrs Seeley is a friend of Wallis Simpson's,' she said, knowing he would be unable to resist inside gossip about King Edward's mistress. 'There are rumours she is seeking a divorce.'

'Who? The Seeley woman?'

'No.' Daphne quelled rising exasperation. 'Mrs Simpson.'

'Is she, by God? That infantile young pup can't be thinking of marrying her, can he?'

'The young pup is forty-two – and he can't marry her. If she divorces, it will be her second divorce. Do be reasonable, Daddy. How can a woman who has been divorced twice become Queen of England?'

'*Tiens!* But she wouldn't merely be Queen of England!' Francine Seeley said an hour and a half later. 'She would be Queen of the United Kingdom and all her Dominions over the Seas, and she would also be *l'impératrice de l'Inde* – Empress of India!'

'A consort,' Lord St Maur said, not overly happy at being told by a Frenchwoman the titles held by the wife of a British king. 'She wouldn't be queen in her own right, Mrs Seeley. She would be a queen consort.'

Francine Seeley gave a Gallic shrug of her shoulders. If Wallis married David – Wallis never referred to the King as anything other than David – then she would wear a crown and even she, Francine, would have to curtsey to her. It would be a great achievement for any woman born a commoner, and an even greater achievement for a twice-divorced American.

Her eyes flicked from Percy St Maur – who must have been in his late forties when Daphne was born, and who was certainly nearer seventy than sixty and therefore of no interest to her – to Daphne. Francine had only ever seen her twice before, and both times only briefly. The first time had been at Buckingham Palace on the day Miranda and Daphne had been next to each other in line, on being presented to the late King George and Queen Mary. The second time had been at Miranda's birthday party, and on that occasion she had only exchanged the most cursory of pleasantries with her.

Sholto, however, had exchanged far more than pleasantries with Daphne St Maur – and was, she knew, still doing so.

Francine's first instinct, when Miranda had told her that Daphne and her father were staying at the Adlon, was to leave the hotel immediately and find accommodation elsewhere. Parisian common sense had swiftly kicked in, ensuring that she hadn't done so. There would be no accommodation elsewhere, or certainly not suitable accommodation. Berlin was bursting to the seams with visitors to the Games.

Besides, she was curious. Although Sholto's romance with Daphne didn't perturb her at a deep level – she knew he had only embarked on it in order to try and make her jealous and because he hadn't been able to handle the knowledge that she had, aeons ago, had an affair with his father – it was a romance now in its fourth month. For an impulsive tit-for-tat gesture, four months was a long time. She wanted to know what it was about Daphne St Maur that had held Sholto's interest for so long; she wanted to know if she should, perhaps, have concerns.

'At present King Edward is on a cruise in the Adriatic with Wallis and a few friends,' she said, wondering if Sholto shared this type of information with Daphne. Her narrow, dark eyes regarded the girl thoughtfully. 'But then you perhaps know that already?'

Daphne didn't. She leaned forward a little in her chair. 'No,' she said. 'Do tell me who the friends are, Mrs Seeley.'

Francine, gratified that Sholto didn't share gossip about Edward and Wallis with Daphne, made a careless gesture with a heavily beringed hand. 'The Coopers. You know the Coopers, *bien sûr*?'

Although they were a generation older than her, Daphne did know the Coopers. As well as having distant royal relations, Duff Cooper was a government minister. He was also a notorious womanizer and, as Daphne didn't find him remotely physically attractive, she had always given him a wide berth. His wife Diana was, though, a delight and one of the most fun-to-be-with people she knew.

'Yes,' she said. 'I know the Coopers. Who else is sailing the Adriatic with the King and Mrs Simpson?'

'The usual group of intimate friends: Lord and Lady Dudley, Lord and Lady Brownlow, Lord Sefton, Lord Beaverbrook's sister-in-law Helen Fitzgerald, Mr and Mrs Herman Rogers.' Seeing that the last two names meant nothing to Daphne, she said, 'When Wallis spent a year in Peking, she lived with Katherine and Herman. Wallis and Katherine have been friends for over twenty years.'

Startled by the mention of Peking, Daphne was about to ask what it was that had taken Wallis to China, when the carefully maintained neutral expression in Francine's eyes slipped, revealing such dislike of her that Daphne was robbed of breath.

Miranda said, 'Mummy would have been aboard the *Nahlin*, too, if it hadn't been for having arranged to be in Berlin for the Games. We're here at the special invitation of a friend of hers, Count von Ribbentrop, who has just been appointed German Ambassador to Britain.'

Aware that some kind of response was needed, Daphne's father said, 'Has he, indeed? Jolly good show.'

Daphne was too shocked by the knowledge that, in twenty minutes of conversation – conversation in which she had said nothing that could possibly have caused offence – she had aroused such a feeling of dislike. It occurred to her that perhaps Miranda's mother was one of those women who, no longer in their twenties, was fiercely jealous of those who were.

Whatever the reason, the knowledge that she was disliked was not pleasant, and she was glad when Francine Seeley rose to her feet, bringing their little pre-dinner drinks party to a close.

*

Later, with the incident forgotten and as the second act of the opera got under way, Daphne's thoughts were all of Sholto.

Ever since she had arrived in Berlin, the fact that Sholto was in the city and unable to spend time with her had been an irritation of mega-proportions; now it was beginning to be more than irritating. It was beginning to be depressing. She loved her father dearly, but spending time with him, especially when the two of them were on their own together, was always an effort. One of the reasons she had allowed him to persuade her to accompany him to the Games was that Sholto was going to be attending them as a representative from the Foreign Office, and she had liked the idea of the two of them being in Berlin at the same time.

It hadn't, though, worked out as she had imagined it would. Instead of being able to leave her father safely tucked up in bed at the Adlon, while she and Sholto went out on the town, all Sholto's time had been taken up with official duties and, as he had told her on the one and only time she had managed to make telephone contact with him, it was a situation that wasn't going to change – which meant that for all she had seen of him, he could have been on another planet.

'I might as well be having a romance with someone who's in trade,' she'd said in comic exasperation.

He'd cracked with laughter. 'I must tell the Foreign Secretary how you regard his diplomats,' he'd said, still chuckling. 'Enjoy the Games, Daphne. I'll be in touch when I'm back in London.'

As a love duet between Tristan and Isolde moved towards an emotional climax, she thought how odd it was that she was still so happily faithful to Sholto. It wasn't as if he slavishly adored her. There were times, such as their recent telephone call, when he was almost offhand. She didn't even seriously mind that, as a career diplomat, his time wasn't his own in the way that the time of her previous boyfriends had been. It meant that although he enjoyed weekend house parties and polo, and everything else that went with being a member of a privileged class of society, he also had interesting and serious issues on his mind, something that couldn't have been said for her discarded exes.

The list of the discarded was, even by her estimation, a long one. However cataclysmic the initial attraction might have been, within weeks, and sometimes days, she had always been too bored to want to continue with the relationship.

Sholto was unique in that he had never yet bored her – and she doubted that he ever would. In Kate's last letter to her, which she'd received just before coming to Berlin, Kate had written:

Has Sholto popped the question yet? In a roundabout way Sam has popped to Ella, by telling her he'll never accept a position abroad without first asking her to marry him. She didn't give him any indication of what, if such a situation arose, her response would be. It wasn't a very romantic way of going about things on his part, was it? But then he's a Yorkshireman and allowances have to be made!

The curtain came down on the second act and Daphne rose to her feet to accompany her father to the champagne bar. There were times when she found keeping in contact with Kate and Ella by letter so unsatisfactory that it hurt. What she wanted was for the three of them to be able to have a good chat over a boozy lunch. That way she would, within minutes, have been able to understand the truth between their often very different accounts of things. For instance, in Ella's last letter to her, Ella had written:

Kate's tension whenever she is working with Lewis Sinclair is so palpable you can almost hear it crackle. It's obviously a huge sexual attraction on her part (he's criminally good-looking), but she won't admit to it, even to me. Apart from one member of the team who is from mainland Greece, the rest are all from Crete and though they obviously find it bizarre having women working on a dig with them, are scrupulously polite about it.

In her letter, Kate had written:

Everything is going wonderfully well out here. That Ella's Greek is pronounced with flat Yorkshire vowels is a source of great amusement to Christos, our site foreman. He vows he's never seen hair her colour of red before and teases her endlessly about it.

In Ella's letter there was no mention of Christos and his teasing, only of the Greek team's 'scrupulous politeness', and in Kate's letter there was no mention whatsoever of Lewis Sinclair.

As she sipped champagne in the crowded bar of the opera house, Daphne knew that when she responded to Kate's letter she would be equally evasive, for although she would write that Sholto hadn't proposed and showed no indications of doing so, she couldn't put down on paper how she felt about that, because she truly didn't know.

Proposals in the past – and since her coming-out she had received quite a few – had always, for her, been the death-knell of the relationship in question. As far as she was concerned, it was too much, too soon. To receive a proposal from someone who barely knew her – one of those who had 'popped' had done so after their first date – was, she felt, more insulting than it was complimentary. Such proposals of marriage were, however, what a debutante's social season was all about, and she had found it annoying that in order to enjoy parties and balls she also had to endure being proposed to by men who, because of the column inches *Tatler* regularly gave her, thought becoming engaged to her would be a social triumph.

Without a shadow of a doubt she knew it wasn't an attitude Sholto would share.

A bell rang, indicating that the third act was about to begin, and she put her champagne flute down and slid her hand into the crook of her father's arm.

Sholto was a world removed from any of the men she had, for however short a space of time, thought herself to be in love with. She had never, she reminded herself, thought herself to be *deeply* in love with any of them. Now she knew that she had never been remotely in love with them; that the only flame that had ever burned had been the flame of infatuation, and even that flame had been exceedingly pale.

As they walked back into the auditorium, excitement spiralled through her that was so intense she sucked in her breath. Of course she knew how she felt about Sholto not yet having proposed to her! It was that he was certainly going to do so one day, and that she wasn't going to spoil the moment when he did, by worrying about how far in the future that moment might be. Why should she, when everything between them was so very, very perfect?

She was still bathed in the joyous certainty of what lay in their future when, later that evening and arm-in-arm with her father, she walked into the Adlon.

Francine, evening-gowned and with her shoulders swathed in white fox furs, was about to enter the lift. Across the reception hall their eyes held. A smile touched Francine's garnet-red mouth.

Daphne was about to respond politely when, with a stab of

shock, she registered the nature of the smile. It wasn't friendly. It wasn't even pleasant. Instead it was a smile full of triumph and malicious amusement.

On the morning when Daphne and her father were due to fly back to England, Daphne took a lone, early-morning stroll along Unter den Linden's tree-shaded boulevard. It was, she thought, the nicest part of the city. There were park benches at strategic intervals beneath the linden trees, and so early in the day the wide central walkway was uncrowded. She paused at the point where Wilhelmstrasse interconnected with the boulevard. Wilhelmstrasse was the city's government district and was also where the British Embassy was situated. Sholto was, she was sure, somewhere tantalizingly near. He wasn't, though, taking an early-morning stroll.

She refused to be disappointed. By the end of the day they would both be back in England and in all probability would have a late-night supper together at the Dorchester, or the Savoy.

He would give her his professional assessment of what the true state of things was in Germany and she would tell him of how, when she had been at the Reichssportfeld, she had seen Hitler close up and had been surprised at how insignificant he had looked. Then, not wanting to waste time talking any longer, they would take a taxi to Sholto's Kensington mansion flat and make delicious love.

Anticipation flooded through her, filling her with such happiness she could hardly bear the intensity of it. One thing she was now certain of was that she had been wrong in thinking there was no hurry for Sholto to propose to her. She now wanted him to propose to her at the earliest possible moment. She wanted his ring on the fourth finger of her left hand. She wanted a huge wonderful wedding at St Margaret's, Westminster, with Kate and Ella as bridesmaids. She wanted the sense of oneness that she felt with Sholto to be a sense of oneness that would last life-long.

'Cooee!' a familiar voice called, breaking in on her thoughts.

Miranda was seated on one of park benches and, to Daphne's relief, there was no sign of her mother anywhere nearby. Walking across to join her, Daphne said, 'We're leaving for the airport in an hour.'

'Lucky you. We're going on to Dresden to stay with friends of the Ribbentrops.'

Daphne sat down beside her. 'Your mother doesn't like me,' she said bluntly. 'Have you any idea why?'

'Well, of course she doesn't like you!' Miranda stared at her in astonishment. 'As things are, why on earth should she? Just remember it was you who suggested we all have pre-dinner drinks together. Why Mummy agreed to it, I have no idea.'

'Why on earth shouldn't I have suggested we have pre-dinner drinks together?'

Miranda raised net-gloved hands in the air in exasperation. 'Because I, for one, found the experience very difficult under the circumstances.'

'Circumstances?' Daphne prayed for patience. 'What circumstances?'

'You and Mummy sharing a lover.'

Daphne burst into laughter. 'Don't be ridiculous, Miranda. I'm not sharing a lover with your mother. I'm in love with Sholto.'

'So,' Miranda said with steel in her voice, 'is my mother.'

Daphne's laughter died. Crossly she said, 'You are a fool, Miranda. Whatever put such a ridiculous idea into your head?'

'Mummy did.'

'Well, it isn't true. How could it be? Your mother is probably old enough to be Sholto's mother.'

'No, she isn't. She's thirty-six and Sholto is twenty-eight.'

'Whatever.' Daphne's irritation was growing. 'The fact remains that Sholto isn't her lover. If Sholto knew what you were saying, he'd be furious.'

'Maybe he would be, but that doesn't alter the fact that it's true. He's been her lover for four years.'

There was a mulish certainty in Miranda's voice.

Daphne stared at her. Then she said, 'You're wrong, Miranda. Sholto and your father are friends. That he was a family friend was one of the first things Sholto ever said to me.'

'If he did, it was a euphemism for being something else, although he *is* on friendly terms with my father. I believe all of Mummy's previous lovers always have been.'

Daphne felt a hideous feeling of doubt stir. 'I don't believe it.' She rose abruptly to her feet. 'Sholto would never be so dishonourable.'

'Why not? He has been before. You're not the first girlfriend he's had during his affair with my mother. If you don't believe me, ask him, but be prepared for him telling you you're making a fuss over nothing. That's what he's said to previous girlfriends when they objected to my mother being the central relationship in his life. I'm sorry if you didn't know about Sholto and Mummy before. I'd always assumed you did and that, as you are so unconventional, you didn't care.' As an afterthought, she said, 'Mummy had dinner with Sholto the night of our pre-dinner drinks party. Perhaps now you understand why she was so cool towards you.'

There was no spite in her voice. Only a truth impossible to disbelieve.

The blood drained from Daphne's face as she finally, and belatedly, understood.

She understood other things as well.

She understood why, late on the night of the pre-dinner drinks party, Francine Seeley had smiled at her with such triumph and malicious amusement.

She understood that although Sholto had said it was impossible for him to see her while he was in Berlin, it had been possible for him to see Francine.

And most of all she understood that for the past four months she had been living in a fool's paradise.

Swamped by tidal waves of rage and pain, her joyous happiness of just minutes ago now dust in the wind, she was certain of only one thing, and that was that after she had confronted Sholto with what she knew – and though it would nearly kill her – she was never going to see him or speak to him again.

Chapter Eight

It was the end of morning surgery and as the last patient closed the door behind him, Sam pushed his chair away from his desk. He had a long list of home visits to make and needed a cup of tea and a biscuit before setting off on them. The practice he had joined as a newly qualified general practitioner was in Scooby, a moorland village close to Richmond, and many patients lived on farms and homesteads in outlying areas. If today's list was anything to go by, Sam knew it would be late afternoon before he was able to sit down to a proper meal.

There was a tap on his door and the receptionist opened the door just wide enough to put her head around it. 'The tea's mashed, Dr Jowett. Shall I bring it in?'

'Yes, please, Jenny. And would you do a favour for me and double up on the biscuits?'

Jenny Gulliver, who was seventeen and who, if he'd asked it of her, would happily have lain down and died for Sam, blushed rosily. 'Course I will. They're chocolate digestives today. Dr Fallow doesn't like them much, but I know you do.'

The door closed and as Sam began checking his doctor's bag to make sure he had everything he needed in it before leaving on his rounds, there was a smile on his mouth. Jenny was pretty and outgoing and someone he would, in the ordinary way of things, have enjoyed having an occasional pub lunch with, or an early-evening drink with. The minute he had realized she had a crush on him was, though, the minute he'd realized he would never issue any such invitation. It would raise hopes he had no intention of fulfilling and he wasn't the sort of bloke to lead a girl on, especially not when the girl was as young and as nice as Jenny.

He put the stethoscope he had recently been using into his bag and, satisfied that everything else he might need was already in it, clicked the bag shut. His desk was clear, apart from Ella's last letter to him. He picked it up and put it in the inner pocket of his tweed jacket. That way, unintentionally but happily, it lay next to his heart. All her earlier letters to him were back at his digs, lying in a neat pile in his underwear-and-sock drawer.

Ever since arriving in Crete she had written to him once a week. It was something he took great comfort from, certain that – busy as she was, and as excited as she was about the work she was doing – she wouldn't write with such regularity unless he was as important to her as she was to him.

Her first letters had been all about the kind of dig it was. In dark blue ink on thin airmail paper she had written:

It's almost like a dig of the last century in that, although being done with Greek government authority, it isn't an official dig being carried out by the British School in Athens (though the British School is taking an interest in it). Instead it's a private venture, although who is funding it is a secret that our charismatic site director is keeping to himself. He excavated in this area a year ago and, though he found a couple of Bronze Age tombs (huge things, built on a great scale – the ground plan of them is square, the front and back walls vertical, the other two walls sloping inwards), he didn't find what he was looking for (which is a small Minoan palace). The existence of such grand tombs does, though, indicate he is right in thinking there was a palace in this area (some of the artefacts found in the tombs are magnificent, especially a couple of incredibly beautiful swords). Where the palace is concerned, all we have to do now is find it!

In July her letters were as much about people and the heat as they were about the excavation work:

Goodness, but it's hot here, Sam! If this had been a regular dig, we would long ago have called a halt till the weather is cooler, but nothing here is like a regular dig. For one thing, there are so few of us on it. Lewis operates very much as a one-man band. How he managed before he took Kate on board, I can't imagine; and as far as he and Kate are concerned – well, I'll come to that another day. All in all, there are ten of us on the team: Christos Kourakis, our site foreman (his family home is within sight of Knossos and he practically grew up on the Palace of Minos dig), Dimitri and Angelos Mamalakis (brothers born and bred in Kalamata), Pericles Georgiou (a mainland Greek who has worked on American digs), Nico Petras (keen, but without much experience), Yanni Zambiakos (Yanni is in his sixties – like Christos, he worked for Sir Arthur Evans on the Palace of Minos dig and has massive practical experience) and finally Adonis Paterakis (he's in his teens and, as his looks live up to his name, he's a great favourite with the village girls). Now that the men's initial unhappiness at working alongside two women has been overcome, we've meshed into a great team. The happiest I've ever been on a dig.

By the end of July Sam knew a lot more about the people she was working with and spending time with. He knew that the Mamalakis brothers were both married with young families;

that Dimitri's wife, Aminta, was sweet-natured; and that Angelos's wife, Rhea, was the exact opposite and the village gossip into the bargain.

Towards the end of the month Ella had written:

> *Despite the site being only a fifteen-minute walk from the village, the village women never visit it. Their menfolk regard the site as a man's province (Kate and me excepted – just) and, in Crete, what men think and say goes. Rhea, however, still gets to know everything that happens on-site and then, heavily embellishing it, broadcasts it far and wide. Fortunately Angelos hasn't cottoned-on to Kate's feelings for Lewis and so hasn't been able to share that with Rhea. If he had, it would be the talk of the village by now. Pericles Georgiou keeps himself to himself, but may not be able to do so for much longer. Apollonia, the widow he is lodging with, is beginning to be very proprietorial about him. There is no work for young men in villages like Kalamata, and so to suddenly have a clutch of single young men lodging in the village has caused a lot of female excitement. Even Yanni is being eyed up by old Zenobia, who tells fortunes and hasn't a tooth left in her head.*

With the practice doors closed until six o'clock, when evening surgery began, Sam's tea and biscuits were now waiting for him on the reception desk. As he drank his tea he reflected on the oddity of how easily Ella had become assimilated into Cretan rural life. When he'd expressed his puzzlement in a letter, she'd responded by writing back:

> *Dearest Sam,*
>   *Bizarrely, I find many aspects of Crete and Yorkshire – and Cretans and Yorkshire folk – similar. Just as Yorkshire is part of England, and yet is viewed by those who live in it*

as a country apart, so Crete, though part of Greece, is
regarded by Cretans as a country apart. And having grown
up in a mill cottage on the edge of the moors, the hardship in
Kalamata hasn't come as a surprise to me. There is, for
instance, no running water in the village (as there wasn't in
the house my granddad used to live in). Lavatories are prim-
itive, dry-earth affairs (something I've had experience of in
the past), and children run barefoot, as did many of my
playmates when I was a child. Just as Yorkshire folk face
hardship with what we call 'Yorkshire grit', so do the people
of Kalamata. All in all – and as I love the work I'm doing
– it's been easy for me to settle in here.

It was a letter that had filled him with disquiet. Though he
didn't want Ella to be unhappy in Crete, neither did he want
her to begin feeling at home there. Filling him with even
greater disquiet was the overall tone of her letters. Chatty and
bubbly, they could have been the letters of a sister to a brother.
In every letter he wrote he told her how much he was missing
her, and of the future he hoped they were going to have
together. In the letters she wrote back there was never a similar
response.

Instead, she wrote about the dig; about how, though they
hadn't yet located a palace, they had located a Bronze Age
villa; and of the hours she had spent under a hot sun scrubbing
sherds in bowls of acid and water to remove the soil from
them; and of the magnificent gold jewellery that Christos had
unearthed, and which was now in the museum at Heraklion.

She wrote about the village and of how there were no paved
streets in it; of how the houses had outside stairs that led to
the living quarters; and of how the ground floors served as
stables for animals.

She wrote of how Andre Stathopoulos, whose *cafeneion* she

and Kate were lodging in, played the fiddle after their evening meals, and of how Agata Stathopoulos fussed over her and Kate like a mother hen.

She wrote about Kate and how, not wanting Lewis Sinclair to guess how she felt about him, she was always coolly polite and distant with him; and she wrote about Daphne, saying that she no longer mentioned Sholto in her letters, and that Daphne's last letter had been posted from Cowes, where she was attending the Regatta with friends.

With the best will in the world, Sam was indifferent as to what was happening in Ella's friends' lives. All he wanted to know, as he finished the last biscuit on the plate and then drained his cup of tea, was what was happening in Ella's own life and, more importantly, what part she envisaged him playing in it.

It was October, and Daphne was spending Friday to Monday at a house party in Derbyshire. All country-house parties in October were shooting parties and although Daphne hadn't the slightest intention of shooting a pheasant, or of following the guns with other non-shooting guests, it was an invitation she had accepted rather than face a weekend without any kind of diversion.

These days, diversion was something she was always in need of.

When she had packed her weekend case, it had been in the hope that at Sherwood Castle she would be able to stop thinking about Sholto; that there would be a man among the other guests with whom she would instantly fall in love; that her heartache would finally shrivel and die, leaving room for joy – or, if not joy, then at least a sliver of happiness.

At the very least it would be an escape from having her flatmate, Sandy Crailsford, constantly trying to lift her spirits by saying, 'Cheer up. It might never happen.'

The first time Sandy had said it, Daphne had pushed her hair away from eyes that were sore with weeping and had said, in agonizing pain, 'But it has, Sandy. It has happened.'

Sandy, incapable of empathizing with anyone's feelings other than her own, had shot her a smile, adjusted the seams of her stockings and dashed from the room to hurry downstairs to where, in the street and in a red sports car, her date for the evening was waiting for her.

By now, whenever Sandy trotted out the same tired platitude, Daphne's reserves of patience were wearing thin.

The bedroom she had been allotted at Sherwood was, like nearly all the bedrooms in England's stately piles, cavernous and chill. She stood at one of the room's massive stained-glass windows, looking out over a topiary garden to a vista of a rolling, immaculate lawn. Since arriving she'd discovered that her fellow guests were all people she knew, which meant an end to all hopes of meeting a handsome dark stranger who was capable of ridding her of thoughts of Sholto.

Sholto.

In the two months since their affair had come to an inglorious end she'd neither heard nor seen anything of him. He'd been nowhere in sight at any of the social events and parties she had attended; there had been no photographs of him in *Tatler*; no mention of him in any gossip columns.

She had told herself that she was glad; that she couldn't care less where he was and with whom – when Sholto was not with Francine – he was spending time.

It wasn't true, though. She cared more than she'd ever thought it possible to care.

In a sea of misery, she thought back to the nightmare scene at the Savoy when she'd faced him with what Miranda had told her. He had already been seated when she had entered the River Room, and she could remember as clearly as if a photograph had been taken the moment when, dinner-jacketed and handsome, he'd risen to his feet to greet her.

At the sight of her there had been naked pleasure in his eyes.

It had been pleasure that hadn't lasted long.

At the expression on her face, he'd said in concern, 'What's the matter, Daphne? Did you hate every minute of Berlin?'

'I hated what I was told there,' she'd said, her voice clipped and curt and filled with almost unbearable tension.

She'd sat down, hoping with every fibre of her being that when she'd said what she had come to say, he would crack with laughter at the ridiculousness of it; that everything in her world would be as it had been before she'd crossed to the park bench in Unter den Linden.

'What was it you were told?' he'd asked. 'Something about Hitler?'

'No.' She'd clasped her evening-gloved hands tightly together in her lap. 'It was about you.'

Apprehension had flared in his eyes, to be immediately chased away, but not before she had recognized it for what it was.

Even before she'd said starkly, 'Is Francine Seeley your mistress?' she had sensed what his answer was going to be.

Instead of leaning forward, removing her hands from her lap, holding them fiercely in his and vehemently denying such a preposterous possibility, he'd breathed in hard and then, without even attempting to deny it, he'd said bluntly, 'Yes, Daphne. She is.'

The wine waiter had approached their table. Abruptly Sholto had waved him away. 'Who told you?' he'd demanded.

'Miranda.' She'd felt so sick and dizzy she'd hardly been able to get Miranda's name past her lips.

He'd said, as if what he was saying was the most reasonable

thing in the world, 'I've known Francine for several years. We have an understanding. That understanding doesn't affect our relationship, Daphne. Or it doesn't, unless you allow it to.'

She'd thought of all the other girlfriends he'd doubtless said the same thing to – the girlfriends who, according to Miranda, he'd accused of making a fuss over nothing – and wondered what their reactions had been. Had they been so besotted with Sholto that they'd accepted the existence of Francine in his life, rather as they might if Francine had been not his mistress, but his wife?

Whether they had or hadn't, she knew one thing for certain: she wasn't going to join their ranks. She'd sucked air into her lungs and had said unsteadily, 'If I'd known you were in a long-term relationship, I would never have flown to Oxford with you, and the last four months would never have happened. I thought you loved me. I thought there were good things waiting for us, and there still could be if . . .'

'If I broke off my relationship with Francine?' he'd finished for her. 'That isn't going to happen, Daphne. I'm sorry. I don't take ultimatums. Not from anyone. Not even from you.'

'And I'm not going to indulge in a *ménage à trois*,' she'd said tightly, 'and especially not with a Nazi sympathizer.'

'What the devil do you mean?'

Abruptly she'd risen to her feet, saying fiercely, 'Don't tell me you don't know! It isn't something Francine or her daughter keep secret. In Berlin, Francine was wined and dined by Ribbentrop, and now that the Games are at an end she and Miranda are still in Germany, staying as guests of Ribbentrop's high-ranking Nazi friends!'

It had, she'd thought, been as good an exit line as any and, taking advantage of it, she'd swung on her heel and stalked out of the restaurant and – as Sholto hadn't come after her – out of the Savoy. Not until she had been in a taxi speeding down the Strand had she given way to scorching, anguished tears.

Now, two months later, the scene was as raw and hurtful as it had been when it had taken place. Bleakly she turned away from the window, walked across to a triple-mirrored dressing table and surveyed herself critically in it. She didn't look like a woman who'd failed to come first in her lover's life. She couldn't imagine any man – other than Sholto – regarding her as being second best. Her evening gown was one of Schiaparelli's slinky slipper-satin numbers, and chandelier sapphire earrings danced against her neck. With her platinum-pale hair falling jaw-length in shiny waves, she looked like a Hollywood movie star, but what was the use of looking like a Hollywood movie star when she had no one in her life to look like a movie star for?

If it had been spring or summer, she would have travelled out to Crete to join Kate and Ella, but it was late October and the year's dig at Kalamata was now at an end. Kate had written to her that, until the following spring, she was going to be based at Knossos, where archaeology work – cleaning and cataloguing – was always ongoing, and that Ella was going to be living in Heraklion, doing similar work at the museum there.

The prospect of joining them in their cleaning and cataloguing didn't appeal, and that was her problem. Since she had ended her relationship with Sholto, nothing appealed.

From the corridor outside her room came the sound of footsteps and laughter, as a group of her fellow guests made their way towards the head of the stairs.

She glanced down at her watch. It was time for pre-dinner drinks in the drawing room. Desultorily she picked up her perfume spray and spritzed her neck and wrists with Guerlain's Shalimar, knowing she'd been a fool to imagine even for one moment that she would meet anyone at Sherwood who would replace Sholto in her heart and in her mind.

Their four months together – the way she had given herself to him with such uninhibited abandon – were not something that could be replicated, and were certainly not something she had previously experienced. Determined to maintain a reputation for recklessness, she had, at Oxford, shed her virginity at the first opportunity. It hadn't been the earth-moving experience she had been hoping for.

Neither had the next experience, or the one that had followed it.

After that – and until she had met Sholto – she had rather given up on sex. And then Sholto, who was experienced in a way that none of her previous boyfriends had been, had introduced her to a whole new, earth-shattering, cataclysmic world. Merely remembering their lovemaking sent a tremor through her body.

Unsteadily she picked up her beaded evening bag. Though their love affair had quite clearly not been a life-defining experience for Sholto, it had been for her. Having experienced what lovemaking could really be like, she knew she was never again going to treat sex casually and cheaply, in the way she had at Oxford. For her, it had become too precious and glorious to want to indulge in it without also being in love.

And she knew something else.

She knew she had been in love with Sholto Hertford.

And that she still was.

Chapter Nine

Although snow in the mountains fell early and heavily and, on top of mountains such as Mount Ida and Mount Dicte, often lingered until June, coastal areas in central and eastern Crete usually only received a light sprinkling.

When Kate woke to a world of whiteness at Knossos on the last day of December, her first thought was that if she wanted to see the Palace of Minos under a covering a snow, this would be her only chance that winter, before tourists spoilt its pristine beauty with their footprints. She had to get there fast.

Ten minutes later, wearing an anorak over a sweater and trousers and with a camera slung over her shoulder, she was hurrying out of the hall as the Squire headed into it.

'Sensible of you to take the opportunity, Kate,' he said, knowing instinctively where she was going and what her intentions were. 'Another hour or two and the snow will have either melted or been trampled into slush.'

Kate liked the Squire. That she was working at Knossos until next season's dig had been entirely down to him, and when he spoke of things Neo-palatial and Post-palatial, it was, for her, the equivalent of being in a highly privileged masterclass. His mother's conversation centred on far different matters.

'Has your friend Daphne sent any fresh news about the King and Mrs Simpson?' Mrs Hutchinson would ask, whenever fresh post arrived from England.

Daphne nearly always had, so Kate had been able to keep Mrs Hutchinson happily abreast of events that the vast majority of British people still knew nothing about. That in November Mrs Simpson had petitioned for a divorce at Ipswich Assizes, and been granted a decree nisi, had concerned Mrs Hutchinson greatly.

'And what is going to happen in six months' time, when Mrs Simpson's divorce is made absolute?' she had asked, her knitting needles clicking fast. 'Surely she can't expect King Edward then to propose marriage?'

On the eleventh of December, and via the radio, Mrs Hutchinson and the rest of the world learned that not only had the King proposed marriage, but that his proposal had been accepted and that, as his government and the Archbishop of Canterbury objected strenuously to having a twice-married American divorcee as Britain's queen consort, he had abdicated. In his speech to the nation and to the Empire, the King – now the ex-King – had sounded isolated and vulnerable, as he had expressed how impossible it was for him to carry the heavy burden of responsibility and to discharge his duties without the help and support of the woman he loved. At the end of his speech, when he had closed with the words 'God bless you all', Mrs Hutchinson had wept. Kate, too, had been deeply moved and had been profoundly grateful that Lewis Sinclair hadn't been there to see her emotional reaction.

As she made the short walk across virgin snow to the Palace of Minos, she wondered when Lewis would be returning to Crete. When the dig at Kalamata had come to an end for the year, and Ella had moved into lodgings at Heraklion and Kate had moved into the Villa Ariadne, Lewis had remained at Kalamata and then, a month ago, had returned to Scotland.

'No doubt in order to discuss with his patron just how long excavation work at Kalamata can continue, without the major find of a palace,' Kit had said to her before he, too, left Crete to spend the winter working at the Ashmolean Museum in Oxford.

As Kit and others left the Villa Ariadne, new people and some not-so-new had arrived. Amongst the not-so-new had been Professor Cottingley with another batch of German students. Occasionally there were distinguished visitors. Lord and Lady Heathcote had been given the privilege of a privately conducted tour of the Palace of Minos by the Squire and, on leaving the Villa Ariadne, Lady Heathcote had left behind her an up-to-date copy of *Tatler*.

Browsing through it, Kate had been startled to see a photograph of Sholto Hertford at a society event, in the company of the new German Ambassador to Great Britain, Joachim von Ribbentrop.

In her next letter to Daphne she had mentioned it; and in her next letter from Daphne, her friend had written:

Sholto's longtime mistress – from years before he met me, but still his mistress – is a close friend of Ribbentrop's. It's become quite the thing in English high society to be cosy with high-ranking Nazis. My poor deluded father thinks them the bee's knees. So, apparently, does Sholto, which is yet another thing I got so wrong about him.

Kate had reached the palace now. The ticket booth wasn't yet open and, even if it had been, having become a member of the ongoing team at Knossos, Kate had unrestricted access and so had no need of it. With no visitors to spoil the sight of snow-covered walls and terraces older than Troy, the palace looked like something out of a fairy tale. For more than an hour, in the eerie silence created by the blanket of snow, she took photographs.

Some shots she took were panoramic views, such as one of snow-capped Mount Juktas as seen from the terrace of the South Propylaeum. Others were of things as small and as perfect as a cluster of snowdrops growing at the entrance to the Throne Room.

Emerging from under a colonnade, she saw that she no longer had the palace to herself, but that she was sharing it with a small group of tourists, all of whom were unmistakably British. The guide showing them around was a Cretan girl, young and slim and very pretty. Few Cretan girls spoke anything other than a smattering of English, but Kate knew this wasn't the case for the girl in question, because Nikoleta Kourakis's English was excellent.

Aware that Nikoleta had not yet seen her, and not particularly wanting to be seen by her, Kate remained motionless. Her initial assumptions about Nikoleta had all been embarrassingly wide of the mark. On the evening when Lewis Sinclair had left the terrace to meet Nikoleta in Villa Ariadne's garden, and the Squire had said, 'The girl will be Nikoleta, Christos Kourakis's sister' and Mrs Hutchinson had added that the family lived close to Knossos, Kate had imagined Nikoleta to be a typical village girl who either helped her mother work whatever small patch of land their family possessed or was, perhaps, one of Villa Ariadne's maids.

During her first few days at Kalamata she had discovered that nothing could have been further from the truth.

'When you take Miss Tetley on her next visit to the Palace of Minos, you must both introduce yourselves to my sister,' Christos had said to Kate, in the days before he had become familiar enough with Ella not only to call her by her first name, but to tease her as well.

'Will that be appropriate, if she is working?' Kate had said

86

doubtfully, not at all sure how she felt about taking him up on his suggestion.

'Of course it will!' Christos's eyebrows had risen so high they'd nearly disappeared into his thick, untidy hair. 'It means Nikoleta will then be able to introduce you to her tour group, and Palace of Minos tour groups love meeting archaeologists.'

Later Kate had said to Ella, 'I'd been told Sir Arthur has always taken a keen interest in the Kourakis family's welfare, but I hadn't realized he'd ensured Nikoleta could speak English well enough for her to take tour groups around the palace.'

'Goodness.' Ella had been entranced. 'How wonderful for her to be taking people around a site that her father spent decades of his life helping to excavate.' Amusement had entered her voice and she'd said, 'What do you bet that, when talking of the excavation work, Nikoleta mentions her father's name just as often as she mentions Sir Arthur's!'

Now, watching Nikoleta lead her little group across the Central Court in the direction of the Grand Staircase, Kate wondered why, when Nikoleta could have no idea of the effect Lewis had on her, her attitude towards Kate was so stiff and guarded. She certainly wasn't stiff and guarded with Ella, or with anyone else Kate had seen her interacting with, but from the first moment they had met, Nikoleta had clearly regarded Kate as being some kind of a threat to her romance with Lewis. As she never spoke an unnecessary word to Lewis and he never spoke an unnecessary word to her, Kate found it all very odd.

'Perhaps she's hyper-intuitive,' Ella had said. 'And you have to feel for Nikoleta. Even her brother suspects she's hopelessly in love with Lewis, but when do you ever see the two of them openly together as a couple?'

'You don't,' Kate had said, 'but if he made a habit of being as indiscreet as he was the night he met her in the garden, it would be shotguns at dawn. Cretan men don't take kindly to having a daughter or sister indulging in romantic relationships outside marriage. In even suspecting his sister is in love with Lewis, Christos is behaving bizarrely – unless, of course, he knows what Lewis's long-term intentions are and is sure that a wedding is in the offing.'

With Nikoleta and her group now out of sight, and with the snow not quite as soft but crunching beneath her feet, Kate walked towards the exit on the outer edge of the West Court. Though she had agreed with Ella that Lewis and Nikoleta never spent time together openly as a couple, she knew they most definitely were a couple, for the week before Lewis had left for Scotland she had seen them strolling together down a street in Réthymnon.

Réthymnon was fifty miles west along the coast from Heraklion and not somewhere they would have expected to have been seen by anyone who knew them. Kate had only been there because she had use of one of the dig's trucks and because, as Réthymnon retained lots of traces of Crete's four-hundred-year occupation by the Venetians and its subsequent two-hundred-year occupation by the Turks, it was a town that interested her.

She had just stepped out of Réthymnon's Archaeological Museum when she had seen them. The street, narrow and lined with small, dark shops selling everything from medicinal herbs to handmade lace, was crowded, but it had seemed to Kate that Lewis and Nikoleta could just as well have been on a desert island, so involved were they with each other.

His head had been bent down to hers, his handsome face – usually so forbiddingly inexpressive – alight with emotions that Kate hadn't wanted to name; and Nikoleta had been laughing up at him, her joy so sizzling it was palpable. The street led down to the Fortezza, the citadel that dominated Réthymnon, and because Lewis was so much taller and broader than the average Cretan, and because the jacket Nikoleta was wearing was a vivid orange, they remained in sight until, at the end of the street, they headed towards the citadel's main gate.

Now, standing in the West Court in front of Sir Arthur Evans's bust – a bust made droll by the snow covering the bronze hair and clinging to the eyebrows – she pondered the oddness of her never having told Ella of how she had seen Lewis and Nikoleta together in Réthymnon and of how, in Nikoleta's company, Lewis had been a changed person. Had she not done so because she hadn't wanted to put into words how Lewis's happiness in Nikoleta's company had made her feel?

She took a photograph of the snow-decorated bust and bit her lip. It hadn't been jealousy she'd felt. She passionately loathed the very idea of jealousy and utterly refused to allow herself to feel it. What she'd felt – and still felt – was a kind of miserable desolation. She was twenty-three and no man she had met had yet had the physical effect on her that Lewis Sinclair had. What if, in the future, she never met anyone who did? Countless times she told herself that no intelligent person fell in love on looks alone and that, as she was intelligent, she hadn't fallen for him. It didn't feel that way, though. It felt as though all she needed in her life to make it utterly glorious and complete was for Lewis Sinclair to look at her in the way she had seen him look at Nikoleta.

She slipped her camera back into its case. The long and the short of it was that Lewis Sinclair did not feel about her as she felt about him; and, after so many months of living together in the close proximity of Kalamata and working together almost every day, he was clearly never going to. That being the case, she had only one option, and that was to get over him – which was exactly what she was determined to do.

*

Nearly two thousand miles away in Yorkshire, Sam Jowett was facing, if not the same situation and conclusion, then one very close to it.

His disappointment that Ella had not come home for Christmas was enormous. What had made the disappointment even deeper was that she hadn't even said in any of her letters how much she would have liked to have come home. All her last letter had been full of was, as usual, the doings of her friends in Knossos and Kalamata.

When she had finished telling him about the Kourakis family, and of how the jewellery that Christos Kourakis had excavated had been elevated to a display case of its own in Heraklion's museum, and of how Christos had gone with her when she'd travelled to Kalamata to visit Apollonia, the Mamalakis families, and Andre and Agata, Ella had written:

> *They are all such lovely people (though maybe Rhea is not quite as lovely as everyone else!) and I am really enjoying my first Christmas here, though it is very different from Christmas in Yorkshire. For one thing, it starts much earlier, on the sixth of December, the Feast of St Nicholas. It's on St Nicholas's Day that Greeks exchange presents. No one had warned me, or Kate, and so you can imagine how surprised we were last Sunday when we were suddenly laden with gifts! Christos's mother, Eleni, is going to show me how to make* Christopsomo *(Christ Bread). It's the tradition to serve it on Christmas Day at the big family meal everyone sits down to, after they've come home from church. So now you know what I will be doing on Christmas Eve. I'll be baking bread!*

She had also told him where she would be spending Christmas Day, and it wasn't going to be at the Villa Ariadne with Kate and the Villa's other guests, nor was it going to be in Heraklion. Ella was going to be spending it with the Kourakis family in Knossos:

Kate is being polite about my doing so, but I know she doesn't much like it, she had written. Nikoleta is almost as cool towards her as she (Kate) is towards Lewis, but as I like Nikoleta and enjoy being in the Kourakis's home, I'm spending Christmas Day with them and that's that.

It was now New Year's Eve, and Sam wondered if, as well as spending Christmas Day with the Kourakis family, Ella would be spending New Year's Eve with them as well. He was honest enough with himself to realize that if it wasn't for Kalamata's dig foreman being the son of the house, he probably wouldn't mind the thought of Ella doing so; but Christos Kourakis *was* the son of the house, and Sam didn't like the number of times his name cropped up in Ella's letters. It was always *Christos has done this* or *Christos has done that.*

In one of her letters she had enclosed a group photograph of the team, taken on a day when Kit had visited Kalamata. Judging their height in relation to Kit's tall lankiness, Sam had estimated none of the Greeks to be over five foot seven. Some of them had a spade in their hands, others a pickaxe. Some of them were bare-chested, others were shirtless, but wearing waistcoats. All of them were wearing disreputable-looking baggy pants, and all of them were heavily moustached.

The photograph had been something of a shock. Although he hadn't expected a group of Cretan workmen to look respectable, neither had he expected them to look like murderous ruffians.

Ella had written their names in pencil above their heads. *Dimitri. Angelos. Pericles. Nico. Yanni. Adonis. Christos.*

Until that moment he'd had a mental image of Christos Kourakis, and his mental image bore no relation at all to the reality. Like his companions in the photograph, Christos was, by Sam's standards, small; probably no taller than Ella herself.

Sam had doubted if anyone could think Christos good-looking, although as his face was dominated by a dark, luxuriant moustache, it had been difficult for him to make an accurate assessment. Having seen the photograph he had, however, felt less anxious where Christos Kourakis's relationship with Ella was concerned, for whatever the nature of it, it was impossible to believe it was romantic; which hadn't meant that he'd been happy about it. And he certainly wasn't happy about the possibility of Ella seeing in the New Year with the Kourakis family and – if he could get away with it – of the ruffian in the photograph giving her a New Year kiss.

He dug his nails deep into the palms of his hands. He was too straightforward a bloke to want to begin playing games, but it wouldn't do Ella any harm to be made aware that she couldn't continue taking him so much for granted. His own plans for the evening had been made some time ago. There was always a riotous, booze-fuelled New Year's Eve party at his rugby club and, come ten or eleven o'clock, that was where he would be. It was a party for wives and girlfriends as well, and suddenly he knew what it was that he was going to do.

He was going to invite Jenny to go with him.

That she would already have made plans for the evening went without saying, but what also went without saying was that once he spoke to her, Jenny would shed her previous plans as fast as light.

The New Year Eve's party at the Villa Ariadne was a very jolly, informal affair, the guests being all those presently staying at the Villa, plus the Villa's staff and their families, local people, and people from Heraklion that the Squire and his mother were on friendly terms with. Inside, the Villa was decorated with gaily coloured paper-chains and boughs of sweet-smelling winter greenery; and outside, on the terrace, there were candles on tables, and in the garden lighted lanterns bobbed amongst trees still sprinkled with snow.

Nikoleta was there, as Kate had known she would be. Kate had smiled across at her and Nikoleta had given her a faint smile in response and had then rather pointedly turned her back. Afterwards Nikoleta was either at the very far side of whichever room Kate happened to be in or was nowhere to be seen at all.

In the drawing room there was dancing. Kate danced a happy quickstep with one of Professor Cottingley's students, and a tortured foxtrot with the professor. When, a little later, the professor again headed in her direction, she was saved by the Squire.

'It's a waltz, Kate,' he said genially. 'I can just about manage a waltz. Are you game?'

He was still waltzing her around the room when she heard someone shout above the noise of the music and the general hubbub, 'Is it true Sinclair is going to first-foot?'

Kate stumbled.

'Oh dear!' The Squire's concern was deep. 'Am I putting you off your stroke?'

'No.' She shot him a reassuring smile. 'I just lost concentration for a moment.'

Ambitiously the Squire attempted a reverse turn.

She said, 'I just heard someone say Lewis was going to be our first-footer. When did he get back?'

'I'm not sure, Kate. It could have been this morning or it could have been yesterday. Being a Scot, he didn't want to put in an appearance at the party until he first-footed. It's something

93

Scots take very seriously. Did you know it's unacceptable for a first-footer to be a resident of the house he first-foots in? And that someone leaving the house after midnight and then coming back in it is not considered to be truly first-footing? Or not by Scotsmen, at any rate.'

Kate hadn't known. What she did know was that a first-footer had to be tall and dark-haired, and that Lewis Sinclair ticked those boxes.

'The music has come to an end,' she said, as the Squire seemed unaware of it.

'Goodness! Has it?' From his gangling height he beamed down at her. 'We did pretty well, didn't we? Next stop Blackpool Tower Ballroom!'

Once mercifully released, Kate leaned against a door jamb and rubbed her bruised toes.

Ella came up to her, a glass of wine in each hand. 'Here.' She handed one of the glasses to Kate. 'Having seen the Squire's idea of a waltz, you need something restorative. Why is it academics are useless on a dance floor?'

'Heaven only knows. Something to do with the job description, I think.'

Ella laughed. 'From the sound of it, it's going to be all reels and jigs after midnight – with a hefty input of Cretan dancing. According to Christos, inebriated Cretans dancing a *maleviziotis* leave in the shade drunken Scots dancing reels.'

'Well, that's certainly going to be something to see. I take it the sedate interlude of ballroom music was a sop in the direction of the Squire and Mrs H.?'

'Something like that.' Ella tucked her free hand companionably into the crook of Kate's arm. 'Don't you think the Cretans look splendid in festive attire?'

'So splendid I've hardly been able to recognize some of them.'

Where the women were concerned, it was true. Eleni Kourakis, who like all Cretan women her age was usually covered from head to foot in shapeless black, was tonight wearing an apron so richly embroidered it dazzled.

It was the men, though, in their traditional baggy *vraka* trousers, wide-sleeved shirts, embroidered waistcoats, purple sashes, knee-high boots and black-fringed head-kerchiefs, who looked truly spectacular. As every man had an obligatory knife at his waist and as they all sported a moustache, they looked more like brigands than archaeological workmen, Villa Ariadne household staff or, in the case of one of them, a much-respected leader of Heraklion's town council.

Midnight was approaching and the noise level grew rowdier. Kate saw Nikoleta squeeze into the crowded room.

'She should wear traditional costume all the time, don't you think?' Ella said.

Kate nodded. In ornately embroidered traditional costume and a necklace of heavy gold coins, Nikoleta looked ravishing. She also looked radiantly happy, her eyes on the door through which, very shortly, Lewis was expected to first-foot.

As the last chimes of midnight died away, mayhem broke out. Champagne corks popped, streamers flew and whistles blew. In the garden Christos and his father let off volley after volley of *feu de joie* celebratory shots with hunting rifles. In the drawing room the English crossed their arms over their chests, joined hands and sang 'Auld Lang Syne' lustily. When as many verses as could be remembered had been sung, the hugs and kisses began.

Kate was laughingly disentangling herself from an over-eager embrace by one of the German students when there came a great hammering on Villa Ariadne's front door.

'It's Lewis!' the Squire shouted, and there was immediately

a general stampede into the hall to see Mrs Hutchinson open the door to him.

Kate didn't join in the stampede and riotous welcome. She was too busy stiffening her resolve never again to allow Lewis to affect her as he had in the past. She was over him, she told herself fiercely; absolutely and utterly over him. The sight of him was no longer going to make her feel weak at the knees. His nearness was no longer going to cause her heart to race. She was a level-headed, intelligent woman, not a schoolgirl experiencing a first passion. She drew in a deep breath, confidence flooding through her. It was a good feeling and she was still savouring it when Lewis, surrounded by the welcoming crush, strode into the drawing room.

In one hand he was carrying a lump of coal for good luck, and in the other he was holding a bottle of whisky by its neck.

And he was wearing a kilt.

It was to have been expected of course, and yet Kate hadn't expected it. The sight of him in kilt and sporran, with a lace jabot at his throat, flounces of lace showing below the cuffs of his jacket and with a dirk tucked into his knee-high right-hand stocking, robbed her of breath. Although the Cretans looked splendid in their national dress, Lewis looked far more than splendid in his. He looked jaw-droppingly magnificent.

The promises she had made to herself were as if they had never been.

With her knees once again weak, and her heart once again racing, she turned away from the sight of him and, threading her way through fellow guests rowdily singing 'For He's a Jolly Good Fellow', made for the nearest door.

It opened into the corridor that led to the Villa's library.

Someone had been in it before her, for the lamps were on and the room was suffused in soft light. She let the door click shut behind her and, leaning against it, her eyes closed, began giving herself a good talking-to. If Lewis hadn't come into the room wearing a kilt, she would not have reacted as she had, and the promises she had made herself wouldn't have been so instantly broken. She would still have her self-respect. She would still be in the good place she'd been in, before he had entered the room. And she could still be in that good place again.

She opened her eyes, fresh determination flooding through her. She could start again. She could make new resolutions this very moment. What had undone her a few minutes ago had been the unexpectedness of seeing Lewis in a kilt. Everyone knew that a handsome Scot in a kilt was damn-near irresistible. And she'd been caught off-guard. Well, she wouldn't be caught off-guard again. She hiccoughed and frowned. She was also slightly tipsy. Where self-control was concerned, it hadn't helped.

The noise of revelry coming from the Villa's gardens was almost as loud as that coming from the drawing room and she began to walk across to the window, intending to look out. The sound of the door opening behind her stopped her in her tracks.

As she whirled around, Lewis closed the door, as she had a little while earlier and, as she had, leaned against it.

'I thought I might find you in here.' He crossed one ghillie-brogued foot over the other and folded his arms across his chest. The lamplight threw a slant of shadow across the hard line of his cheek. There was no smile on his face, but then she could never remember Lewis smiling towards her. She could only ever remember him smiling towards Nikoleta.

'I didn't come in here to be found.' Her voice was so taut she scarcely recognized it. 'And I would now like to return to the party. So if you don't mind . . .' She made a gesture with her hand indicating that she would like him to step aside, so that she could leave the room.

He made no attempt to move. It was as if he had settled there for the night.

'It's the first few minutes of the New Year.' His speech was slightly slurred and she realized that he was on his way to being drunk.

As it was New Year and he was a Scot, it was no very great surprise. With the exception of Mrs Hutchinson, she doubted if anyone in the Villa was still completely sober, and that included herself. The turbulent emotion Lewis was arousing in her was joined by a new one: a flickering of apprehension. He had always been an unknown quantity, and that had been when he was sober. Now that he was sober no longer – and in a very odd mood – she didn't know the best way of responding to him, without triggering something she sensed it would be best not to trigger.

But what was that? His temper? Although she had never seen Lewis lose his temper, she had always sensed that it was often held on a very short leash. But why should he be on the verge of losing his temper with her, when he hadn't seen her in over a month? Or was his mood occasioned by something that had happened while he had been in Scotland, in discussions with the patron who was financing the dig? Was that why he had sought her out alone? In order to break the news that there wasn't going to be another season's dig at Kalamata?

Fighting down the sense of menace that the closed door – and the way he was preventing her from opening it – was giving her, she said, struggling to bring a sense of normality to their unexpected *tête-à-tête*, 'Is there bad news about next season's dig?'

'Next season's dig?' He quirked an eyebrow. 'No. What bad news could there possibly be?' He shifted his stance so that his weight was now on both feet. The lamplight fell on the dirk, making the steel gleam like silver

Kate averted her eyes from it. 'Then if you haven't sought me out to talk about the dig, I would like to return to the party.'

'If you hadn't left the party, I wouldn't have had to come in here to wish you a happy New Year.'

There was a hot flush at the back of his eyes and his voice was even thicker than it had been a minute or so earlier, but she no longer had any sense of foreboding. If all Lewis wanted was to wish her a happy New Year, then the sooner she wished him one, the sooner the present bizarre little scene would be over.

She put an unconcerned smile on her face. 'A happy New Year,' she said, closing the distance between them, expecting to be wished a happy New Year back, and for him to either open the door for her or at least step aside so that she could open it herself.

He said, 'I think traditional New Year's greetings are the best' and, instead of opening the door or moving aside, he caught hold of her, pulling her hard against him.

She cried out in shocked protest, struggling to prise herself free. She might as well have been trying to free herself from a vice. Her cry of protest was even less effectual, silenced instantly as he brought his mouth down on hers in swift, unfumbled contact.

To her horror, she knew that although she was struggling against him, she was doing so without any real conviction. Even worse, her lips parted willingly as his tongue slipped past hers.

It was a long, deep, passionate kiss, and only as he finally raised his head did Kate summon the willpower to push herself violently away from him. It was easy to do, for his arms were no longer holding her. Instead, as if nothing out of the ordinary had occurred, he merely held the door open for her.

Kate forced her legs to take her out of the room. The drawing room was the obvious place to head for, but then it would also be the obvious place for Lewis to head for, and she couldn't face the thought of having to meet his eyes – and wasn't certain when she would be able to.

With her mouth still scorched by his kiss, and her legs still trembling, she made for the garden, which was where the Cretan contingent were singing and dancing their hearts out and was where, if the Kourakis family were in the garden, she expected also to find Ella.

Beneath the light of lanterns in the trees and to the accompaniment of a violin and lyre, a long line of dancers were holding each other by the shoulders and enthusiastically beating out a rhythm with their feet, eight steps forward, eight steps back. Ella was at the end of the line, next to Christos. She was the only woman in the line who was not Cretan, but if it hadn't been for her red-gold hair, it would have been hard to distinguish her as a foreigner.

Kate stood still, watching and realizing for the first time that Ella had assimilated herself into life on Crete in a way she hadn't yet done. She'd come to find Ella, in order to tell her of the scene in the library – and to try and make some sense of it. Had Lewis been merely drunk? Was it something he wouldn't even remember when he sobered up? Or had he kissed her as he had done because he had wanted to? Had perhaps wanted to for some time? The thought sent tingles all the way down to her fingertips.

The music changed and, moving even faster, the dancers drew into a circle. Ella was laughing, her head thrown back as the steps of the dance became yet more fast and furious. It occurred to Kate that Ella's friends and family in Yorkshire would scarcely recognize her, if they could see her now. It also occurred to her that this was no time to be trying to have the kind of talk with Ella that she wanted to have. It was a conversation that was going to have to wait.

She turned and began making her way back into the Villa. Lewis wasn't an easy person to read, but after what had just happened between them, surely – for her – that would now change? She wondered if she'd been a fool to push him away as violently as she had? But how else, when he'd previously given no indication of feeling an iota of desire for her, should she have reacted? If he'd kissed her in a moment of drunken aberration, then when he remembered it – *if* he remembered it – he would also remember that she hadn't been a totally willing party; that way, she might at least be saved the humiliation of Lewis realizing what her true response to him had been.

And if he had kissed her for other reasons? At the thought of things that once seemed impossible now being possible, the pulse in her throat pounded and the blood surged through her veins in a hot tide.

Although the party in the garden was still as raucous as ever, inside the house it had calmed down, and as Kate approached the double doors of the drawing room she could hear Irving Berlin's 'What'll I Do?' being played on the gramophone. If Lewis was in the drawing room – and surely he had to be, for he hadn't followed her out to the garden – then his body language was bound to indicate whether or not his kiss had been given in the way she so fervently hoped it had been given.

In the drawing room, people were still dancing.

Mrs Hutchinson was dancing with Professor Cottingley. One of the German students was dancing with Nikoleta. The leader of Heraklion's town council was waltzing with Christos's mother.

Lewis was standing at the far side of the room, talking to one of the students, a glass of whisky in his hand. Sensing her presence in the doorway, he looked across at her.

Their eyes met.

Then, as her heart began slamming in short, quick strokes, he put down his glass of whisky and began walking across the room in her direction. Professor Cottingley and Mrs Hutchinson skilfully avoided him. The leader of the town council was a little more clumsy in getting out of his way.

Kate was on a knife edge, certain that the next few moments were ones she would remember lifelong.

The disillusionment, when it came, was shattering.

Lewis came to a halt, tapping on the arm the student who was dancing with Nikoleta, cutting in on him.

With a radiant smile, Nikoleta slid into his arms.

Nothing he could possibly have done could have signalled more clearly that what had happened between them in the library had no meaning for him whatsoever.

For a second, Kate thought she wasn't going to be able to breathe; then, drawing in a shuddering gasp of air, she swung on her heel, breaking into a run, with the strains of Judy Garland singing, 'When I'm alone, With only dreams of you, That won't come true, What'll I do?' following her all the way to her lonely bedroom.

Chapter Ten

Kit rested his arms on top of the *Boringia*'s deck rails, watching Southampton harbour fade from view in the early-evening twilight. The *Boringia* was a cargo ship en route to Piraeus and points further east and was Kit's preferred way of travelling, when returning to Crete. As Kate and Ella had when travelling by train, once in Piraeus he would board a night-ferry to Heraklion.

He had enjoyed his few months in Oxford. Though he'd been born in Canterbury, and that was where his parents still lived, ever since his university days he'd thought of Oxford as home turf. He had, however, spent a weekend once a month with his parents. Both he and Kate had always had a good relationship with them and, with Kate still in Crete, he'd felt it was the least he could do. He'd spent Christmas with them as well, taking great pleasure in attending the singing of carols in the Cathedral on Christmas Eve and, as was tradition in the Shelton family, attending morning service there on Christmas morning.

Unlike his parents, Kit wasn't a regular churchgoer, but the knowledge that people had been worshipping in Canterbury Cathedral for more than a thousand years, combined with the stunning beauty of the building and its ancient stained glass, always moved him deeply.

The *Boringia* had now reached open water and sea spray had misted his glasses. He took them off, wiping them with a handkerchief. The sea journey, with its stops at Oporto, Gibraltar and Naples, was lengthier than the train and sea route that had been Kate and Ella's choice, but he loved being at sea and, given the opportunity, would quite happily have remained aboard the *Boringia* all the way to its final port of call in India.

In his many journeys on cargo boats he had never been the only passenger, and he wasn't the only passenger this time. A middle-aged married couple were travelling as far as Oporto, where their daughter and Portuguese son-in-law lived. An elderly, white-bearded gentleman had announced that he would be disembarking at Gibraltar.

'From where I will then,' he had said ponderously, 'cross to Morocco and travel to the Rif Valley, in order to study the Berber tribe who live there.'

Kit's fourth and last fellow passenger was a slim blonde-haired woman probably in her late twenties or early thirties. He had been close behind her as she had boarded and he'd noticed, as she'd shaken hands with the ship's captain, that she hadn't been wearing a wedding ring. The absence of a wedding ring didn't arouse his interest. The fit-looking purser standing to one side of the captain was of far greater interest to Kit, although long practice had ensured that he hadn't let his interest show.

He turned away from the sight of the English Channel and leaned his back against the rail. Ever since puberty he'd found his sexual interest in his own sex a burden, and it had been his constant hope that one day he would find a woman he could desire enough to be able to live life relieved of that burden. On the few times he had embarked on an heterosexual relationship the women in question had always, before too very long, sensed his true nature and, although they had then seemed to view it as something of a challenge, Kit hadn't wanted to be seen as a challenge. What he had wanted was to be perceived as uncomplicatedly heterosexual and, once the charade was over, he'd found the relationship pointless.

In Nikoleta Kourakis, because of her youth combined with her sexual inexperience – Cretan village girls nearly always went to their marriage beds virgins – he had rather thought that, if he could engage her interest, the outcome might be exactly what he was looking for, for who would suspect Kit of being a celibate homosexual, if he had a wife as startlingly beautiful as Nikoleta? And unlike the women he'd previously had brief affairs with, he doubted if Nikoleta would be worldly enough to recognize in him what they had.

That was the fear he lived with: being recognized for what he was. Whenever he'd read of some poor devil standing in the dock, accused of what was termed 'an act of gross indecency', he'd been determined never to risk being in the same situation. To be an active homosexual was to risk a ruined life; a destroyed reputation; blackmail. A criminal act, homosexuality led to two-year prison sentences. Given a choice, it wasn't something any sane, responsible person would opt for.

But what if you weren't given a choice? What if you simply *were*? Then the only answer, as far as he could see, was to find the right sort of wife, have children and shut the door on your natural inclinations once and for all.

There was a huge snag, however, where Nikoleta was concerned: for all the interest he held for her, he could have been a plank of wood. The only person Nikoleta had eyes for was Lewis. And why wouldn't it be? He'd seen Lewis walk down a street in Heraklion turning female heads all the way. In his favour was that he'd seemed totally oblivious of the admiration he was attracting.

Still leaning against the deck rail, Kit reached into his jacket pocket for cigarettes and a lighter. As he lit up and blew a plume of blue smoke into the air, he wondered if the way Lewis never gave anything away about himself was also a challenge to women; the kind of challenge they perhaps found hard to resist. When it came to personal information, Lewis was extremely close-mouthed.

Even after nearly two years, Kit knew little more about him than he had at their first introduction – which was that Lewis was a Scot who hailed from Sutherland. A direct question had elicited that he was neither an Oxford nor a Cambridge man, but that Lewis had gained his first-class honours in archaeology at the University of the Highlands and Islands. Kit, whose college had been Christ Church, Oxford, and who had left with first-class degrees in both Mods and Greats, had had to fight hard to hide his surprise – and had immediately been ashamed of his rare attack of snobbishness. If Lewis had ever been aware of it, he'd shown no sign.

Fairly regular social meet-ups over dinner with Lewis at the Villa Ariadne hadn't added to his spare bank of knowledge about him. If Lewis had hobbies and interests other than Minoan Crete, he never mentioned them and certainly didn't devote time to them. His one overriding passion was his work, but even there, there was a large element of mystery. The days of privately funded Victorian and Edwardian digs were long over, yet the Kalamata dig was as near to being one of them as made no difference. When the subject of funding came up, Lewis was always nonchalantly evasive, and if the Squire knew the identity of Lewis's wealthy patron, he wasn't admitting to it.

Kit took a last draw on his cigarette and, turning once more to face the English Channel, tossed the butt into the heaving grey waves and then, pushing his hands deep into his trouser pockets, made his way towards the companionway and his cabin, reflecting that Lewis never even gave any information about his family. If he had parents who were still alive, and if he had siblings, he never mentioned them. He could, for all anyone knew, even be married.

Kit bit the corner of his lip. If Lewis was married, it would explain why the nature of his relationship with Nikoleta was such a mystery. Was it a mutual passion, and were they enjoying a very discreetly conducted love affair? Or were Nikoleta's blatantly romantic feelings for Lewis one-sided, as Mrs Hutchinson so staunchly believed? Whatever the truth of the matter, the bottom line was that Nikoleta was infatuated with Lewis and that even if her feelings were unreturned, she was never, in a hundred years, going to feel anything similar where he, Kit, was concerned.

Lewis slung his rucksack to the ground and, with his legs apart and his hands on his hips, surveyed the view. It had been a hard climb, but it had been worth it. He was high enough now to see, to the north, a glittering glimpse of sea. To the west was the great mountain range of Ida, its many peaks still covered in snow. To the east, but unseen because of the rugged landscape, was Mount Juktas.

He sat down on a boulder and took a bottle of water out of his rucksack. After a long drink he reached for the letter he'd come so far to read for a second time. It was from Tom Wilkinson's father.

Dear Lewis,

It is with a breaking heart that I write to tell you I have received news of Tom's death in Spain. He died in a bombing raid carried out by Germany's Condor Legion. What will happen to the world, now that Hitler and Franco are in league together, is a horror too great for me to imagine. The

attack took place on the outskirts of Gerona two months ago,
but the situation with the International Brigades is such that
I have only just received the news from the Foreign Office.
You were his closest friend for so long – at school, at uni-
versity and later in Crete – that hard and painful as this
letter is to write, I knew I couldn't let you continue believing
Tom was still alive when he lies buried far from home, in
Spanish soil. Thank you for being such a good friend to my
boy. Take care of yourself, lad.
    Harry Wilkinson

As well as the bottle of water, Lewis had also brought a bottle
of King Minos red wine with him and, his face white and set,
he uncorked it and raised it high.

'To you, Tom,' he said, looking out over the magnificent
panorama of mountains. Then, after pouring a libation to the
gods, he drank deeply, remembering the day just before Tom
had left for Spain, when the two of them had climbed to where
he was now sitting and, while talking of their great hopes of
discovering a palace to rank alongside those of Phaistos and
Mallia, had demolished a bottle of King Minos between them.

That had been just under a year ago, and all he had to show
for last season's dig were a few tombs and a villa. The Neo-
palatial tombs were, it was true, grandiose and indicative of a
palace nearby; the villa, too, had been pleasingly substantial and
of the same period; and the necklace that Christos had knifed
free from thirty centuries' weight of earth had been equal in
beauty and workmanship to jewellery found at Knossos. But the
villa hadn't been a palace, and if the palace wasn't found this
year, then it wouldn't be found at all – or at least not by him.

The Greek government had already informed Nathaniel
they would be reviewing his permit to excavate for a third
year; and, even if they had not, his godfather's seemingly

bottomless purse wasn't literally bottomless, although there were many people in the international world of high finance who, Lewis knew, would find that hard to believe. As far as finding a Minoan palace was concerned, this coming season was going to be a case of make-or-break.

He took another swig from the bottle of King Minos, reflecting on how relatively easy things had been for Sir Arthur Evans. Tradition as far back as Homer's *The Odyssey* stated that the palace of the Kings of Crete had stood on Kephala, a hill at Knossos. Heinrich Schliemann, the archaeologist who had found Troy, had visited Kephala twice in the 1880s, but Crete had still been under Turkish control and he had been refused permission to excavate. In 1897 an uprising against the Turks brought about the end of Turkish rule, and two years later Sir Arthur bought the site. Together with two fellow archaeologists and a team of local workmen, Evans's first trial-pit had been sunk on the twenty-third of March 1900.

On the second day, his team had uncovered the remains of an ancient house with fragments of frescoes. Another four days, and the team were clearing the top and part of a terrace. From then on, discovery followed discovery. There was a great paved area with stairways; a fresco of olive sprays in flower; tablets of baked clay covered in strange symbols; a great relief in painted stucco of a charging bull. Within a month, a labyrinth of buildings was revealed and Sir Arthur knew he had found a palace – a palace more than three thousand years old.

Lucky old Arthur, Lewis thought grimly, re-corking the bottle and putting it back into his rucksack. No couple of tombs and a villa for him, after a season's work. Sir Arthur had found what he had hoped he would find, and it had been the find of a lifetime; or, as the great man had written in his diary at the time, 'a find one could not hope for in many lifetimes'.

Lewis rose to his feet. He, too, for his own sake and his

godfather's sake, was hoping to make the find of a lifetime – and this season he would have a friend joining the team whose judgement he trusted implicitly.

He'd first worked with Helmut Becke when, fresh from university, he'd gone out to join a dig in Mesopotamia, at Uruk. Helmut was only two years his senior and they had bonded immediately. Later, in northern Greece, they had worked together again. When Tom had left the Kalamata dig to fight in Spain for the Republican cause, Lewis had contacted Helmut to see if he was interested in joining him on Crete. Helmut had been keen, but his present contract had had another twelve months to run. With the contract now nearly at an end, he had contacted Lewis; and just before Lewis had begun his return journey to Crete, they had met up in the bar of London's Victoria Station.

'I'll be with you by the first week of April, Lewis,' Helmut had said, only a slight guttural accent betraying his nationality. 'But as the last two Kalamata digs were void – void of a palace at any rate – where is your last-shot dig going to be?'

Lewis had swirled the brandy around in the glass he was cradling. 'There's a small upland plain a thirty-minute climb higher than the Kalamata village plateau. I'd like you to see it.'

'And when I see it, what will make me think it could be the bullseye?'

Lewis had taken a drink of brandy and had said, 'There's a palace in, or near to, Kalamata, Helmut. I can practically smell it. As I've failed to find it on the plateau itself, it's the only other place it can be.'

'Knossos isn't halfway up a mountain. Neither is Phaistos or Mallia.'

'Maybe not, but they are all on high ground. And the plain

above the plateau gives a stupendous view north, south, east and west. Strategically, it ticks all the right boxes.'

'And?' Helmut had asked.

'And there is the fact of tombs, which can only be described as royal, being found not too far away on the village plateau. And the villa, too, of course, and the sumptuousness of the necklace found in the villa.'

'And?' Helmut had said again.

Lewis had grinned. 'And there is a two-acre area knee-deep in fennel.'

Helmut had cracked with laughter. 'So we are now trusting in peasant folklore, are we?'

'Why not?' Lewis's voice had been full of answering amusement. 'Vegetation always gives clues, and both you and I know from experience that fennel grows rampant where the earth has been deeply disturbed, even when the disturbance was thousands of years ago. Think of the fennel at Uruk.'

Helmut had thought of it and had said in mock resignation, 'Okay, *lieber Freund*. I will be with you on Crete in the first week of April, though I will take care, I think, not to arrive on April Fool's Day!'

When they had said goodbye to each other, and before he had boarded the boat train, Lewis had gone to a call box on the station concourse and telephoned his godfather.

'Helmut Becke will be joining the team in April,' he had said, his satisfaction obvious.

'I hate to doubt your judgement,' his godfather had said, from the suite at Claridge's that he always stayed in when in London, 'but is bringing a German aboard wise, when the political situation is as it is?'

'Helmut isn't a Nazi. Do you think I would have any truck with an admirer of Hitler's?'

'And he'll fit in with the team?'

'As easy as clockwork,' he'd said reassuringly.

'Then all good luck with things, Lewis. Perhaps you would give Sophie's double a special good wish from me?'

There had been a catch in Nathaniel's aged voice as he'd uttered the name of his late god-daughter.

'Yes.' There had been an answering catch in Lewis's voice. 'Of course I will. Goodbye, Nathaniel. I'll write.'

His hand had been slightly unsteady as he replaced the receiver on its rest.

Six years ago, Lewis's sister and his parents had died in a sailing accident off the isle of Islay in the Hebrides. Sophie, who'd been five years younger than him, had been seventeen. He'd had no other siblings. No other family. His South African godfather, a childless bachelor, had stepped into the breach and, with his help, Lewis had eventually found life bearable again. And then, on Crete, he'd met Nikoleta; and Nikoleta, with her heart-shaped face, tumbling hair, dark-blue eyes, wide smile and vivacious personality, had seemed such a reincarnation of Sophie that when he'd first met her, he'd thought his heart was going to fail him.

He'd sent a photograph of her to Nathaniel; and Nathaniel, too, had agreed that the likeness was extraordinary.

Right from the beginning Lewis had known the thin ice he was skating on, but hadn't been able to help himself. Being with Nikoleta had been like being back in the past. There had been times when he'd almost been able to believe that his parents weren't dead; that Sophie wasn't dead; that everything was as it once had been.

The complications had set in almost from the beginning. When it was obvious that Nikoleta's feelings for him were overwhelmingly romantic, he'd gently explained to her that she was too like his dead sister for him ever to be able to reciprocate them. She hadn't cared that she reminded him of

Sophie and, to his horror, he realized that he'd been lying to her; that it would be terrifyingly easy to respond to her in the way she wished him to and that, if he did so, the complex incestuous feelings that would follow would be more than he could sanely manage.

He'd known for months that he should begin seeing less of Nikoleta, but doing so would, he knew, be like cutting off his right arm.

And then, as if his private life wasn't in enough of a shambles, in the first minutes of New Year's Day he'd added to his difficulties by drunkenly kissing Kate Shelton on the mouth.

What in the world had possessed him? It wasn't as if there'd been any likelihood of her laughing the incident off. There had never been any camaraderie between them, and for that he had been initially at fault when he'd been so unenthused at the thought of having her as a replacement for Tom – and for letting his lack of enthusiasm show. From then on, Kate had combined the scrupulous correctness due to him as director of the dig with the kind of chilly frostiness that would have done an ice-queen credit.

He slung his rucksack over his shoulder. When Helmut joined the team, it wasn't a frostiness that would extend to him. Kate was far too professional not to want a good working relationship with all of her fellow team members. Only with him was she Alaskan ice personified.

And yet . . . And yet . . .

When, in his befuddled brain, it had seemed a good idea to begin the New Year by kissing her in the manner he had, there had been a long, unforgettable moment when her mouth had opened beneath his and her response had been all he could ever have desired. Or at least he'd thought it had been.

It hadn't been a thought that had lasted for long.

There had been no mistaking the violence with which she

had wrested herself free of his embrace, or the nature of her whirlwind exit from the room. Since then he had only seen her twice, both times at the Villa, and if she had been expecting him to apologize for his behaviour at New Year, she had been disappointed.

He hadn't apologized and had no intention of doing so, which meant that when the dig began again in a few weeks' time, it would again be a case of scrupulous, icy correctness on her part, and indifference to her iciness on his.

As he began making his way back down the mountain he wondered if, where he and Kate were concerned, he should have put Helmut in the picture, and then he shrugged the thought away. Mentioning it would make it important – and it wasn't important. All that was important was that this season he found a Minoan palace: a palace that would make his name as an archaeologist known worldwide.

Chapter Eleven

''Bye, Agata!' Ella called out cheerily as she ran down the last of the *cafeneion*'s outside steps.

'Goodbye,' Agata shouted back from where, in a wired-off area, she was milking a goat. 'God be with you!'

With Agata's daily blessing ringing in her ears, Ella set off through the village in the direction of the mule track that led to the mountain's small upper plateau. Once on the track, the way was steep, but she was young and fit and, just as important, after three weeks on the dig she was already getting used to the daily climb.

Usually she set off for the upper plateau with all the other members of the team, but this morning, because she had been doing paperwork for Lewis, she was an hour or so behind them and the mid-morning sun was hot on her back.

She adjusted the strap on her haversack so that it would fit more comfortably and, as she did so, the engagement ring on the fourth finger of her left hand sparkled and shone. Even though she had been wearing it ever since her trip home six weeks ago, the sight of it still gave her a jolt of pleasure and surprise.

How had it happened? She had certainly not had the slightest intention of becoming engaged to Sam when, in late March and before the year's dig had begun, she had left Crete to spend ten days with her parents and granddad. As well as looking forward to seeing them, she had, of course, also been looking forward to seeing Sam. Ever since they had first met there had never been a time when she hadn't looked forward to seeing him. She hadn't been expecting to become engaged to him, though. At the time she had left Crete for England, nothing had been further from her mind.

She paused in her climb in order to gain a little more breath, before setting off on the last part of it, thinking back to her ten days at home. As it had been Easter, and a warm, sunny Easter, Wilsden had been looking its best. The fields had been full of young lambs, the roadside verges had been thick with primroses and even though it was far too early in the year for the heather to be in bloom, in the near distance the sunlit moors were as inviting as ever. Her mother had baked a whole shoal of Tetley favourite recipes. Ale-and-walnut bread, currant teacakes, oatcakes, parkin and last, but by no means least, curd tarts.

'It's going to take till Whitsuntide to eat this lot up,' her father had said, cutting a thick slice of the ale-and-walnut bread and then breaking off a piece of Wensleydale cheese to eat with it. He had looked across at her and winked. 'It's your mother's way of tempting you back home, lass. I can't say I mind it. Your mother's the best baker of bread and cakes this side of Hebden Bridge.'

Sam had motorcycled all the way from Scooby, and her mother had laid on a Yorkshire high tea in his honour. The minute she had heard Sam's bike roar past the Ling Bob, Ella had run out of the house to meet him. To her exasperation, her mother had followed hard on her heels, and her father and granddad had followed them as far as the open front door.

She had been sure this meant she was going to be cheated of a proper reunion, but Sam had leapt from his bike, pushed his goggles high into his thatch of straw-coloured hair and, uncaring of their audience, had pulled her joyfully into his arms and kissed her soundly.

If it had been anyone else, her parents and granddad would, she knew, have been outraged by such behaviour in public, but as they read Sam's action as indicating that an engagement was in the offing, not even her granddad frowned or clicked his tongue.

Instead, standing on the doorstep in trousers held up by a broad leather belt without the benefit of belt loops, and a striped collarless shirt, he had called out wheezily, 'Come on in, lad. Tea's on t'table.'

'No need to tell the entire street,' her mother had said chidingly, as she had ushered them all into the house.

Her father had dropped his arm in a matey way around Sam's shoulders. 'Mother's made curd tarts,' he'd said, referring to Alice in the way most West Riding men of his age referred to their wives. 'She makes 'em with rosewater, not currants. They're so soft and creamy you've never tasted the like of 'em.'

An hour later, after a salad of Yorkshire ham helped down by all the sweet foods Alice had prepared, Sam had to agree with Alfred: where Alice's curd tarts were concerned, none he'd ever tasted had been even half as good – and being Yorkshire-born, he'd tasted a good many.

''Ow abaht an 'and of gin rummy, lad?' her granddad had said to Sam, as the plates were being cleared from the table.

Ella, impatient to have some time with Sam on her own, had raised her eyes to heaven.

Reading her mind, Sam had looked across at her and grinned. 'Maybe another day, Mr Tetley,' he'd said to Jos, rising to his feet. 'For now, I'm going to take Ella over to the Easter Fair in Manningham Park.' He'd turned to her mother and said, 'Thank you for the grand tea, Mrs Tetley. Living in digs in Scooby, I haven't had a tea like that in a long time.'

Her mother had flushed with pleasure. 'You're very welcome, lad,' she'd said. 'It's always a pleasure to see you. Don't leave it too long before you're back.'

'I won't,' he'd said, picking up his cycling jacket and shrugging himself into it. And then, to Ella, he'd said, 'Put on something warm, love. It may be lovely and sunny now, but it will be late tonight before we're back, and it will be chilly riding pillion.'

It had been as good a way as any at letting her family know they needn't wait up for her and, as she'd run upstairs for her coat, Ella had had a happy smile on her lips.

The first thing he'd said to her when they'd left the house, and even before she had got on the bike, had been, 'I've missed you badly, Ella.' There had no longer been easy affability in Sam's eyes and voice. 'I can't get used to you being so far away, and for such long stretches of time.' His eyes had been dark with intensity, his voice fierce.

Her blissful happiness had faded. The conversation was one she'd known they were bound to have, but she hadn't expected him to embark on it so soon, or that he would do so with such unnerving urgency. Worse, she hadn't known how to respond. She'd known that Sam wanted her to say that she wouldn't return to Crete, and it was something she couldn't say because she *was* going to return there – and she was going to remain there for as long as there was a dig to work on.

He'd taken hold of her hands, holding them so tightly he'd bruised the backs of them.

'Let's have this conversation a little later,' she'd said, knowing that to anyone seeing them, it would look as if they were having a heated argument – and that they were in fact on the verge of one.

She'd shot a quick look towards the house and seen a net curtain fall quickly back into place.

'Mum's already giving a running commentary,' she'd said, 'and I don't want her, Dad and Granddad worrying that we're at odds with each other. Give me a hug. It will set their minds at rest.'

He'd looked towards the house and seen a curtain twitch. 'You win,' he'd said reluctantly, giving her the hug she'd asked for.

When he'd released her, Sam straddled his bike, his face sombre. 'But we're going to have to talk about this, Ella,' he'd said, putting his goggles on. 'We can't go on as we have been doing. Either we are a couple, or we're not. And if we're not . . .'

As she'd made herself secure on the pillion, he'd given an expressive shrug of leather-jacketed shoulders.

'And if we're not,' she'd said, filled with a hideous sense of unease, 'what then?'

'Then you can't expect me to be here waiting for you, whenever you choose to spend a few days of the year at home.' And with that, he'd kicked the bike into life and the noise of the engine had made any response impossible.

Bradford's Manningham Park was a good twenty minutes away, and in those twenty minutes Ella had had a lot to think about. In all the time she had known Sam, she had never known him sound so determined, or so grim, and she hadn't had a shadow of doubt that he'd meant every word he'd said. If she didn't accept that they were a couple – and by that, she was certain Sam meant an engaged couple – then he wouldn't be there for her the next time she came home.

To her startled surprise, the prospect had appalled her.

She'd thought of how she would feel if, next time she returned to Yorkshire, Sam was dating someone else: if he had become engaged to someone else, someone he had met in Scooby. The picture it conjured up was so unpleasant it made her feel queasy.

She'd thought about what becoming engaged would mean for her, and decided that although it would, of course, mean that she and Sam would eventually get married, their getting married wasn't something that would happen within a year, or perhaps even within two or three years. What Sam wanted from her was a public declaration that they were a couple, and she'd known from the way she'd looked forward to seeing him again that their being a couple was what she wanted, too.

She'd also known that once they were engaged, and though he would miss her, Sam would accept her need to return to Crete to finish the Kalamata dig; and that he would accept other digs in the future as well, just as long as they were either near to home or, if abroad, digs of reasonably short duration.

No longer feeling a hideous sense of unease, no longer appalled, she had tightened her arms around his waist, hoping to indicate to him that everything was going to be all right.

The noise of the fair had been audible long before they reached it. Sam had slewed the motorbike to a halt in a street thronged with people making their way towards the park entrance.

'Before we go into the park, I have to finish saying my piece,' he'd said when he'd dismounted, his shoulders tense, his face set and pale. 'I'm not a bloke that goes in for demands and ultimatums, but as I said before, I can't go on like this.'

'I understand, Sam,' she'd said.

It had been as if she hadn't spoken.

'I could endure being apart from you for months on end, if there was a proper understanding between us.' His eyes had been agonized, his voice resolute. 'But if there's never going to be one . . .'

'There is, Sam.'

'. . . then I have to feel free to be courting elsewhere.'

'No, you haven't—'

Again, he hadn't let her finish and he'd made no move to take her in his arms, or even to hold her hands.

'There's a girl at Scooby, Ella,' he'd said. 'Her name is Jenny Gulliver and she's the receptionist at the surgery. I've taken her out a few times . . .'

Ella had heard enough and hadn't wanted to hear any more. Closing the small gap Sam had so carefully ensured had been between them, whilst he'd said what he'd had to say, she'd slid her arms around his neck, saying, 'Don't take her out again, Sam; at least not in a romantic way. As your fiancée, I wouldn't like it.'

It had, she reflected now, been a reckless thing to say. What if, in Sam's eyes, being a couple was a far different thing from their becoming engaged? What if he'd no longer had marriage in mind?

The worry had been unnecessary.

'Fiancée?' Disbelief had flashed through his eyes, and then understanding. With a whoop of exultation he'd lifted her off her feet, whirling her round and round. When he'd finally set her unsteadily back on the pavement, he'd said, a broad grin splitting his face, 'Can we have a replay of the last few minutes, Ella love? I'd like to propose properly. On one knee. And more than anything else in the world, I'd like to actually hear you say "Yes".'

'You can't propose on a crowded pavement,' she'd protested, laughter in her voice.

'Oh, but I can,' he'd said.

Dropping down on one knee and causing a man with a child riding high on his shoulders to sidestep him adroitly, Sam had taken her hands in his and said, his voice choked with emotion, 'My dearest, darling Ella. I love you more than anyone – or anything – in the world. Will you marry me, and let me love and care for you always and forever?'

'Yes,' she'd said, filled with the happy certainty that she had made the right decision: the decision her parents had always hoped she would make.

Six weeks later, it was the way she still felt. Both Kate and Daphne had taken the news that she was engaged to Sam as if it was news they had long expected and, once she had told them it was going to be a long engagement, had made all the right noises. Agata had kissed her on both cheeks, saying with deep affection, 'Happy I am for thee. A good husband is a gift from God. From God such men come.' On a visit to the Villa Ariadne, Ella had been toasted in champagne by Kit and the Squire. All the team, apart from Pericles and Christos, had teased her mercilessly. Not being teased by Pericles was no surprise, as he rarely joined in any team jollity, but as Christos had teased her almost from the first moment they had met, she had found his not doing so disconcerting, until Kate had pointed out that one-to-one teasing was different from team teasing and that, as Christos was site supervisor, he had probably felt it was something he should keep aloof from.

Her way up the track now was intermittently edged with clumps of paper-white cyclamen, their beauty compensating for the many mule droppings she had to avoid. The mules accompanied the team every morning, carrying picks, buckets, spades and other gear necessary for the day's work.

Faintly, in the crystal-clear air, came the sound of men's voices. Though she couldn't be sure, she thought two of the voices – who sounded to be arguing over a football result – belonged to Nico, one of the youngest members of the team, and Yanni, the oldest member of the team. Someone else was whistling. Ella smiled, certain the whistler would be Adonis. Christos had told her that Adonis's constant whistling was an irritation to Lewis, but she liked it. Her dad was a whistler, and Adonis's cheerful whistling reminded her of him.

The path finally crested the rim of the plateau. A hundred yards or so away, beneath the soaring silver-grey and silver-white upper ridges of the mountain, was the beginning of the site, a large area that over the last few weeks had been arduously cleared of all undergrowth and was now beginning to be criss-crossed with trial-pits. So far none of the pits had yielded any signs of ancient walls or terraces, or any signs of anything ever having been built there. 'Which means,' Christos had said to her glumly, 'that Lewis's gut feeling is wrong once again.'

No one else on the team had put that thought into words, but Ella knew it was something they were all beginning to fear.

She had arrived just as most of the men had temporarily downed tools for a tea break. Dimitri was the self-appointed tea-maker and, as she drew closer, she could smell the distinctive aroma of the aptly named Mountain Tea brewing.

'Does Dimitri call it "Mountain Tea" because we're drinking it halfway up a mountain?' she had asked Christos the first time she had tasted it.

Christos had laughed so much he'd given himself a stitch. 'No, Ella,' he'd said at last, when he'd finally been able to speak. 'He calls it "Mountain Tea" because it's made from *Sideritis* leaves, and *Sideritis* only grows at a height of over three thousand feet.'

Later, Lewis had told her that in Crete, Mountain Tea – as well as being a popular daily drink – was also regarded as a cure for all kinds of ailments and was part of every family's medicine chest. 'But it needs to be served with a spoonful of honey and a dash of lemon,' he had added, shooting her one of his rare smiles. 'It's a challenge to the tastebuds to take it neat.'

Before meeting Lewis, and because of what Kate had told her about him, Ella had been prepared to find him difficult to work for, and hard to like. It had taken only a couple of days on the dig for her to find out how wrong her expectations had been. Lewis certainly wasn't a hearty 'treat-me-as-if-I'm-just-another-member-of-the-team' kind of employer and site director, but she didn't mind that. Once he had told someone what he wanted from them, and knew them capable of it, he let them get on with it, without unnecessary interference, and his work team treated him with confidence and respect.

Everyone was enjoying their tea break apart from Kate and Christos, who were still a distance away, working beneath a shade cloth on trial-pit five, and Lewis, who was seated at a camp table covered in survey maps and ground plans.

She had just been about to join the tea-drinkers, two of whom were still arguing about football, when Lewis noticed her arrival.

'A minute Ella, please.'

His voice was grim and, with nothing found to indicate building of any era, let alone the Neo-palatial era, she knew the reason why. It was still early days, though, and at the thought that he might be about to write off the dig, her tummy muscles knotted with tension.

'Look at these results, Ella.' Lewis indicated the daily reports on the trial-pits. 'They're not encouraging.'

'No,' she said cautiously. 'They're not. But the present pits aren't sufficient in number to mean the plateau is void. Are we going to be extending the area of search?'

'Yes. And with a bigger team.'

Before she could make a response, Helmut Becke walked up to them, carrying a mug of tea for Lewis. 'Are you beginning to lose heart, *mein Freund*?' he asked sympathetically, handing him the mug.

'I'm disappointed.' Lewis ran his free hand distractedly

through his hair. 'I'd expected we would at least be finding pottery sherds by now.'

Helmut moved some papers to one side and perched on the corner of the table, one leg swinging. 'I overheard Ella say that the present trial-pits aren't sufficient to come to any kind of a conclusion, and she's right. A bigger team would move things along faster. What do you think, Ella?'

Ella, who had been wondering if it was perhaps time for her to excuse herself, decided it wasn't. 'A big team always moves things along faster, but only if it means the extra men are as experienced as the team we already have.'

This was so true that neither Helmut nor Lewis disagreed with her, but the expression on their faces told her that assembling a bigger experienced team wouldn't be easy.

Lewis pushed his camp chair away from the table. 'For now, we'll begin digging new trial-pits on the western edge of the site,' he said, his voice indicating that, for the moment, there was nothing more to be said.

As Ella began walking away in the direction of the pit that was her responsibility, Helmut fell into step beside her.

'Not easy for Lewis, is it?' he said, his thumbs tucked into the pockets of dusty khaki shorts. 'If this was a straightforward British School dig, it would have been called off by now.'

Ella, who had forged an easy relationship with Helmut, said wryly, 'But then the British School would never have sanctioned it, would they?'

'*Zu blutig wahr!*' he said, laughing. 'Too bloody true!'

She laughed with him. Before Helmut had arrived, Dimitri and Angelos had been very unenthusiastic about having a German as a member of the team. 'The Germans we worked with at Olympia were no fun,' Angelos had said glumly. 'They were as stiff as sticks and nothing ever made them laugh.'

'How unfortunate,' Helmut had said, when Adonis had told

him of what they had been expecting. 'Quite obviously the Germans you speak of were not from Berlin. *Ich bin Berliner*, and Berliners have a very relaxed attitude.'

He was a typical north German in looks: tall and lean, with a narrow, high-cheekboned face and blond hair.

Ella thought his hair colour very like Sam's, but where Sam's hair was a thick, coarse thatch, Helmut's hair was fine, straight as a dye and cut *en brosse*.

She was just about to ask him how long he thought they could continue working the plateau, without a find of any kind to encourage them, when he suddenly said, 'Look, Ella! A lammergeier!'

High in the sky, a bird with an enormous wingspan was circling over one of the topmost ravines.

Ella stood still, looking in the direction he was pointing. 'It's huge!' With rising excitement she shaded her eyes from the sun. 'Are you sure it's a lammergeier, Helmut? They're terribly rare. Perhaps it's an eagle?'

'Wrong colouring and shape. And can you see a flash of orange on its chest? Lammergeiers get that distinctive coloration from rubbing against ferrous rock. *Ist es nicht wunderbar?*'

It was indeed a wonderful sight, and by now everyone else near them was looking up and enjoying the sight as well. So much so that when Christos came sprinting towards them, no one took the slightest notice of him, until he shouted: 'Kate's uncovered ashlar masonry! It's limestone and looks like walling!'

The impressive sight of a lammergeier was forgotten in an instant.

'*Jesus Gott!*' Helmut broke into a run, heading for trial-pit five with everyone else running in his wake, apart from Lewis, who was already yards ahead of him.

Kate was squatting beside the masonry she had uncovered,

a mattock in her hand, her forehead and cheeks streaked with dirt and a smile of huge satisfaction on her face.

Lewis jumped down beside her, running his hand reverently over stone whose surface had been precisely cut, in exactly the same way that stone at Knossos and Phaistos and Mallia had been cut.

'Bloody marvellous, Kate!' His eyes blazed with exhilaration. 'You've saved the day! This is a moment I'll never forget.'

Kate flushed scarlet, and for a moment Ella thought Lewis was so relieved at having his instincts about the site proved right that he was going to kiss her until she was breathless.

She was fairly sure Kate was thinking the same thing, and then Lewis checked himself. 'Let's start digging,' he said exultantly to the rest of the team. 'Let's find out how far this thunderingly beautiful line of ashlar extends!'

Chapter Twelve

Christos was sitting on a rickety metal chair on the patch of ground that served the Kourakis family as a garden. It was July and the first time since Kate's find that he had been back home and able to share all the excitement of the last few weeks with Nikoleta and his mother.

'The expertly cut walling Kate found stretched for an incredible fifteen yards,' he said ebulliently, as scrawny hens pecked their way around them, 'and in one of the new pits to the west of it, Helmut and Pericles uncovered a limestone door lintel.'

'A door lintel?' The query came from Eleni. Though Christos and Nikoleta were sitting in their garden, Eleni was seated in the open doorway, spinning. 'A door lintel is a door lintel.' She paused in what she was doing, in order to gesture expressively. 'Georgio's shepherd's hut has a door lintel. Perhaps from a shepherd's hut it came?'

Christos shook his head. 'This door lintel had an outline of a Minoan double-headed axe engraved on it.'

Nikoleta gave a cry of satisfaction and Eleni nodded, understanding at last the lintel's importance. At the Palace of Minos there were many carved depictions of double-headed axes. Kostas had told her that, to the ancient Minoans, the double-headed axe was a symbol of sacred royalty and power. If it had been found on a lintel at the Kalamata dig, then it meant Lewis

Sinclair had at last found the palace he'd been searching for; it also meant that just as her husband had once been part of a dig of historical importance, so her son might also now be discovering a palace that, like Knossos, Phaistos and Mallia, would be in all the guidebooks.

'And artefacts? Has Lewis found artefacts?' Nikoleta asked, eager to bring Lewis's name into the conversation. Since Kate Shelton's find, she hadn't seen him. Like Christos and the rest of his team, Lewis had spent each and every day in further excavation of what the team were now referring to as a summer palace.

Christos, who knew that by 'artefacts' Nikoleta was thinking of jewellery similar to the magnificent gold necklace he had unearthed when excavating the villa on the village plateau, said, 'Nothing to match the necklace, but it's still early days. What is important is that we're uncovering something bigger than a villa. This week we found part of a drainage system full of pottery fragments and bits of fresco. The bits aren't enough for us to know what the fresco depicted, but Ella thinks they are part of a woman's hand and that she is holding the section of a stem – perhaps the stem of a flower or a spray of leaves.'

'She is smart, the little Ella. Smart she is.' From a fleecy-white mass, Eleni was again pinching wool on to the leader cord of her spinning wheel. 'In August, when heat puts an end to work at Kalamata, will she stay in Heraklion?' she asked, her fingers moving as fast as light, while at a slower rhythm her feet worked the wheel's treadle. 'In Heraklion will she stay?'

Nikoleta waited for Christos's reply with interest. In the manner of brothers, he had never spoken to her about any girl in whom he had been romantically interested, and he had certainly never spoken to her about Ella. She knew, though, that Ella mattered to him. When Ella had returned to Crete with an engagement ring on her finger, Christos had been so subdued that their mother had thought he was sickening for something.

He said now, carefully not catching her eye, 'No. I do not think so. I think that now she is engaged, she will return to England until the weather is cooler and work on the dig begins again.'

'And when it is winter?' Eleni asked, hope in her voice, for last winter, when Ella had lodged in Heraklion, she had visited their home often. 'In winter will she again stay in Heraklion?'

He rose abruptly to his feet. 'Perhaps.' He ran a hand through his unruly hair. 'Or perhaps she will return to England and marry.' He turned to Nikoleta. 'Lewis is at the Villa, giving the Squire and Kit Shelton an update on the progress we have made.'

Nikoleta's face lit up in eager anticipation. 'Did he tell you to let me know he was at Knossos?'

Christos nodded, not wanting to say anything in front of their mother that would alert her to the true nature of Nikoleta's feelings for Lewis. Shrewd though she was about many things, the fact that Nikoleta had hopes of marrying Lewis would be as incomprehensible to their mother as if, years ago, a village girl had fallen in love with the widowed Sir Arthur Evans and had lived in similar hope. Lewis was a foreigner and, as director of a dig, a man of importance. No matter how friendly men like him became with the island's peasant families, they didn't marry into them.

Having worked for Lewis for two years, Christos felt that the tradition of their not doing so was one that might be about to be broken. It wasn't a thought he'd shared with Nikoleta. Simply by accepting the close nature of her relationship with

Lewis, he was acknowledging that such a possibility existed and, more importantly still, that he was happy with it.

'Come on,' he said now to Nikoleta. 'You may as well walk to the Villa with me. A handful of Mrs Hutchinson's roses are still in bloom, but once it's August they'll be gone. This may be your last chance to see them.'

Nikoleta leapt to her feet with alacrity. The Villa Ariadne's garden had always served as a trysting place for her and Lewis, and it would be where he was expecting to find her. When he did, he would tell her, as Christos had, all about the find at Kalamata. The difference would be, though, that Lewis would be able to tell her things Christos hadn't been able to. Lewis would be able to tell her if the find on the upper plateau meant he would now be in Crete for years to come, and not just for the remainder of the present season.

When Sir Arthur Evans had discovered Knossos he had made a home for himself at the Villa Ariadne, and throughout all the years of Nikoleta's childhood he had returned to Crete year after year, extending his area of excavation, reconstructing, restoring, struggling to make unity out of a dizzying array of pottery and stone, walls and pavements.

And that was how she imagined it would now be for Lewis. In future years he wouldn't be excavating in fresh places – places like Egypt or Iraq – places so far away from Crete that she might never see him again, and where, in time, he would forget her. Instead his work would continue to be in Crete: at Kalamata. The prospect made her heart soar with joy.

It was scorchingly hot and when they reached the side gate leading into the Villa's rear garden, Christos said, 'I'm going to the cafe to buy cigarettes and have something to drink in the shade. Once Lewis has caught up with you, he's heading into Heraklion and, as I'm going with him, this is goodbye for now.'

She nodded understandingly and as, with a wave of his hand, he continued up the dusty road towards the Palace of Minos's entrance and the tourist cafe opposite it, she opened the gate and walked up the tree-shaded path and into the garden.

Lewis was already there. He had been sitting on one of the wrought-iron garden seats, one arm resting along the seat's back, a cigarette in his hand. The minute he saw her, he crushed the cigarette out and jumped to his feet.

'Lewis!' She ran straight towards him and into his arms. '*Lewis!* Do you know how long it's been? Over six weeks! Nearly eight.'

He hugged her tight. 'Is that all?' There was amusement in his voice. 'And in that short space of time I've found a palace.'

'Have you?' She pressed her hands against his chest so that she could look up into his eyes. 'Have you really? Is it going to be as big a palace as the Palace of Minos?'

'God, no.' His amusement deepened. 'Nothing again could ever be so big.' At the immediate disappointment in her eyes, he kissed the top of her hair. 'And it doesn't have to be so big to be of major importance, Niki. Hazarding a guess, I'd say I'm in the early stages of finding a palace similar to Mallia.'

Mallia was the third-biggest Minoan palace yet found. As a matter of course, tourists who flocked to the Palace of Minos afterwards visited Phaistos, the next-biggest palace, and then they visited Mallia. If the palace at Kalamata proved to be anything at all like Mallia, then Lewis's reputation as an archaeologist would be internationally respected. At the thought of how the wife of such a man would be regarded, the blood sang through her veins.

'I want to know exactly what has been found,' she said, as he took hold of her hand and tucked it into the crook of his arm. 'And I want to see the site for myself. Can I go back with you today, Lewis? Will you show me the palace today?'

It was a question he had been expecting and as they sat down, shaded from the heat by the wide-spanning branches of an urn-potted mulberry tree, he said, 'Not today, Niki,' knowing the kind of prurient speculation such a visit would arouse in some members of his team. 'When you first see the site, I'd like you to do so when more of the palace has been uncovered. Because we're a small team it's going to be a long process. It's impossible to work at speed, when the tiniest thing found has to be measured and recorded on a grid sheet so that later, when it's being studied off-site, the exact location of where it was found is known; and the artefact, even if it's as small as a pottery sherd or a flake of fresco, can be tied to its context within the site.'

Nikoleta knew the kind of grid sheets he was talking about because Christos had once tried to explain to her the way a Cartesian coordinate system worked, but she hadn't been interested then, and she wasn't interested now.

The finer mechanics of excavation work bored her. She only liked the final, wonderful results, and then only truly responded to them when, as at Knossos, the site had been partially reconstructed. She wondered if, at Kalamata, Lewis would reconstruct in the same way.

Christos had told her it was something that was never likely to happen. 'Lewis is too much of a purist,' he'd said, when she had brought up the subject with him. 'He appreciates that Sir Arthur's reconstructed pillars and frescoes enable visitors to more easily envisage what the Palace of Minos looked like three and a half thousand years ago, and although such reconstructions weren't frowned upon in the 1920s when the work took place, they are now. Even if the Greek government sanctioned it, it isn't a route Lewis would want to go down.'

His arm was around her shoulders. Nikoleta leaned into him, enjoying the faint tang of lemon aftershave. All the Greeks were heavily moustached and after working on the dig – and apart from Adonis – were bearded as well. Even Helmut now sported a light-blond beard. She tried to imagine what Lewis would look like, moustached and bearded, and knew that he would look Greek.

It wasn't something she wanted. She liked the fact that he wasn't Greek; that he was Scottish, although a Scot with no discernible Scottish accent. Ella had told her that not only was Scotland far colder than Crete – something she did, of course, already know – but it was even chillier and wetter than England. The thought of living there wasn't enticing. As he told her of the flakes of fresco that had been found, she listened with only half an ear, pondering the problem of Scotland's disagreeable climate.

She most certainly would never want to live there, but as Lewis's habit was to return home only for a short visit at the end of each season's dig, it was a prospect that might never arise.

'. . . As far as I can tell at this stage, the layout at Kalamata is going to prove to be the same as at Mallia,' he was saying, unaware that he had lost her attention, 'four wings set around a rectangular central court.'

'Lewis,' she squeezed hold of his hand, another thought occurring to her, 'when the site is fully excavated and the tourists come, can I be the palace's chief guide?'

'Guide?' Startled, he broke off from what he had been saying. 'There will never be a need for a full-time guide at Kalamata, Niki. The site is simply too difficult to reach for it to attract visitors in the numbers that Phaistos and Mallia do.'

She pulled away from him, deeply shocked. 'But if it is not to be famous, what is the point of it?'

Lewis didn't know whether to be amused by the naivety of her question or despairing. He reminded himself that her knowledge of the Palace of Minos wasn't down to an academic archaeological education, but due to her father having been a member of the palace's excavation team throughout all the years of her childhood, and of Nikoleta having been practically brought up on the site.

'The point of it is what it will tell us about a society that lived more than three thousand years ago,' he said patiently. 'And the palace at Kalamata is going to throw an entirely new angle on what we've learned from previous palaces, because no way can it have been intended to fulfil the same functions they did. All three previous palaces were easily accessible. This one isn't. Knossos, Phaistos and Mallia are all near the sea. Knossos is not quite as near it as Phaistos and Mallia, but near enough for its closeness to have been taken into account when the palace was built. Phaistos has not just one port, but two. At Mallia there is a road still intact that leads from the sea directly to the palace. There's no such sea access for Kalamata. It's been built as far away from the coast as, in Crete, it's possible to get.'

Nikoleta was uncaring as to how near, or far, Kalamata was from the sea. What mattered to her was that it should become a world-famous site, for if it didn't, how could Lewis's name become world-famous?

'A road,' she said. 'A road must be built from Kalamata village to the palace.'

At the idea of a road being hacked out of the upper reaches of Kalamata's mountain, Lewis winced. 'Any road leading to the upper plateau would have to wind around the mountain almost vertically, and no government would even consider a project so mammoth and costly.'

'But of course they would, if they realized the palace would be a second Knossos and if . . .'

Lewis drew in a deep breath, belatedly realizing that the excitement Nikoleta felt at the finding of the palace was far removed from the kind of excitement he and his team felt.

Giving her hand a squeeze to show he hadn't fallen out of patience with her, he said, 'I thought I'd made it clear that whatever has been found at Kalamata, it isn't a second Knossos, or even a second Phaistos or Mallia. The double-axe engravings in the stonework, the indications of a great central courtyard and the traces we've found of a sophisticated sewage and drainage system indicate beyond any possibility of doubt that we've found a palace. But please, Niki, get any idea that it's a second Palace of Minos completely out of your head.'

'But . . .'

'And get the possibility of a road being built from Kalamata village to the upper plateau out of your head as well. It isn't going to happen, and it's the last thing on earth I would want to happen.'

'But why?' Her bewilderment was total. 'So many people would be able to see what you have found. Thousands of people.'

'They will be able to experience the palace by reading about it and seeing photographs of it.' Despite his best intentions, Lewis couldn't keep the exasperation from showing in his voice. 'There doesn't need to be a monstrous road disfiguring the mountain for them to appreciate the palace's significance – a significance that's still unknown.'

She withdrew her hand from his, hoping it would indicate the depth of her disappointment and that, once he realized it, he would begin thinking differently.

Instead of showing any signs of doing so, Lewis rose to his feet.

'I have to be in Heraklion for twelve. Christos is coming with me. Do you want to come into the Villa to say goodbye to us both?'

'No.' Her voice was petulant and she didn't care. 'I have already said goodbye to Christos, and I think you will find him not in the Villa, but at the bus-stop cafe.'

He waited for her to rise to her feet so that he could give her a goodbye kiss on the cheek, as he'd always given Sophie.

She didn't do so, and although he knew she was waiting for him to sit down again beside her, he didn't. When a teenage Sophie had behaved childishly, he had refused to be manipulated and had ignored her fits of pique until she was over them, something that had never taken very long.

Taking the same kind of action now, he said, 'Give my best wishes to your parents Niki, and to Georgi, and when you next see your brother tell him that when he isn't tending sheep he's very welcome at the dig.' Then, as she still stubbornly made no response, he turned away from her and, with his fists shoved deep into the pockets of his trousers, headed in the direction of the side gate.

Tears stung the back of Nikoleta's eyes. More than anything in the world she wanted to run after him, but pride, and the bewilderment and frustration she felt, prevented her. Fiercely she told herself that she had done and said nothing wrong. It was Lewis who was in the wrong. She had been so looking forward to his taking her back with him to Kalamata; to their walking around all that had been excavated so far and to his explaining it all to her; and yet when she had asked that he take her to the site, he had refused. True, he had been going into Heraklion with Christos, but he could have called for her on his way back to Kalamata; and if he couldn't have done that, he could have said he would take her to the site later in the week – or perhaps even next week – instead of which he had put her off indefinitely.

And then when she had asked Lewis if, when the site was opened to tourists, she could be its chief guide, he had said that because the site was one it was so difficult to reach, he didn't envisage it ever being opened to tourists – certainly not in the numbers that would require the kind of guide she clearly imagined herself being.

Her bewilderment and frustration turned into resentment. How could what he had said be true? What was the point of discovering a palace if no one could visit it?

A petal from one of Mrs Hutchinson's roses fell on to her hair and crossly she brushed it away. Tourists would want to see the palace, even if it meant them having to be taken to it on the backs of mules. She certainly intended to see what Lewis had found and, just to show that she wasn't entirely dependent on him saying that she could or couldn't, she wanted to see it now. How, though, was she going to be able to do so?

The door leading from the Villa into the garden opened and then closed. Footsteps came down the shallow flight of stone steps and then came to a sudden halt.

As the footsteps weren't Lewis's, Nikoleta didn't trouble to turn around.

Kit hesitated. He knew Lewis and Nikoleta were in the habit of meeting in the garden, but there was no sign of Lewis being there now, and there was nothing happily expectant about the set of Nikoleta's shoulders. Instead she was leaning forward a little, as if her hands were clasped in her lap, and suddenly he was certain that far from being expectant, she was deeply despondent.

He cleared his throat. 'Nikoleta?'

He walked towards her, and it wasn't until his shadow fell across her that she finally made a response. 'I'm just leaving,

Mr Shelton.' She rose to her feet, aware that as she was neither a resident nor a guest at the Villa, she had no real right to be there.

'There's no need for you to leave.' He wished she would refer to him as Kit, but though he'd asked her to do so several times, she'd never yet taken him up on the offer. 'Are you waiting for Lewis?'

'No. I've already seen him.'

Now that they were face-to-face, Kit was appalled to realize that his assumption about Nikoleta's unhappiness had been correct. There was none of the usual sparkle in her eyes, and the fizzing gaiety that was so much a part of her personality was entirely absent.

'You're upset,' he said bluntly. 'Is there anything I can do to help?'

Behind the lenses of his horn-rimmed spectacles, his eyes were full of concern.

For as long as she had known him, Nikoleta had barely acknowledged Kit's existence. Now, though, she found his concern comforting.

'I was hoping Lewis could take me today to see the site at Kalamata, but he has business in Heraklion.'

Both statements were true and, even though the conclusion Kit would reach about them was false, they did at least save her pride. She wasn't going to let Kit know that Lewis had no intention of showing her the site until more of it had been excavated.

Relieved that the cause of her unhappiness wasn't too dire, Kit smiled.

'That's a problem easily solved,' he said, uncaring that he had been about to set off for a day's work at the necropolis site in Fortetsa. 'Let me take you up there.'

Nikoleta's frustration vanished in a flash. If Kit took her to the site, she would not only have her passionate desire to see it fulfilled, but she would also be showing Lewis that he should have more regard for her; and that, if he didn't, then someone else just as important as he was did.

At the thought of making Lewis even a tiny bit jealous, Nikoleta's spirits soared.

'Now?' she said eagerly. 'This minute?'

'Of course this minute.' Kit felt a surge of satisfaction. He would take her up there in the Sally and stay there with her for as long as Lewis remained in Heraklion.

'You are very kind, Mr Shelton.'

'Kit,' he said. 'Please call me Kit.'

'You are very kind, Kit,' she said, and as they began walking out of the garden to where the Villa's transport was parked, she not only smiled at him, but slipped her hand into the crook of his arm.

It was all Kit could have asked for.

Chapter Thirteen

Kate had written to Daphne in her distinctive scrawl:

*It's already October, and by the end of the month we will
again have to halt work on-site, this time not just for a
month, as in August, but until next March – or, if the winter
is a bad one and the ground is exceptionally hard, until next
April.*

*What we have found so far this year is really quite
amazing. A section of courtyard still paved in mesmerizing
blue schist stone; footings of storerooms on the west side of
the courtyard; and intermittent three-foot- and four-foot-
high walls of what we are almost sure is a royal apartment
and a sacred area on the east side of the court. What is
intriguing is that there only seems to be the one royal apartment. Knossos, Phaistos and Mallia all have two megara
complete with porch, vestibule, large hall and central hearth,
but not so at Kalamata. Or, at least, not so far.*

Daphne paused before reading more. It was so long since she
had been on a dig that she could scarcely remember what being
on one felt like. She was alone in the mansion flat she shared
with Sandy in Kensington, and rain was beating against the
multi-paned windows. She wondered if it was raining on Crete,
or if, in October, the weather was still dry and mild. She had

been meaning to visit Crete all summer and perhaps work alongside Kate and Ella for a week or two on the dig. Where the dig was concerned, she had quite obviously left things too late, but it wasn't too late to make a trip out there in order to spend time with Kate and Ella – provided, of course, that Kate and Ella were staying on in Crete, as they had last year.

She returned her attention to the letter, to see if Kate had written anything about her own and Ella's intentions:

The work on the site has been totally engrossing, so apologies if I don't have too much other news. At one time I thought I might have, because in the summer I had several dates with Helmut. He's very attractive in a raw-boned, blond, blue-eyed German kind of way, but much as I like him (and I like him an awful lot), there were no sparks (at least not for me), and so instead of blossoming into a red-hot romance it's settled into good solid friendship. (As far as red-hot romances go, I sometimes wonder if I'm ever going to know what one is like).

Daphne knew what one was like.

She bit the corner of her lip, overcome by memories of her romance with Sholto and the cataclysmic way in which it had ended so abruptly. Where was Sholto now? As it was October and a weekend, he was most likely out of town and at a North Country house party, shooting pheasants. Or perhaps he was in Paris with Francine. Her stomach muscles tightened in a painful knot. If he wasn't in Paris with Francine, perhaps Sholto was somewhere else with her. Perhaps they were even now in London together, enjoying lunch at the Ritz or the Dorchester.

It was just over a year since the nightmare scene in the Savoy's River Room when she had so dramatically and finally broken off her relationship with him. Why was she not yet over Sholto? Why was the memory of him – prior to her finding out about his long affair with Francine – still the yardstick by which she judged all the other men who came her way? There had even, God help her, been moments when she'd wondered what would have happened if she'd never let him know that she knew about Francine. If she'd continued with their affair as if Francine didn't exist. Would Sholto's need of her then have become so great that Francine would now be nothing but a distant memory, both to him and to her?

Fiercely closing her mind against the thought, she returned her attention to the letter. At the start of a new paragraph, Kate had written:

Ella spent August at home in Wilsden. She came back seriously out of patience with Sam, her parents and her granddad. Apparently they all think Christmas a perfect time for a wedding, and the Christmas they have in mind is this Christmas. When Ella got engaged at Easter she was anticipating being engaged for two or three years. She says that there's no Christmas wedding pencilled in her diary and that, despite a mammoth amount of persuasion, she's not about to pencil one in! The engagement is still on, though. Ella says she never really spelled out to Sam that she expected to be engaged for far longer and that, as she hadn't done so, she is partly to blame for the misunderstanding. However, there is now pressure for her to agree to a wedding date. Her mother says an Easter wedding would be the next best thing to a Christmas wedding, and Sam is saying if not Easter, then June.

Despite the melancholy she'd been plunged into by thoughts of Sholto, Daphne felt a flash of amusement. A wedding in

June would fall smack in the middle of next year's season at Kalamata, and she could no more imagine Ella taking time off from it than she could imagine Ella flying to the moon.

The dig is clearly going to be one of major archaeological importance and next year's team needs to be far bigger than our present team. As the site is so isolated, and as Kalamata village is small and the present team are already occupying all the available lodgings there, for newcomers it's going to be a case of tented accommodation on the upper plateau.

It's all tremendously exciting and I do wish you were a part of it. (Don't panic at the thought of being in tented accommodation with thirty men halfway up a mountain! Another bed can be squeezed in our room at the cafeneion*). Please give it some thought, Daphne. It's been way too long since Ella and I last saw you and if you don't flex your archaeological muscles soon, you won't be able to remember what a mattock is for!*

In a week or two, when this year's dig is finally over, I'll be moving with Ella to Knossos, so that together with Lewis and Helmut – and in the facilities provided by the British School – we can study what has been found at Kalamata. I'll be staying in the Villa Ariadne's hostel with whatever British School students happen to be there, and Ella is going to be lodging with the Kourakis family.

Love you lots, Daph – and think about Crete for next year.

Kate

Daphne *was* thinking about Crete – and not for next year, but for what was left of the present year.

She sprang to her feet, seized with an overwhelming passion to see for herself what had been excavated on Kalamata's upper plateau; to meet Lewis and Helmut and Christos; to see the *cafeneion* and meet Andre and Agata, and drink raki beneath the shade of the *cafeneion*'s shabby awning; to throw sweets to the children as, according to Kate, Lewis did; and, most of all, to visit Knossos. How could she have lived so long and yet never have visited Knossos? How could she have known Kate for so many years and yet never have met Kit?

As she shrugged herself into a chinchilla bolero and snatched up a lizard-skin clutch bag, she thought of Crete's fabled White Mountains; of Mount Dicte, where the ancients believed the great god Zeus had been born; of snow-capped Mount Ida, where they believed he had been reared.

As Daphne went down in the lift, her head was full of lammergeiers with ten-foot wingspans – surely it was a lammergeier Ella had written of seeing? Of small plains dense with white-sailed windmills, and of elderly peasant women dressed from head to foot in black, smiling toothlessly as they rode on the backs of donkeys. It was all going to be utterly magical and, once there, she could stay for as long as she wanted.

She stepped out of the lift and ran out of the building into Kensington High Street. Maybe she could even help puzzle out the significance of a Minoan palace without sea access and with only one royal apartment. Sir Arthur Evans's excavations at Knossos had shown that Minoan kings were also priests, and that their queens were priestesses. What it would be interesting to know was if the apartment found at Kalamata was that of a priest-king or a priest-queen. If it was that of a priest-queen, it might have been that the queen in question had fallen out of royal favour. In medieval times, discarded queens were traditionally sent to nunneries. Maybe the palace found at Kalamata was the Minoan equivalent of a nunnery?

With all kinds of possibilities racing through her head as

to how she could be useful to Lewis Sinclair and his team, she ran into the first travel agency she came to.

'I want to go to Crete!' she announced breathlessly to the young man seated behind a desk in one of three booths, the sides of which were high enough to give privacy. 'I want to go now, and I want to get there in the fastest time possible!'

'Cr . . . Crete, Gr . . . Greece, Miss?'

Stammering wasn't a habit with the young man in question, but he couldn't help it. It was as if a combination of Marlene Dietrich and Jean Harlow had dramatically sat down opposite him. Her silver-blonde hair was worn close to her head in shining finger-waves. Her eyes, framed by soot-black mascaraed lashes, were the most amazing colour he had ever seen, for surely no one could have amethyst-coloured eyes?

Before he could decide that they could, the goddess opposite him said crossly, 'Well, of course Crete, Greece! What other kind of Crete is there? '

Seriously flustered, he began dragging heavy timetables out from under his desk.

'Per . . . perhaps the *Orient Express* as far as So . . . Sofia and then . . . and then a standard train down to Thessaloniki and a boat from Thessaloniki . . .'

Daphne regarded him pityingly. 'Sofia is in Bucharest, not Greece, and a boat to Crete from Thessaloniki would take forever.'

Aware that her astonishingly coloured eyes and hourglass figure were fast making it impossible for him to behave intelligently, he heaved another tome, this time the *Thomas Cook Continental Railway Timetable*, on to his desk.

As he rifled through it with unsteady fingers, there came the sound of someone entering the next booth.

Whoever it was, Daphne wished them better luck than she was having.

'The boat train from London to Paris?' her pimply-skinned advisor suggested. 'And then a train from Paris to Milan, where you would need to change trains again, this time taking a train down to Brindisi, from where you can get a steamer across to—'

'Piraeus, from where I can get a steamer to Heraklion,' Daphne snapped, remembering the long, time-consuming journeys Kate and Ella had made. 'I know all that and it takes forever. What I want is to get to Crete in the fastest time possible, and I want to set off now – today. Or,' she added as he looked as if he was about to pass out, 'at the very latest, tomorrow. And why,' she added sternly, 'are you not suggesting that I fly to Paris, in order to cut down the travelling time it takes to get there? There are regular air flights from Croydon Airport to Le Bourget and . . .'

'And they are not half as much fun as flying across the Channel in a two-seater Leopard Moth,' a dark, rich voice said from the next booth.

Daphne sucked in her breath.

Unseen, but only a couple of feet away from her, there came the sound of a chair being scraped backwards from a desk; of someone rising to their feet.

'Fly to Paris?' The young man who was causing her so much irritation looked bewildered. 'But the boat train arrives at the Gare du Nord, which is where trains for your ongoing journey leave from. It is m . . . m . . . much more convenient and . . .'

Daphne was no longer listening to him.

As far as she was concerned, he no longer existed.

Dry-mouthed, she rose to her feet and very slowly, her heart feeling as if it was beating fast and light somewhere up in her throat, she turned around.

He was wearing a dove-grey three-piece suit, a trilby tilted at a rakish angle and black leather shoes that had clearly been handmade. There was a suspicion of a smile at the corner of his mouth and he looked, as always, heart-stoppingly gorgeous. She wanted him so much she could barely stand.

'The Leopard Moth,' Sholto said again. 'It's far more fun. Sadly, Crete is out of its range. However, Imperial Airways have just started a flying-boat service to Cape Town and one of the refuelling stops is Athens, so that might be a possibility. If it isn't, then there's a seaplane crossing from Athens to Crete, which would shorten your journey time by several hours.'

Resisting the urge to throw herself into his arms, Daphne said hoarsely, 'What are you doing here?'

Her puzzlement was genuine. A travel agency in Kensington High Street was one of the last places anyone would have expected to find Sholto. As Daphne knew from the months they had spent together, Sholto travelled only on private transport. Private planes, private yachts and possibly – when he visited the ex-royals of Europe, several of whom were his friends – private trains.

'You're still wearing Shalimar,' he said, ignoring the question.

Equally inconsequentially, she said, 'You've grown a moustache.'

It was a very neat pencil moustache and it made him look very much a diplomat. No one, she thought looking at him, would suspect how much of a bohemian he really was. And then, because she couldn't stop herself, she said, 'Does Francine like it?'

'I've no idea. She's no longer part of my life.'

Blood began beating in Daphne's ears. 'She's left you for someone else? Someone in Hitler's hierarchy?'

'No. Or not in the way you think. We fell out over her politics. Nazi Germany has never been a joke. Now it's reached a pitch where no one is justified in continuing to be friends with Hitler's henchmen.'

'And Francine still is?'

'Yes.'

Daphne let out a deep, long sigh.

Their eyes held.

'You asked me what I was doing here.' His voice had become taut and, with a stab of shock, she realized he was as nearly thrown off-course by their unexpected meeting as she was. 'Now that Hitler and Mussolini are hunting as a pair, the workload at the Foreign Office is manic. Before I expire beneath it, I thought I'd take a short cruise to Madeira.'

'By yourself?' Her throat was so tight she could barely get the words past her lips.

'That was the original plan. Now I think a double suite would make far more sense.' The heat in his eyes left her in no doubt as to what he was suggesting.

Never before had Daphne hesitated when faced with a major decision. Her choice of what to do, no matter how reckless, had always been instant, made on nothing more than gut instinct.

Now, to her own amazement, she hesitated.

Although Francine was no longer a part of Sholto's life, it didn't change the fact that eighteen months ago, when faced with a choice between her and Francine, he had, without a moment's hesitation, chosen Francine. And when he had finally ended his long affair with Francine he hadn't taken steps to seek her, Daphne, out. His meeting with her now was entirely accidental; his invitation a purely spur-of-the-moment thing. As the blood continued thundering in her ears, she asked herself if she really wanted to rekindle an affair with a man who had treated her so cavalierly in the past and who, given the chance, would probably do so again in the future.

No answer to her question came.

In a voice that didn't sound remotely like hers, she said,

'What makes you think that, after the decision you made the last time we were together, I should now be interested in a double suite on a cruise to Madeira?'

The air between them was so charged with sexual tension it was palpable.

In their booths, the young men they had been dealing with held their breath.

'This,' Sholto said masterfully, pulling her into his arms and kissing her hard on the mouth.

It was a deep, forceful kiss. She couldn't have pushed him away even if she had wanted to – and she didn't want to. She could no more have stopped her arms from winding around his neck, and her mouth from opening beneath his, than she could have stopped herself from breathing.

The young man in booth one began making out a double booking form.

The young man in booth two began sliding heavy railway timetables back beneath his desk. It was obvious that his client was no longer interested in travelling to Crete; so obvious that he doubted if she even remembered it had ever been her intention.

Chapter Fourteen

Ella woke to the sound of tin buckets clanging against knee-high boots and knew that Christos was walking back towards the house after milking the Kourakises' bad-tempered goats. She looked across the small whitewashed room and saw that Nikoleta's bed was empty, which meant that she had overslept. It didn't matter. She wasn't expected in the workrooms this morning. It was a free day and, as it was also a free day for Christos and as free days didn't come round very often, he had suggested they make full use of it by borrowing one of Villa Ariadne's spare trucks and driving to Kalamata to visit Dimitri and Angelos Mamalakis and their families. Unspoken had also been the possibility, if the weather conditions permitted, of not only visiting Kalamata village, but also the excavation site.

'Just to make sure that no one has helped themselves to any ashlar blocks,' Christos had said, only half-teasing.

'They won't have,' she'd said, for Yanni Zambiakos, whose marksmanship with a rifle was legendary, had appointed himself the site's guardian and, with typical Cretan toughness, had moved into a cave overlooking it for the winter.

Looking forward to the day ahead of her, Ella dressed swiftly in the same kind of clothes she wore when on-site, the only difference being that now it was November, her dungarees were denim, not cotton; and bearing in mind how high in the mountains Kalamata village was, she'd taken the precaution of wearing a polo-neck sweater beneath her lumberjack chequered shirt.

The room she shared with Nikoleta wasn't far different from the room she'd shared with Kate at the *cafeneion*. There was a handmade rag rug on the floor, striped woven coverlets on both beds, an oil lamp on a chest of drawers and an enamel bowl and ewer on a washstand. The only major difference was the number of hooks that had been hammered into the walls in order to accommodate Nikoleta's prized collection of citified dresses, for Nikoleta liked to dress in a way that made her stand out from other village girls and, because of her guiding work, could afford to do so.

Ella's clothes took up hardly any room at all. Her dungarees, shorts, T-shirts and sweaters were kept neatly stacked in a cardboard box beneath her bed; her underwear and nightwear were in a second cardboard box; and two wall hooks took care of everything else.

Bearing in mind that it was now the rainy season, she took a waterproof jacket from one of the hooks and, carrying it over her arm, ran lightly down the stairs to the family living quarters.

There was no sign of Nikoleta, which meant she was already taking a small group of tourists around the Palace of Minos: a small group because in November all tourist groups were small.

A breakfast of hard toast and honey was waiting for her on the table that stood in the centre of the stone-floored room. When she had first moved in with the Kourakis family, Ella had thought she would never get used to having hard toast. Now she never gave it a thought, just as she had long ago stopped giving a thought to having everything cooked in lashings of olive oil and eating omelettes served with jam.

Having deposited the buckets of foaming goat's milk in the lean-to where Eleni would turn it into cheese, Christos was now, by the sound of the splashing that Ella could hear, having what her granddad called a 'swill-down' at the garden pump. This meant he would be bare-chested, and Ella – though it was a secret she kept to herself – liked the sight of a semi-naked Christos performing his daily ablutions.

With a slice of toast in her hand, she walked across to the window that looked out on to the water-pump. Clad only in the baggy breeches that all Cretan men wore, and which were tucked into his boots, Christos was vigorously splashing water on to his face and then on to his olive-toned and well-muscled chest, shoulders and arms. Finally he bent his head low so that the water drenched his hair. There was something very primitive about seeing a man washing himself in the open air and, watching Christos, it occurred to Ella that although she and Sam were engaged, she had never seen him splendidly bare-chested as, nearly every morning, she saw Christos.

Returning to the table to spread honey on a second slice of toast, she reflected that for an engaged couple, the level of intimacy between herself and Sam had barely moved off the starting blocks – something that wasn't, she reminded herself, Sam's fault. She had been the one who, for an agonizingly long time, had refused to accept he even came into the category of being a boyfriend; and when, six months ago, she had realized that she *did* have romantic feelings for him – and that she certainly didn't want him having romantic feelings for anyone else – she had taken him completely by surprise by accepting his proposal and had then promptly returned to Crete.

Since then she had been back home only once, in August, and most of that time had been spent trying to come to an agreement as to when they were going to be married. Never had they had any real courtship time, so it was understandable that Sam was anxious for a wedding as soon as one could be arranged. Seen in that light, Sam being prepared to forgo the Christmas wedding that he and her parents had originally been hoping for, for a June wedding in eight months' time, really wasn't all that unreasonable. Or wouldn't be, if it wasn't that the dig on Kalamata's upper plateau was turning into the dig of a lifetime and she absolutely did not want to miss a minute of it.

Ella wondered if her lack of urgency about tying the knot with Sam indicated that she was sexually frigid. She hoped not, because it would be so unfair to Sam if she was. How, though, was she to know? Although she'd had a handful of dates when she was at St Hugh's, none of them had developed into a regular boyfriend/girlfriend situation. She'd been far too focused on getting a good degree to be interested in a social life. She'd had her friendships with Kate and Daphne, and that had been enough.

It had been the same when she had been at grammar school. Other than Sam, boys had never featured in her existence. She had been far too busy, nose to the grindstone, swotting to get a place at Oxford. And as her friendship with Sam had had no romantic overtones, or at least hadn't had any for her, it had never interfered with her school work.

They had met in Bradford's Central Library when she was fourteen and he was seventeen. She had been carrying a far-too-large pile of books and had dropped them. He had picked them up for her. From then on, they had seen each other regularly and were now, thanks to her realization that Sam was an integral part of her life and that she didn't want to lose him, far more than friends.

They were not, however, yet lovers. Not in the fullest sense of the word. At twenty-three she was still a virgin, a not-uncommon state of affairs for an engaged girl of her class, when virginity was the only sure-fire way of not becoming pregnant. Only moneyed and reckless upper-class girls were able to escape the consequences of an illegitimate pregnancy by disappearing for the duration to somewhere like Switzerland; and could then, with the baby adopted, return to the hectic whirl of their social lives as if nothing untoward had happened. Even if she'd been born into money, it wasn't behaviour she would want to emulate.

As she now put the jar of honey back on a shelf that formed part of Eleni's pantry, Ella turned her thoughts back to Sam. Christmas wasn't too far away and if she went home for it, the two of them would at last be able to have some proper courtship time together.

Christos stepped into the room, buttoning a waistcoat that was shiny from wear over a shirt that was the same dark blue as his distinctive Cretan breeches.

'I've had breakfast,' she said to him with her usual sunny smile, 'and so I'm ready to leave whenever you are.'

'I'm ready also.' He wound a long mulberry-coloured sash several times around his waist and, as he always did, rammed a lethal-looking long knife into it. Although he wasn't in full Cretan heroic dress – he would have had to be wearing a bobble-trimmed sleeveless jacket and a fringed bandana for that – the sash and knife were a part of heroic dress that, like all the other Cretans on the dig, Christos wore as naturally as he wore breeches and boots. Unlike his father, Yanni and a hefty proportion of the island's male population, he didn't, though, always have a rifle slung over his shoulder. Even if he had, Ella had grown so used to the sight of village men carrying hunting rifles that she wouldn't have found it at all odd.

As they reached the parking area Ella said, 'Will Georgio have brought his sheep down from summer pasture by now?'

'Probably. He winters them on the green coast.'

She stepped into the truck. 'Is that far away?'

'It's the area around Canea.' He slammed the truck into gear. 'I'll take you to see him one day, if you would like?'

'Yes, I would. I would like that very much.'

His mahogany-tanned face split into a wide grin. 'I warn you, though, that Georgio is not like me. Even at eighteen, he is still very shy. It is why a shepherd's life suits him.'

A shepherd's life would not, she thought, suit Christos, who was the most gregarious, outgoing person imaginable.

The truck bucketed out of the parking area and on to the road and she said, 'Have you heard from anyone what Lewis's reaction was, to Kit having shown Nikoleta around the site at a time when he wasn't there?'

'No. Have you?'

'No. That's why I asked. And I thought that if Lewis was going to give his opinion about it to anyone, he would have given it to you.'

'He hasn't. Are you thinking that perhaps it annoyed him? Because if you are, I think you are barking up the wrong bush.'

'Tree.'

'Tree.' Christos was still occasionally stumped by English idioms. 'Why should Lewis be annoyed by it? Nikoleta is naturally curious, and it was a kind thing for Kit Shelton to have done.'

'Yes, it was.' As Christos obviously didn't think, as she did, that Kit's kind action had probably annoyed Lewis, she changed the subject. 'I've finally decided what I'm going to do for Christmas, and I'm going to spend it at home. Two Christmases away in succession would be a bit much, don't you think? Especially as I'm an only child.'

Christos's hands tightened on the steering wheel. By spending last Christmas with his family, Ella had made his

Christmas extra-special and he had been hoping she would be making it extra-special again this year.

'Your fiancé will be pleased,' he said – only the hardening of his jaw indicating how he truly felt. 'It is right that you should be spending Christmas with him. I would certainly not want my fiancée to be spending Christmas nearly two thousand miles away from me.'

By now well aware of the fiery temperament where romance and the Cretan male were concerned, Ella could well believe it. Nikoleta had told her that only a week ago, in a mountain village not far from Kalamata, a young girl had been 'bride-abducted'.

'It is a tradition in Crete,' Nikoleta had said. 'If a man wishes to marry a girl badly enough, and if the family of the girl objects, then sometimes a man will abduct his bride. It is not, I think, something that happens in England?'

'No,' she had said drily, 'it is not something that happens in England.'

The apparent habit of bride-abduction was something she intended asking Christos about, although not just yet, when she had important news to share with him.

As they left the narrow streets of Archanes behind them, she said, 'I've something to tell you. I meant to keep it as a surprise, but I can't, because if I don't tell you I shall burst.'

'Burst?' Beneath his luxuriant moustache, Christos cracked a smile. 'What is this burst? It sounds painful.'

'It means I can't keep the news to myself for another minute.' Ella had always found it more comfortable, when travelling in the truck, to do so with her legs bent and her feet pressed against the dashboard. They were on the dashboard now and, with clasped hands, she hugged her knees. 'We are about to have a visitor from England: someone who has never before been to Crete.'

Christos's amusement vanished. He could only think of one person who fitted that description and whose imminent arrival would cause Ella so much excitement, and that was her Yorkshire fiancé. His hands tightened on the steering wheel. Why was Sam Jowett coming out to Crete now, in late November? Was it because he didn't yet know of Ella's intention to return home for Christmas? And where was he going to stay? He wasn't an archaeologist and, as he had no links to the British School, it was unlikely he would be staying at the Villa Ariadne.

As if reading his thoughts, Ella said, 'Which is the nicest hotel in Heraklion? I want one with recognizable plumbing.'

At the thought of a man caring about the plumbing, when snatching a few days with the woman he was to marry, Christos made a disparaging sound in his throat and was tempted to give her the name of the biggest flea-pit he knew of. Fighting the temptation and keeping his eyes fixed firmly on the road, so that she wouldn't see the expression in them, he said, 'The Astoria,' and then, 'when will your visitor be arriving?'

'At the weekend. She had been going to visit last month, but she had a wonderful reconciliation with an old boyfriend and, instead of coming to Crete, the two of them went off to Madeira together.'

'She? It is a woman visitor you are expecting? Not your fiancé?'

'Of course it isn't my fiancé! Sam is a doctor. He can't just take time off on the spur of the moment.'

'And your friend can?' For Christos, the world was suddenly a bright and beautiful place again. If he hadn't been driving, he would have hugged her.

'Daphne is the daughter of an earl and can do pretty much what she wants, when she wants.'

They were driving westwards now, deeper into the mountains. 'And her boyfriend? If they have just had a – how do you say? – a reconciliation, will he not mind her travelling to Crete without him?'

'No. He works for the Foreign Office and when she will be in Crete, he will be in Geneva attending a meeting of the League of Nations.'

'And at Christmas?'

'By Christmas they will be together again, but I don't know where. Maybe they will be in London, or maybe they will be in the country with either her family or his, or maybe even in another country.'

Christos had never been further than mainland Greece and the very idea of travelling the world with the ease with which Ella's friend, and her friend's boyfriend, travelled it staggered him.

It was not, however, something he would want to do himself, and especially not at Christmas time. That foreigners didn't always display the same kind of fierce attachment to the land of their birth as Cretans did was a perpetual mystery to him.

He said now, thinking of Kate and Kit and Lewis, 'And is Kate going home for Christmas?'

'Yes. She would have been leaving any day now, but because Daphne is coming out, she's staying on and will be leaving when Daphne leaves, which is what I will be doing as well.'

The terrain was becoming ever steeper, winding between cliffs of granite studded with oak and chestnut trees, the leaves of the trees glowing every possible shade of red and gold.

'And Kit?' he asked, changing into a still-lower gear. 'Will he be spending the winter at the Ashmolean Museum in Oxford, as he did last year?'

'He'd planned to, but he's now changed his mind. Instead he's going to spend the winter here, writing a book about the necropolis sites.'

Christos said nothing. Although he had never said so to

Ella, he'd always sensed an undercurrent of professional rivalry between Kit Shelton and Lewis; and, as Lewis was also going to be spending the winter at Knossos, he wondered if, in such close proximity, the rivalry might begin to show.

Ella quite obviously had no such misgivings about Kit and Lewis's relationship. 'It's nice that Kit and Nikoleta occasionally spend time together, isn't it?' she said, as the track neared the lip of the village plateau. 'It means Lewis won't have to worry about Nikoleta moping, when he leaves for his yearly visit to his sponsors in Scotland.'

Christos gave her a look of startled surprise. 'In what way will Lewis not have to worry? And I don't think the excavation's sponsors are situated in Scotland. I think last year Lewis's meeting with them took place in London.'

'Did it?' Lewis was always so close-mouthed about the financing of the dig that Ella was amazed Christos knew even that much. Equally amazing was that he didn't seem to realize that, while Lewis was away, Kit would try to cheer up Nikoleta – and would probably do so by taking her out for the occasional meal in Heraklion.

By the time she had explained this to him they were on the plateau, and the village, surrounded by its fields and cluster of white-sailed windmills, lay before them.

She gasped with pleasure at the sight of it, as if she was returning after months away, not just a few weeks.

Christos looked across at her and then, overcome by feelings he could no longer contain, brought the truck to a sudden, shuddering halt. 'So already you have missed the village?' he said, an arm across the wheel as he swung round to face her. 'Think how one day you will miss Crete! And that is because you belong here. You belong here in a way that – though they have a love of Crete – Lewis, Kit, Kate, Helmut, the Squire and Mrs Hutchinson do not. You should be marrying a Cretan, not an Englishman who is happy to see you only a couple of times a year.'

It was said with such passion that Ella's eyebrows flew nearly into her hair. 'That isn't fair!' she protested. 'Sam *isn't* happy that I'm working so far away from him and—'

'If he is not happy, why has he never come here and taken you back to England with him?' Christos's eyes, usually so full of laughter, were fierce. 'A Cretan would not behave so. *I* would not behave so!'

Ella could well believe it. She said, 'Just because Sam doesn't react to things in the way you would react doesn't mean he doesn't feel things just as deeply. Englishmen aren't known for showing emotion – and Sam is a Yorkshireman, and men from Yorkshire are the worst of all when it comes to keeping their feelings to themselves.'

She remembered the recent incident of bride-abduction that had taken place not far from Kalamata and said with amusement, hoping to put things between them back on an even keel, 'You wouldn't want Sam to bride-abduct me and race off with me on the back of a horse, would you?'

For once she received no answering smile. Instead, grim-faced, Christos slammed the truck into gear. 'No, I wouldn't,' he said, revving the engine. 'But if I was engaged to you, it is what I would do!'

Even though she knew he was teasing – for he had to be – it was teasing that left her with a very odd sensation in the pit of her tummy. The sensation didn't go away and she didn't attempt to analyse it, for she had long suspected that analysing her feelings where Christos was concerned would be a very, very dangerous thing for her to do.

Chapter Fifteen

With only a month until Christmas, the weather at Knossos was still warm and Kate wasn't wearing a jacket as she drove the short distance from the Villa Ariadne to the Kourakises' cottage. Daphne was arriving in Heraklion by seaplane in just over an hour's time, and Kate was hoping that she'd made it quite clear in her last letter that although the weather was mild in areas near the coast, the temperatures were different inland, and especially so in mountain villages such as Kalamata. She had added in a postscript:

> *It snowed at Knossos last December, and the palace looked so beautiful under snow that I'm hoping it will snow again this year, so bring suitable clothing just in case, and especially bring boots for the upper plateau climb.*

Daphne's plan was to stay for two weeks, and Ella and Kate's plan was that they would return to England with her and that, once there, Ella would travel north to spend Christmas in Yorkshire, and Kate would head south-east for a family Christmas in Canterbury.

Apart from the fact that Daphne had chosen a very odd time of the year to visit Crete and was doing so for what was, in Kate's eyes, an almost unforgivably short period, there was the advantage that the major Minoan centres of Knossos,

Phaistos and Mallia would be less crowded than they would have been if Daphne's visit had been made in the spring or the summer. The downside was that as excavation work on Kalamata's upper plateau was at an end until March or April, there would be no chance of Daphne joining them on-site and having her passion for archaeology reawakened.

When they had been at St Hugh's, they had talked constantly of a time when the three of them would be working on a dig together in Egypt or Greece, and ever since the find of the palace Kate had held hopes that when Daphne visited Crete, she would be so dazzled by the work taking place on the upper plateau that she would want to stay and become part of the team. With Sholto once again in Daphne's life, it was a scenario that was beginning to seem unlikely.

'She's fathoms-deep in love with him,' Ella had said, after reading the letter Daphne had posted from Madeira. 'And unlike all the previous men in her life, it appears that Sholto is the one calling all the shots – something I'm finding very difficult to get my head around.'

It was something Kate, too, found it very difficult to get her head around, and it wasn't the only thing that was baffling her, for Ella had also begun behaving out of character. Usually full of fun and chat, and someone who, once she came to a decision, stuck with it, for the last two weeks Ella had been unusually quiet and had not only changed her mind about a wedding date once, but had changed it twice.

First of all, after being adamant that she wanted a long engagement of two years, possibly even three years, she had suddenly announced that she'd written to Sam telling him that, after having had time to think things over, she was now happy to go with next June as a wedding date. And then just yesterday, after a long day in the workrooms with Christos and without any explanation, she'd said that the June wedding was now off, in favour of Easter, a date that would be even more pleasing to her parents and to Sam.

'But why, Ella?' Kate had asked, bewildered.

Without lifting her head from the notes she was writing, on a Neo-palatial clay vase with a linear inscription engraved on its shoulder, Ella had said, 'I just think it's best, and don't go badgering me as to why, Kate. If you do, I might bring it even further forward and opt for a Register Office wedding while I'm home for Christmas.'

A flock of sheep were now taking up the whole width of the road and Kate slowed to a snail's pace behind them, pondering the irony that although Daphne and Ella's love lives were seemingly going great guns, her own love life was at its usual barren standstill. Common sense told her it wasn't because men found her unattractive; men's reaction to her was invariably one of immediate interest, or had been until she had joined Lewis's team at Kalamata, and Lewis – the first man she had ever passionately wished *would* fall head-over-heels for her – had so very clearly not done. It was something she had come to terms with, telling herself resolutely that it was his loss, not hers; and over the summer Helmut's interest in her had gone a long way to restoring her self-esteem. Like her relationships at Oxford, it had, though, ended up going nowhere because although she found him attractive and good company, she hadn't fallen in love with him. The spark simply hadn't been there.

Lodging in a village as isolated as Kalamata, and working long hours halfway up a mountain with a team of Cretan workmen, didn't offer much opportunity for meeting eligible men; and as Kate didn't see her pattern of living and working changing in the foreseeable future, there was nothing she could do but accept that while she had a very satisfying work life, her love life was a non-event – and looked like remaining so.

The young boy herding the sheep finally succeeded in mustering them to one side of the road, leaving a hair's breadth of room for her to drive past them. She did so deafened by their baa-ing protests.

Half an hour later, with Ella sitting beside her and with a disconcertingly large clump of wool clinging to the left side of the truck, Kate was heading through Heraklion's crowded streets in the direction of the harbour.

'Apparently the only other person the Squire can remember arriving by seaplane was Sir Arthur Evans, when he came for the dedication of his bust in the Palace of Minos's West Court-yard,' Ella said, her mane of fiery-red hair held away from her face by tortoiseshell combs. 'I don't think it's a regular service and, even if it is, if that is the way Daphne intends returning to Athens, then she'll have to do it without me. The fare must be eye-watering.'

'I expect it is, but it isn't an issue. We'll all be leaving together on the ferry. Daphne wouldn't want it any other way. You do realize she's going to arrive looking a million dollars, don't you? Which will be a bit of a contrast to us. I think it's safe to say that a season of digging has taken its toll on the clothes we arrived with.'

Ella turned her face up to the winter sun. 'It's not going to matter. We're not going to be partying in Heraklion and I do have a dress, for if we're invited to dinner at the Villa. To be honest, because you've stuck to skirts when not wearing shorts, you never look disreputable. Whereas I . . .' She looked down at the dungarees she was wearing and which, after giving her great service during the months of the dig, could only be described as well-worn and shabby. 'I always look as if I've just come off a Bradford building site.'

'You look like an archaeologist,' Kate said firmly, as she

turned a corner that opened to a view of the harbour and the great fortress that, centuries ago, had been built to defend it.

She brought the truck to a halt. 'There's a silver dot on the horizon, which I think is the plane. We're going to be on the jetty in time.'

The imminent arrival of the small seaplane was already arousing interest, and people were gathering on the harbour walls to watch it land. In mounting anticipation, Kate and Ella weaved their way down to the jetty and stood, shading their eyes from the glare of the winter sun, as the plane came nearer. When it touched down on the smooth water within the harbour and began taxiing towards the jetty, a great cheer went up.

'What do you think?' Ella said to Kate. 'Is Daphne going to be first off, or last?'

'First. She won't have the patience for anything else.'

A member of the crew jumped out of the seaplane, ready to steady passengers as they stepped onto the gangplank, and seconds later Kate was proved right.

Daphne, having taken Kate at her word that it would be pleasantly mild in late November, was wearing the kind of patent-belted, figure-hugging sweater that the film star Lana Turner had made famous. In Daphne's case, the sweater was pillar-box red and with it she was wearing white slacks and white wedge-heeled sandals. A white jacket was around her shoulders, and tucked under one arm was a lizard-skin clutch bag. Behind her was another crew member, this time carrying a sizeable piece of Louis Vuitton luggage.

'Daphne!' Kate shouted, waving furiously. '*Daphne!*'

Daphne, accustomed to managing the difficult descent from Sholto's Leopard Moth, made easy work of the unsteady gangplank. With a shriek of delight she broke into a run, barely slowing down as she ran up the jetty steps.

Kate and Ella met her with open arms, hugging her

enthusiastically as the crew member who was carrying her suitcase asked, 'Is a car or a taxi waiting, *Kyria*?'

Daphne quirked an eyebrow at Kate.

'I'm driving a truck,' Kate said. 'It's parked about fifty yards away.'

Daphne linked arms with her and Ella. 'Then let's go,' she said exuberantly. 'The hotel first, and then where? To meet Kit, Lewis, Helmut and the Squire at the Villa Ariadne and then to the Palace of Minos? I'm simply *aching* to walk the ground Minoans walked over three thousand years ago. Then perhaps a trip into the mountains to Kalamata, to be introduced to all the locals, and after that the upper plateau? Or is that impossible all in one day? The trouble is I'm in a fever of impatience to see everything and meet everyone, from Andre and Agata to Ella's Christos.'

'Christos isn't *my* Christos,' Ella said immediately and with great emphasis.

Kate and Daphne raised their eyebrows.

Ella flushed. 'There's no need for both of you to look at me like that. I just don't want there to be any misunderstanding. I'm engaged to Sam, remember?'

'Okay. Got it.' Daphne was unfazed. 'Is this the truck? I'd better warn you, I was travel-sick crossing the Channel and queasy on the plane.'

'No problems,' Kate said, as the obliging crew member heaved the suitcase into the truck's rear and Daphne tipped him lavishly. 'As the three of us are going to be squashed up front in the cab, Ella had better sit in the middle and then – if you want to be sick, Daphne – all you need do is hang your head out of the window.'

At a zippy speed Kate drove away from the harbour and into 25 August Street. 'Named after the date of a massacre that took place in it in 1898, and which led to the ending of the Ottoman occupation,' she said, adding, 'Your hotel is at the far end of the street, close to the lion fountain.'

It took Daphne barely five minutes to check in.

'Where to now?' she asked as, back in the truck, they drove past the fountain and its water-spouting lions. 'The Villa Ariadne? The Palace of Minos?'

'The Archaeological Museum.' Kate narrowly avoided a lorry piled high with golden melons. 'The necklace Christos unearthed on the lower plateau is on display there, and the museum is so near, it would be a sin not to stop off and have a look at it.'

Grateful to Kate for drawing attention to Christos's spectacular find, Ella said, 'The necklace is so gossamer-fine, and was in such a fragile condition, that you would have thought a breath of air would have damaged it, yet Christos retrieved it without breaking even one of its delicate links.'

Daphne was impressed, and she was even more impressed when, in the museum, she stood before the glass case displaying it. On a small card in front of it was written: 'Neo-palatial Period 1650–1450 BC. Discovered 1936, Kalamata.'

Ella said, 'Lewis wanted the museum to add Christos's name to the card, but the museum authorities said it wasn't their habit to display the name of the finder, when the finder was the member of an official archaeological dig. Lewis is going to have a word with the director of the British School in Athens, to see if he can persuade the museum authorities to think differently.'

'I hope he succeeds. As for Lewis . . . I'm looking forward to meeting a dig director who takes that kind of trouble.'

'That's one thing you're unlikely to be able to do while you're here. Lewis is in London, giving his yearly report to the dig's sponsors.'

Daphne said a rude word, seriously miffed. Of all the people she had been looking forward to meeting, Lewis Sinclair had been top of her list. 'Is there any likelihood of his returning while I'm still here?'

'Not if last year is anything to go by.' Kate's voice was carefully expressionless. 'Last year he didn't return until after Christmas.'

'He arrived on New Year's Eve,' Ella added as they began walking away from the display case, 'just in time to first-foot at the Squire's New Year's Eve party. No one knew he was back until he knocked at the door at five past midnight and entered the house, looking absolutely magnificent in full Highland rig.'

Reminded of Lewis's fierce, scorchingly deep New Year's kiss in the Villa Ariadne's lamplit library, Kate breathed in hard and then, when she could trust her voice, changed the subject, saying briskly, 'Next stop is Knossos and the Kourakis household. Eleni is home and waiting in great impatience to meet you – as is Kostas, which is a great compliment. Cretan men of his age are rarely to be found at home, but Ella has told him you are aristocracy and, as he has never been introduced to the daughter of an earl before, he's greatly looking forward to meeting you. When we left he was already sprucing himself up for the occasion.'

'Good heavens! I hope he's not expecting ermine and pearls.'

'I think he is,' Kate said as Ella began laughing, 'so you're going to be something of a shock, although in that tight sweater, not a total disappointment.'

The visit to the Kourakises' home was a resounding success, just as Kate had known it would be. Kostas was in full historic dress, his baggy blue breeches tucked into knee-high boots, a mulberry-red sash wound around a belly where once a waist had been, the obligatory knife tucked between its folds. Over a full-sleeved shirt he was wearing an embroidered sleeveless jacket, and the crowning touch was a black bandana tied rakishly over still-thick white hair. Although his reaction when he first saw Daphne was one of almost pathetic bewilderment, it was a bewilderment he soon recovered from. Within minutes he was as beguiled by her as old Jos Tetley had been.

Eleni had fussed around Daphne, plying her with little cakes and pastries until at last Daphne had said apologetically, 'Enough, Eleni. I've had travel-sickness these last few days and it's still lingering.'

'You need a glass of Mountain Tea,' Eleni had said firmly. 'Mountain Tea is what you need.'

Later, with Daphne revived by the tea, and when they were en route to the Villa Ariadne, Ella said, 'It's a pity you haven't yet met Nikoleta, although we'll probably run into her later this morning when we take you to the Palace of Minos.'

'And Christos? When are we likely to run into Christos?'

Ella's pale skin always flushed easily and it warmed now as she said, 'Oh, we'll probably run into him at the Villa. I expect he'll be in one of the workrooms, doing an honest day's work on the Kalamata palace finds.'

Twenty minutes later they were in the Villa Ariadne's drawing room where, after Daphne had been introduced to the Squire, Kit and Helmut, they were all drinking the dry sherry Mrs Hutchinson thought suitable for the occasion.

The atmosphere in the Villa was always one of relaxed informality and Kate perched on the arm of a chintz-covered sofa, amused by the effect Daphne was having, not only on Helmut, but on the Squire as well.

'I understand you are an archaeologist?' the Squire said to her.

'Only technically.' She smiled encouragingly at him, sensing that he was shy with women he didn't yet know well. 'Since leaving university I haven't worked as one.'

Helmut, who was as far from being shy as it was possible for a man to get, said, 'There's no reason why you shouldn't.'

He was leaning against the corner of the fireplace, one foot crossed over the other, his arms folded, his eyes riveted admiringly on her. 'Next season's dig at Kalamata is going to be *gewaltig*,' he continued. 'Tremendous. I know I can speak for Lewis when I say a position on the team would be yours for the asking.'

'That's very gratifying, but I shan't be asking, although I am agog to see the site.'

'You'll need different clothes and shoes. It's a steep climb.'

'I have different clothes and shoes.' Daphne looked away from him and towards Kate. 'For today, I'm going to be satisfied with being shown around the Palace of Minos, but tomorrow I'll be all rigged out ready for the upper plateau, if that's okay with you and Ella?'

'Absolutely okay. We can't wait to show it to you, and for you to meet Andre and Agata, and Dimitri and Angelos and their families.'

Half an hour later, accompanied by Kit and Helmut, they walked the short distance from the Villa to the palace's paved West Court. Due respects were paid to Sir Arthur Evans's bust on its granite pedestal and then Kit, the only one among them who was an official member of the Knossos team, acted as a guide to Daphne as they walked through the ruined remains and the restorations of halls, courts, staircases, royal rooms, priestly ceremonial rooms, storerooms, workrooms and porticoes that had once formed the palace where, according to Homer and legend, King Minos had conversed with the god Zeus, and his daughter, Ariadne, had rescued Theseus from the Minotaur.

Later in the day, though this time without Kit or Helmut, they drove up into the mountains to Kalamata village where, with troops of excited children following in their wake, Daphne was introduced to Andre and Agata, to the two Mamalakis brothers and to Apollonia, Pericles Georgiou's landlady. Then it was back to Heraklion and dinner in a candlelit taverna looking out over the harbour.

The following week and with Lewis still in the UK, they visited the palaces of Phaistos and Mallia; returned time and again to the Palace of Minos; and spent long hours in Heraklion's Archaeological Museum, where Daphne was mesmerized by a fresco that, three thousand five hundred years ago, had decorated a wall in the West Wing of the palace.

It depicted three pale-skinned young women of the court against a dazzling blue background, their jet-black hair jewelled and coiled in intricate ringlets, their tightly bodiced dresses impossibly narrow at the waist and open above to reveal pert, bare breasts. All three ladies had enigmatic half-smiles on their faces, and to Kate and Ella's hilarity, Daphne had declared that the painting was of the three of them when, in a different incarnation, they had been Minoan priestesses.

Afterwards they had walked the entire length of Heraklion's great fifteenth-century walls. Another day they had motored out to Réthymnon. Every evening they sat over glasses of King Minos, talking about everything under the sun, but always ending up discussing their private lives.

'Though, from the sound of it, I'm the only one whose private life is interesting,' Daphne said late one evening as, in her room at the Astoria, the three of them sat cross-legged on her bed. 'Ella has spent just days with Sam, since becoming engaged to him – and that was way back in August – and what were you doing, Kate, letting a hunk like Helmut Becke slip through your fingers? That striking blond hair, those wonderfully broad shoulders, that powerful, careless charm? He's such a perfect specimen of handsome masculinity that if I wasn't so madly in love with Sholto, I'd be making eyes at him myself.'

Lifting the bottle of wine from the floor, Kate topped up their glasses. 'He is dishy, isn't he? Especially so since he shaved off his beard. I thought I'd finally struck lucky, when we first began dating. It was very gratifying being wined and dined in Heraklion by such a good-looking man, and especially one who is intelligent into the bargain.'

'So what went wrong?'

Kate pushed a wing of jaw-length hair back behind her ear. 'Nothing, except that on my part there was no overwhelming sexual chemistry, and Helmut is thirty-one and expects a little more from a girlfriend than I was prepared to give.'

'And so what is Helmut doing now, for female companion-ship? He doesn't strike me as the kind of man to settle for long periods of celibacy.'

'I don't think he is, and I don't think he has. Though he hasn't said so to anyone, I rather think he's found himself a girlfriend in Heraklion. He drives there alone one or two evenings a week, but I doubt if he's alone once he gets there.'

'And Lewis Sinclair?' Until now it had been a subject that had only been skirted around, and Daphne was determined to skirt around it no longer. 'What's the state of play there?'

Kate took a drink of her wine and then said, with studied carelessness, 'The state of play is that he did once have a shat-tering effect on my peace of mind, but that he does so no longer.'

'And so you're now on the same kind of friendly terms with him that you're on with Helmut?'

'No. But then Lewis is the dig's director and, coupled with that, he doesn't have the kind of personality that encourages easy friendliness.'

Out of the corner of her eye Daphne saw Ella roll her eyes. Ella, she knew, had a very easy relationship with Lewis.

'And Nikoleta? Are she and Lewis really a hot number?'

'Nikoleta and Lewis's relationship is a complete mystery. And if they are hot lovers, they win top marks for discretion.'

Ella put her wine glass down and shifted position so that she was lying on her tummy, with her weight resting on her arms. 'I share a room with Nikoleta, and I know no more than Kate. What I do know, though, is that Christos is beginning to doubt there will ever be wedding bells.'

'And I think Kit,' Kate said, 'is hoping there won't be.'

'Heavens!' Daphne's violet eyes widened. 'Is Kit besotted with Nikoleta as well?'

'He's begun paying her a lot of attention, and Nikoleta doesn't seem to object to it.'

'Goodness! What a hotbed of action the Villa Ariadne is! What about the Squire? Is his love life equally interesting?'

'The Squire,' Kate said in amusement, 'is as unworldly as he looks and lives a life of perfect probity.'

'I rather thought so, which leaves only Ella's love life to be discussed. Now that you are engaged, Ella, and there is a wedding in the offing – at which I assume Kate and I will be bridesmaids – have you finally joined the ranks of the deflowered?'

Scarlet banners flew in Ella's cheeks. 'Absolutely not! Sam and I don't lead the racy lifestyle you and Sholto lead, staying in grand country houses for long weekends, where bedrooms are conveniently next door to each other and everybody, married as well as single, bed-hops. I expect that in London, Sholto has a very smart flat . . .'

'He most certainly does. It's a mansion flat in Knightsbridge.'

'Well, Sam doesn't have a mansion flat – in Knightsbridge, or anywhere else. He lives in digs in Scooby, North Yorkshire, and when I'm in Yorkshire I live at home with Mum, Dad and Granddad. Neither place is a likely setting for a seduction;

and before you rhapsodize about hay lofts and river banks, forget it. Sam is a Yorkshireman and a Methodist. He takes it for granted that when he marries, his bride will be a virgin. And I'm happy with that. I don't want to shame my family by being pregnant when I walk down the aisle of Wilsden's Methodist church.'

'You've no need to. No one has, if they live within travelling distance of a Marie Stopes Mothers' Clinic.'

Kate put her wine glass down. 'That's not true, Daphne.' There was affectionate exasperation in her voice. 'The clinics are for married women, hence their name. They aren't for single women. They aren't even for single, about-to-be-married women.'

'And so you put a wedding ring from Woolworths on your finger, register as "Mrs" – and Bob's your uncle. You come away with a Dutch cap in a tin box, and no fears of becoming pregnant.'

She swung her legs from the bed. 'Of course using it can be a pesky nuisance, and when you are invited to as many country-house weekends as I am – and as Sholto is – it's hard to remember, when you leave, that it's still in its tin box in a bedside drawer. I'm forever forgetting about it and leaving mine behind.'

'And what happens then?' Ella was riveted, despite her determination not to be.

Daphne shrugged. 'I trot along to the Stopes clinic in Camden, admit to being unforgivably careless and come away with a replacement.'

Looking across at Ella, she said, stark truth in her voice, 'I don't know how you do the remaining-a-virgin thing, Ella. I'm so totally, utterly, completely in love with Sholto, I just can't keep my hands off him – and I don't want him to keep his hands off me. It's as if all other men are a dull grey, and Sholto is in glorious, stupendous, sensational Technicolor.

Every time I see him, my heart leaps and I want him so much I can hardly breathe.'

Later, as Kate drove Ella back to Knossos in the Sally, she said, 'Is the way Daphne feels about Sholto the way you feel about Sam?'

For a long moment Ella didn't answer, and then she said, 'No. Not quite. We've known each other for such a long time, and that long friendship is what lies at the heart of our relationship. I know it sounds dull, compared with how Daphne describes her relationship with Sholto, but perhaps their relationship won't last, whereas I know my relationship with Sam will, because, quite simply, it's impossible for me to imagine him ever letting me down. He would cut his throat first.'

It was so unexpectedly dramatic, coming from Ella, that Kate sucked in her breath.

'And for that reason,' Ella added fiercely, looking out of the Sally's window so that there was no opportunity for their eyes to meet, 'I'm determined not to let him down. Not ever.' And in her lap her hands were clasped so tightly together that her knuckles were bloodless.

Their plans for the next morning were to visit the necropolis site in Fortetsa, but even before Kate was dressed, a fellow guest at the hostel knocked on her door to tell her there was a phone call for her.

The communal telephone was in the hall and, tying the belt of her dressing gown around her, Kate hurried down to the ground floor.

'It's me,' Daphne said unnecessarily when Kate picked up the receiver. 'I'm sick again, so don't hurry over. Give me an hour.'

Kate made a suitably sympathetic noise and said, 'You were perfectly okay last night. Did you eat anything after we left?'

'No, but I had something called "green pie" for breakfast. The waiter in the hotel's dining room told me it was a traditional Cretan breakfast dish. God only knows what was in it.'

'In spring and summer it would be any green vegetable or salad leaf. Now, in November, your guess is as good as mine. Would you rather we called Fortetsa off?'

'No. The way I feel at the moment, there could be no better place for me than a necropolis. I might just ask to be left there.'

Beneath the black scarf covering her head and shoulders, Eleni's sun-wrinkled face was concerned when, forty minutes later, Kate told her that Daphne had been sick after eating green pie for breakfast. Clicking her teeth together, she said, 'Green pie, cheese pie, whatever kind of pie, it would make no difference. What she needs to drink – what all women in her condition need to drink – is plenty of Mountain Tea.'

Realizing the assumption Eleni had come to, Kate said, amused, 'Daphne isn't having a baby, Eleni. She's simply eaten something that has disagreed with her.'

'And when she felt sick the day she arrived?'

'She was travel-sick. Lots of people get travel-sick.'

'And lots of women are sick when they first fall. Nikoleta's cousin in Canea was sick every day for a week. For a week she was sick, even before she missed her time. And the Lady Daphne has the look.'

'The look?' Ella asked, stuffing the things she needed for the day into a haversack.

With a gnarled hand, Eleni gestured expressively. 'When a woman is making a child there is always a look. And Lady Daphne has the look. Let me parcel some Mountain Tea for you to take to her.'

As Eleni set about spooning dried *Sideritis* leaves from a large jar into a paper cone, Kate and Ella stared at each other, transfixed.

'It's possible,' Ella said at last. 'Especially if she was as careless with her little tin box as she said she was.'

'But surely she'd know if she'd missed a period?'

'Maybe she hasn't. Maybe, like Nikoleta's cousin, she's simply begun being sick from day one.'

Ella drew in a deep, steadying breath. 'Do we tell her? Do we tell her Eleni thinks she could be suffering from morning sickness?'

'It can't do any harm, can it? Even if she began being sick almost from day one, this is the second week she's felt regularly queasy. She must already have missed a period, or be on the point of missing one. If she hasn't, or isn't, it doesn't matter, does it? And if she is . . . well, the sooner she's aware of it, the better.'

They barely spoke to each other on the short journey into Heraklion. As they entered the town's narrow, busy streets, Ella finally voiced what they were both thinking. 'If she *is* pregnant, what on earth will she do?'

'God knows.' Kate slewed the Sally around the lion fountain in Platía Venizélou. 'But whatever it is, it's bound to be a nightmare.'

'I'm over it,' Daphne said as she opened her room door to them. 'Why anyone would serve a pie filled with unnameable greenery for breakfast is beyond me. I should have had more sense than to have eaten it. Why are you both looking at me like that?'

'Because you're being sick so often.' Kate sat down on the edge of the still-unmade bed, adding bluntly, 'Eleni thinks it might be morning sickness.'

'And she's sent you some Mountain Tea,' Ella added, handing it over.

Daphne took it from her. 'That's very kind of Eleni, but please tell her I am most definitely *not* suffering from morning sickness.'

'Great.' Ella's relief was instant.

Kate, not so easily reassured, said, 'When was your last period, Daph?'

'God, I don't know, Kate. I never pay them a thought, but to humour you . . .' Daphne lifted her clutch bag from the dressing table and, taking a slim pocket-diary from it, sat down on the room's only chair. 'I know I had the curse when I was at Cliveden, the weekend before my reunion with Sholto, and I was at Cliveden . . .' she flicked carelessly through the diary's pages, 'I was at Cliveden the weekend of the sixteenth of October.'

There was silence.

At last Kate said unsteadily, 'And it's now the end of November, Daphne.'

'Yes.' Daphne's voice was odd, as if she still hadn't grasped what the dates meant.

Ella, terrified of Daphne's reaction when she did grasp their meaning, said, 'Don't panic, Daphne. If you panic, you won't be able to think clearly and . . .'

'I'm not panicking.'

Letting her breath out slowly, Kate said, 'Good. The question now is: what are you going to do about it?'

'Do about it?' Dazedly Daphne looked across at her and then, instead of breaking down in hysterics, a slow, joyful smile spread across her face. 'I'm going to leave for England now, immediately, so that I can be there to greet Sholto when he returns from Geneva. And then – together – we're going to plan a perfect, splendid, beautiful Christmas wedding!'

Chapter Sixteen

Daphne's confidence concerning how Sholto would greet the news was absolute. In the weeks since their reconciliation, he had left her in no doubt as to how passionately he felt about her and how bitterly he regretted what he now declared to be his insane refusal to end his affair with Francine.

'I don't take kindly to being given ultimatums,' he'd said wryly, his arms around Daphne when, aboard their cruise ship and in bed, she had thought she deserved an explanation. 'I don't have any other explanation for you, darling. Just damnable Hertford pride. It's been our downfall ever since 1689, when Tobias Hertford left it a little too late in bowing the knee to William of Orange. If he'd been quicker off the mark, my father could well have inherited an earldom, like yours, and not a mere marquessate.'

His hand had caressed one of her small, high breasts, his thumb tantalizingly brushing and circling her nipple and, with familiar delicious sensations spiralling through her body, Daphne had no longer cared about the Hertford pride; all that had mattered was that Francine was ancient history and that Sholto was, for the second time in an hour, about to make blissful, rapturous love to her.

Now, once again, she crossed by seaplane from Heraklion to Athens, but as there were no seats available on the next day's Imperial Airways service from Cape Town to London via Athens, she was reduced to crossing to the foot of Italy by ferry and then travelling the rest of the way by train. All through the long, tedious journey her initial certainty concerning Sholto's reaction to her news never wavered. She simply didn't allow it to.

From the moment she had laid eyes on Sholto at Miranda's party, she had known that she wanted him, and that she would always want him. Even when she had issued her ultimatum about Francine and he had refused to accede to it, it had made no difference to the fundamental way she felt about him. Her own pride had ensured she'd been hesitant when, in the travel agency, Sholto had suggested that she join him on the cruise he was about to take; but even when she had been hesitating, she had known it was a hesitation that wouldn't survive his touch – and it most certainly hadn't survived his kiss.

Although their reconciliation was still only weeks old, Daphne didn't have a shadow of doubt that she was destined to spend the rest of her life with him. All her many previous love affairs were as if they had never been; her only love, now and forever, was Sholto.

As the train halted at the Swiss/German border for passports to be checked, she reflected on how instant her reaction had been, to the realization that she had definitely missed her period. The joy that had sung through her veins at the certainty that she was carrying Sholto's child had been primeval in its intensity.

Her passport was returned to her and, as she put it back in her clutch bag, it occurred to her that as men were physically and emotionally wired differently from women, Sholto's reaction would not be primeval in the same way hers had been. He knew she used a Dutch cap, so he would be disbelieving when she first told him he was going to be a father; but hard on the heels of his disbelief would come the realization that, as their engagement would have been announced sometime over the next few months – for how could it not be, when they were so crazily in love with each other and there could be no family objections? – all it meant was that things would now be speeded up.

In leaving Crete immediately, as she had done, she would be home in time to meet him when his plane from Geneva touched down at Croydon in two days' time.

As the train ate up the miles across Germany she pondered whether Croydon Airport was the best possible place to tell him that she was having a baby and decided, fifty miles short of the border with Belgium, that it wasn't.

Where then was?

The most likely thing Sholto would have in mind, when she telephoned him to let him know she had come back from Crete several days early, was to ask her where she would like to dine that evening. Her usual answer was Quaglino's and, after they had dined and caught up on each other's news, he would expect it to be post-haste either to her flat, if Sandy was absent from it, or his mansion flat in Knightsbridge. And then it would be bed, glorious bed.

She thought about bed, glorious bed for a long time and, as they neared the Belgian border, began pondering as to whether Quaglino's was any more suitable for her purpose than Croydon Airport. It was a wonderfully intimate and atmospheric restaurant, but it was also a public place and, though it may have been a suitable place for her to break the news of her pregnancy if they'd been married, it wasn't the most suitable venue when Sholto's initial reaction was going to be one of incredulity, bordering on disbelief. That being the case, Quaglino's was out.

Bed, though, was still very much in, and the most perfect place possible for her to break her momentous news. The snag of the arrangement was the time that would be spent over the dinner preceding it, when she would be longing to share her news and yet having to keep it to herself.

It wasn't until the train approached the Belgian border and she again took her passport out of her clutch bag that the solution stared her in the face. Dinner would simply have to be skipped. She would still have to allow Sholto to book their regular table at Quaglino's, for if she didn't, it would arouse more questions than she could answer. She would then, after her telephone call to him – and a good hour or so before their arranged meeting time, when he would be getting showered and changed, in readiness for the evening ahead – arrive on his doorstep unannounced.

His flat, wonderfully private and full of memories of the many times they had made love in it, was the perfect place for what was surely going to be a moment they would remember lifelong.

Sholto's briefcase was bulging as he stepped into the Foreign Office's chauffered car waiting for him at Croydon Airport. Top of the list of his many files was one labelled 'ITALY'. Mussolini, long in cahoots with Hitler, had, in a rabble-rousing speech, threatened to withdraw from the League of Nations. No one in Geneva had been overly surprised at his threat, but it was yet another ominous indication of the way the world was moving inexorably, step by step, towards war.

The car sped out of the airport and on to the main road leading into central London and he shaded his eyes with his hand, appalled at the blindness of his country's pacifists. Only in the Foreign Office were the true dangers of the international situation recognized; and the Prime Minister, at loggerheads with his Foreign Secretary and bent on a policy of appease-ment with Hitler, had not called a Foreign Affairs Committee meeting since early summer.

He looked down at his watch. It was ten past two. The first thing he had to do was check in with his superior at the Foreign Office, but he had no intention of being caught up in early-evening meetings. The time he had spent in Geneva, painfully aware that the League of Nations was spectacularly failing to either deter or to halt aggression, had exhausted him. What he needed was a hot bath, a light meal and a couple of large, restorative malt whiskies. Something that would have restored him even more than the whiskies was taking Daphne to bed, but Daphne was still on Crete, and would be for another long, tedious week.

'I'm afraid it's the usual crawl, sir,' his chauffeur said apologetically as heavy traffic slowed them to a snail's pace.

With a motion of his hand Sholto indicated that it didn't matter. A sensible thing for him to do with the extra time he was being given was to reread one of the files in his briefcase, but as they all made such dismal reading he didn't have the heart for it. What he needed to jolt him out of his sombre mood was Daphne's lively sparkiness and, as that was denied to him, he decided the next best distraction would be an evening at his gentlemen's club.

It was six-thirty and he had just stepped out of the bath when the telephone rang.

'Darling! Surprise, surprise!' Daphne's husky voice was full of bouncy vivacity. 'I'm in London. Isn't that super? I was simply missing you far too much to stay away a moment longer.'

Relief and pleasure flooded through Sholto.

'Splendid,' he said, too sophisticated to allow the intensity of his feelings to show. 'Where would you like to have dinner?'

'Quaglino's.'

'Quaglino's it is. I'll book a table for eight o'clock.'

'Super. Till eight, then.'

'Till eight,' he said.

Replacing the receiver on its rest, he secured the bath towel around his waist a little tighter and, whistling, poured himself one of his promised malt whiskies. The evening was going to be a good one. He grinned to himself as he walked in the direction of his bedroom. If the size of his erection was anything to go by, the evening was going to be stupendous.

With a fur coat around her shoulders, Daphne ran out of her block of flats, flagged down a taxi and, ten minutes later, was pressing a bell at the entrance to Sholto's mansion block.

'*C'est moi*,' she said when he answered its ring, her voice full of excited anticipation.

'Daphne? Why on earth . . . ?'

'I've something to tell you that can't wait till eight o'clock. Something absolutely blissy. Let me in, darling, will you?'

The door buzzer was activated and seconds later she was inside, blowing a kiss to the porter and heading for the ornately mirrored cage-lift.

Even before she reached the door of his flat, Sholto opened it to her, the top buttons of his shirt undone, his bow-tie hanging loose around his neck.

'What news is so important it couldn't wait another hour?' he said, amusement thick in his voice as Daphne threw herself into his arms. 'Is your mother getting married for the third time? Are you going to return to Crete as a full-time archae-ologist? Have you fallen in love with a Cretan shepherd and are about to give up everything to live in pastoral poverty halfway up a mountain?'

'Idiot,' she said, and then, as the door closed behind them and his mouth came down on hers, was unable to say anything for several delicious, spine-tingling moments.

When he finally raised his head from hers, she said, her

eyes sparkling, 'My news is going to be an even bigger surprise than any of the far-fetched things you've thought of.'

'Then it must be outlandish.'

He slid his hands down over the slippery satin of her evening gown and cupped the cheeks of her voluptuous *derrière*.

'You're making it very difficult for me to concentrate,' she said in mock complaint, as he pressed her against the hardness of his erection.

'I could make it even more difficult, but may I remind you that we have a table booked for eight o'clock, which is . . .' he glanced down at his wristwatch, 'in a little less than an hour's time. However, if you're not worried about being there for eight, then I'm not.'

'We may not get there at all.' She pressed the palms of her hands against his chest, her eyes meeting his. 'Not after I've told you my news.'

'Which is?'

She let the moment spin out, before saying simply, 'I'm having a baby.'

The expression on his face didn't change. 'Not funny,' he said, 'though you were right that such a piece of news knocks my suggestions into a cocked hat.'

Realizing she hadn't yet finished teasing him, he released his hold of her.

'Do you want a drink, before continuing with this a little longer? A pink gin? And while I'm mixing it, why don't I have another stab at guessing the cause of all this excitement? Is your father finally to get his heart's desire and be made Speaker of the House of Lords?'

Just making the suggestion amused him. As with the Speaker in the House of Commons, the first requirement of the Speaker in the House of Lords was that he remain impartial at all times. And the 9th Earl of Dugdale was renowned for being biased, prejudiced and partisan to the point of imbecility.

'No, he isn't – or not that I know of. And I don't want a pink gin. Not just yet.' She wound her arms around his waist. 'I wasn't teasing when I said I'm having a baby, Sholto. I really am. I only found out a couple of days ago – and wouldn't even have known then, if it wasn't for a very wise old peasant lady who could tell I was pregnant, even before I realized I'd missed my last period.'

Very few people had ever seen a stunned expression on Sholto Hertford's face, but there was a stunned expression on it now. With a nerve pulsing at the corner of his jaw, he said, 'Say that again, Daphne. And this time say it very slowly.'

Her arms tightened around him. 'Sholto, darling. I'm pregnant. And let me tell you that no one is more surprised about it than I am.'

'Oh, I think they are.' There was a note in his voice that was a world away from what she had been expecting. 'I am, for a start.'

'Well, of course you are! But when the news sinks in, you'll realize it's all rather blissy.'

'Blissy?' Incredulity took over from stunned disbelief. '*Blissy?* Are you completely out of your mind? How the *hell* can you possibly be pregnant, when you always took precautions? Or always said you took precautions?'

'Well, accidents happen, and I expect I must have been so carried away in the heat of the moment that I forgot all about the pesky cap – and to be honest, darling, it isn't such a great tragedy, is it? I rather love the thought of our having made a baby. Such a clever thing for us to have done, don't you think?'

He unwound her arms from around his waist. 'It's a bloody fiasco,' he said bluntly. 'Hell, we've only been together again a few weeks. I'll make all the arrangements, of course.' He clenched his teeth, trying to control the anger and revulsion he felt at being, because of Daphne's carelessness and foolishness, put in the position of arranging to have a child of his aborted.

If, of course, the child was his.

Under the circumstances, it was a reasonable suspicion to entertain, but he closed his mind to the possibility, almost as soon as it came. Daphne was a lot of things, but she wasn't duplicitous.

'I doubt there'll be a suitable slot at St Margaret's.' A small frown wrinkled Daphne's forehead now. 'Christmas is always a preferred time of year for weddings, and we're not in a position to wait long for an available date, are we? That being the case, we may have to settle for having the wedding in the Dugdale parish church.'

For a second Sholto was so disorientated that he felt as Alice must have done, when she tumbled down the hole in the wake of the White Rabbit. Then, aware of how hideously deep the gulf of misunderstanding between them was, he said tautly, 'I'm not talking about arrangements for a wedding, Daphne. I'm talking about an abortion.'

'An abortion?' Her disbelief was total. 'But I don't want an abortion! I'm *happy* about this baby. How could I not be?'

Sholto could think of a score of reasons, but instead of listing them, he said in a voice brooking no argument, 'I'm on the verge of thirty, a member of the aristocracy – minor though a viscount may be, in your family's eyes – a respected diplomat in His Majesty's Foreign Office, with an outstanding career in front of me. So far in life I have managed – by hook or by crook – to retain a reputation unsullied by scandal, and I am not prepared to blight it by marrying because a shotgun's been slammed into the middle of my back.'

Daphne stared at him, trying to make sense of what he'd

said. For several seconds, as the world shifted on its axis, she struggled to unscramble his words and rearrange them, and to make the sense of what he'd said quite different. It wasn't possible. She tried to suck air into her lungs and couldn't. It was as if she was once again facing him in the Savoy's River Room, knowing that he wasn't going to change his mind; that the future she'd been so certain about simply wasn't going to happen. He had let her down not once, but twice. And this time was far, far worse, for this time he was letting down their unborn child, too.

When she could speak, it was to say in a voice she didn't even recognize as hers: 'You don't love me.'

It was a bleak, bare statement of fact. She lost her balance slightly and put a hand out to the back of a chair to steady herself. 'If you loved me, you might very well be angry at my having been so careless – and at your having to marry me before you'd got round to thinking what a jolly good idea marrying me would be – but you would never, *never* suggest that I have an abortion.'

He opened his mouth to speak, but before he could do so she cut across him. 'And I'm not going to have an abortion. I'm going to have this baby – and I'm not going to hide myself away. No doubt I'll be the talk of high society, but do you know something, Sholto? I don't care what people say. I never have. You may not want our baby, but I do.'

And she did what she had done a little over a year ago in the River Room restaurant.

She turned her back on him and walked out of the room.

He made no attempt to stop her.

He heard the hall door close. A couple of moments later he heard the sound of the lift gates rolling open and then closing; heard the unmistakable sound of the lift returning to the ground floor. He didn't hear the double doors of the mansion block being opened and then closed after her by the porter, but he crossed the drawing room and, from a window that looked down into the street, saw her cross the pavement and flag down a taxi.

She was crying. He was certain she was crying.

'Oh, *God!*' he said savagely. 'Oh, *hell!* Oh, *shit!*' He spun on his heel and picked up the nearest thing that came to hand. It was the heavy cut-glass tumbler that had had whisky in it and, with all the force he was capable of, he hurled it against the nearest wall. The glass splintered and shattered; ten-year-old Laphroaig malt trickled down Italian wallpaper that had cost an arm and a leg at Harrods.

Sholto didn't care. How could Daphne have been so careless about something so important? And why had she been so provocatively *happy* at having become pregnant? Why hadn't she been able to see it for the disaster it was?

And it was a disaster. A mega–mega–disaster.

Any other woman, on realizing he wasn't going to be so easily bamboozled into a shotgun wedding, would have been only too grateful to have had him make the arrangements for an abortion. Not that he'd made such arrangements before, because he hadn't. He had always conducted his private life far too circumspectly for such slipshod, messy accidents to occur. Daphne, though, had been adamant that her Dutch cap was far less intrusive than old-fashioned French letters and, as he had agreed wholeheartedly with her on that score, he had been more than happy to let her take the precautions.

Except that she hadn't.

He sank down on the sofa, his head in his hands. Not for a minute did he doubt that Daphne would stand by everything she had said. She wasn't a woman for meaningless threats. If she said she was going to have the baby, then – gutsy, reckless and as uncaring of the consequences as she always was – she would have the baby.

He couldn't even begin to imagine the consequences.

With perspiration sheening his forehead, he forced himself to imagine them.

His father and Daphne's father were fellow members of the House of Lords. There were many occasions – pheasant-shooting in Yorkshire, for one – when they socialized together. Neither man would stand idly by while a grandchild was born illegitimately.

He thought of his career; the career that meant so much to him. There would be no continuing spectacular advancement in the Foreign Office, once it became known that he hadn't made an honest woman of the Earl of Dugdale's daughter.

And then he thought of something else – something that twisted his stomach muscles into heaving, griping knots. The Foreign Secretary, Sir Anthony Eden, was a close chum of Percy St Maur. Once St Maur told Eden the situation – and he would – then Sholto's career in the diplomatic service would be as good as over.

And for what?

His hands bunched into fists.

It wasn't as if he didn't care for Daphne. He did. Another year down the line and their engagement would, no doubt, have been announced in *The Times*. Six months later there would have been a high-society wedding at St Margaret's, Westminster. There would have been a couple of hundred guests, including of course Sir Anthony Eden and, quite possibly, King George and Queen Elizabeth.

And it would all have taken place when he, Sholto, had been ready for it to take place.

He thought of his ancestor Tobias Hertford refusing, because of pride, to bow the knee to William of Orange. Tobias had not exactly ruined his life, but with a little less pride, he could certainly have risen to greater social heights than he had done.

Was he about to make the same kind of mistake Tobias had made? Was he falling into the 'no one gives me an ultimatum' trap again?

He groaned, thinking of his options, of which he could only see two. The first was to persist in the stance he had already taken. The results of this, where his career and personal reputation were concerned, were bound to be calamitous. The second was to marry Daphne, which – apart from the embarrassment of a precipitously early wedding – would not be very calamitous at all.

Slowly he unclenched his hands and, resentment burning in him like hot coals, reached for the telephone and took the receiver from its rest.

'I never thought we'd be walking down the aisle as bridesmaids during our Christmas holidays,' Ella said to Kate, as she settled herself in the front passenger seat of Kate's father's Riley.

Kate turned the key in the ignition. 'According to Daphne, there were a ghastly forty-five minutes when she didn't think she'd be walking down the aisle, either.'

'Did he really suggest that she have an abortion?'

Kate let out the clutch and pulled away from the front of King's Cross Station. 'Apparently. But Daphne says that was just a knee-jerk reaction to the shock. By the time she arrived home, after telling him what he could do with such a suggestion and walking out on him, the phone was ringing; and seconds later he was making things right pretty damn quickly.'

She overtook a lorry and was then baulked as a bus pulled out in front of her. 'Did your parents mind you taking three days out of your time home, in order to travel south to be a bridesmaid?' she asked, hoping that getting out of London wasn't going to take her longer than she'd anticipated.

'No. They know how important it is that we are bridesmaids for each other.'

'And Sam?'

Laughter was thick in Ella's voice. 'Sam wasn't remotely understanding, nor was he mollified at being included in the guest list. There was an awful lot of talk about the high-handedness of the aristocracy; the impossibility of a country GP being able to drop everything at little more than a moment's notice, for a top-hat-and-tails shindig in Wiltshire; how, even if he'd been able to accept, he wouldn't have been able to lay his hands on a morning suit; and last, but by no means least, that even if he had been able to lay his hands on one, he would have looked like a stuffed penguin wearing it.'

'So no top hat and tails at the Methodist chapel at Easter, then?'

'Goodness, no, though I have a sneaking suspicion my future in-laws would quite like that kind of formality. I can't imagine my dad or granddad in top hat and tails, though, can you?'

'No.' There was amusement in Kate's voice as, still in heavy traffic, she continued heading west, out of town. 'I can't. What did you say, to explain the suddenness of it all?'

'I told Sam the truth, and gave my parents and granddad the same explanation that Daphne's parents – according to Daphne herself – are giving everyone: that her eighty-year-old grandmother has only a short time left to live and that, before she dies, she wants to see her granddaughter walk down the aisle as a radiant bride.'

The next day when, on the arm of her father and to Wagner's 'Bridal Chorus' from *Lohengrin*, Daphne walked down the aisle of the fifteenth-century church she had been christened in, there was no hint of how little foreknowledge of the occasion there had been. The bride's antique-lace wedding gown was the same gown her maternal grandmother had worn. Her veil was held in place by a coronet of orange-blossom, its long length embroidered with crystals and seed-pearls. Behind her, Kate and Ella were wearing dresses of eau-de-nil velvet made for them by a London dressmaker, and which they had only tried on for the first time two hours earlier. Pale winter sunlight streamed through the exquisite stained-glass windows. White hot-house roses filled the air with heady fragrance.

As Daphne relinquished her father's arm and, at the foot of the chancel, took her place next to Sholto, Ella couldn't help thinking about her own wedding, now only four months away. It would, of course, be very different from today's wedding. Being a Methodist service, not an Anglican one, the liturgy would be far simpler and there would be far fewer people in the congregation: just her family and Sam's, a couple of the friends she had grown up with in Wilsden and a clutch of Sam's rugby-playing friends. It would, though, be perfect, or as perfect as a wedding could be, without any of her Cretan friends present.

'Who giveth this woman to be married to this man?' the minister was now saying.

The Earl of Dugdale stepped forward.

Ella's thoughts continued to drift. She thought of her Cretan friends: Kostas and Eleni; Andre and Agata; Nikoleta; Apollonia; Pericles; Nico; Yanni; Adonis; Dimitri and Aminta; Angelos and Rhea. If she had been marrying Sam on Crete, they would all have been there, magnificent in their heroic costume, the men carrying rifles in order to fire into the air volley after volley of celebratory shots.

Christos wouldn't have been there, though.

'I take thee, Sholto Edward Henry Hertford,' Daphne was

saying in her distinctively husky voice, 'to be my wedded husband, to have and to hold from this day forward . . .'

Christos. Ella's fingers tightened on her posy of lilies-of-the-valley and stephanotis. Why was Christos invading her thoughts now, at this of all moments?

Only yards away from her, Sholto Hertford was sliding a wedding ring on to the fourth finger of Daphne's left hand.

'With this ring I thee wed.' His voice was perfectly steady, his eyes, as they held Daphne's, unreadable. 'With my body I thee worship, and with all my worldly goods I thee endow.'

Ella tried hard to stop thinking of Christos, but now that she had started, she couldn't stop.

With Daphne and Sholto now kneeling before him, the minister exhorted the congregation to join him in prayer.

Dutifully Ella bowed her head, but although she tried hard to concentrate on the words of the prayer, she couldn't stop the thought that even if she had been marrying in Crete, Christos would not have come to her wedding; not unless it had been in order to bride-kidnap her, before Sam's ring had slid upon her finger.

The minister joined Daphne and Sholto's right hands together, saying: 'Those whom God hath joined together let no man put asunder.'

Ella gave a sigh of relief as deep as if the words were being said over her and Sam.

For this was the moment that she wanted – the moment when she and Sam were married and when she would, she was sure, be beyond all temptation, where Christos was concerned.

Chapter Seventeen

JANUARY 1938

Lewis walked out of King's Cross Station and towards the taxi rank, a leather travel bag in one hand, a briefcase in the other. He had come down from Sutherland on the overnight sleeper after spending Hogmanay with the aunt who took care of his home during his long absences from it, and with his godfather who, this year, had decided to forsake Claridge's for the snow and icy chill of the far north of Scotland.

'The Travellers Club, Pall Mall,' he said, stepping into the back of a black cab.

He had booked in for two nights, long enough for him to take care of his residual business in London before, on Wednesday, he left on the boat train for the beginning of his journey back to Crete.

That his godfather was pleased with the results of the year's dig at Kalamata was an understatement. 'It's far, far better than I could possibly have dreamed of,' he'd said as, with snow falling steadily outside, they'd sat nursing brandies before a pungent-scented log fire. 'A palace! Who would have thought there would have been another Minoan palace still to be found?'

'I would,' Lewis had said, a rare smile creasing his face. 'But be warned, Nathaniel, even though we still don't know the full

196

extent of what we've got at Kalamata, it can't be over an acre in size. The plateau isn't big enough for anything larger.'

'How big is Phaistos?' Nathaniel had asked.

'One-point-eight acres.'

'And Mallia?'

'A tad smaller, although not much. And both Phaistos and Mallia had been, like Knossos, the centres of small townships. The upper plateau at Kalamata isn't large enough for that situation to have existed there. In being situated where it is, and in being so isolated, the palace at Kalamata is unlike any other palace so far found.'

And that, for Lewis, was what made it so exciting.

As the taxi headed now in the general direction of Blooms-bury, he again pondered his theory that the palace at Kalamata had never been built to serve the same purposes as the other excavated palaces. Whereas they had all quite clearly been not only the residence of a priest-king and a priest-queen but also administrative and storage centres, so far only one royal megaron, or central hall, had been discovered at Kalamata; and, of the artefacts found there, there was nothing to indicate whether the occupant of it had been male or female.

Helmut's theory was that Kalamata had served as a pleasant occasional retreat from the official residence – a residence that could, because of Kalamata's geographical position, have been any one of the other three palaces. It wasn't a theory Lewis shared. The retinue that would of necessity have accompanied a priest-king and -queen could not have been accommodated at Kalamata. And always the mystery came back to the one royal suite of rooms, when every other palace had two.

As the taxi entered the maze of little streets that made up Covent Garden, Lewis continued pondering the mystery. Had the personage for whom the palace had been built been living in some kind of exile? And, if so, what new light would that shed on the culture and lifestyle of the ancient Minoans? Was he going to find himself at odds with Sir Arthur's conclusions about them? If he did, the resulting academic furore could last for years – and would do his reputation no harm whatsoever.

In Pall Mall the taxi drew to a halt and, in high spirits, Lewis paid the cabbie and strode up the steps and into the familiar ornate reception hall.

'It's good to see you again, sir,' the middle-aged man on the desk said, handing him his room key. 'And there's post for you.'

He handed Lewis four envelopes. Lewis flicked through them. One was from the Royal Archaeological Institute. Two were in handwriting that was familiar to him, and which he had been expecting. The fourth envelope had just his name on the front and had been hand-delivered.

Seeing his frown of perplexity, the uniformed figure manning the desk said, 'The messenger-boy who delivered it was most particular that you should receive it the instant you arrived, sir.'

Lewis pocketed his room key and then opened the envelope. It had come from an unspecified government department in Whitehall and the name of the sender – Julian Kermode – was unknown to him. It read:

> *Dear Mr Sinclair,*
> *I would be most grateful if you would find time this after-noon to meet me at the above address. Three o'clock would be convenient to me, but I shall be here until five.*

Lewis slid the letter into his pocket and made his way to his room. Once in it, he dropped his travel bag and briefcase on the bed, walked into the bathroom, put the plug in the bath and turned the hot tap on. Then he walked back into the bedroom, took the letter out of his pocket and read through it once again.

There was no hint at all that Julian Kermode wished to see him in connection with his working life; and if the meeting wasn't in connection with the dig at Kalamata, then what was it in connection with? And how had Julian Kermode known of his imminent arrival at the Travellers Club? It was all so high-handed and cavalier that Lewis's first instinct was to screw the letter up and lob it into the nearest bin.

He didn't. It was too intriguing. Instead he shrugged himself out of his jacket, undid his tie and went back into the bathroom to check on the bath water.

At five past three he was at the required office in Whitehall. It wasn't what he had expected.

Though the exterior of the building was grandiose, the part of the building that he was directed to was a rabbit warren of small, functional numbered offices. In growing bewilderment and certain that his time was being wasted, Lewis came to a halt outside the door he'd been searching for and knocked.

No one called out for him to enter.

Instead the door was flung open by a man he judged to be not much older than he himself was. Nothing about him spoke of being a Whitehall mandarin. Instead of being formally suited, he was wearing flannels and a shabby but very good-quality tweed jacket. In one hand he was holding a pipe; the other was thrust out towards him.

'Julian Kermode,' he said, giving Lewis a vigorous handshake. 'Good of you to come. Sit down and I'll get to the point straight away.' Once behind his desk, and with Lewis seated at the far side of it, he went on, 'You're a classicist, right?'

Lewis nodded.

'And you've spent the last two years working in Greece?'

'Yes,' Lewis said, equally brief. 'Crete.'

Julian Kermode sucked on his pipe and then said, 'Do you find familiarity with classical Greek gets you around in modern-day Greece?'

'Yes, but I don't have to rely on it. I speak modern Greek. Before this goes any further, would you mind explaining just what this is about?'

'Ah, yes. Sorry.' A smile tugged at the corner of Julian Kermode's tough-looking mouth. 'Although you wouldn't think it, looking at this cubbyhole I've been allotted, I'm attached to the War Office – and the War Office is interested in recruiting persons with special knowledge and languages of the Mediterranean area, in the event of war breaking out.'

Lewis looked beyond Julian Kermode to the large map of the Mediterranean area that had been pinned to the wall.

'And if war breaks out, how does Crete fit into the scenario?'

Kermode rose to his feet and turned to the map. 'Being halfway between Europe, North Africa and the Near East, Crete is strategically a time-bomb. Whoever controls it and has use of its deep harbour at Suda Bay controls the Mediterranean. This means that if war is declared, it is highly likely the Germans will try to occupy it. Because of this possible eventuality, Military Intelligence is looking to recruit people like yourself who have an intimate knowledge of Crete, for what can best be described as special operations.'

'But if war is declared, I'll no longer be in Crete. I'll be back in Britain, seeking a commission in the army.'

'Why – when you will be in a unique position to serve your country by laying the foundations of Cretan resistance? You'll be supplying intelligence; sounding out which local leaders can be trusted and which can't; preparing groups to resist invasion; and, if it is invaded, you'll lead the resistance in an area of the island you know like the back of your hand.'

Already knowing what his answer to Julian Kermode's proposal was going to be, Lewis said, 'And I'd be doing this under whose authority?'

'You'd be operating under a newly formed branch of Military Intelligence, the Special Operations Executive, usually referred to simply as SOE. For now, and until you are contacted to the contrary, we'll want straightforward intelligence. Who on the island has influence, lists of who is pro-British and who is anti-British. That kind of thing.'

'And when I'm contacted?'

Kermode grinned. 'Then you'll have more action on your plate than you'll know what to do with.'

Fifteen minutes later, and walking down Whitehall in the direction of Trafalgar Square, Lewis was still trying to get his thoughts in order. It had been obvious to him for months that Prime Minister Neville Chamberlain's appeasement policy with regard to Hitler was never going to have a happy outcome, and that war with Germany was inevitable. What he had never faced up to previously was where a war between Britain and Germany would leave Greece and, in particular, Crete.

He thought of his friends on Crete. He thought of the precious artefacts in Heraklion's museum, and of bombs being dropped on Heraklion; of bombs even, perhaps, destroying the irreplaceable, reconstructed Palace of Minos. He thought of the Kalamata dig and of how war would bring an end to it. He thought of Helmut. Helmut wasn't a Nazi, but if his country was at war, he would return to it in order to fight. His friend would become his enemy, and the thought made Lewis feel physically ill.

A number-eleven bus thundered past. Outside the Whitehall Theatre a ticket-tout tried to waylay him. Ahead of him the sun shone on Nelson, as he stood on top of his column. England's green and pleasant land was green and pleasant still; but for how much longer? Sometime soon, perhaps within months, Hitler would go a step too far and all appeasement would end. And if war came to Crete?

As he turned left into Pall Mall he felt a spasm of certainty. If war came to Crete, Hitler would find that he'd bitten off more than he could chew. In Crete every male over the age of twelve could handle a rifle and bring down a bird with a single shot. And it wasn't only rifles that were commonplace.

Muskets – relics from the Greco-Turkish War of forty years ago – still hung on the inner walls of many Cretan cottages. Shotguns were legion. Although Cretans were the most generous, gregarious people in the world to those they regarded as their friends, no quarter was ever given to an enemy. They were natural brigands. In the line of mountains that ran from east to west of the island, lawlessness was a rule of thumb. Sheep were still rustled. Honour-killings still took place. Brides were still occasionally abducted. No matter what other country in Europe Hitler rode roughshod over, he wouldn't be able to ride roughshod over Crete. When it came to Homer's sea-girt isle set in a wine-dark sea, the Führer would find every man and woman armed to the teeth and ready to fight to the death. And he, Lewis, would be shoulder-to-shoulder with them.

Chapter Eighteen

It was nearing the end of February, and Kate and Ella had been back on Crete for just over a month. Although the dig wasn't officially to start until March, because there was so much work to do preparing tented accommodation for the new team of workmen who were about to arrive, they were back in their familiar lodgings at the *cafeneion*. Lewis, Helmut and Christos were also back at Kalamata, as were Nico and Adonis. The Mamalakis brothers both had family homes in the village and so had never left it, and Yanni had moved in as a lodger with Dimitri and Aminta Mamalakis. Of the original team, only Pericles was still to arrive.

Ella's relief at having moved out of the Kourakises' small house was vast, as it meant that now they were no longer living beneath the same roof, she spent far less time in close proximity to Christos. Whereas she had once enjoyed the sight of Christos washing at the pump, she did so no longer. The feelings he aroused in her were far too disturbing and filled her with too much guilt and confusion. How was it possible for every fibre of her being to react to Christos as it did, when she loved Sam and, in just two months' time, was going to marry him? And when Sam was, in every possible respect, the perfect person for her to marry?

All her life she had behaved with great common sense. Unlike Daphne, Ella had never acted impulsively or recklessly.

Ever since junior school she had slogged hard to make her parents and granddad proud of her, and to achieve her personal ambitions. And she had attained those ambitions. She had won a place at Oxford. She had left with impressive letters after her name. She was an archaeologist, and an archaeologist working on what would, when the work on it was published, be a site of worldwide repute.

She had only ever had one boyfriend, and that boyfriend had never let her down. Although Sam didn't share her passion for the far-distant past and for unearthing artefacts and the remains of buildings thousands of years old, he understood how important her work was to her. As a GP, he had every right to expect that when they married she would be a support to him in his medical practice, and would show that support on a daily basis by answering the phone, taking messages and generally being a familiar face, where his patients were concerned; and yet Sam had agreed that instead of being an adjunct to his career, Ella should continue with her own career. All he had asked was that she didn't accept archaeological digs so far away that she wouldn't be able to get home from them easily and often.

Her mum, dad and granddad all thought Sam wonderful, and would have done so even if, like generations of Tetleys before them, he had been a rag-and-bone man or a mill worker. That Sam was a doctor did, though, give him added lustre, especially in her mother's eyes. If, when she had been home over Christmas, Ella had heard her mother say proudly once, in a conversation with a neighbour, a shopkeeper or absolutely anyone at all, 'Ella's fiancé is a doctor. A *proper* doctor. A GP in Scooby', she had heard her say it a hundred times.

Everyone loved Sam and thought he was right for her. *She* loved Sam and thought he was right for her. Why, then, was she still so dangerously and overwhelmingly attracted to Christos?

All the while she was thinking, she was making her way to

the upper plateau. Everyone else, apart from her, was already there, getting the campsite ready for the men who were about to arrive. Although in coastal areas such as Knossos the weather was beginning to be milder, it was still chilly in the mountains and she was wearing several layers of suitable clothing.

It wasn't, she thought as she reached the approximate halfway point, where chestnut trees hemmed the steep path, as if – were she to give way to temptation, where Christos was concerned – anything could come of it. Though gifted at what he did, he wasn't academically educated. She tried to imagine telling her parents and granddad that, after all the sacrifices they had made for her education, she was going to jilt Sam because she was in love with a Cretan workman who had had no more education than an English junior-school child. Then she thought of trying to tell them that Christos wasn't a Methodist, and wasn't even a Protestant. Whether or not they would understand what being Greek Orthodox meant, she didn't know, but she did know that the chances of them being happy about it were on the scant side.

And when it came to trying to imagine what it would be like being married to Christos – supposing Christos should ever ask her to marry him – her imagination simply wouldn't stretch that far. For one thing, Christos would never take the same under- ' standing attitude towards her career that Sam had taken. He would probably be happy for her to continue working as an archaeologist, but only if the digs in question were on Crete. Anywhere else, even mainland Greece, would be out of the question. If one thing had become obvious to her during her time on Crete, it was that Cretan wives didn't have a life of their own. They looked after the family's animals, made cheese, dug fields, tended crops, marketed home-made produce, bred children, led hard lives and were at the beck and call of their menfolk.

She came to a halt and pushed her mane of Titian hair back

over her shoulders. Even daydreaming about jettisoning all that she had going for her, in order to join the ranks of Crete's womenfolk, was insanity. What on earth was she doing, even contemplating such thoughts?

Jilting Sam and marrying Christos was a scenario that was never, *never* going to happen. She was a level-headed, down-to-earth Yorkshire girl. Rational behaviour was in her blood and bones, and just because she'd discovered within herself a capacity for lust that was giving her wakeful nights and troubled days, it didn't mean she had to give in to it – and she wasn't going to give in to it.

From further up the track came the sound of someone coming down it at a fast pace. Her heart began drumming in her chest. It could only be a member of the team, but which one? What if it were Christos? She remained standing still, half in desperate hope, half in sickening apprehension.

When the figure rounded a bend in the track and became visible, Ella sagged, her reaction again one of opposites – this time relief and disappointment, for it wasn't Christos. It was Lewis.

'Ah,' he said, coming to a halt in front of her. 'You're just the person I wanted to speak with.' He took off his jacket, slinging it over his shoulder, holding it by his thumb. 'During the winter Yanni found another cave within a stone's throw of the summit. Although we've found nothing but animal bones in the cave he's been camping in, I'm wondering if the cave he's found will prove to be a sacred one.'

He didn't have to explain to her what the relevance of such a find would be. The palaces at Knossos, Phaistos and Mallia were all in alignment with a sacred cave or peak sanctuary. If the small palace of Kalamata had also been built in alignment with a sacred cave, it would be further proof that, though much smaller than the other three palaces, Lewis was quite justified in believing that what they'd found at Kalamata was, indeed, a Neo-palatial palace.

His hair had fallen low across his forehead and he pushed it back with his free hand. 'It's certainly worth checking out, and I want you and Christos to climb up to it tomorrow.'

At the prospect of a whole day high on the mountain alone with Christos, alarm flooded through Ella. 'Perhaps Adonis would be a better choice,' she said, trying to keep her voice steady. 'Or Nico.'

'Nico doesn't have the experience for anything other than digging under direction, and Adonis is supervising the erection of the tents. Besides, you and Christos work well together, and you'll both know what to look for. Neither Nico nor Adonis would.'

'But . . .' Desperately she tried to think of another objection, but couldn't.

'Thanks a lot, Ella. I've already spoken to Christos. You'll have a steep climb in front of you, but Yanni says it doesn't need mountaineering skills. Sacred caves are always accessible. They had to be, in order for worshippers to reach them.'

He shot her one of his rare smiles and, without waiting for any comment from her, set off once again, covering the rough ground in fast, easy strides.

Ella watched him with a troubled heart, certain that all the Fates of Greek mythology were conspiring against her.

'And so there it is,' she said late that evening as she sat at one of the *cafeneion*'s outside tables with Kate, 'a whole day tomorrow with Christos. Believe me, it's the very last thing I need.'

Kate topped up their glasses with Agata's home-made wine, so dark a red it was almost black. 'Are you sure you should still be sticking to an Easter wedding date, when the man dominating all your waking thoughts – and I dare say your dreams at night as well – isn't Sam, but Christos?'

'Of *course* I should be sticking to the arranged wedding date! I wish now that I'd agreed to an even earlier date. Only when I'm married to Sam will I feel safe.'

'I don't follow your logic, Ella, and neither does Daphne.'

'Daphne,' Ella said with great feeling, 'is hopeless. Her only advice has been that I should have a full-on affair with Christos before the wedding. She says: that way, he'll be past history by the time I marry Sam, and no longer a torment.'

'She may be right.'

'Really? And is that what you would do?'

'Of course it isn't.'

'And it's not what I'm going to do, either. How could I keep my having had a love affair with Christos a secret from Sam? Especially when it would have been a love affair that had taken place in the run-up to our marriage? I would have to tell him. There's no way I could *not* tell him. To not tell him would mean our life together would be built on deceit, and I couldn't do that. Not to Sam. And if I have to tell him I've been unfaithful to him, he'll be so devastated there will probably be no marriage at all. He'll most likely call the whole thing off, and who could blame him?'

She took a sip of her wine and then pushed the glass away from her, saying fiercely, 'If I give in to temptation where Christos is concerned, then one way or another my marriage to Sam will be off. And I don't want that. It would break my mum and dad's hearts. It would break Sam's heart.' She rose to her feet. 'Sorry, Kate. I'm going to bed. I need a decent night's sleep, if I'm to climb higher tomorrow than I've ever done previously.'

Kate tilted her head to one side, watching as Ella walked off in the direction of the steps leading to the *cafeneion*'s living quarters. Although Ella seemed unaware of it, there had been a rather huge omission, when she had listed the people whose hearts would be broken if her marriage to Sam was called off. Intentionally or unintentionally, she had never said that her heart, too, would be broken.

They met outside the *cafeneion* just after dawn.

'It's going to be a long day,' Christos said, without shooting her his usual brilliant grin.

Ella adjusted the straps of her rucksack more comfortably on her shoulders. Christos's moods were always mercurial, and as they crossed the scrubby ground of the village square she did so certain that he wouldn't be out of sorts for long.

It was so early there were very few of Kalamata's villagers up and about, and their booted feet crunched loudly on the cobbles as they walked up the steep street leading out of the village.

By the time they were on the wooded mountain track, Ella – who in the past had often welcomed a break from Christos's teasing chit-chat, in order to remind herself that it was Sam whose company she was supposed to be so happy in, not Christos's – no longer wanted time in which to think. Thinking was dangerous. It could all too easily lead to a very wrong decision.

'Do you think Lewis is right, and that the cave Yanni has found will prove to be a sacred cave or a peak sanctuary?' she asked as, half an hour later, they skirted the Little Palace plateau and began the climb to the summit.

'But of course!' He didn't break stride. 'Every royal palace has either one or the other. And when we find whichever it is, and dig and find the offerings that have been left there, then the mystery of the Little Palace having only one royal megaron will be solved.'

'I'm not sure how votive offerings will solve that mystery,' she said, and found that Christos had stepped in front of her and she was talking to the back of his neck.

The back of his neck was an extremely attractive part of Christos's very attractive anatomy, because it was where his shock of blue-black hair curled the thickest, the curls so tight that she itched to hook her fingers into them. She fought the thought away, furious at her inability to be physically indifferent to him.

He came to a sudden halt and swung around. 'And I do not want to talk about votive offerings,' he said explosively, unable to keep quiet any longer about what it was that had been tormenting him for days. 'I want to talk about your method wedding!'

They were on a flank of a mountain thick with shale, and as she came to an answering halt, Ella slipped. Christos's arm shot out to steady her and, regaining her balance, she wrenched her arm away from his hold and said between clenched teeth, 'And it's a *Methodist* wedding, Christos. Not a method wedding!'

'And how many best men will there be?'

'One. There is only ever one best man at a Methodist wedding, or at a Protestant, Anglican or Roman Catholic wedding too, come to that.'

'At a Cretan wedding there are nearly always two best men. Sometimes, as when Angelos married, there are more. How long is a Method*ist* wedding ceremony?'

'Thirty minutes, perhaps a bit less.'

'*Ba!*' Christos was even more unimpressed. 'A Cretan wedding is an hour, sometimes—'

'Sometimes longer,' Ella finished for him, not hiding how unwelcome the conversation was to her. 'Do you think we could talk about something other than wedding ceremonies?'

'But why?' Beneath winged eyebrows, his near-black eyes flashed with emotions she didn't want to recognize. 'You are to be married soon. You have chosen your wedding dress, yes?'

She had. When she'd been home at Christmas, she and her mother had gone shopping in Bradford and had chosen a dream of a dress. It was ankle-length and made of white silk chiffon, with crocheted lace detail on the bodice and a full foot of the same lace above the hem.

'Yes,' she snapped back at him. 'Though what my wedding dress has to do with you, Christos, I really don't know.'

There were thick clusters of yellow and white anemones growing amongst the shale and Ella tried to concentrate on them. Christos didn't let her do so.

'You know why!' he said abruptly, coming to a sudden halt and swinging her round to face him. 'You know it is not the right thing for you to do! You say that after you have married you are coming back to Crete. Back to the dig. But will you? And if you do come back, for how long will you be back? Will you be here next year? No, of course you will not! And will you be happy away from Crete? Away from all the friends you have made in the village? Away from Andre and Agata? Away from Eleni and Kostas? Away from *me*?'

She pushed past him, walking as fast as she could over the steep ground.

He was beside her almost instantly. 'You can run away from me, Ella, but not from yourself.'

'You talk rubbish, Christos Kourakis. Do you know that? We should be talking about how we're supposed to find this cave – and why isn't Yanni with us? He would have been able to take us straight to it.'

'Yanni gave me enough directions to make his presence unnecessary.'

'And what are the directions? Second to the right and straight on till morning?'

'*Oriste?* And you say I talk rubbish? What kind of rubbish talk is that?'

Ashamed at having descended into the kind of sarcasm he couldn't possibly understand, she said, 'It's Peter Pan talk. It was the directions Peter gave for flying to Neverland.'

The expression on Christos's face was one of utter bewilderment.

'*Peter Pan* is a book,' she said, as the volatile atmosphere between them eased and, despite their mutual intentions, they found themselves sliding back into their usual camaraderie. 'It's about a little boy who doesn't want to grow up and who lives in a magical place called Neverland.'

'Okay. I understand. The book is to the British what Homer's *Odyssey* is to the Greeks.'

'Not quite,' she said, amused, even though she didn't want to be. She came to a halt, looking westwards to where, in the far distance, dark clouds had begun obliterating the snow-covered peaks of Mount Ida. 'It looks as though a storm is coming in,' she said, her amusement dying fast. 'Have we time to get back to the dig and shelter, before we get caught in it?'

Since setting off from the upper plateau, all Christos's thoughts had been centred on Ella's forthcoming wedding and how he could dissuade her from going ahead with it. Now, for the first time, he noticed the drop in temperature and the change in the light. As he looked towards Mount Ida, there came the rumble of distant thunder. Grim-faced, he looked back the way they had come, and then upwards. If the landmarks Yanni had given him were correct, they were far nearer to the cave than they were to the plateau.

'The cave is our best bet,' he said, taking hold of her hand, 'but we need to move fast. We have minutes – maybe only ten – until the storm reaches us.'

Ella didn't need any encouragement to move fast. The last thing she wanted was to be caught in a Cretan thunderstorm, high on an open mountainside.

As the minutes ran out and the storm drew closer she saw, fifty yards or so ahead of them and just below the summit, a shelf of rock jutting out over giant boulders and half-obscured by bushes of spiny yellow broom.

'Is the cave there? At the back of the shelf of rock?' she gasped, as Christos continued hauling her after him at break-neck speed.

'Yes,' he said as lightning forked above their heads.

She was just about to say she didn't think she was going to be able to climb the boulders, when her right foot gave way beneath her, twisting at a sickeningly ugly angle and pitching her forward onto her knees.

Her cry of pain was almost, but not quite, drowned by the crash of thunder that followed the lightning.

'*Holy Virgin!*' As rain began knifing down on them in torrents, Christos dropped to his knees beside her. One look at her sheet-white face, and the way she was struggling not to follow her first shout with further cries of pain, was enough to tell him she couldn't put weight on her foot, let alone walk.

He readjusted his *sakouli*, the embroidered woollen knapsack Cretan men carried on their backs instead of a rucksack, and then, with rain saturating his hair and streaming down his face, swung her up into his arms.

'You can't . . . carry me . . . over the boulders.' Her words came out in short, sharp gasps.

'I won't need to. The gaps between them make a passageway.'

Ella's head sagged against his chest, his shirt and sleeveless jacket as wet against her face as if they had been submerged in water.

'If your arms were around my neck, it would make carrying you a little easier.'

'Yes. Sorry.' She did as he suggested and immediately sensed that although it was doing nothing for her peace of mind, she had lightened his load.

Because of the way Christos was carrying her, she had no clear view of the boulders as they approached them, but she could certainly feel the rain stinging every inch of her exposed flesh. 'Stair-rods,' she said.

'Stair-rods?'

'Stair-rods. They're brass rods that hold stair carpeting in place, and it's a Yorkshire expression for rain like this – rain that lashes straight down with heavy force.'

As she spoke, she winced.

Aware of the pain she was in, and aware that until he could look at her ankle properly he still didn't know how badly sprained, or perhaps even fractured, it was, he said, 'In Crete we also have a name for rain like this, but it is not one we say in front of young women.'

She knew that he was trying to make her laugh, but she was in too much pain to do so.

For another ten minutes they continued on in silence and then he said, 'We've reached the boulders, Ella, and Yanni is right. There's a narrow gap leading up between them.'

He entered it, the rain still sluicing down on them, the ground rising steeply.

'Will it bring us out at the side of the rock shelf or in front of it?' she asked, anxiety for him obvious in her voice, for she could tell by his increased breathlessness that he wasn't going to be able to continue carrying her for much longer.

'The edge – and we're nearly there.'

There was another crack of thunder, this time directly overhead.

'And the rain is still stair-pods,' he added as, with a last manful effort, he stepped out onto the ledge.

'Stair-*rods*,' Ella said, and then forgot the pain she was in, for the shelf of rock wasn't level, as they had supposed. Instead it sloped backwards into the cliff face, and at the bottom of the slope, and beyond a natural channel carrying rainwater away, there was the mouth of a cave.

'Goodness!' Still held in Christos's arms, Ella stared at it, mesmerized. 'Who would have dreamed what the boulders hid from sight?'

'Not me,' Christos said truthfully. In arms that felt as if they were breaking, he began carrying her down the slope. 'Although if it proves to be a sacred cave, it wouldn't always have been hidden from sight. It would once have been visible from the palace. The boulders and rock shelf will be the result of one of Crete's many earthquakes.'

The rain, although light in comparison to what it had been earlier, was still falling, with drops dripping from his hair into his eyes. He blinked them away as best he could and then, in vast relief, stepped across the channel of fast-running rainwater and into the shelter of the cave.

Gently he lowered Ella to its sandy floor and, with her back supported by the cave wall and bending down on one knee beside her, said thickly, 'Okay, Ella, *agápi mou*. Now let me see what you've done to your ankle.'

Ella knew what the words *agápi mou* meant. They meant 'my love'. She braced herself for an examination that she was sure was going to be agonizingly painful, but what she had forgotten was Christos's reputation for having the gentlest, most careful hands in the world. Within seconds she realized his reputation didn't apply only to the handling of artefacts lost for thousands of years, but to sprained ankles as well.

'For it is a sprain,' he said in relief, 'not a fracture, and certainly not a break.'

Their eyes held. 'It may only be a sprain, but there's no

way I can put weight on it and get myself back down to Kalamata,' Ella said.

'You may be able to, once I've put an ice-cold bandage on it and made you a crutch.'

Christos shrugged off his jacket, folded it into a makeshift cushion and put it behind her back. Then he took off his shirt and, with the knife he kept in his sash, began ripping the material into broad strips, saying as he did so, 'Before I strap your ankle up, there are a couple of things I have to do. First, I'm going to soak the bandaging in the channel of rainwater. It will be icy enough to reduce the swelling. Then I'm going to see if there is dittany growing amongst the broom.'

'Dittany? What's dittany?'

'It's a herb that's known for its healing powers. If I find some, I shall make a poultice of it.'

He stood up and, as bare-chested as when he took a morning wash beneath his family's pump, smiled down at her. 'When Georgio's sheep injure themselves, they rub against dittany.' He shrugged expressively. 'And if it is good enough for a sheep . . .'

'. . . then it must be good enough for me,' she finished for him, laughter in her throat despite her pain.

'I would tell you not to move while I look for it, only it is so obviously unnecessary.' He picked up the strips of linen that had once been his shirt and thrust them through his knife-sash. Then, wearing only sash, breeches and boots, he strode out of the cave and, because of the upward angle of the rock shelf, was almost immediately lost from view.

Ella took in a deep steadying breath and looked around at what she could see of the cave. There was no discernible end to it. The roof was high, and from where she was sitting she couldn't see any markings on the walls that would instantly stamp it as a sacred cave. There were no double axes carved into the stone; no carvings of any kind. She reminded herself that from where she was sitting she had a very restricted view, and that carvings so near the cave's mouth would, in any case, be unlikely. There was a torch in Christos's *sakouli* and with it he would, when he returned, be able to do as thorough a search of the cave as time permitted.

She regarded her swollen ankle malevolently. If she hadn't sprained it, they would have been able to do the torchlit search together. As it was, Christos would not only have to do the search on his own, but would also have to cut it short, for there was now the extra time it was going to take getting her back to Kalamata to factor in, and that was something that couldn't even be guessed at.

Considering everything, she knew she ought to be feeling wretched, and yet she wasn't. She was disappointed they couldn't use the best part of the day to search the cave together; she was sorry she was causing Christos so much trouble and anxiety; she didn't like the wincing pain she felt whenever she tried to put weight on her foot; but she didn't feel wretched. Instead, with her head and back resting against the wall of the cave, waiting for Christos to return to her, she felt the opposite of wretched. She felt light-headed and trouble-free, as if she'd been lifted out of normal space and time.

The Minoans had deemed such caves sacred because of their special atmosphere and the otherworldly sensations they aroused in those who entered them. Was that why she had this curious feeling of well-being? She'd once heard the Squire say that the Minoans considered sacred caves to be the connecting point between this world and the next – a place where humans could contact the normally inaccessible spirit world. It was something Ella found easy to believe. Just as she was pondering what the manner of Minoan worship might have been, there came the sound of boots on stone, and a second later Christos's shadow fell across the entrance. In one hand he was carrying the makeshift bandages, now all dripping wet; in the other, a clump of not very inspiring-looking greenery.

'Dittany,' he said, going down on one knee beside her. 'I found it growing in the same cleft of rock as the yellow broom.'

His knee was pressed close against her thigh, the throb of sexual tension between them so strong it seemed to Ella that the very air was thick with it. He was sweating from the exertion of his climb and as a bead rolled down his chest, she had an overpowering urge to lick it away. Half-senseless with desire, knowing that to give in to it would be to open floodgates that could never be closed, she dug her nails into her palms and struggled to focus on the plant he was holding.

It was very unprepossessing. There were no flowers on it, although as March was still a couple of days away, that was perhaps not surprising. Its leaves and stems were coated in tiny white-grey hairs, giving the impression that it was covered in velvety-white down.

Taking the silence of her private battle as disappointment in the plant, Christos said, 'It's very rare, Ella. It grows only in Crete and only in high, hard-to-reach places. As well as being famous for its healing powers, it also symbolizes love. Men have died climbing mountainsides and deep gorges in order to give it to their sweethearts as love tokens.'

Full of deep intensity, his eyes held hers, and even before he spoke again she could feel passion rising within her, in a tide so vast and violent she knew that this time it was going to be unstoppable.

'Ella, *agápi mou*, I have brought dittany to you to speed the healing of your ankle, but I also bring it as a love token – and if it had been necessary for me to risk my life in order to bring it to you, then I would have risked it not once, but a score of times – a hundred times.' His voice cracked and broke. 'I love you, little Yorkshire girl. You are like no other girl I've ever known, or ever will know. You are not meant to return to England and marry. You are meant to stay here, on Crete, and marry me.'

In the pale shafts of light now spilling into the cave, Christos had never looked more Greek. Wearing only breeches and boots, his tightly curling hair falling low over his forehead, his skin a sun-bronzed mahogany, his moustache as dark and luxuriant as that of a bandit, he confounded Ella with desire; desire that overruled all common sense. He was what she wanted, and nothing else – Sam, Yorkshire, a career as an archaeologist in parts of the world other than Crete – mattered.

In that moment she abandoned the battle she had waged for so long. With her eyes holding his, she slowly and steadily slid Sam's engagement ring off the fourth finger of her left hand and into her jacket pocket.

With a groan that seemed to come from the very centre of his being, he pulled her into his arms, saying hoarsely, 'I love you, Ella. I will always love you. There is nothing you could ever do that would stop me from loving you.'

She could feel hot tears on her cheeks and didn't know if they were her tears or his.

His mouth was on her temples, her eyelids and then, just as she had dreamed of for so many months, at long last on her mouth. As his hands moved to her breasts, she made no move to stop him. Between them there were now no limits, and when Christos made love to her on the hard floor of the cave, it was an experience of such deep commitment, such perfect joy that Ella knew she would remember and treasure it lifelong.

Chapter Nineteen

Daphne had written in her distinctive scrawl:

Dear Kate,

I received your letter and Ella's letter in the same post and I'm utterly speechless. I've always thought myself remarkably free of snobbery, but now I'm no longer sure that's true. If Christos was a pukka archaeologist, it would be different. But he isn't. I know Lewis, Helmut, Kit and the Squire all think very highly of him, but he has no professional qualifications. Being foreman on a dig is as high as he can ever go, and I suspect he wouldn't be foreman on the Kalamata dig if it wasn't that both he and his father had worked on the Palace of Minos site and that the family was well known to the Squire. It was the Squire who recommended him to Lewis, wasn't it? I think Ella's making a huge mistake, but as she's already written to Sam – and returned his ring by post – there's no point in my telling her so, as it can't, now, change anything.

As for me, I'm gloriously happy and, at six month's pregnant, I'm beginning to look like a ship in full sail. Sholto is now very enthused at the prospect of becoming a father and refers to my lump as 'the sprog'. He's assuming the sprog will be a boy and, if it was possible to put his name down now for Eton, he would have. As it is, if it is a boy, Sholto will be

*doing so the day Caspian (not my choice, but I like it) is
born. I, of course, am hoping for a girl and am already
thinking up lots of delicious names for her. Theodora, Perseph-
one and, with a nod to Crete, Ariadne being top of the list.*

*Returning to Ella and this month's unlikeliest wedding of
the year . . . Even though I think she's making a ghastly
mistake marrying Christos, I would still have liked to have
been a bridesmaid (now I'm married, 'matron of honour', to
be more correct), but because of the sprog it simply isn't
possible. (And anyway Ella made it sound very compli-
cated.) Can't get my head around the fact that you can be a
bridesmaid/matron of honour if you're not Greek Orthodox,
but not a* koumbara *– who, apparently, is the person who
really matters. As the* koumbara *is to be Nikoleta, I'm not
sure I'd appreciate playing second fiddle to her – and don't
expect you will, either!*

*Sholto is in a state of cold, icy anger at the way the
Austrians have embraced Hitler so wholeheartedly. Austria is
now just another province of Germany. Can you believe it?
What life must now be like for Austria's Jews, I can't imagine.
Sholto says the Foreign Office is inundated with immigration
applications. The latest obscenity is that German and Austrian
children are no longer allowed to play or speak with Jewish
children. If that doesn't make people's blood boil, nothing will.
The sooner Herr Hitler is drummed into outer darkness, the
better it will be for the world; and if it takes a war to get rid
of him, then so be it, although I hate the thought of a war in
which the charming Helmut Becke will be the enemy. Is much
said on the dig about the war clouds hanging over Europe, or
are you all in your own private little bubble on Crete?*

Sombrely Kate put the letter down, reflecting that, totally
immersed in excavation work, they were indeed living in their

own private little bubble. It was the excitement of the palace and of the now-confirmed sacred cave that took up conversation at mealtimes, not politics. Or it had been, until Christos and Ella had announced they were going to marry.

She was taking a mid-morning break, sitting beneath a tented awning with what, on the dig, passed for a cup of coffee. Not far away from her Yanni, the dig's self-appointed cook, was tending a pot of lamb stew over a fire of pungent-smelling juniper wood. The rest of the team had already had their mid-morning breaks and were all hard at work in different sections of the site.

The progress that had been achieved since the dig had begun again was phenomenal. Thanks to the extra workforce, in a score of deep pits and trenches the entire outline of the palace was now clearly visible. Although patchy in lots of places and built on a more modest scale than the other Minoan palaces, there were now identifiable remains of a central court, west court, a royal megaron, a small tripartite shrine and what had once been a three-columned portico. Down the east side of the central court a long line of what appeared to have been storerooms were, after three and a half thousand years, emerging into twentieth-century daylight.

Dimitri, Angelos, Pericles, Nico and Adonis were excavating a series of galleries abutting the west court. Something that was a feature of other palaces, and which had not yet been found, was a broad ceremonial staircase; and the new work team, under the direction of Helmut, were a little distance away, digging trial-pits in a likely area.

Kate watched them, her thoughts not on the dig, but on the difficult atmosphere that had existed on it, since Ella and Christos had announced they were a couple.

She and Ella had always enjoyed an easy-going camaraderie with the work team, but since Ella's engagement to Christos, the team's behaviour towards her had become awkward and strained.

Lewis, who liked a congenial atmosphere on his digs, had solved the problem by handing Ella responsibility for the most important artefacts, which, when found, were taken to a workroom at the Villa Ariadne where they could be kept safe, studied and the notes on them written up. Ella now undertook these tasks full-time, driving herself there and back daily in one of the dig's small trucks; and although she usually had a lunch of sandwiches in a corner of the workroom, there were many days when she joined Eleni, Kostas and sometimes Nikoleta for a lunch of soup, salad and a hunk of Eleni's home-made cheese.

That the Kourakis family were happy about Ella and Christos marrying was a source of great relief to Kate. Nikoleta, she knew, had reasons of her own for being happy about it, for Christos and Ella were setting a precedent for her and Lewis. Eleni and Kostas's happiness had no ulterior motive. Quite simply, because of the winter months Ella had spent living in their home and because of their affection for her, she was, in their eyes, already one of the family.

Kate rose to her feet and began walking in the direction of the partially excavated storeroom trenches, enjoying the sight of mountains as far as the eye could see, certain that May had to be the most wonderful month of the year in Crete. The sun wasn't yet too hot for comfort, and the island was a riot of wild flowers. Even high on the upper plateau it was hard to walk without crushing sweet-smelling thyme and sage underfoot. On the edges of the site were carpets of white, pink and purple anemones and, a special joy to Kate because of their rarity value, thick clusters of wild tulips, their petals the palest lilac, their hearts the deepest indigo. Whoever the chief occupant of the palace had been – and, like Lewis, Kate's instinct was that it had been built for a priestess-queen – the person in question had lived amidst great beauty.

What she dearly wanted to discover was some inscription on pottery or stone that would solve the mystery of the palace's single royal suite of rooms and confirm the sex of whoever it was who had occupied them.

Yesterday, in one of the storerooms in which excavation had only just begun, the rims of three great stone jars had begun appearing and, with the help of one of the new team members, she was in the middle of exposing them fully. When that was done she would carefully remove the earth still clinging to them and it was then that inscriptions, if there were any, would be revealed.

As she bypassed what had been uncovered of the stone-paved central court, she saw Lewis striding purposefully towards her from the opposite direction. Her stomach muscles tightened as they always did when the two of them were in an unexpected one-to-one situation.

'I've just been looking at the *pithoi* you're unearthing,' he said, referring to the stone jars and coming to a halt in front of her. 'They'll help confirm that the area was used for storing produce – in this case, probably oil and wine.'

'Yes.' She wondered what was going to come next. Lewis rarely commented on the obvious. She didn't have to wonder for long.

His shirt sleeves were rolled up to the elbows and he was wearing the kind of blue jeans American cowboys wore.

'I want to talk to you at length about the dig and what is concerning me.'

'Fine.' She waited expectantly.

'Not here and now. It's the kind of conversation best done over dinner. If you've no objections, I'll pick you up at the *cafeneion* at seven. Will one of the restaurants around the harbour suit?'

'In Heraklion? Yes. Fine.'

He gave her a nod, hooked his thumbs in the pockets of his jeans and strode off.

It took her several seconds to steady her breathing. In the almost two years they had worked together, Lewis had never made such a suggestion before. Discussions to do with the progress of the dig were either solely between him and Helmut, or were group discussions in which they all – Lewis, Helmut, Christos, Ella and Kate herself – took part. As she climbed down the earth steps of the trench, she wondered if perhaps the mysterious sponsors of the dig had run out of money; if the dig was perhaps going to be prematurely terminated. Was Lewis going to fire her, in one of the harbour's candlelit restaurants?

That evening, on the drive into Heraklion, he said very little. He asked Kate about the four-foot-high jars and shared her disappointment that, now they were totally uncovered, there was no sign of inscriptions on them. 'It was perhaps too much to hope for' was all he said as he drove through Archanes, scattering hens right and left.

She didn't fill the ensuing silence with chatter. If he didn't wish to talk, then it was all right by her. She wasn't going to allow him to make her feel uncomfortable. Neither did she want to give the impression that she thought there was a social aspect to their evening. They may have been going out for a meal together, but she hadn't dressed as if they were out on a date. She was wearing a pleated skirt that could have passed for a work skirt, a sweater and cardigan, as it could be cool around the harbour in the evenings, and low-heeled sandals. She had put on pearl earrings, but then, deciding they made it look as if she was making too much of an effort, had taken them off again.

He parked in one of the harbour's side streets and led the way into a restaurant she hadn't been in before. Immediately they stepped over the threshold, she regretted not having worn the earrings. She had been expecting that they would eat somewhere casual, but the restaurant he took her into was far from casual. It oozed formality and expense.

When they were seated he said, 'Would you like something to drink, before we order?'

'I don't know.' She was thrown off-balance by the unexpectedness of the white napery and heavy silverware. 'Perhaps a raki.'

He ordered two rakis and asked for the menu. Then he said, 'What I'm going to say this evening must remain between the two of us, Kate. I don't want you to talk about it to anyone, not even Ella.'

Her sense of foreboding escalated.

The waiter came with the aperitifs. Another waiter came with the menus.

'Let's choose and order,' he said, 'then we'll talk.'

She sipped her raki, chose figs oozing with goat's cheese for a starter, and lamb braised with quince for a main course.

What she didn't do was immediately start showering him with questions.

Lewis was grateful, but unsurprised. He'd long ago got over his annoyance at Kit Sinclair for having thrust Kate on him as a member of his team. Since that inauspicious start to their relationship, she had rarely irritated him and, apart from the previous year's New Year's incident in the Villa Ariadne's library, never disappointed him. That being the case, it was unlikely she was going to start doing so now.

He said flatly, 'I don't think we're going to be able to

complete the excavation of the palace, Kate. I thought it only fair to let you know.'

So he was about to fire her. Kate's stomach muscles tightened. No more Crete. No more living at the *cafeneion*. No more camaraderie with the team. No more Little Palace and sacred cave; blissful sunshine; snow-capped mountains; fields and fields of wild flowers; hot sun; lammergeiers hovering against brassy blue skies; and last, but by a long way not least, no more Lewis.

She said, trying not to let the violent emotion she was feeling show in her voice, 'Is this because the funding is to be withdrawn?'

'No. Funding is the least of the problems. A major problem is that now the importance of the dig is so clearly evident, there is no avoiding the British School becoming more and more involved in it, and that would radically change the nature of the dig – something I very much don't want. But there is something else, something graver and equally likely.'

He paused, frowned, picked up a knife from the table and replaced it.

At last he said, 'The likelihood of war with Germany is overwhelming, Kate. Hitler may have walked into Austria without a shot being fired, but it won't be the same with his threatened invasion of Czechoslovakia. Prague has already ordered troops to what is now the Austro-German border, and all Czechs from the age of six to sixty have been ordered to have defence training.'

They had been served their first course. He pushed it away, untouched.

'I don't know how much you're keeping up with world events – it's not easy here, when British newspapers don't reach Heraklion until the news in them is well out of date

– but Britain has just signed a pact with France to defend Czechoslovakia from any aggression by Germany.'

Kate thought of Kit and Lewis returning to Britain to serve in the armed forces and, with a sickening inner lurch, of Helmut returning to Germany to serve in the Wehrmacht. In those circumstances, of course the dig would come to an end. How, unless the British School in Athens took it over, could it continue?

The wine steward poured their wine and she said apprehensively, 'We will be able to finish this year's dig, though, won't we?'

'Yes, and thanks to the new team who are working together very well, we're going to get a lot done. Hopefully we'll find a ceremonial terrace and artefacts that will explain the mystery of the palace's single-megaron layout, and its setting halfway up a mountain.'

Kate took a drink of her wine. It was like nectar. Far superior to the King Minos that was her usual tipple.

'If there is a war, then afterwards – and if the British School hasn't taken over – surely you will be able to return to Crete and, if the excavation was left unfinished, finish it?'

He liked the fact she so utterly assumed that, if war came, it was a war Britain would win.

'Probably,' he said, deciding to leave it until the end of the meal before he put his proposition to her.

When their meal was over and coffee had been served, he said, 'I'd like to return to what we were talking about earlier, Kate. The strong possibility of war, and the possible scenario with regard to the dig.'

'You mean about it being on hold until you return, once the war – if there is one – is over?'

'No,' he said. 'I mean earlier.'

She waited for him to explain.

He hesitated, aware that what he was about to suggest could have all kinds of repercussions, especially if Julian Kermode's prediction was correct and the Germans tried to occupy Crete. Although he didn't think such an attempt would succeed, there could well be fighting on the island; fighting that Kate could easily be caught up in. Was that a risk he was willing to run, for a woman about whom he had such complex feelings? There was, however, always the chance that such a situation might never come about and, in that case, as long as he put her fully in the picture, he saw no reason why he shouldn't give her the chance of at least considering his suggestion.

He went on, 'If war is declared, the only reason excavation will come to a standstill is because both Helmut and I will be serving our countries.'

He didn't need to spell out that they would be serving them on different sides; nor, aware of the Official Secrets Act that he had signed before leaving Julian Kermode's office, did he tell her where his war service would be carried out.

'In theory,' he continued, 'excavation work could continue under someone else's direction – someone who was already familiar with it; someone who could be trusted.'

'Christos?'

'No, I have something else in mind for Christos.'

'But there isn't anyone else who is both familiar with the site and has the necessary experience.'

'Yes, there is Kate. You.'

She drew in a sharp breath.

'There is a major drawback you need to be aware of. Although Greece pitching in, if war is declared, is unlikely, it *is* likely, because of her strategic position, that she will become involved in it against her will; and as Crete possesses the biggest harbour in the Mediterranean, it particularly applies here.'

'You mean the Germans will try to take over the island?'

He nodded. 'If a German invasion became a strong possibility, I think all British civilians on the island would be taken off it by the Royal Navy, although that couldn't be guaranteed.'

'And so I could find myself sitting out the war under German occupation, alongside Ella and Christos, Agata and Andre, Eleni and Kostas, and everyone else who I think of as being part of my extended family?'

'Yes.'

Her mouth tugged into a smile. 'Then in that case, it's a risk I'll take.'

He smiled back. She'd never seen him smile with his eyes before. Desire shot up like a flame inside her. She fought it down fast, before he could become aware of it.

'Let's take a stroll around the harbour,' he said, signalling for the bill.

Once outside, they began walking along the road skirting the harbour. Everywhere couples hand-in-hand, or arm-in-arm, were doing the same thing. The difference was that although she and Lewis were walking close together, unlike everyone else they were carefully not touching. She said suddenly, asking him something she would never have dreamed of asking him only hours earlier, 'Are there going to be long-term difficulties for Ella, once she is married to Christos?'

'No. I don't think so. The present difficulty is because the work team are embarrassed. Suddenly they don't know how they should be treating her. Unspoken barriers have been breached, and it's going to take a little time before they feel at ease about it.'

She wanted to say, 'And will you meet the same reaction, if you marry Nikoleta?' but it would have been a pointless question. He wouldn't; she didn't have any doubt at all about that. Instead she said, 'What is so special about the role of a *koumbara*? What differentiates her from other bridesmaids?'

'You mean why couldn't you be Ella's *koumbara*?'

They had reached the harbour's causeway, the water at their feet an inky, glittering black.

She nodded, and he said, 'The role of the *koumbara* is a very important one, extending far beyond the wedding day. The reason she has to be Greek Orthodox is that she will act as a godparent to the couple's first child.'

The late-evening breeze had turned chilly and he came to a halt. 'I think it's time we were heading back. Not a word to anyone of what I think the future may hold, Kate. It may never happen.'

'I hope it doesn't.' Her voice was fervent, but there was also something else in it, for because the possibility of war had been brought up between them – and because of what Lewis had suggested to her, and the trust it showed he placed in her – their relationship with one another had been entirely reshaped.

Somehow, over the last couple of hours, the seemingly impossible had happened. A link had been forged between them and, if friendship was perhaps too strong a word for it, it was something very close to friendship; something that hadn't been there before; something that, to her, meant a very great deal.

Chapter Twenty

It was September and an Indian summer. Daphne was seated in a deckchair in the rear garden of the Cadogan Square house that she and Sholto had moved into immediately after their wedding. Some yards away, in the shade of a tree, Caspian was in his Harrods perambulator, blowing bubbles and kicking legs that were blissfully unencumbered by sheets or a shawl. If his nanny had been on-duty she would have objected to his lack of coverings, but to Daphne's great pleasure, nanny was having an afternoon off.

Deirdre Holbeck-Pratchett, also in a deckchair and separated from her by a small garden table on which stood an ice-bucket holding a bottle of white Bordeaux, said, 'Toby and I had been thinking of driving down to the South of France and sailing across to the Porquerolles Islands. Apparently they're known locally as the Isles of Gold. They sound dreamy, don't you think?'

'Yes, Dee. They sound lovely.' Deirdre never allowed anyone to call her by her full name as she said it sounded too like 'dreary', something she most certainly was not. 'However, I'm not tempted by anywhere abroad at the moment. It would mean leaving Caspian behind and, much to Sholto's irritation, I'm not ready to do that yet.'

Dee, who had barely seen her children until they left the nursery – and not very often then – thought she'd never heard anything quite so ridiculous, but kept her thoughts to herself.

Daphne was also keeping her thoughts to herself. Dee was wearing a shocking-pink dress – the colour, and the silver buttons in the shape of tambourines, shrieking that it had come from Paris and that the designer had been Elsa Schiaparelli. Perhaps, Daphne thought, she could tear herself away from Caspian long enough to make a short trip to Paris? The House of Schiaparelli was now *the* Parisian fashion house and she hadn't yet stepped foot across its threshold.

Dee gossiped on, this time about how Toby, who was senior to Sholto at the Foreign Office, was hoping to be posted to the British Embassy in Cairo. 'He thinks sitting out a war in Cairo will be far preferable to sitting one out in London. And he may be right. I believe Cairo nightlife is *very* lively.'

Daphne said she'd heard the same thing, but her thoughts weren't on Cairo and certainly not on Toby, whom she found a pretentious bore; they were still on Dee's shocking-pink dress. Shocking pink was a difficult colour to carry off, if the wearer was the teeniest bit overweight, and though she had lost a noticeable amount of weight since Caspian's birth, Daphne still wasn't exactly svelte. Dee was. Dee was as svelte as a whippet. So, where a Paris dress was concerned, perhaps not one in the newest, latest colour for herself; perhaps lime-green instead. Certain shades of green had always suited her near-white blonde hair.

Dee was now talking about someone other than her husband, and not doing so in a very complimentary way. Daphne sometimes wondered why she persisted in the friendship. Dee was a good ten years older than her, and the friendship had begun only because of Sholto's working relationship with Toby.

Dee had now moved on to a christening party they were both invited to. 'It's bound to be tedious. Everything the Carringtons do is tedious. All that money, and no style. Tragic, absolutely tragic.'

Daphne had forgotten all about Albert George Henry

Carrington's christening party. Would Sholto have bought a suitable christening gift? No, he wouldn't. Not without having mentioned it to her. Would he assume she had bought a suitable christening gift? Yes, of course he would. It was the kind of thing wives were expected to do.

Sholto had gone to Asprey's for Caspian's christening present. Asprey's had been the royal jewellers for more than two hundred years. If she went to Asprey's for Albert George Henry's christening present, she couldn't possibly go wrong.

She was still thinking about the christening present when Dee had said her goodbyes. What should she buy? A christening mug? But usually only parents and godparents gave christening mugs. A silver baby rattle? But perhaps a baby rattle was a tad *déclassé*? Apostle spoons? Apostle spoons were definitely not *déclassé*. Apostle spoons it would be, then. And as Sholto had an account at Asprey's, all she need do was make a phone call.

'The entire set of twelve, Lady Hertford?' the male assistant at the other end of the telephone wire asked, 'or the four?'

'The four?'

'The four is a Matthew, Mark, Luke and John set.'

'Dear me. Only four spoons seems a little on the mean side.'

'Believe it or not, Lady Hertford, we are occasionally asked to supply just one spoon – although only ever, of course, in situations where the baby's first name is also the name of one of the apostles.'

Daphne never minded being pleasantly chatty to sales staff and said, with amusement in her voice, 'Fortunately that isn't the case with this particular baby and so I can fight temptation. The full set, please, delivered to my London address.'

'Certainly, Lady Hertford. And the initials and birth date for the engraving?'

'A.G.H. The fourteenth of July 1938.'

'And would you like the same font style as on your husband's last purchases?'

'I expect so. Can you remind me what his last purchases were?'

There came the sound of paper rustling and then the young man – Daphne was sure he was young, from his voice and manner – said, 'A Georgian silver christening mug, a silver bracelet and a gold-and-emerald tiger brooch, although only the christening mug and bracelet were engraved.'

Daphne frowned. That only Caspian's christening mug and the bracelet had been engraved made sense. The gold-and-emerald tiger brooch had been Sholto's present to her when Caspian had been born, and nowhere on it would engraved initials have been suitable. She knew nothing about a silver bracelet, though.

She felt an unpleasant tightening sensation, deep in the pit of her stomach. Why, when buying the brooch, would Sholto also have bought a second piece of jewellery – a piece of jewellery that he hadn't given to her? And what had he had engraved on it?

'What type of font was used on the items my husband bought?' she asked, wondering how she could find out who the bracelet had been bought for.

'The font used on both items was cursive, Lady Hertford.'

'Then I'd like cursive used again.' She hesitated and then said, her voice as casual as before, 'Am I right in thinking there was a little difficulty with the spelling on the bracelet?'

'I don't think so, Lady Hertford. There may been a query about it from our end. Pet names and foreign names are often checked, just to be on the safe side. Foreign names can be especially difficult.'

Indeed they could. The name Francine, for instance. An engraver not over-familiar with French might well have telephoned Sholto to check whether or not a cedilla was to be used beneath the letter c. After all, the French name Françoise was spelled with one.

Francine. Was that who Sholto had bought the bracelet for? If so, when had he restarted his affair with her? Obviously it had only happened after their marriage. Her head swam. Their passionate lovemaking had come to a temporary halt in the later stages of her pregnancy. 'I'm sorry, sweetheart,' he had said, lovingly apologetic. 'I believe some men find heavily pregnant women erotic, but I'm afraid I'm not one of them.'

Why hadn't it occurred to her that, if he wasn't making love to her, Sholto was most likely making love to someone else? And surely the most obvious person was Francine. Francine who was, no doubt, still associating with high-ranking Nazis.

'Was there something else, Lady Hertford?' the sales assistant prompted.

'Yes.' She thought fast on her feet. 'I'm curious as to the near-miss spelling mistake on the bracelet. What exactly was it?'

'There wasn't one, Lady Hertford, though there could quite well have been. The name "Dee" could so easily have been mistaken for the initial D, couldn't it?'

'Yes.' The world rocked around her, the breath suddenly so tight in her chest that she didn't know how she was continuing to breathe. 'Yes, it would have been an easy mistake to have made. Thank you for all your help.'

Before he could tell her what a pleasure it had been, she'd dropped the receiver heavily back on its rest.

She was shaking from head to foot.

There could only be one Dee. Deirdre. Of all the people to have been having an affair with, Sholto had opted for the most trite option: a woman who was one of his wife's friends. Or had it been Deirdre who had made a play for Sholto? Either way, it didn't matter very much. The result was the same.

Sholto had been unfaithful to her. Worse – he had been unfaithful to her when, in the run-up to Caspian's birth, she had thought the two of them so deliriously happy.

Since Caspian's birth, their lovemaking was again enthusiastically back on keel – so did that mean his affair with Dee was over, or was it still continuing? Either way, what was she going to do about it? Trembling violently, she sat down on the nearest of the drawing room's three lavish sofas. If the affair was still continuing, she would bring it to a very abrupt halt, even if it meant shooting Sholto in the kneecaps to do so. And if the affair was over? Then a lot would depend on how contrite he was. One thing was a given: their marriage would continue. No one in her parents' families had ever been divorced, and neither had anyone in Sholto's family. She was all for being innovative, but she wasn't going to be so where her marriage was concerned. There was also the question of her pride. How could she allow a woman ten years her senior to derail her marriage? The answer was that she couldn't. It would be just too utterly shaming.

She glanced down at her watch. It was nearly five o'clock and if she didn't go up to the nursery, she would miss out on Caspian's bath time. Not only that, but she and Sholto had been invited to the French Embassy for early-evening cocktails, and no matter what kind of a scene took place between them beforehand, she had every intention of still putting in an appearance at it. That they did so was important to her: a statement that no matter what might or might not change within their marriage, it was a marriage that was going to continue.

At six-thirty, when Sholto walked into the house, Daphne was wearing a black Balenciaga cocktail dress, artfully designed to disguise the fact that she hadn't quite lost all of the weight she had put on when pregnant. She looked gorgeous, and knew it.

Sholto popped his head around the drawing-room door. 'Goodness, sweetheart,' he said appreciatively, 'you're going to knock the French for six tonight. I'll be with you in thirty minutes.'

Seconds later Daphne could hear him running up the stairs and calling for Barak, his valet. She crossed to the cocktail cabinet and made herself a pink gin. By the time she was seated, drinking it, she could hear Sholto's bath water being run.

She remained where she was, her stomach cramping with nerves. Only when she had judged that Sholto was out of the bathroom, back in the bedroom and had nearly finished with Barak's services did she rise to her feet and, her heart slamming against her breastbone, her palms slippery with sweat, make her way upstairs.

Sholto looked up in surprise as she entered the bedroom. 'Nearly there, Daphs,' he said, putting in a cufflink and then saying, as Barak finished brushing the shoulders of his evening jacket, 'Thank you, Barak. That's all.'

Barak left the room. Sholto gave a last look in the cheval glass and saw how unnaturally pale Daphne was looking. 'What's the matter?' he asked, turning towards her in concern. 'Are you under the weather?'

'No. Yes.' She steadied her voice. 'I ordered a christening present for the Carringtons' baby this afternoon.'

Sholto slid a slim cigarette case into his inner breast-pocket. 'Surely that wasn't enough to make you feel out of sorts?' There was mild amusement in his voice.

'I ordered it – a set of apostle spoons – from Asprey's.'

'On the account?'

'Yes.'

'Then what's the problem? Why are you looking as if the world has come to an end?'

'Because it might have.'

Their eyes held. She could see him rapidly making the connections: Asprey's – his account – the bracelet.

'That's a rather extreme statement, Daphne,' he said cautiously. 'D'you mind explaining?'

'I was trying to make up my mind about the style of font for the engraving. The sales assistant asked if I would like the same style you had asked for on your last purchases, and I asked him to remind me what those purchases had been.'

The room was suddenly so charged with tension it was if all the air had been sucked out of it.

'He had to refer back to your account and he said you had bought a christening mug, a brooch – my gold-and-emerald tiger brooch – and a silver bracelet.'

'Ah!' The smile he gave her was perfectly steady. 'And you were wondering why I hadn't yet given you the bracelet?'

She knew if she said 'yes' she would, by lunchtime tomorrow, be receiving a bracelet purporting to be the original, although this time with her name engraved on it.

The sense of betrayal, and the bitter disappointment she felt in him, flooded through her with such intensity that she didn't know how she was remaining upright.

'No, Sholto. I wasn't wondering that. I know why you didn't give me the bracelet. It was because it hadn't been bought for me.'

'Absolute rubbish.' The skin had tightened over his cheek-bones and a muscle had begun ticking at the corner of his jaw.

'No, it isn't. You had it engraved. And the name you had engraved wasn't mine.'

Sholto was temporarily robbed of speech. At last he said, his voice full of disbelief, 'An *Asprey* employee *told you* what I'd had engraved on it?'

'Only because I tricked him into doing so and because, as my Christian name begins with the letter D, he obviously thought the bracelet had been meant for me and there was no harm in divulging the information. Only it wasn't meant for me, was it?'

The game was up and Sholto knew it. 'No, it wasn't.' Stalling for time, he ran a hand over his hair and then, determining to have the sales assistant instantly fired, said, 'I can understand you being angry and a little hurt Daphne, but there's no real reason for either emotion.'

It was a reaction so unlike the one she had been expecting that she gasped.

'A little hurt?' The self-control she'd been hanging on to with such difficulty finally deserted her. 'A *little* hurt?' her voice broke on a sob. 'While I'm pregnant with our baby, you begin an affair with the wife of a colleague – with a woman who professes to be a friend of mine – a woman at least ten years older than I am – and you say you understand if, on my finding out about it, I'm a little hurt! Well, I'm a damn sight more than a little hurt!'

'Let's get one thing straight.' There was no remorse or contrition in his voice. Instead, to her utter incredulity, he sounded exasperated. 'It wasn't an affair. It was barely a fling. If it wasn't for the fact that you were so close to having Caspian, it wouldn't even have been that. What's more, it's a fling that is over. So can we now please draw a line under it? We're due at the French Embassy in twenty minutes.'

She felt as if the floor was moving beneath her feet. Nothing had been as she had imagined it would be. Sholto hadn't been horrified at being found out. He hadn't been overcome with remorse. He hadn't begged her forgiveness. Instead, he was behaving as if his adultery was of no consequence whatsoever.

As if reading her thoughts, he said placatingly, 'Come on, darling. No matter what you might think, it isn't the end of the world. All married men have flings, and most of the time they are meaningless. Mine certainly was. Jackson will have brought the car round to the door by now. Collect your stole and let's go.'

She didn't move. She couldn't move. She said slowly, 'And is that what you anticipate doing throughout our marriage, Sholto? Having little "flings" whenever the mood takes you?'

This time she had truly expected a vehement denial. Instead he said, clearly out of patience with the fuss she was making, 'Be reasonable, Daphne. Why not? Our marriage is a marriage I was dragooned into, because you were pregnant. Amazingly, it's working out quite well, but under the circumstances I think I deserve to be cut a little slack now and again, don't you?'

She slapped him hard across the face. For a moment she thought he was going to retaliate, then she saw him master his reaction. Breathing hard, he said tersely, 'At least the ground rules are out in the open now. This evening the two of us are going to the French Embassy cocktail party – and we're going to leave for it right now.'

Daphne didn't argue. After all, attending the party, no matter what the outcome of her confrontation with Sholto, had been what she had intended all along. What she had never envisioned, though, was their confrontation ending the way it had. How could Sholto not love her, the way she loved him? On unsteady legs, with tears of anguish scalding her cheeks, she turned away from him, blind, deaf and dumb with the pain of all that had been lost between them in a few mere moments.

As she picked up her white fox stole, one thing only was obvious to her. She needed her friends. She needed Kate and Ella. She was going to overcome her scruples about leaving Caspian and would go to Crete, and while there she would think very hard about the ground rules for their marriage, as Sholto saw them; for if they applied to him, she saw no reason why they shouldn't apply to her.

But they weren't the ground rules she had wanted.

Not even in the smallest way were they what she had sought.

Chapter Twenty-One

'That's the most disgraceful thing I've ever heard!' Ella's delicately featured face was white with outrage.

It was eleven o'clock on an October morning, and she and Kate were sitting around one of the *cafeneion*'s zinc-topped tables with Daphne, who had arrived by plane from Athens a few hours earlier. The temperature was in the mid-sixties, warm enough for Daphne to be wearing a sleeveless cotton dress, and they were outside, beneath the awning.

Neither Kate nor Daphne disagreed with her, and Ella said vehemently: 'From what you say, it isn't even as if he was in love with this Deirdre person and, when it comes to the two of them, I'm not sure which of them has behaved the worst. How could she pretend to be a friend to you, when all the time she was . . . she was . . .' Words failed her.

'When all the time she knew how my husband kissed? How he made love?' Sunglasses hid Daphne's eyes, but her voice was thick with the hurt and anger she still felt. 'I don't know. Deirdre Holbeck-Pratchett is a bitch. What makes a hideous situation even more hideous is that she moves in the same social circles that Sholto and I move in. Forgetting she exists is impossible.'

Kate said, 'But you are still together? You haven't left Sholto? He hasn't left you?'

'Oh no,' Daphne's voice was bitter. 'We're still together. Aristocracy doesn't divorce. Socially, a divorce would be the end of us. It would certainly be the end of Sholto's high-flying career at the Foreign Office.'

'And the Royal Enclosure at Ascot would be barred to you,' Ella said, concerned.

Coming from Ella, the remark was so comical that for the first time since her phone call to Asprey's, Daphne came very close to laughing. 'Too true, Ella. I mustn't forget the truly serious aspects of divorce. Changing the subject to something far happier: tell me all about your wedding. I hated not being here for it, but in June I was the size of a house, and Caspian could have been born at any moment.'

Ella pushed her coffee cup to one side. 'My wedding was wonderful, Daphne. Andre stood in for my father and gave me away and, before I put in an appearance, Christos led a parade to the church, accompanied by musicians singing wedding songs and playing lyres. In the parade were his family and all the local villagers. There must have been three hundred people in total, and when you add in all the villagers who came from Kalamata, the full number of guests must have been close to six hundred.'

'Great Scott! Where on earth was the reception held?'

'Where nearly all Cretan wedding receptions are held – in the village square.'

Remembering the Kourakis family's extremely modest income, and knowing how unlikely it was that Ella's parents had contributed to a wedding she knew had disappointed them deeply, Daphne was dumbfounded. 'But who paid for all the food and drink?'

'The guests.' Kate raised her face to the warmth of the sun. 'It's the tradition for Greek wedding presents to be gifts of money, and a relative of the bride or groom stands at the exit of the church holding a special tray, on which guests place money-filled envelopes called *fakelaki*.'

'And in the evening,' Ella said, 'when Christos and I opened the dancing, guests pinned even more money on my dress. All of which meant there was no problem at all, when it came to paying for the food and drink.'

'How practical. And what about the wedding service? What did your *koumbara* have to do?'

Kate pushed her chair away from the table. 'While Ella tells you, I'll bring fresh coffee out.'

As Kate headed into the *cafeneion*, Ella said, 'When the priest had blessed our wedding rings and placed them on the fourth finger of our right hands, Nikoleta exchanged the rings three times to symbolize how, in marriage, the weakness and imperfections of one of us will be compensated by the strength of the other. And then she performed the crowning.'

'The crowning?' Daphne's eyes widened.

'Crowning symbolizes the establishment of a new family under God. Our crowns were made of plaited flowers, and represented the new kingdom of our marriage and of our being the king and queen of our home and of our family to come; and, just as she had with the rings, Nikoleta exchanged our crowns three times.'

'It all sounds very beautiful – and not at all like a Methodist ceremony.'

'Oh, there were some aspects that wouldn't have been out of place at a Methodist ceremony. There was a reading from St Paul's Letter to the Ephesians, and another New Testament reading from John. Plus the service and the symbolism and the words used were so beautiful I didn't mind it not being a Methodist service. As each day goes by, I'm beginning to feel more and more Greek. I haven't converted to the Greek Orthodox Church yet, but I'm happy for the children we'll have to be Greek Orthodox and – who knows? – perhaps before too long I will be Greek Orthodox as well.'

Happiness and contentment radiated from her.

Daphne wondered if, before the Asprey's phone call, she too had radiated the same happiness and contentment. Certainly she had felt it and, just as certainly, she didn't feel it any longer. As Kate came out of the *cafeneion* with another pot of coffee, she wondered if she would ever again feel that level of heedless, glorious happiness that she had felt in the first nine months of her marriage to Sholto.

Kate set the jug down on the table, saying, 'I can hear a truck coming up the mountain and I think we're about to be joined by Lewis and Helmut. They've been in Heraklion and it can't be anyone else, as everyone is either at the palace or the cave.'

Now that they were no longer talking, both Daphne and Ella could also hear the faint sound of an approaching vehicle.

Daphne said, 'Is it the usual end-of-season scramble to get things done, before you abandon the sites for the winter?'

'Something like that.' The sound of the engine changed as, still out of sight, the truck crested the lip of the plateau. 'The team that was new to us in May has already left and won't be back until next March or April. Only the hard core are still here: Angelos and Dimitri Mamalakis, Pericles, Nico, Yanni and Adonis. Yanni wants to do exactly as he did last year, which is keeping an eye on the palace site by camping out in a cave overlooking it. Pericles will be leaving for his home on the mainland in a couple of weeks' time. Nico and Adonis will be leaving for their homes in western Crete. Dimitri and Angelos live in Kalamata, and they'll be on hand if Yannis should need them.'

'And what will you and Ella do, from November to next spring?'

'I shall be at Knossos, using the facilities in the workrooms to study and date the huge number of vases we've found. One black-figure vase depicting Theseus fighting the Minotaur is almost exactly the same as one found at the Palace of Minos by Sir Arthur Evans, but other scenes aren't so easy to decipher, and the pieces of pottery waiting to be pieced together are in the thousands and could keep me busy for years.' Kate pushed a heavy fall of glossy hair back behind her ear. 'And I'll go home for Christmas, spend time with my parents and come back at the end of January, or early February.'

'And my plans aren't much different.' Ella refilled their coffee cups. 'I'll be going to Wilsden, although for New Year, not Christmas, and I'll be staying there for as long as it takes to bring Mum, Dad and Granddad round to accepting Christos as a son-in-law and being happy for us.'

Privately, Daphne thought Ella unlikely to achieve her aim. Secretly sympathizing with the feelings of Ella's parents and granddad, she said, 'Perhaps when they meet Christos and see how happy the two of you are . . .'

Her voice tailed away and Ella said carelessly, 'Oh, they won't be meeting him. Not this coming New Year, at any rate. When I suggested that he come with me to Yorkshire, he was appalled. You would have thought I'd suggested that he take a trip to Outer Mongolia.'

Daphne carefully kept her eyes from meeting Kate's, fairly sure she would read the same expression in Kate's eyes that she was suppressing in hers. 'Oh, well,' she said laconically, making a joke of it, 'there are lots of people in southern England who have exactly the same thoughts as Christos, where Yorkshire is concerned.'

The sound of the truck speeding towards them through the village brought the subject to a halt. It burst into the square, a couple of barking dogs racing in its wake.

Nikoleta was leaning out of the passenger side window, her riotous mass of dark hair windblown. It was rare to see a Cretan woman with her head uncovered, and Daphne knew immediately that Nikoleta was still determinedly dressing city-style.

'Daphne!' Nikoleta jumped from the truck wearing high-heeled sandals and a turquoise linen dress that wouldn't have been out of place in London. 'Lewis told me you had sent a telegram saying you were on your way here.' She dragged a chair up to the table, positioning it next to Daphne's chair.

Lewis shot Daphne one of his rare smiles. 'Welcome back to Crete, Daphne. Kate may already have told you we're in the last week or so of closing down the site, and unfortunately I need her and Ella to be up there for the next few hours. If you want to come with us, you're very welcome.'

His thumbs were hooked in the pockets of narrow denim trousers and he looked so slim-hipped and virile that Daphne could well understand why, even after all this time, Kate was still so dazzled by him.

'Not for the first time I'm wearing the wrong kind of shoes for a hike to the upper plateau.' There was wry laughter in Daphne's voice. 'Perhaps tomorrow – and perhaps I could help with the work?'

'Christos could certainly find you something to do.' He looked across at Kate. 'Sorry to do this to you, Kate, when Daphne has only just arrived, but I really do need your help for a couple of hours.'

'That's okay.' Ella had already risen to her feet, and now Kate rose to hers.

'And I don't mind,' Daphne said, 'although I might, if you rob me of Nikoleta's company as well.'

'I won't be doing that. Her shoes are just as unsuitable for mountain-climbing as yours are.'

'That's true.' Nikoleta was deeply gratified by the similarity. 'And so the two of us will stay here and drink coffee and talk.'

Helmut said, 'I would also like to drink coffee with you, Daphne, but perhaps I can do so later?'

His eyes held Daphne's, the expression in them telling her

that he was still as smitten with her as he had been on her previous visit. Then, although she had flirted with him, she had been too much in love with Sholto to give him any serious encouragement. Now she didn't see any reason why things shouldn't be a little different.

'Coffee would be lovely.' Her voice, like his, was carelessly light, but as her eyes met his, they held a look of encouragement he couldn't possible mistake.

'*Gut.*' His mouth crooked into a smile, '*Ich freue mich darauf.*'

He walked away, falling into step beside Ella, and Nikoleta said, 'Why does he sometimes speak in German? What did he just say?'

Daphne's German wasn't very good, but what Helmut had said hadn't been too hard to interpret.

'He said he was looking forward to having coffee with me.'

Nikoleta was no longer listening. With long strides, Ella and Helmut had disappeared into the steep street that led out of the village and to the track leading to the upper plateau. Kate and Lewis were still crossing the square, walking at a much slower pace, their heads close together in deep discussion.

Watching them, Nikoleta said bleakly, 'For months now it has been the same. Always it is Kate he discusses things with. He never used to discuss things with her, and so why does he do so now? Why are Englishmen so strange? Why is it you can never know what is going on inside of them?'

Considering the events of the last few days, it wasn't a question Daphne felt qualified to answer. Sympathizing with Nikoleta's bewilderment, she said truthfully, 'I don't know. I wish I did. But Lewis isn't an Englishman, Nikoleta. He's a Scotsman.'

'But Scotland is part of England.'

'No, it isn't. England is England, and Scotland is Scotland. And both countries are a part of Great Britain.'

'Then it is all the same thing, and I do not understand him. Why does he not ask me to marry him? The whole of central Crete believes I am betrothed to him, and I am not. What will my reputation be, if Lewis never asks me to marry him? I will be laughed about from here to Réthymnon. And Kit, who is very, very all-English – he is just as bad. I have been spending time with him to make Lewis jealous, but Lewis is not jealous. And Kit, who I know wants to marry me, never does more than kiss me like a friend and put his arms around me. He is attentive and kind, but he has no . . .' She struggled for a suitable word. At last she said despairingly, 'He has no *sizzle*.'

That Lewis had plenty of sizzle was something too obvious to need to be stated.

'A Greek man would not treat a woman he loved as Lewis and Kit treat me,' Nikoleta continued glumly. 'With a Greek man, a woman knows where she is.'

Daphne didn't think this was necessarily true, but didn't think it the right time to say so. She glanced down at her watch. 'The sun is over the yardarm. What's your preference, Nikoleta? Wine or raki?'

'Wine, please. And when you come back with it, we will talk of English things – of Harrods, and King George and Queen Elizabeth and the little princesses. If I was married to Lewis or Kit and lived in England, would I see the King and Queen and the little princesses often?'

It occurred to Daphne that Nikoleta had rather a distorted view of what life in England would be like, if she should ever find herself living there; and that she would be doing Nikoleta a big favour if she replaced fantasy with a little reality.

For the next two hours she did her best, but Nikoleta wouldn't be budged from believing that marriage to Lewis or Kit would automatically mean her seeing a lot of the royal family.

'Sir Arthur did,' she said stubbornly. 'He once told me how, when he was with the King's father, the King's father said to him how very interested he was in all things Cretan and how, one day, he would like to visit Knossos.'

Daphne was quite willing to believe that Sir Arthur had had a conversation with George V, but as the King had been known to have no interests other than stamp-collecting and shooting, she didn't for a moment believe that his expressed interest in all things Cretan had been genuine, or that he had spent a moment pining to visit the Palace of Minos.

She was just about to say so when they heard someone approaching the square from the street leading to the track.

Nikoleta immediately lost interest in their conversation, hoping it would prove to be Lewis.

Daphne was rather hoping it would prove to be Helmut.

Moments later Helmut stepped from the shadow of the street into the sunlight and Nikoleta's shoulders sagged in disappointment.

'Helmut on his own means Ella and Kate are going to be longer than Lewis had thought they would be,' she said desultorily. 'He will have come to offer us lifts back to Knossos and Heraklion.'

Daphne took off her sunglasses. 'Well, if he has, it's an offer I'm going to accept. I haven't had much sleep since I left London, and I'm ready for a nice hotel room and a comfortable bed.'

Any doubts Daphne had, where her intentions with Helmut were concerned, vanished as she watched him cross the square towards them. Tall and toughly built, he moved with an athlete's muscular strength and coordination. She wondered if he played rugby. He looked like a rugby player, although one without a broken nose or cauliflower ears.

'Lewis apologizes,' he said as he walked up to them, 'but he'd miscalculated the length of time things were going to take, and Kate and Ella are going to be at least another two hours. That being the case, would the two of you like lifts back to Knossos and Heraklion?'

Without a second's hesitation Daphne rose to her feet. 'Lovely,' she said, swinging her bag over her shoulder.

Nikoleta, who would have far preferred it to have been Lewis who was offering the lift, rose to her feet with much less enthusiasm.

The bench seat in the truck's cab seated three people, but only at a pinch. As Helmut opened the truck's passenger door, Daphne climbed in first, determined to be seated in the middle, in order that she would be thigh-to-thigh with Helmut.

As she had known it would be, it was a very arousing experience.

He slammed the truck into gear and, as they sped out of the village and bucketed across the plateau towards the dirt road leading away from it, she knew he was as taut with sexual tension as she was.

She closed her eyes. There had been a time when it would never have occurred to her to be unfaithful to Sholto; but a month ago he hadn't been unfaithful to her with Deirdre Holbeck-Pratchett. She needed to do what she was about to do, in order to inflict on Sholto the same pain he had inflicted on her. As far as she was concerned, that way the continuation of their marriage would at least be starting from a level playing field.

'I do not like the winter,' Nikoleta said half an hour later, as they reached the road leading north-east towards Archanes. 'I do not see why Lewis always returns to Scotland for weeks in the winter.'

'Presumably he returns for the same reason I go back to Germany. He returns because it is his home.' There was nothing in Helmut's voice to indicate the effect that the pressure of Daphne's body against his was having on him. Ever since they had left Kalamata he had refused to allow his eyes to meet hers in his driving mirror. To have done so would have been to risk driving the truck off the road.

From Archanes to Knossos, Helmut continued making small talk with Nikoleta about local things. Of how Rhea and Angelos Mamalakis were finally about to become parents; of how, when the palace dig finally came to an end, a new wing would have to be added to the Heraklion Museum, in order to cope with all the precious artefacts that had been found.

They sped past the entrance to the Palace of Minos and, a few hundred yards further on, drew up outside the Kourakises' cottage.

'Will I see you tomorrow?' Nikoleta asked Daphne, before jumping down from the cab.

'Maybe tomorrow evening, but during the day I'm going to be working on the site with Kate and Ella.' Although Daphne now had room enough to put a little space between her and Helmut, she didn't do so.

'Oh, the site – always it is the site.' Nikoleta had long ago lost enthusiasm for the site at Kalamata. Before its discovery, her relationship with Lewis had been exciting and full of the hope of an engagement. Now, because he was always at Kalamata and only rarely at Knossos, she did not see him as often and, when she did, her hopes of an engagement only grew fainter, not stronger.

Helmut waited until a disconsolate Nikoleta had bypassed a tethered goat and had closed the door of the house behind her and then he said abruptly, his voice thick with tension, 'Which hotel?'

'The Astoria.'

She laid her hand on his thigh. 'Drive fast.'

He covered the three miles of narrow road in under four minutes.

Chapter Twenty-Two

MARCH 1939

The temperature in Cairo was seventy-two degrees Fahrenheit: hot, but not yet unbearably so. Daphne was seated in a wicker chair on the shaded terrace of Shepheard's Hotel in the centre of the city, waiting for Sholto to join her for lunch. That it was Sholto who had been posted to the British Embassy in Cairo, and not Toby Holbeck-Pratchett, had pleased her enormously. It had been one in the eye for Deirdre, who, Daphne knew, had been much looking forward to Cairo; and Egypt had the wonderful advantage of being only a sea crossing from Crete.

Pulsating and exciting, Cairo was a city she had immediately felt at home in. There was a crazy energy about it that suited her personality. Although Egypt was no longer a British Protectorate, Britain still had the right to intervene in Egyptian affairs if her interests were threatened, and large swathes of the city were as much British as they were Arab.

The diplomatic community either lived in Garden City, close to the British Embassy, or at Zamalek, which was situated on an island in the Nile and had the advantage of being within a stone's throw of Cairo's exclusive Gezira Sporting Club. The large, airy house she and Sholto had moved into was at the far end of one of Zamalek's broad boulevards. From her bedroom windows, Daphne could see the white sails of feluccas navigating the Nile and, when the breeze was in the right direction, hear the cheers from the Sporting Club's stands when a six was scored at cricket.

The terrace at Shepheard's looked out onto a busy street and, for most people seated on it, that only added to its attraction. It was fun to wave to friends trundling past in horse-drawn gharries; to notice who was being accompanied by whom in a smart diplomatic motor-car; to watch the antics of the monkey seated on the shoe-shiner's shoulder at the foot of the steps leading on to the terrace.

It was also quite acceptable for a woman to be seated at a table unaccompanied, as she waited to be joined by a woman friend or, as this was Cairo and not much shocked anyone, a man friend.

A taxi swerved to a halt in front of the hotel and a friend of Daphne's stepped from it, accompanied by a spruce-looking gentleman wearing the uniform of a British brigadier. Lady Vanessa Dane was married to a high-ranking government official and held a senior position in the St John Ambulance Brigade. Mindful of fast-thickening war clouds, Daphne had joined the St John Ambulance Brigade in London and, when she had arrived in Cairo, Vanessa had been one of the first friends she had made.

As Vanessa crossed the terrace with her escort, she dropped Daphne a wink. Daphne knew exactly what the wink signified. It meant that Vanessa was embarking on a new love affair.

Daphne lit a cigarette and blew a plume of blue smoke into the air, well aware that to have been in Cairo for three months and still have no lover labelled her as being something of a slouch.

She didn't care. Her experience with Helmut had taught her a lesson. Extramarital sex was explosively dangerous. She hadn't thought it would be, because it had never occurred to her that she wouldn't be in total control of the situation. How could she not be, when it was to be a one-off with a man she need never meet again, if she didn't want to? When the dig was over, Helmut would disappear to another dig: one in Iraq, or Syria, or Persia. He wasn't a friend of Sholto. He wasn't in their social circle, or even on the fringes of it. What repercussions to a one-night stand or, as it had turned out to be, a one-day stand could there possibly be? In retrospect, the sexual electricity between the two of them should have told her exactly what kind of repercussions there could be, but Daphne had been so determined to pay Sholto back in his own coin that she had been blind to them.

She chewed the corner of her lip, thinking back to the moment when, with a screech of tyres, Helmut had brought the truck to a halt outside Heraklion's Astoria Hotel. They had run across the pavement into the foyer and she had asked for her room key, without even attempting to explain Helmut's presence. In the slow, creaky lift he had pulled her into his arms and kissed her deeply. Then it had been another sprint along a corridor to her room. When they reached it, he had kicked the door shut behind them and then, without even pausing to remove all her clothes or his, or to make it to the bed, he had made love to her on the hard floor.

It had been lovemaking that was as violent as a battle.

The second time, naked and in bed, had been different. Like Sholto, Helmut was an accomplished lover and this time he made love to her with careful expertise, as well as raw need. Her response had been total – so utterly without restraints of any kind, mental and emotional as well as physical, that she'd forgotten all about her reason for being in bed with him. Sholto might just as well have not existed. All that mattered was Helmut and the all-engulfing pleasure he was giving her.

It was only later that, still in each other's arms, exhausted and sheened with sweat, he'd said with great depth of feeling, 'I knew making love to you would be like this, *mein Liebling*. I knew it would not be for once, or for just a few days. I knew it would begin something serious for me.' Then finally, and at long last, warning sirens had exploded in Daphne's head.

Even now, thinking about that moment, her stomach tightened. Her cheek had been pressed against his strongly muscled chest and she had made a sudden, decisive movement, breaking free of his arms and pushing herself up against the pillows.

'It can't be something serious,' she'd said, panic-stricken at how very easily it could be. 'I'm in love with Sholto. We have a much better marriage than most people I know. And there is Caspian. I would never risk Sholto having grounds to divorce me and suing for custody of Caspian.'

Helmut had sat up with even more suddenness than she had. 'Then why this?' he'd demanded. 'I thought it was because you knew, from your last visit, the effect you had on me and that you now felt the same about me. If this was just a one-off holiday adventure, then I need to know, because it wasn't a one-off holiday adventure for me!'

She'd swung her legs from the bed and reached for the kimono she used as a dressing gown. Rising to her feet, knowing that he deserved an explanation, she'd wrapped it around herself and turned to face him. 'I love Sholto,' she'd said, 'but when I was in the final months of my pregnancy with Caspian, he did something I've found very hard to forgive.'

'He had an affair?'

She'd nodded and said, 'It's over now. The woman in question wasn't important to him. But I just wanted to . . . needed to . . .'

'Even up the score?' His face had drained white beneath his suntan. 'Well, you've certainly achieved that.' He'd vaulted to his feet and had begun dressing with sharp, angry movements. 'I'm glad I was so useful to you. I'd like to say I was lying, when I said I'd thought making love to you would be the beginning of something serious for me, but I wasn't.' He'd zipped up his trousers and pulled his shirt on over his head. Tucking it into his trousers, he'd said savagely, 'Now I know how women feel when they say a man used them. *I* feel used! And, *Gott im Himmel*, it is not a good feeling.'

She'd said unsteadily, 'Although at first I had an ulterior motive for wanting you to make love to me, once it started – and even before, when we were still at Kalamata – that motive no longer even entered my head. From the moment I stepped into the truck, everything that has taken place between us has, for me, been genuine and true.' A sob had risen in her throat and she'd choked it down. 'And because it's been genuine and true, and for all the reasons I've already given, it can't continue, no matter how much I may want it to.'

The depth of her sincerity and distress was palpable.

Helmut had said, sensing she wasn't going to change her mind, 'Then if all we have is today, *meine Liebe*, let us at least have the full day together.'

She had known what her answer should be, but she hadn't had the willpower to say it. Instead, when he'd stepped towards her, she had entered his arms like an arrow entering the gold, overcome by the vast, unspeakable relief that there were still hours and hours before the day was over.

'More coffee, Madame?' asked a waiter wearing a tasselled fez.

Daphne glanced down at her watch. Sholto was now ten minutes late, but she knew from experience that he wouldn't be much longer.

'No, thank you,' she said, and as the waiter turned away to attend to another table, Sholto emerged from the crowd of pedestrians on Ibrahim Pasha Street and took the steps leading to the terrace two at a time.

Her heart flipped. Vanessa was welcome to her brigadier. Her marriage to Sholto had its tensions and wasn't quite as she had envisioned, but then all marriages had their difficulties. She knew, from reading between the lines in Ella and Kate's letters to her, that Ella's marriage wasn't entirely problem-free. She was also certain that, like her, Ella wasn't going to allow the problems to destabilize her marriage.

Where her own marriage was concerned, it was Helmut who had the power to wreck it and so, while Helmut was still on Crete, she wasn't going to visit again. Exerting a great deal of willpower, she did not, in her letters to Kate and Ella, ask for news of him.

'Sorry I'm late, Daphs.'

As she rose to her feet, Sholto kissed her on the cheek and then, pushing Helmut firmly to the back of her mind, Daphne slipped her hand into the crook of his arm and walked with him into the hotel's deliciously cool, Moorish-decorated dining room.

Ella stared at Christos in despair. 'But a house in Archanes would be perfect for us! With two of us working, we could afford the rent and . . .'

'No,' he said emphatically for the third time. 'No. It is customary for a man of my village to live with his wife in the family home, at least until a child is on the way. For us to move out now would be to hurt my mother's feelings.'

They were sitting on a large boulder a little distance from the excavation site, sharing a lunch of rolls, cold lamb and olives. A hundred yards away everyone else was taking their lunch break communally. Only if their conversation developed into a full-scale row would anyone overhear them.

Determined not to let it develop into a full-scale row, Ella said, keeping exasperation out of her voice with difficulty, 'I think Eleni understands that because I am English, our marriage will not always be like other local marriages. Archanes is only a fifteen-minute drive from Knossos, and it is a pretty house, Christos. It has a little courtyard and there is a cypress tree in it for shade and . . .'

'No!' He cut across her yet again, running a hand despairingly through his pelt of curls. 'What is it you do not understand about how wives should behave? Surely even in Yorkshire wives do not argue back to their husbands?'

Well aware that in Yorkshire there were countless wives who would have received very short shrift, if they had tried arguing back, and also knowing that there were many other wives – like her mother – whose views, reasonably expressed, often changed their husband's way of thinking, Ella said, 'In a good marriage, and when the wife has a sensible point to make, they do.'

'That is not the case here, in Crete.' His trousers were tucked into the tops of his knee-high boots, and beneath an unbuttoned waistcoat his shirt sleeves were rolled up to his elbows, revealing forearms brown and knotted with lean muscle. Christos reached into one of his waistcoat pockets for the small block of cheese he always carried with him. He broke it into pieces and offered her one of them. It was his way of being conciliatory.

Aware of it, Ella accepted a piece and said, 'Think how much more room your parents and Nikoleta would have, if we were to move out. Nikoleta would be pleased as Punch.'

'Punch?' Christos's eyebrows flew together in immediate suspicion. 'Who is this Punch? I do not know him.'

Not wanting to be sidetracked into a long explanation, Ella said, 'He's a popular British seaside wooden puppet. About the house at Archanes, Christos. At least come with me to look at it.'

'No.' As mulishly stubborn as he had been about not accompanying her to Yorkshire in order that he could meet her family, he rose to his feet, saying on a note of finality, 'And when we do move into a house of our own, I will be the one to find it. And when I find it, it will not be in Archanes.'

He walked off, expecting her to hurry after him. Ella didn't do so. What she would have done, if there had been a suitable object to hand, was throw something at him in utter exasperation. The little house at Archanes was perfect for them. The plumbing was basic, but she had been brought up with plumbing that was basic. It was near enough to the Kourakis family home for them to be in almost constant touch, and far enough away for them to have much-needed privacy. Making love in a room sandwiched just thin walls from where Nikoleta, Kostas and Eleni slept was so inhibiting that she felt hot with embarrassment, just thinking about it. It would all be so different in a little home of their own, and she couldn't for the life of her understand why Christos didn't realize that.

She chewed the corner of her lip. Perhaps what was needed was for her to go on strike in the bedroom. If that didn't make Christos change his mind about their having a house of their own, nothing would.

Christos was now a good forty yards away from her and, aware that she wasn't, as he had expected, about to run up to his side, he came to a halt and turned round, spreading his hands out expressively. 'Why aren't you with me?' he shouted. 'It's lonely walking on my own.'

He looked so bewildered that much as she would like to have held on to her exasperation, she couldn't do so. Brushing crumbs from her lap, she rose to her feet.

His face split into a wide grin.

The fact that, after they had been at odds with each other, his sunny nature always reasserted itself so speedily was one of the things Ella most loved about him. Exasperating as he was, she loved him in a way she knew she could never love anyone else, and she could no more imagine living without Christos than she could imagine flying to the moon.

She broke into a run. Making love in the Kourakis family home wasn't ideal, but it was a thousand times better than their not making love at all. As she hurtled into his arms, she was confident that it wouldn't be long before he saw the sense of having a home of their own. The bedroom regime she was about to instigate would see to that.

Together with Kate, Lewis walked out of the Archaeological Museum in Heraklion and across to the side street where he had parked the truck. Their meeting with the museum's curator and board of directors had gone well. With Europe so clearly on the verge of being set to the torch, they were just as passionately anxious as he and Kate that all the artefacts found at Kalamata, both at the palace and in the cave, should be stored in absolute safety.

Kate opened the passenger door of the truck, saying, 'Now Hitler has marched into Czechoslovakia without a finger being lifted to prevent him, is he likely to believe that Poland will be any different, if he attempts the same thing there?'

'He may hope so. Why shouldn't he, when Britain and France have let him get away with so much?' He put the truck into gear and pulled away from the kerb. 'Where Poland is concerned, though, he'll be making a huge mistake. Even Chamberlain has realized that no further compromises are possible. The pledge to defend Poland is a pledge Britain will keep.'

He had come to value the occasions when she accompanied

him on site business. He enjoyed the conversations they had on archaeology and the disastrous state of world politics. Their conversation never turned to anything personal. The fierce physical attraction he felt for her was something he kept under tight control. He'd had one rebuff, although as he'd been drunk when he'd kissed her, it was a rebuff he'd deserved; and, until he'd resolved the awkward nature of his relationship with Nikoleta, he was in no position to try his luck with Kate a second time.

He drove down the street named after Sir Arthur Evans and through the gate in the city walls leading out on to the Knossos road. When he came to the Fortetsa turn-off he took it, saying, 'Kit will be at the new tomb site and I want to have a word with him. I'm interested in what his plans are, for when the balloon goes up.'

What he really wanted to know was whether, as Kit Shelton's knowledge of Greek was equal to his own, he too had been interviewed by Julian Kermode, in an unprepossessing White-hall room.

The new necropolis site, still only in its early stages, was a couple of miles south-west of Fortetsa village and as they bumped over rough ground towards it, they could see against the banked earth a giant chamber tomb completely exposed and, a little distance from it, a handful of men shovelling and sifting earth as they dug down towards another one.

Kit was overseeing the dig, with a small scruffy dog of indeterminate parentage by his side. Further away, near where the Sally was parked, Nikoleta was perched on a camp stool, brushing three thousand years of compacted earth from a large burial jar. It was a task that needed carrying out with great care. By the look of it, that was exactly what Nikoleta was doing, but it still disturbed him that Kit was allowing her to be so hands-on with a jar that only a qualified archaeologist should have been handling.

As they come to a dusty halt, Kit turned his head towards them, Nikoleta dropped the brush she had been using and jumped to her feet, and the dog bounded towards them, barking furiously.

'Tinker's okay,' Kit called out, walking up to them. 'It's happy barking. He likes visitors.'

Lewis hadn't thought the barking to be anything other than happy, especially as the dog was now licking the back of his hand.

'Who does Tinker belong to?' He put an end to the licking by giving the dog a friendly pat.

'No one.' Nikoleta had joined them. 'He's a stray. He comes here because there's food.'

Her disparaging tone of voice reminded him that the British attitude to dogs was far more indulgent than that of the average Cretan. 'Sensible dog,' Lewis said, knowing it was only due to Kit that Tinker wasn't scavenging Fortetsa's waste tips in order to stay alive; and then, to Kit, 'Kate and I have just left the museum. The curator went to great lengths to assure us the building is relatively earthquake-proof. Hopefully that might go for bombs too, should there be any.'

'It needs to be earthquake-resilient in a country as earthquake-prone as Crete, but why should Heraklion be bombed? It's Poland Hitler is threatening. Not Greece.'

'Yes, you're right,' he said easily. 'There's no sense my making the scenario worse than it already is.' He was no longer wondering if Kit had had an interview with Julian Kermode, for he so very clearly hadn't. 'What will you do, when push comes to shove? Stay on here, or join up?'

'I shall join up.' They began walking in the direction of the camp kitchen, where folding canvas chairs were conveniently scattered. Tinker saw a rabbit and, his welcome duties at an end, raced excitedly after it. 'As I have a background of Eton and Oxford, I imagine I'll be earmarked for officers' training. What about you?'

'Pretty much the same thing.' Having found out what he'd wanted to find out, Lewis changed the subject. 'Is the cemetery here the same age as the one at Fortetsa?'

'No. The tomb we've found is much earlier.' Just as Kit began explaining his reasons for thinking so, there came noise of a disturbance from the far side of the site where the ground rose into a rocky hillock.

Glad of the distraction, Lewis said, 'I think someone's found something.'

'I shouldn't think so – not there.' Kit shaded his eyes against the sun. Some of the men, all of whom had been standing in a circle looking down at the ground, began walking back to the tomb they'd been in the process of uncovering. One of them called out, 'It's no problem, Kyrie Shelton! The dog has fallen down a hole – that is all!'

Kit rose to his feet in alarm. 'Is he still in it?'

The man nodded. 'Yes! A long way down. Too far to be reached.'

Kit swore and broke into a sprint, Lewis and Kate hard behind him.

The boulder-strewn hillock was deceptive, for though on the near side the rise was gentle, the far side plunged steeply. Beyond the plunge were the olive groves and vineyards of the people of Fortetsa. At any other time it would have been a view to be enjoyed. Now, though, all Lewis had eyes for was the gap running part of the way between the base of one of the giant boulders and the ground. Coming from it was faint, frantic barking.

Kit fell on his knees, thrusting his arms as far inside the gap as he could reach. 'I can't feel anything. Just empty space!'

One of the workmen said unhelpfully, 'It is always the same, when dogs fall into holes such as this one. They go straight down and the dogs cannot scramble out. There is nothing that can be done.'

'There must be!' Kate's eyes were wide with horror. 'We can't leave him to starve to death in the dark.'

'What else is there to do?' Nikoleta had joined them. 'This kind of thing happens. Dogs chase rabbits into holes, and sometimes the hole is not a rabbit-hole.'

Still on his knees, Kit turned a white face to where Lewis was standing, a foot or so away from him. 'What can we do, Lewis? How the hell are we going to get him out?'

It was something Lewis had been thinking about ever since they had reached the boulder. Turning to one of the workmen, he said, 'When a sheep gets trapped, can the shepherd judge how far it's fallen by the faintness of its bleat?'

'Of course, *Kyrie*. My father is a shepherd and always he can tell.'

'Can you tell? From the sound of its barking, can you tell how far down the dog is?'

The man listened to Tinker's pathetic barking attentively and then said, 'Fifty feet, *Kyrie*. Maybe a little more.'

Lewis turned back to Kit. 'Do you have cordoning-off rope on-site?'

'Yes, but . . . ?'

'Then get it. I'll slide through the gap and you can lower me down to him.'

Kit clambered to his feet, dizzy with relief at having a plan of action. 'Let me go down! My shoulders are narrower than yours. Getting through the gap will be easier for me than for you.' He took off his horn-rimmed glasses, signalling how ready he was to launch himself on a rescue mission.

Hideous as the situation was, Lewis felt a flash of amusement. Kit possessed a lot of admirable qualities, but gung-ho recklessness wasn't one of them. 'Thanks for the offer, but I don't imagine you've done much potholing or mountain-climbing. I have.'

Nikoleta stared at Lewis as if he had lost his mind. 'You cannot mean to do this thing! You may become trapped. The rope may break. To risk your life for a dog is craziness. It is not even your dog. It is no one's dog.'

He looked at her for a long moment, aware that something had finally ended for him, and then he said, his voice raw, 'It is a dog that doesn't deserve a long, terrifying death, if he can be saved from it. That's why I'm doing it, Nikoleta. And I'm sorry you don't understand that.'

To Kit he said, 'Fetch the cordoning-off rope and a torch – and get the other workmen back here.'

To Kate, he said, 'Find a sack Tinker can be hauled up in.'

As Kit and Kate set off at a run to do as he'd asked, Nikoleta said yet again, 'But the dog isn't yours, Lewis! And although Kit is happy for it to run around on the site, it isn't his dog, either. It has no value – not even the value of a sheep or a goat. Why are you and Kit and Kate making so much fuss about it?'

It was a question he had answered once and had no intention of answering again.

Aware that he was no longer listening to her, Nikoleta erupted explosively, 'A Cretan would not do what you are going to do. A Cretan would have more sense.' And she spun on her heel, heading in the direction of the Sally.

He didn't go after her.

Thirty minutes later, Lewis was being lowered into the hole. He had a torch in one of his pockets, and a sack to put Tinker in was shoved down his shirt front. One end of a long coil of rope was attached to his right wrist; the end of another coil of rope was knotted around his waist. The rope attached to his wrist was held at the other end by Kit's foreman and was the rope Tinker would be hauled up by. The rope around his waist was the one that was his lifeline, and which Kit and his workmen were paying out, inch by inch.

With movement above him, Tinker's barking grew enthusiastic.

Lewis fervently hoped Tinker's expectations were going to be justified, for the hole, small at the outset, was growing increasingly narrow. His shoulder hit the side and a scattering of loose stone and earth showered down. Fearful of causing an avalanche that would bury Tinker, and might cause the upper sides of the hole to weaken and cave in on top of both of them, Lewis gave a jerk on the rope, indicating that he wanted a temporary halt.

'Are you okay, Lewis?' Kit's voice was fraught with tension.

'Yes!' he shouted back. 'Just give it a minute.'

Tinker was now yelping, but as far as Lewis was concerned, a sound of any kind from the dog was a good sign.

There was no further fall of loose stone and he gave another jerk on the rope to signal that lowering could start again.

Slowly but surely he neared Tinker; then finally, with swamping relief, his feet touched damp solidity and, in the inky blackness, Tinker jumped into his arms, licking his face, overjoyed at having company.

Lewis got his torch out of his pocket and, by its light, managed to get an uncooperative Tinker into the sack and tie the top tightly, with the length of rope that had been attached to his wrist. He then gave the rope a tug to indicate that Tinker was ready for his journey to the surface.

Tinker went up a lot more quickly than he, Lewis, had come down.

When he heard cheering, he stuffed the torch back into his pocket and gave a sharp tug on the rope.

'Ready, Lewis?' Kit yelled down to him.

'Ready!' he shouted back.

Fifteen minutes later, several pairs of hands were hauling him through the gap into brilliant sunshine. He stood up, pushing the hair out of his eyes, his face and clothes streaked with sweat and dirt. A miraculously unhurt Tinker raced towards him, skittering around his ankles. Kit threw an arm around his shoulders. Members of the work team – all of whom had earlier shown little interest in Tinker's plight – clustered around him, shaking his hand and slapping him on the back.

Only one person remained outside the congratulatory circle, and that was Kate.

And Kate was the only person he wanted to be with.

Pausing only to say to Kit, 'Get the men to block the gap', Lewis broke free of the crush and walked swiftly towards her. The agonizing tension she had been under still showed on her face and he felt his heart tighten within his chest. She had cared about his safety; had cared about it to the extent that, although now vastly relieved, her face was still drained of colour.

She said unsteadily, 'That was a very long half-hour.'

'Half an hour?' His eyes smiled into hers in a way he had never allowed them to do before. 'It felt like half a day.'

'If you're looking for Nikoleta, she's gone back to Knossos.'

'I'm not looking for Nikoleta. The person I most wanted to see, when I stepped back into the sunlight, wasn't Nikoleta. It was you.'

She drew in her breath and he said, with a different expression in his eyes now, an expression she couldn't possibly mistake, 'There's a lot I want to say to you, Kate, and it can't be said in front of an audience. Let's go back to Kalamata – that is, if you don't mind being trapped in the truck's cab with someone in my filthy condition?'

'No.' Colour was edging fast into her face. 'No, I don't mind.'

Both of them were aware that something profound and irrevocable was changing between them.

'Let's go,' he said, and as they turned to walk together towards the truck, he slid his arm around her shoulders, pulling her close against him.

There was a brief second when he felt her almost stop breathing and then she leaned into him, sliding her arm around his waist.

It was a good feeling.

It was the most stunningly good feeling he'd had for a long, long time.

Chapter Twenty-Three

It was early morning on the third of September and Kate's thoughts, like that of every other British subject, were on whatever messages were being passed between Prime Minister Neville Chamberlain and Chancellor Adolf Hitler. In May, Hitler and Mussolini had signed what was being called a 'Pact of Steel'. The Italian army had occupied Greece's next-door neighbour, Albania. Despite Britain and France's pledge to defend Poland if Germany attacked her, Hitler had continued to threaten Poland.

Two days earlier he had acted, his armies storming across the Polish frontier, his air force destroying the Polish railway system and shooting the Polish air force out of the sky.

If Britain was to honour its pledge to defend Poland – and it was unthinkable that it wouldn't – then they were living through the last few hours of peace. Determined to make the most of them, Lewis had suggested that he and Kate take a picnic and their swimming things and drive westwards along the coast road in the direction of Canea and Kastelli.

'I'd like to have a second look at the ground around Suda Bay and the airfield at Maleme,' he'd said, 'and this may be my last chance before leaving for Cairo.'

Cairo was where he had been ordered to report for a crash course in Special Operations training, the minute war was declared. After that, he would return to Crete, without the

Greek authorities having known he'd left. Where Germany and Italy were concerned, Greece was struggling to remain neutral, and Lewis's cover – his being an archaeologist with legitimate business in Crete – was essential if he was to successfully carry out his task of secretly organizing resistance groups in case of a German, or Italian, invasion.

They had been lying in bed in the house in Kalamata village that Lewis had, at one time, shared with Christos and Helmut. Since Christos and Ella had moved into their own home in Archanes, and since Helmut had agreed to help Dimitri and Aminta Mamalakis financially by moving in with them as a lodger, the house was one Kate often visited. When she did, she did so discreetly, knowing how unhappy any gossip about her would make Andre and Agata.

Her own moral standards hadn't changed. She was twenty-six and losing her virginity had seemed quite reasonable to her, especially when it was to a man she was so seriously in love with, and whom she had known for more than three years.

She'd dropped a kiss on to his naked shoulder. 'When do you want to leave for Suda Bay and Maleme?' she'd asked.

'Now,' he'd said decisively. 'Don't bother making the picnic. We'll buy bread, cheese and wine en route.'

The road to Suda Bay was narrow, full of potholes and frequently clogged by sheep and donkeys – the donkeys being ridden by peasant women sitting sideways, feet dangling. West of Réthymnon wasn't a part of Crete that Kate knew well, and with the windows of the truck as far down as they would go, she enjoyed the views as the road first hugged the coast, then deviated inland for several miles, giving spectacular views of the fabled White Mountains, and then dipped back to the coast to run along the side of the gigantic bay. Longer than it was wide, the bay was overlooked on all three sides by gentle hills.

It was the hills that interested Lewis – the hills and the access points to them and the cover they gave. The truck was used to rough country, and Kate was used to being bucketed about in it. There were stops for photographs; stops while Lewis took notes. Then it was on to Maleme, where Lewis unobtrusively took another sheaf of photographs, both of the airfield itself and of the ground surrounding it.

At last he said, with the smile that used to be so rare, but was now, when he was with Kate, so frequent: 'Duty done, I think.' He rested his hand on her bare leg. 'Let's find a beach.'

It didn't take them long. Akrotiri, the peninsula that formed the north side of the bay, was full of secluded coves of glistening white sand, and hand-in-hand they scrambled down to one of them. As they swam, picnicked and made love, it seemed impossible to believe that twenty-five years after the outbreak of what had been believed to be the war to end all wars – and thanks to Hitler – Europe was poised once again on the edge of chaos and horror.

As they lay, their bodies entwined on the sand, Lewis looked at his watch. By now Hitler must either have acceded to the ultimatums Chamberlain would have sent over the last forty-eight hours, demanding that he cease hostilities against Poland, or ignored them. And if he'd ignored them, then Britain could now be at war with Germany.

In the curve of his arm, Kate was asleep. He looked down at her, knowing he loved her in a way he had never come close to loving Nikoleta. It was Nikoleta's physical likeness to Sophie that had mesmerized him and been the reason he had so enjoyed being with her. A brother-and-sister relationship had not, though, been what Nikoleta had wanted; and there had been a time when Lewis, too, had thought romance a reasonable next step in their friendship. By the time he realized it wasn't, her family and village had all assumed he was going to marry her. Cretan honour had been at stake and, knowing he was responsible, his own sense of honour had come into play. Only the relationship that Nikoleta had struck up with Kit had saved him from making what would have been the biggest mistake of his life.

He wasn't making a mistake now. For the first time in long years, his personal life was as rewarding and as uncomplicated as his professional life. What had annoyed him when they had first met – the way Kate had capitalized on being Kit's sister, in order to get herself a position on a Minoan dig – now amused him. He was honest enough to admit that if he'd been in her position, he would have done exactly the same thing. As well as her ambition, he loved lots of other things about her. He loved the beauty of her high-cheekboned face; the heavy, shiny swing of her hair; the intelligence in her eyes. He loved her innate self-confidence; her generous nature; her caring heart.

It had been her caring heart that had been the defining moment for him: her reaction when Tinker was barking frantically from the bottom of the hole, compared to Nikoleta's reaction. It had been then that he'd known Nikoleta would never again remind him of Sophie. Sophie would have been as incapable of Nikoleta's fatalistic reaction as Kate had been.

Now he shook Kate's shoulder gently, saying, 'Wake up, Kate. We need to be back at Villa Ariadne, listening in to the BBC.'

Accepting the inevitable, she rose to her feet, knowing they were lucky. War would part hundreds of thousands of couples, but although Lewis would leave immediately for Cairo, he would soon be back in Crete. The same couldn't be said for Helmut and Kit. Goodbyes would have to be said, and saying them wouldn't be easy.

*

The drawing room at the Villa Ariadne was full of tense, silent people. The focus of attention for all of them was the room's wireless. The announcement they were waiting for wasn't long in coming.

'The Prime Minister will now broadcast to the nation. Please stand by.'

Kit shot a look towards the Squire. He was standing in front of one of the room's glass-fronted bookcases, his arms folded, face grave.

Mrs Hutchinson, who had been knitting as they had waited, laid down her knitting and clasped her hands tightly together in her lap. Some of the archaeologists from the British School who were crowding the room put out their cigarettes; others lit them. All of them were between the ages of eighteen and forty-one. All of them would find themselves fighting in one capacity or another, if war was declared.

Intermittent reception ratcheted up the tension. There was a lot of static. Then, as it mercifully cleared, Mr Chamberlain's voice came clearly over the airwaves: 'This morning,' he said slowly, his voice heavy with the burden of his message, 'the British Ambassador in Berlin handed the German Government a final note stating that, unless we heard from them by eleven o'clock that they were prepared at once to withdraw their troops from Poland, a state of war exists between us.'

The pause that followed seemed, to Kit, to go on forever.

The finger of history lay heavy on the room.

'I have to tell you now,' Mr Chamberlain continued sombrely, 'that no such undertaking has been received, and that consequently this country is at war with Germany.'

Mrs Hutchinson gave an anguished cry.

'About bloody time, too!' someone said explosively.

'Shut up and listen to what else he has to say,' someone from the British School snapped, their nerves raw.

'We and France,' Mr Chamberlain continued, 'are today, in fulfilment of our obligations, going to the aid of Poland, who is so bravely resisting this wicked and unprovoked attack on her people. We have a clear conscience. We have done all that any country could do to establish peace . . .'

Kit didn't wait to hear any more. He'd heard all he needed to hear, and he wanted to be on his own. Leaving the room, he made his way up to the Villa Ariadne's flat roof and lit a cigarette. The die was cast. The world had changed. Nothing would be quite the same ever again.

He leaned over the balustrade, occasionally flicking ash onto the terrace below. He would do what he had told Lewis he would do. He would return to England and apply for officers' training. The thought made the muscles in the pit of his stomach clench. He wasn't a coward, but the thought of killing another human being was so abhorrent to him that he couldn't imagine ever doing it.

And then there was Nikoleta. Once he left Crete to serve his country, there was no telling when he would see her again. Would she marry him, if he asked her? With her hopes of marrying Lewis now at an end, he rather thought she would. Until now he had always thought it was what he wanted, but in a moment of blinding clarity he knew Nikoleta would never be the right sort of wife for the kind of marriage he needed. No matter how hard he tried, she would physically want from him far more than he could give. She would be unhappy – and so would he.

Now that push had come to shove, and he had to either marry in haste or not marry at all, he knew with utter certainty what it was he must do – or rather, what it was he must not do.

He ground out his cigarette and glanced down at his watch. Kate, Ella, Lewis, Christos and Helmut had all been conspicuously absent from the gathering in the drawing room – Helmut, for obvious reasons. Kit didn't know where he would find Kate and Lewis, but he rather thought he'd find Helmut at Ella and Christos's little house in Archanes. The house didn't possess a wireless and so someone needed to tell them all the news; and that someone might just as well be him.

'*Für die Liebe Christus!*' Helmut brought his fist down so hard on Ella's wooden kitchen table that crockery on the dresser behind him rattled. 'It needn't have come to this. And now, because Hitler doesn't know when to stop, Germany is at war with Britain and France.'

'What will you do?'

Helmut's eyes met Kit's. 'Do?' he demanded, despair in his voice. 'I will do what you will no doubt do. My country is now at war, and I shall return to it in order to fight in its defence.'

'Against Britain and France?'

'Yes. *Jesus Gott*, Kit! It is Britain and France who have declared war on Germany. It is not the other way around. What else can I do but fight for my country?'

Kit wanted to shout at him that he could be a pacifist; that as he was living and working in a neutral country, Helmut could remain living and working in a neutral country. He didn't, because he knew such suggestions would fall on deaf ears. Helmut was not the stuff that pacifists were made of, and neither was he the kind of man to sit a war out in safety.

Christos put a bottle of raki and glasses on the table. Pouring the raki into the glasses, he said with a gravitas that sat oddly on him, 'Friends cannot become enemies just because their countries are enemies. Between us – and between us and Kate and Lewis – there will always be friendship. If it were not so, it would be a crime against heaven.'

It was something they all – even Ella – affirmed by knocking the fiery spirit straight back. Ella said, her eyes watering from its effects, 'I don't know where Kate and Lewis are, but I'm certain they'll be with us soon. I'll make something to eat while we wait for them.'

They were halfway through a meal of lamb rissoles flavoured with herbs and served with rice when there came the sound of the truck rumbling to a halt outside.

Helmut pushed his chair away from the table. Facing Lewis when, because of Hitler's invasion of a peaceful Poland, Britain had had no alternative but to go to war was going to be one of the most difficult things he'd ever had to do. He felt ashamed – not of his country, he could never be that – but of the Nazi dictatorship governing it.

The first thing Lewis said when he walked with Kate into the house was, 'We've just left Villa Ariadne. We've heard the news.'

Helmut rose to his feet.

Christos set another two glasses on the table and poured more raki.

Kit took off his spectacles and pinched the bridge of his nose. 'Then you'll know it's goodbye time. There's no telling for how long travel across Europe is going to be possible and so I'm not going to waste any time. We'll be leaving for England tomorrow.'

'We?' Lewis looked at him questioningly. 'You're taking Nikoleta with you?'

Kit flushed. 'No.' He avoided looking in Christos's direction. 'But at a time like this, Kate will want to be in England . . .'

'But I don't.' When they had entered the room, Kate had walked over to Ella and they were standing in front of the room's stone sink, their arms linked. 'I'm going to remain in Crete.' As she saw her brother about to object, she added firmly,

'Greece isn't at war. I'm safe here, and as the Luftwaffe will soon be dropping bombs on London and on towns near to the coast, such as Canterbury, it makes sense for me to remain here. The parents won't expect me to return and will have far fewer anxieties about me if I don't.'

The image she had conjured up of bombing raids on civilian targets was so nightmarish that for a long moment no one spoke. Then Helmut said tautly, the skin tight across his cheekbones, 'And the RAF will soon be dropping bombs on German towns.'

Kit pushed his chair sharply away from the table and rose to his feet. 'I can't stand this any longer. I'm going to say my goodbyes now. Keep safe, Helmut. Technically you may now be an enemy, but that is never how I will think of you.'

Visibly moved, Helmut said thickly, 'Nor I you, Kit.'

To Christos, Kit said, 'That I am not taking Nikoleta with me is for the best, Christos. I wouldn't have been able to make her happy. I'll be telling her so myself, before I board the ferry to Piraeus.'

He said goodbye to Ella and kissed Kate on her temple, a mark of brotherly affection that she could never remember him having shown before. 'I'll give your love to the parents,' he said gruffly. 'Look after Tinker for me.'

To Lewis he said simply, 'Look after Kate.'

And then, without looking back, he walked out of the house.

Helmut broke the silence that followed. 'I, too, must now leave.' Turning to Christos, he said, 'Don't get into trouble in my absence, you rascal.'

Inches taller than Christos, he ruffled the Cretan's hair, gave both Ella and Kate a goodbye kiss on the cheek and finally turned to Lewis.

'And so it is goodbye to you as well, *mein Freund*. By this time tomorrow I will be halfway to Italy and a train back to Germany.'

Overcome with emotion, they hugged each other hard.

'Till we meet again,' Lewis said as they broke apart. 'Good luck, Helmut. Stay safe.'

'And you, too, Lewis. *Auf Wiedersehen.*'

And then, as Kit had done, he walked out of the house without looking back.

There was a long silence.

It was Kate who broke it. 'Tomorrow night?' There was a catch in her voice. 'So soon?'

Lewis nodded.

She intertwined her fingers in his. Until now, because she hadn't wanted Andre and Agata to be made unhappy by gossip, she had never spent the entire night at the house Lewis rented from the former mayor. As his fingers tightened on hers, she knew that tonight was going to be different, just as so much else was going to be different. Village gossip no longer mattered. What mattered now was her parents remaining safe until the world was at peace again, and Kit and Helmut remaining safe. What mattered was Greece remaining out of the war, and the resistance groups Lewis was forming never seeing action. And what mattered was believing implicitly that right would prevail. Any other outcome was beyond imagination.

Chapter Twenty-Four

It was Christmas Eve, and in the little house in Archanes that, with great persistence, she had persuaded Christos they should move into, Ella was making *Christopsomo* bread. As she did so she was thinking of her mum, dad and granddad, and of what Christmas preparations would now be taking place in the little house in Wilsden. She knew from her mother's letters that her father had begun keeping hens and was fairly sure one of them would be on the Tetley Christmas dinner table tomorrow. Tonight, as the village children came door-to-door singing carols, her mother would be at a carol service in Wilsden's small Methodist church. When she had been living at home, Ella and her mother had always gone to the carol service together, while her dad and granddad had taken the opportunity of having a Christmas drink in the Ling Bob. On Christmas morning everyone in the house would be up early, exchanging presents.

Presents would not be being exchanged tomorrow morning in Cretan villages, where it was traditional to exchange them on the sixth of December, St Nicholas's Day. Another Christmas tradition she had always loved – Christmas trees – also played no part in a Cretan Christmas, but Christos had brought in a few small branches of evergreen laurel to give their home a festive feel.

Her dough had risen and she added sugar to it, and then a teaspoon each of cinnamon, coriander, crushed cloves and *mahlepi*, a Greek spice with a distinctive, fruity taste. As she did so, she was overcome by an intense wave of homesickness. When she had first come to Crete she had been worried at how little homesickness she had felt, and when she had married Christos she had felt herself to be almost as Cretan as she was English.

Since war had been declared, all that had changed. Now she felt British to the bone and her thoughts were continually with her mum, dad and granddad – and, if her grandad's old mare Bessie had still been alive, they would have been with her as well. They were certainly with Sam. Was he still practising as a doctor in Scooby, or was he now in the army, serving in a medical corps? Her mother hadn't known, but in a letter sent before war had broken out, she had written that Sam had visited them and that he'd had a young lady with him. In pencil on thin airmail paper she had written:

Her name is Jenny and it's quite clear she thinks the world of Sam. I suppose he'll marry her and she'll have the life we thought you would have. I don't truly think I'll ever get over the disappointment, Ella, but it's a comfort to us that Kate lives so near to you.

Kate didn't live near her, in the sense her mother meant, but as it made her mother happy to think they were practically next-door neighbours, Ella hadn't corrected the misunderstanding.

She began kneading the dough again. It was three months and three weeks since war had been declared and since then, although tension ran high, not a lot had happened. It was beginning to be called the 'Phoney War'. No blitzkrieg had been unleashed on Britain, as had been expected, and although a British Expeditionary Force of four divisions had been despatched to France, they hadn't as yet engaged with the enemy. *It's a bit of a rum do, lass,* her granddad had written as a postscript to one of her mother's letters, *but yon bugger Hitler will show his hand soon, and then we'll nab him!*

On Crete, life was going on as normal. As usual when it was winter, excavation work had finished until the spring. Lewis was back from Cairo and, although based at the Villa Ariadne, he spent most of his time in other parts of the island, meeting local leaders; getting to know who could be depended on, if the worst should happen, and who couldn't.

Kate had moved in with Kostas and Eleni. It wasn't something she could have done if Nikoleta had still been living at home, but when Kit had left for England without her – and made it clear he wouldn't be sending for her – Nikoleta had said she never wanted to see another Englishman ever again, and that she was going to live and work in Athens and find herself a wealthy Greek husband. 'Or even a Turkish husband!' she'd stormed as she'd packed her suitcase. 'Even a Turk would be an improvement on Englishmen and Scotsmen!'

With the dough now ready for its second prove, Ella covered it with a cloth. Leaving it in a warm place, she poured herself a glass of wine and, putting a jacket around her shoulders, went outside to sit beneath the cypress tree. Christos had been away for a couple of nights with Lewis, but as it was Christmas Eve he would be back later in the day. She didn't know where they had gone or who they had been seeing and, unless he told her when he returned home, she wouldn't ask. She didn't like being reminded of clandestine preparations being taken in case of an enemy invasion.

Her thoughts flicked back to Kate. At one time it had always been Daphne's recklessness that had caused her concern. That Kate, usually so sensible and level-headed, should now be causing her similar concern was something she had never anticipated, but how could she have foreseen Lewis making a clean break with Nikoleta, and Kate and Lewis becoming lovers? Lewis had never paid Kate any romantic attention previously. The first year they had all been working together he'd barely spoken to her, unless it was about something work-related.

'It isn't as if you're in London, Kate,' Ella had said, when she'd first realized how full-on Kate and Lewis's relationship was. 'There isn't a Marie Stopes clinic you can pop into to be fitted for a Dutch cap. There won't be a woman on the island who has even *heard* of a Dutch cap.'

Kate had been unnervingly unperturbed. 'There's no need to worry about my becoming pregnant,' she'd said, raising her face to the sun, eyes closed. 'Lewis has told me not to worry. He won't let it happen.'

'*Millions* of women have been told that and have then fallen pregnant. Are you an intelligent woman or are you not? How can you run such a risk?'

Ella had received no answer, and another thought had struck her. 'Have you reason to believe he'll marry you, if you do? Has he spoken of marriage?'

'No.' Kate had opened her eyes and looked towards her. 'He hasn't had any need to, Ella. It's something both of us are taking for granted.'

'*You* may be taking it for granted,' she'd said, her exasperation boundless. 'I doubt very much if he is! I think Lewis likes his freedom too much ever to want to marry – look how he backed out of marrying Nikoleta when it became obvious he was expected to.'

'You don't understand, Ella,' Kate had said patiently. 'For Lewis, romance wasn't what his relationship with Nikoleta was about. He sought her out, wanted to be with her, because she reminded him of his sister – and before you make the kind of remark you'll regret, let me explain.'

It was then that Kate had told her of the sailing accident

in the Hebrides, and of how Lewis's parents and Sophie, his sister, had drowned.

'Lewis wasn't on board,' Kate had said, 'and wishes he had been. He feels if he had been, he might have been able to save them. He has no other family, apart from a great-aunt and a godfather who lives in South Africa. Nikoleta was seventeen when he met her, the same age Sophie was when she died – and she's Sophie's double. For Lewis, being with Nikoleta was like being with Sophie again. In the beginning, romance didn't come into it.'

'And later?' she'd prompted, and Kate had said, 'Yes, a little. From the beginning, and even though Lewis had told her about Sophie, romance was what Nikoleta had always thought they had. Eventually, of course, there was romance. He's only human and, with a girl who looks like Nikoleta, how could there not have been? But it was never a full-on love affair, as ours is. Her likeness to Sophie made that impossible for him.'

It was a conversation that had explained a lot about Lewis, but it hadn't stopped Ella worrying about what the outcome would be, if Kate should fall pregnant.

Ella took another sip of wine, reflecting on the irony of worrying about Kate becoming pregnant, when her other worry was that she didn't seem able to become pregnant. Christos, of course, seemed to think it a slight on his manhood that they still weren't parents, or even prospective parents. In one of her letters, her mother had told Ella that it was far too soon to begin worrying about it, and that worrying would make conceiving even less likely.

She was trying to take her mother's advice, but Christos's mercurial temperament wasn't a great help. Lately he had begun questioning any time she spent in ordinary friendly conversation with Adonis. When the dig had come to an end for the winter, Adonis hadn't returned to his home on the mainland. Instead he had moved into lodgings in Heraklion and taken a job in one of the bars lining the harbour.

In his free time he sometimes cycled out to Knossos and helped with the sorting of sherds in the Villa Ariadne's workroom. All the members of the team, with the possible exception of Pericles who kept himself to himself, were like family, and laughing and joking with Adonis was second nature to Ella. Now, and ridiculously in her eyes, Christos had taken exception to it. 'Now that you are married, it isn't proper for you to laugh and joke with a young man who is a bachelor,' he had said. At first she had thought he was teasing her, but he wasn't. She had no intention of altering the innocent, friendly way she had always interacted with Adonis, and had told Christos so. It had led to a row of spectacular proportions, which had, in turn, led to a reconciliation of such equally spectacular proportions that as they had lain in sweat-sheened exhaustion amidst a tangle of sheets, the row had seemed positively worthwhile.

It was always the same. No matter how he might exasperate her, she was never exasperated with him for long. She couldn't be, for he was incapable of sulking, or of holding a grudge, and even when she was determined not to laugh, Christos would make her laugh and then they would be in each other's arms again and his mouth would be hot and sweet on hers, and whatever it was that had exasperated her would be forgotten.

Judging that her *Christopsomo* dough would now be ready to bake, she went back into the house, divided the dough into four round pieces, placed a halved walnut in the centre of each and sprinkled them with sesame seeds. She'd just closed the door of her wood-burning stove when Christos burst into the house.

Joyfully she ran into his arms. Holding her tightly, he lifted her off her feet, whirling her round and round. When at last he set her back on her feet – and after he had kissed her until she was breathless – he pulled an envelope out of his jacket pocket.

'It's for you,' he said, handing her it. He shrugged himself out of his shabby jacket. 'It came care of the Villa Ariadne. Lewis gave me it.'

She looked down at it, puzzled. Her mother's letters were always sent to the *cafeneion*, which acted as Archanes's post office. Post addressed to her any differently was a rarity.

And then she recognized Sam's handwriting – and saw that the letter had been opened.

Shock went through her like an electric current.

'You've opened it!' She stared at him in disbelief. 'It was addressed to me and you opened it. I can't believe you'd do such a thing.'

He looked at her in genuine perplexity. 'You are my wife. and so of course I opened it. What else would you expect of me? And there is nothing of importance in the letter. The Yorkshire doctor writes only to say that he has married. Of what interest is that to you? I do not know why he would trouble to tell you. And I am behaving very well, Ella. I am behaving as Lewis and the Squire have told me to behave. I am not blaming you and giving you a beating, that you should receive such a letter. I am behaving like an English gentleman.' His eyebrows pulled together suddenly. 'But I would not behave thus, if the fellow was on Crete. If he was on Crete, I would take my hunting rifle and I would kill him for his impertinence – and not one single Cretan would blame me.'

On an island famed for feuds and lawlessness and where, especially in mountain villages, vendettas and honour killings still took place, Ella could well believe it.

She struggled for self–control. It was Christmas Eve. They were about to spend their first Christmas together as a married couple. They could not have a row. They absolutely could not. By opening her letter, Christos had only behaved as the majority of other Cretan men would have behaved. And in not entering the house in a furious temper over it, he was behaving better than any Cretan man she knew would have behaved. Allowances had to be made for their very different cultures, upbringings and expectations.

Not for the first time, though, she was finding it harder than she'd once thought she would, to make those allowances. With great effort she steadied her breathing, knowing what the wisest course of action now was.

'You're right.' She handed him the letter back, without even looking down at it. 'I don't know why Sam would trouble to tell me, either. Do you want to know what I've been baking while you've been away?'

Highly pleased at her reaction to the letter, Christos screwed it into a ball and tossed it into the heat of the oven.

Averting her eyes from its destruction, Ella said, 'I've made a walnut spice cake, sesame baklava, *melomakarona* biscuits, English mince pies, Yorkshire parkin—'

'And *Christopsomo* bread?'

'Of course. That is what is baking now.'

He shot her the impish, face-splitting grin she'd never been able to resist. 'Then there's nothing more for you to do.' He held her close so that she could feel his erection. 'All that is left is for us to go to bed.'

Although she was as ablaze with desire as he was, she couldn't resist saying teasingly, 'At two o'clock in the afternoon?'

'Of course at two o'clock in the afternoon. I've been away two nights!' Carrying her in his arms, he strode purposefully towards the alcove that was their bedroom, saying, his honey-brown eyes dark with heat, 'We have a lot of time to make up for, sweetheart – and we have a Christmas baby to conceive!'

Chapter Twenty-Five

It was the first week of April, and Cairo was suffering from the *khamaseen*, the hot, dry wind that blew in from the south, carrying with it suffocating quantities of sand and dust from the deserts. 'How long does this hell go on for?' Daphne asked Adjo, her head housekeeper, after having had to make a run from her car to the house through choking dust.

Adjo, imperturbable in an ankle-length royal-blue *galabiyeh*, said, 'In Arabic *khamaseen* means "fifty", my lady. Once the *khamaseen* comes – and it comes nearly always in April – it continues for over fifty days.'

Daphne, who treated her staff in Cairo with the same easy familiarity she had always treated her staff in England, gave a shriek of horror and then said flatly, 'If what you are telling me is the truth, Adjo, I shall never survive it.'

'Apologies, my lady.' There was affectionate amusement in Adjo's eyes. 'What I should have said is that it continues on and off for fifty days.'

'Indeed you should!' Daphne's relief was vast.

'Lord Hertford is home, my lady.'

Daphne blinked and looked down at her watch. 'But it isn't even lunchtime! Where is he? His study or the drawing room?'

'The bedroom.' The amusement in Adjo's eyes had been

288

replaced by slightly anxious curiosity. 'Barak is packing a suitcase for him.'

Barak was the houseboy who acted as Sholto's valet.

As a diplomat's wife, Daphne was accustomed to Sholto often leaving at short notice for weekend conferences and meetings, but there had been no suitcase-packing since their posting to Cairo.

Full of curiosity, she ran up the stairs to the enormous bedroom that looked out over the garden towards the shimmering olive-green river.

'Where are you going?' she asked, grateful for the rotating paddles of two large ceiling fans, 'because if it's out of the country, I'm coming as well. Adjo says it could be the end of May before the *khamaseen* comes to an end. I need every break from it that I can get.'

Sholto shot her a regretful smile. 'I'm afraid you're in for a disappointment, Daphs. I've been summoned on a five-day turn-around trip to London. It obviously means a posting elsewhere – and hopefully further promotion.' His attention flicked back to Barak. 'Not the grey linen suit, Barak. April in England can be freezing.'

'Freezing sounds wonderful to me. Raincoats, umbrellas, gloves. Air you can breathe. Bluebell woods and primroses in hedgerows. I can't wait.'

'You're going to have to.' He slid his zipped silver-backed hairbrush and clothes-brush set into the open suitcase.

He might as well not have spoken. Daphne was already making plans. Five days would give her time to look up a couple of old friends. She might even fit in seeing *Gone with the Wind*. It had just opened in London and apparently everyone was raving about it. Five days wouldn't be a long break, but it would be a change of scene. Cairo social life was lively enough, but as far as Daphne was concerned, the city also had more than its fair share of drawbacks – chief of which was the pitiful sight of overloaded donkeys, beggars covered in sores and children with flies crawling around their eyes and mouths.

'When are you leaving?' she asked, wondering if she would also be able to fit in a quick visit to Ella's parents in Yorkshire, and perhaps even a fleeting visit to Kate's parents in Kent.

'This afternoon.'

'Then I'd better get a move on, although I won't need much. Not for five days.'

Sholto signalled to Barak that he had finished with his services and, as Barak left the room, said exasperatedly, 'This trip is work, Daphne. Not a pleasure jaunt. And Britain is at war, remember?'

'She may be at war, but at the moment – apart from at sea – nothing much is happening. There have been no air raids as yet, and I don't see why Hitler should begin them now, just to spite me.'

'And Caspian?'

'Caspian will be as safe as houses with his nanny. I dare say that when I come back, he won't have realized I've been away.'

'The answer is still no.' He snapped his suitcase shut. 'How the devil would I account for your presence on a Royal Air Force flying-boat?'

'A flying-boat?' Daphne's eyes sparkled. 'How brill! And you won't have to account for my presence, if you have permission for it, and you can get that by telling Ambassador Lampson that your trip gives me the opportunity to have a last visit with my dying mother. Under his forbidding exterior, Sir Miles has a very soft heart – and he also has a soft spot for me. He'll be happy to give permission.'

'You don't have a dying mother. She died years ago.'

'Miles Lampson doesn't know that.'

Sholto ran a hand distractedly over shiny-smooth hair. The trouble with Daphne was that when she got the bit between her teeth, there was simply no gainsaying her. 'And if I don't?'

Daphne stood on tiptoe and kissed him on his nose. 'If you don't, then at Saturday's Red Cross Ball I shall tell Ambassador Lampson how ghastly it has been – you travelling to England and, in the circumstances of my mother's failing health, my not being able to accompany you.'

Sholto gritted his teeth. Sometimes Daphne's high-spirited quirkiness vastly amused him, and sometimes it didn't. This was one of the occasions when it didn't. Unless the subject was Farouk, Egypt's twenty-year-old king, Sir Miles Lampson was known for being reasonable, and Sholto knew that if he asked permission for Daphne to accompany him on compassionate grounds, the answer would most probably be 'yes'. He also knew that if he didn't ask, and if Daphne did as she threatened – which she would – he would lose points with Lampson for being an unthoughtful husband.

Bad-temperedly he capitulated. 'Okay, Daphs. You win. But don't expect to have my company in London, because I won't have any free time.'

'And neither will I – not with all the plans I've already made.'

'Plans?' As he looked at her, he wasn't sure which emotion was uppermost – despair or a familiar surge of amusement.

'I shall spend a day in London seeing a couple of friends and going to the cinema. Then the next day I'm going to travel to Yorkshire by train and . . .'

'Yorkshire?' He couldn't have been more bewildered if she'd said Tibet.

'Yorkshire. Wilsden, to be precise. And then I might try and fit in a trip to Canterbury.'

'Which is at the other end of the country. I'm getting the

picture. Just make sure you're back in London in time to meet up with me, for the car ride to Poole.'

'Poole?' It was Daphne's turn to be bewildered, but it was interested bewilderment.

'The flying-boat flies into – and out of – Poole harbour.'

'This is going to be such fun!' She slid her arms around his waist and gave him another kiss – this time on the mouth. 'You're such a sweetheart to have suggested it. I'll be packed and ready to go in under an hour.'

The flying-boat wasn't quite as Daphne had expected it to be. A year ago a London friend had written to her about her experience of travelling from Southampton to New York by flying-boat:

> *It was utterly luxe, Daphne. The passenger cabin had easy chairs and sofas and when we flew over the Atlantic at night, the sofas converted into beds. Being a Pan Am Clipper flight, it was all very American. Wonderful service, as you might expect. Champagne all the way. You simply must give it a try when Sholto's Cairo posting comes to an end (and wouldn't it be heaven if his next posting turned out to be Washington and I could visit you there?).*

The RAF flying-boat left from Alexandria on the coast and possessed none of the luxuries of the Pan Am Clipper. It was very basic and very uncomfortable. Their fellow passengers – five of them – were all high-ranking British army personnel. All of them gave Daphne disapproving looks when she boarded what was an official flight and, as they made their disapproval felt by not engaging in conversation with her, Daphne resorted to reading the Agatha Christie book she had brought with her.

*

When it came to travelling by train to Yorkshire, she bought another book at King's Cross station, this time Eric Ambler's *The Mask of Dimitrios*, reflecting as she did so that the atmosphere in London wasn't at all as she had expected it to be. She had expected a pervading feeling of, if not fear, then at least tension. There wasn't. Only the compulsory gas masks everyone was carrying, the sandbags staked around the entrances of shops and public buildings and, when night fell, the strictly adhered to blackout regulations indicated that the country was at war.

Another thing that indicated the country was on a war footing was the number of troops on the train travelling north to Catterick Camp. It was standing room only, although not for Daphne, as the minute she stepped foot on the train, every man in the nearest carriage sprang from his seat.

'Going far, Miss?' asked the soldier whose window seat she accepted.

'Leeds.' Daphne paused. Normally she was happy to chat with anyone and everyone, but a near three-hour train journey was a little long to be trapped in banter with an admiring squaddie, and so very firmly she took out her book.

At Leeds she changed trains for Bradford. As she travelled the short distance from one soot-blackened city to another, it occurred to her that she might have been a little precipitate in setting off for Wilsden when she hadn't been able to warn the Tetleys that she was about to do so, but arriving unexpectedly couldn't be helped. A letter had been out of the question, as it wouldn't arrive until after she'd been and gone; the Tetleys – and probably everyone else who lived in Wilsden, apart from the local doctor – weren't on the telephone; and the arrival of a telegram would have terrified them.

The only way out of Bradford was uphill, and the taxi she took from the station wheezed up succeeding inclines until, with the city behind them, the road curved down through open country and a magnificent view of moorland towards the Ling Bob pub and Wilsden village.

'Are you sure this is where you want to be?' the taxi driver asked as he pulled up outside the Tetleys' little terraced cottage.

'Absolutely.' Daphne could understand the doubt in his voice. Having come straight from London, she was wearing a pearl-grey suit with a nipped-in waist and arrow-straight skirt, sheer stockings and peep-toed, high-heeled shoes. It wasn't the kind of outfit often seen – if ever – on the streets of Wilsden.

As she paid the driver, curtains in the houses on either side of the Tetleys' twitched. A woman a couple of doors down who had been on her knees, white-stoning her doorstep, heaved herself to her feet in order to get a better look.

Before Daphne could even knock on the door, it flew open and, wearing a sleeveless paisley-patterned overall Alice Tetley seized her by both hands, saying with a beaming smile, 'As soon as I heard the taxi come to a stop, I knew it must be you! My, you're a rare treat for the eyes. Alfred! Dad! Come here and see what the wind's blown in.'

Alfred, who had been in the kitchen doing home-made repairs to a pair of work boots, strolled into the room that opened on to the street and was always referred to as the parlour, saying teasingly, 'By 'eck, Alice luv. From the fuss you're making, I thought King George was paying a visit.'

Alice began patting the cushions smooth on the well-worn moquette sofa and Daphne said, 'Can we sit in the kitchen, Alice? It's sunnier in there, isn't it?'

'Indeed it is, lass.' Alfred led the way, past the foot of the stairs and into the sunlit back room. 'Nah then, Alice. Put t'kettle on for a brew and I'll give Dad another shout. He's in t'shed,' he said explanatively to Daphne, 'and 'e's deaf into t'bargain now.'

As Daphne sat down at the well-scrubbed kitchen table, Alfred opened the back door and hollered, 'Dad! DAD! We 'ave a visitor! One you'll want ter see!'

'Now, you'll know the news about Ella having a baby, won't you?' Alice said, filling the kettle. 'September it's due.'

'I know. It's brilliant news. I'm so happy for them.'

'Them?' Alice paused in what she was doing.

'Ella and Christos.'

'Oh, aye. Truth to tell, Daphne, I try to forget about him as much as I can. It wasn't what we wanted for her, and now she's not only near two thousand miles away from us for a season of work, she's near two thousand miles away permanently.'

Daphne was spared the awkwardness of having to make a suitable reply by Jos stomping up the garden path and into the house. 'We'd gi'en you up fer lost,' he said, grinning toothlessly. ''as Cairo gone over to 'itler's mob, then? Is that why you're back in God's own country?'

Daphne grinned back at her old sparring partner. 'My husband is in London for a few days and I was able to cadge a lift on his flight. This is only a fleeting visit. We fly back to Egypt the day after tomorrow, and I want to fit in a visit to Kate's parents in Canterbury, too.'

'That's very considerate of you, lass.' Alfred Tetley sat down at the table opposite her. 'So tell us all yer news. What's life like in Cairo? Blooming 'ot, I should think.'

'It's nearly always hot, and at the moment there's a windstorm blowing from the Sahara. I've been glad to get away from it for a few days. Before I tell you my news – and I haven't really a lot – tell me all yours.'

Swirling hot water around in a teapot, Alice said, 'Mine is that I have a ration book. I don't know how people who don't keep hens manage, as the egg allowance is only one egg a week.

How can anyone do a week's baking on only one egg a week? We're all right because we have hens, but people living in Bradford back-to-backs can't keep hens, can they?'

She tipped the water down the sink and spooned tea into the warmed pot. 'And Sam Jowett has wed. She's a nice lass – he brought her to Wilsden to meet us – but if Ella had behaved differently, it would have been Ella he'd married.'

For a dreadful moment Daphne thought Ella's mother was about to burst into tears.

'Nah then, luv,' Alfred said gruffly. 'The lass is 'appy. You can tell by her letters that she's 'appy, and that's what counts.' To Daphne he said, 'Sam's joined up. He's in the Royal Army Medical Corps. Lots of young men in Wilsden 'ave joined up as well. Most of 'em in West Yorkshire regiments. If I'd bin a bit younger, I'd 'ave joined up meself.'

'And then 'itler would 'ave 'ad summat to worry abaht, wouldn't 'e?' Jos cackled with laughter. 'Accordin' to t'*Telegraph & Argus*, there's goin' ter be local Defence Volunteer units formed all over t'country. I'll join the Wilsden one, Alfred. I want ter do me bit, just as much as you do.'

With the tea now mashed, Alice put the teapot on the table and sat down, saying, 'Tell me what it's like living in Cairo, Daphne. Are you near the Pyramids? Are there camels in the streets?'

'We are near the Pyramids and from certain parts of Cairo there are spectacular views of them, and there are camels in the streets, though not as many as there are donkeys.'

'And what do you do with your time? Do you go to lots of parties?'

'A fair few.' Daphne thought of the near-continual round of parties that made Cairo such a lively and scandalously racy diplomatic posting. 'But I do other things as well. Donkeys and mules have a grim time of it in Cairo, as the Egyptians don't have the same attitude to animals that we have. A British general's wife has founded a hospital to care for the city's ill-fed and exhausted animals and, along with other volunteers, I help out there a couple of afternoons a week. I also do voluntary work at an Anglican orphanage. Orphaned children in Cairo have as hard a time of it as the animals do.'

'Aye, we're lucky to have been born British,' Alfred said fiercely. 'And we're not going to let 'itler overrun us, like he's overrun the Poles. We've not been invaded since 1066 and we're sure as 'eck not goin' to be invaded again!'

'And especially not by a little bloke with a funny moustache!' Jos added, bringing his fist down hard on the table.

The crockery jumped and, anxious for its safety, Alice changed the subject. 'You'll stay for tea, Daphne? It won't be anything fancy. Tinned salmon with some of Dad's home-grown cucumber, and a mint-and-currant pasty made this morning.'

'Sounds heaven.' Having previously enjoyed slices of Alice's mint-and-currant pasty, Daphne spoke with sincerity. 'But I'll have to leave in time to catch the seven o'clock London train.'

'And until then you can tell us all about your little lad,' Alfred said. 'Our Ella said in one of her letters that 'is name is Caspian. Now 'ow in the name o' glory did you come up wi' a name like that?'

The next afternoon Daphne was two hundred and fifty-six miles away, in Canterbury. She had only ever met Kate's parents a few times, and always only when they had travelled to Oxford and St Hilda's to visit Kate. Unlike the Tetleys, they were, though, expecting her as Daphne had telephoned them from London.

Hilda Shelton hadn't been interested in the Pyramids or camels. What she had been interested in was British diplomatic social life in Cairo, and whether Daphne and her husband had met the Egyptian royal family.

Truthfully, Daphne had been able to tell her that they had. 'Although where King Farouk is concerned, only at official diplomatic gatherings. Unfortunately, Farouk and Sir Miles Lampson – Sir Miles is Britain's Ambassador – don't see eye-to-eye. Farouk is too pleasure-loving for Sir Miles's taste, and meanwhile Farouk resents Britain's presence in Egypt.'

'And why are we there, Daphne? I don't understand.'

Daphne was saved from giving Kate's mother a mini-history lesson by her husband saying gently, 'Egypt used to be one of our country's many colonies, Hilda. After the last war we granted it independence, but because the Suez Canal is so vital to British interests, we've continued to keep a military presence there, isn't that so, Daphne?'

Daphne said that it was so. In order to avoid being roped into explaining just why the Suez Canal was so vital to Britain's interests, she turned the subject back to royalty. 'The greatest royal party-giver in Cairo is Princess Shevakier. She was King Farouk's father's first wife and is very pro-British.'

'Then I don't suppose,' Kate's father interjected, 'that she appreciates Egypt remaining neutral in the war we're now engaged in. I find doing so very shabby, Daphne. Very shabby indeed.'

Daphne found it very shabby as well, and rather than give Mr Shelton more cause for concern, she didn't mention that it was the general opinion in Cairo that if Egypt was to abandon its neutral stance, it wouldn't be to come out on the side of Britain and France. It would be to come out on the side of Germany.

*

The train journey to London from Kent was much shorter than the train journey back from Yorkshire had been. With her self-appointed visits over, and feeling sure that both Kate and Ella would be glad she had made them, Daphne began thinking about Sholto and his intriguing summons to Whitehall.

Sholto was thirty-four; too young yet for an ambassadorship. Or was he? Someone would have to be the youngest UK ambassador ever, and why shouldn't it be Sholto? As the Kent countryside flashed past the train windows, reality kicked in. There were other ranks still to achieve, before Sholto could hope for an ambassadorship. Presumably, though, after the meeting he had been asked to attend, he was now another rung closer to achieving his long-term aim. The question now was: with Europe in such disarray, where would his new posting be?

'Well?' she said as they met in the Dorchester hotel's cocktail bar. 'Is it promotion within the embassy at Cairo? Or are we on our travels again?'

'We're on our travels again,' he said, an odd note in his voice.

It took quite a lot to discompose Sholto and she felt the first faint flickers of anxiety.

'Am I going to need a stiff gin before you give me the news?'

'Very probably.'

'Dear God! It isn't Berlin?'

'Don't be an ass, sweetheart. The Berlin Embassy hasn't been operative since the outbreak of war. Let me get a couple of drinks in and then I'll tell you.'

With rising impatience she waited until their drinks had been served and then said again, 'Well?'

'For a start off, I'm not being posted to an embassy. I'm being posted to a consulate.'

'A consulate?' Daphne stared at him in disbelief. 'But isn't that some kind of demotion? And what as? A consul?'

'A vice-consul.'

She stared at him. There was concern on his face, but she could tell his concern wasn't for himself, but for her, and how she was going to feel about being a consulate wife and not an embassy wife.

For several moments she fought an inner struggle. Privately she was appalled, but how could she let Sholto know that? For his sake, she had to be philosophical about it and make the best of a bad job.

Slipping her hand into his and feeling that she was behaving exceptionally well, she said, 'Where is this consulate that's so lucky to be having you?'

At the loyal way she had taken his news, the tension he'd been feeling eased. All he had to do now was give her the second part of his news. And he had no qualms at all about how she was going to receive it.

He savoured the moment for a few seconds longer, and then said: 'Heraklion.'

Her jaw dropped. 'Heraklion? Heraklion, *Crete*?'

He nodded.

She gave a whoop of such delight that heads turned and the buzz of conversation and laughter around them came to a temporary, startled halt.

'Oh, but that's *brilliant*, Sholto. Absolutely stupendous! I'll be able to see Kate and Ella all the time.'

'Not *all* the time. As a vice-consul's wife, you will have duties.'

'And whatever they are, I'll perform them superbly.'

Knowing the reason for his posting to Crete, he felt a flash of guilt. It was one he quickly suppressed. However strategic the island, the likelihood of an attack on it by Germany was, surely, remote – and he was going there with the promise that, in the event of a threatened invasion, Daphne and Caspian would, along with all other British women and children, be speedily and safely evacuated to Cairo.

'And it is absolutely necessary that your wife accompanies you,' the Foreign Secretary had said when Sholto had met him. 'Greece is sticking to its neutral stance and the slightest indication that we are compromising its position by filling the island with British intelligence personnel – and legitimate personnel who are also fulfilling that role – would be disastrous. There will be no such suspicion if you take up your new posting accompanied by Lady Hertford.'

Daphne's euphoria at the thought of being reunited with Ella and Kate on a long-term basis lasted all the way on the train journey to Poole, and all the way on the flight back to Alexandria.

At Alexandria they were met by an official chauffeur-driven car and the first thing the chauffeur said, as he opened the limousine's rear doors for them, was, 'Bad news this morning, sir. Hitler's invaded Denmark and Norway.'

Sholto blasphemed, and then said, tight-lipped, 'Any news of what sort of resistance is being put up?'

The chauffeur waited till the car's doors were closed and he was behind the wheel and then said, 'They were blitzkrieg attacks, like the attack on Poland, sir. No warning. Denmark has been overrun, but the Norwegians are still resisting.'

Sholto swore beneath his breath and, as the car began speeding through the city streets in the direction of the road to Cairo, Daphne said apprehensively, 'What does this mean for Britain, Sholto?'

'It means we'll go to Norway's aid,' he said, his handsome face grim. 'It means that the Phoney War is finally over.'

Very little else was said between them on the car ride into Cairo. All Daphne's joy at the thought of going to Crete had vanished. All she could think of was the horrors now taking place in Denmark, Norway and occupied Poland.

Once in Cairo, the driver dropped Sholto off at the embassy and then drove over the Bulaq Bridge to Gezira Island and Zamalek.

Adjo greeted her with his usual tranquil smile. 'Welcome home, my lady. Barak has some good news for you.'

'Has he? I could do with a little bit of good news. What is it?'

'Your earring, my lady. It had dropped into the breast-pocket of his lordship's dinner jacket. Barak has left it on your dressing-table tray. I told him that on no account was he to touch your jewellery boxes.'

'Thank you, Adjo.' Earrings were something Daphne regularly mislaid as she wore clip-ons and often, when a clip became uncomfortable, she would take the earring off and drop it into her purse or somewhere else equally convenient. In this case the convenient place had apparently been Sholto's breast-pocket.

Once in the bedroom, she put her handbag down and slipped her feet out of her shoes. On the cut-glass dressing-table tray the earring lay in solitary splendour.

She crossed the room, intending to put it in one of her jewellery boxes with its partner.

It was a very pretty earring: a drop pearl surrounded by diamonds, and certainly not the kind of earring she would have wanted to lose.

She didn't move to pick it up, though.

She couldn't move, because there was something very, very wrong with the earring.

It wasn't hers.

Chapter Twenty-Six

Although there was an autumn chill in the air, the pavements of Athens were as noisy and as crowded as ever that October. There was, though, one significant difference. Because of the war raging in Western Europe, the people in the crowds were nearly all Greek and the foreign tourists who would have been patronizing the smart dress shops in and around Monastiraki Square, which was where Nikoleta worked, were noticeably absent.

Nikoleta's salary was modest, but that hadn't mattered when she had first begun working at Athiná Módas, because she also earned commission – and the dresses she sold were all high-fashion, expensive dresses. Now, though, very few dresses were being sold and it mattered, especially as her hopes of a rich fiancé had never materialized.

It was her lunchtime and she was in a cafe sipping a coffee that had been served with a tumbler of water. Although she didn't admit it in her letters to her parents and to Ella, she was lonely. The other assistants at Athiná Módas hated the way her sales figures so consistently outstripped theirs and, being jealous, were unfriendly. She missed the gregariousness that had come with always being made welcome at the Villa Ariadne, and the sense of importance given to her by being a Palace of Minos tourist guide. None of the Greek men who had flirted with her had interested her. Her upbringing, living cheek-by-jowl with the constantly changing occupants and visitors of the Villa Ariadne, had given her expectations that it now seemed were never going to be fulfilled.

The world-famous Sir Arthur Evans had for years behaved towards her with all the kindliness of a godfather, when she was a small child. It had made Nikoleta feel special and different, as had her growing ability to speak English. As a young woman, the archaeologists who came to the Villa Ariadne from the British School in Athens had, in her eyes, all possessed not only foreign glamour, but intellectual glamour. It was something Cretan young men at home – and now the young men she had met in Athens – had so far failed to deliver.

Life was not panning out as she had expected it to. Worse, the neutrality that Greece had clung to with such determination was crumbling fast. Italian forces had massed on the frontier with Albania. A Greek ship had been sunk in the harbour by an Italian submarine, and the announcement of an all-out attempted Italian invasion was expected at any moment.

She stubbed her cigarette out. Twice she'd been tempted to leave Athens for home. The first time had been when Ella had written to her with the news that Daphne's husband had been posted to the British Vice-Consulate in Heraklion, and that Daphne was with him; the second had been when she had received a telegram telling her that Ella had given birth to a healthy baby boy. Now had come a temptation that she had no intention of fighting. Crete was the biggest and most strategic of all the Greek islands and, when the Italians invaded, Crete was where she had to be.

She rose abruptly to her feet.

Athiná Módas was going to have to manage without her. She was going home.

*

'So when did Nikoleta arrive home?' Daphne asked Ella as, despite autumn temperatures and a cloud-covered sky, they sat companionably in the little courtyard that Ella had made pretty with pots of flowers and shrubs.

'Yesterday morning.'

'So she was still in Athens when the Italians invaded?'

Ella pulled her cardigan a little closer around her shoulders. 'She was. And she was amongst the crowds outside the British Embassy when our ambassador made an appearance on its balcony. She said the cheering he received was deafening.'

'Rightly so – especially as the RAF were straight off the mark, giving support with squadrons of both fighter planes and bombers.'

Ella looked across at her, impressed. 'As Sholto's wife, do you always get to know things like that before anyone else? And do you get to know what is happening in Britain as well?'

At the mention of Sholto's name, Daphne's face tightened, but her voice was steady as she said, 'I don't get to know anything that's classified as being secret, and the despatch of RAF fighters and bombers to the Albanian frontier isn't secret – rather the opposite, as it's news that will bolster public confidence.'

No Greek Ella had ever met had been in need of having their confidence boosted, but she didn't say so. Instead she said, 'And the situation back home? Do you know more about it than we're told in the newspapers and over the wireless?'

'No. Sholto might, but I don't, although I may get news a little earlier. Southampton suffered yet another God-awful bombing raid on Saturday night, as did a whole clutch of other industrial towns – though not Bradford,' she added quickly, as Ella sucked in her breath. Bradford had been bombed in August, with some bombs falling on the side of the city closest to Wilsden. 'As for London . . .'

She fell silent. Since the Blitz had started two months ago, there simply weren't words enough to sum up the hell Londoners were enduring night after night.

When she finally spoke again, she changed the subject. 'When is the baby to be baptized?' she asked, as contented mewling sounds came from the crib positioned in the open doorway. 'And who gets to be his godparents – and why, when he's six weeks old, has he still not got a name?'

'Taking things in order. The baptism will probably be next week. We couldn't have had it earlier because it's Greek tradition that they don't take place until forty days after the baby has been born. Question number two: as Nikoleta was *koumbara* at our wedding, she will be baby's godmother and Georgio, Christos's brother, will be his godfather. Sorry, Daphne, but as with bridesmaids, godparents have to be Greek Orthodox. Thirdly: it's tradition that the baby's name isn't spoken until after the priest has given him, or her, the name at baptism.'

'But you have chosen a name?'

'Yes, although I can't honestly say we *chose* it.'

Daphne rolled her eyes. 'Don't tell me! Traditionally he has to be named after the priest who baptizes him, or a saint, or . . .'

'. . . or his paternal grandfather,' Ella said, vastly amused by the expression on Daphne's face. 'So his first name is to be Kostas and, as what is good for the goose is also good for the gander, I've insisted that his second name is Alfred, after my dad.'

'So no imagination called for at all?'

'Not even a tad.'

They looked at each other and burst out laughing.

Later, when they were back in the house and she was breast-feeding Kostas Alfred, Ella said tentatively, 'Is everything okay, Daphne? You look as if you have a lot on your mind.'

'Well, who wouldn't have, with Britain fighting for her life and so very little good news?'

'Yes, I know. But is there something else as well? I don't mean to pry, but between the three of us – you, me and Kate – we've always told each other everything and—'

She broke off as Daphne made an odd sound in her throat and then said with deep feeling, 'Oh God, you're right, Ella. I do have something on my mind.'

To her horror, Ella saw that Daphne was fighting back tears. She removed Kostas Alfred from her breast, saying as she burped him, 'What is it, Daphne love? Whatever it is, it can't be so bad, surely?'

'It is. Sholto is having another affair. After his affair with Deirdre Holbeck-Pratchett, and a brief, intense affair that I had in retaliation, I truly thought we'd drawn a line when it came to being unfaithful – but although I have, he hasn't.' Her voice was thick with disillusionment and hurt. 'I don't understand it, Ella, because we're good together, both in bed and out of it; and the worst of it is, when I confronted him about this latest affair, he admitted to a string of previous affairs, or "flings" as he prefers to call them, as if they didn't matter at all. And perhaps, to him, they don't. But they matter to me.'

Ella was at a loss to know what to say. She couldn't even begin to imagine how she would feel if Christos was unfaithful to her, but then neither could she imagine him ever being so. She laid Kostas Alfred back in his crib and then, wishing she could box Sholto Hertford hard around his aristocratic ears, gave Daphne a long, loving, sympathetic hug.

After Daphne had left and when she was baking Christos's favourite cheese pasties, Ella realized she had never asked Daphne just who it was that she'd had her brief and intense love affair with.

She pressed the edges of the pasties together with the flat of her thumb and then she stopped what she was doing. When Daphne had learned about Sholto's affair with Deirdre Holbeck-Pratchett, she had immediately left for Crete. It was then that she had told her and Kate about it. And as her own affair had been in retaliation, had it happened while she had been on Crete?

In sudden shock she stopped what she was doing.

If Daphne's affair had taken place on her visit to Crete, there was only one likely person for her to have had it with, and that was Helmut.

Helmut had never hidden how smitten he was with Daphne.

With a heavy heart she wondered where Helmut was now. Was he in a Panzer division? Or in the German navy, serving on a battleship or a U-boat? Or perhaps he was a pilot in the Luftwaffe?

She closed her eyes, trying to shut hideous possibilities from her mind, knowing only that she hoped he was still alive and that the day would come when, in a world that was at peace again, they would once more meet as friends.

Lewis and Christos were striding up a track that led from the small village of Kefalari to the slightly larger village of Aroania. Both villages were in a valley in western Crete in an area of the White Mountains that Lewis was unfamiliar with. Since the Italian invasion at the end of September, when British troops were welcomed into Greece as allies, he'd had no need to conceal why, or in what capacity, he had remained behind, when Kit and other archaeologists had left in order to enlist in the armed forces. One of his first tasks had been to familiarize himself with the entire island until he knew it, as Christos did, like the back of his hand. Because of its mountainous terrain, Crete was extremely difficult to travel around in – something in its favour if enemy troops were to try and occupy it, but not very convenient when Lewis needed to meet the leaders of remote scattered villages, sounding out which of them could be relied upon as future guerrilla leaders.

Daphne's husband, Viscount Hertford, a man he had never met until Hertford had taken up his position in the vice-consulate, had sought him out immediately after his arrival on Crete.

Hertford had been disarmingly direct. 'I've heard a lot about you from my wife and from Julian Kermode,' he'd said, his manner as easy as if they were chatting in a rugby locker room and not the formal setting of the consulate. 'That you can speak Greek like a true Cretan is going to be a great help to me. I have a little classical Greek, but it's rusty and I understand there's a dialect I'll have to get to grips with.'

'There is,' he'd said, 'but it's not much different from standard Greek.'

Hertford had shot him a grin. 'That's a relief. I know from Kermode how helpful you've already been, and how much valuable information about the island you've already delivered. Under cover of my official position, I'm here to liaise with you. Your days of being a one-man band are over.'

He'd paused long enough to pour two generous-sized Laphroaig single malts.

'The pace is hotting up,' he'd continued when they were both nursing Lewis's favourite whisky. 'As the Greeks are so far holding the Italians at bay, there's no likelihood at the moment of an Eyetie invasion of Crete, but Germany is another matter. Needing Suda's deep natural harbour, so their navy can control the Med, means the Krauts could attempt a sea landing at any time. We need to be prepared for the worst.' He'd grinned, and Lewis had realized that Heraklion's new and relatively young vice-consul was a man of quite devastating charm. 'Only fair to mention that organizing bands of partisans for armed resistance is against international law,' he'd continued, 'but what the hell – here's to being ready to give any invading bastards a greeting they won't forget in a hurry!'

As he and Christos continued now up the narrow valley so that he could meet a retired former governor of the island, Lewis knew that in Sholto Hertford he had met a kindred spirit. Sholto was a man he had immediately liked; a man far different from the usual run of pompous civil servants; a man he was certain would be equal to anything.

Christos broke into his thoughts. 'Not much further now. And we are lucky that the way is clear of snow. Usually, by November, the snow on the path to Astrakos is deep.'

Lewis could well believe it. Every peak soaring around them was covered in snow so blindingly white it hurt the eyes to look at it.

His thoughts returned, as they did constantly when he was away from her, to Kate. At the moment she was doing the winter close-down of the palace and cave digs at Kalamata.

Reading his thoughts, Christos said, 'Kate will be managing well. She has Dimitri and Angelos, and they are good, those brothers. Pericles and Yannis are good workers, too, despite Pericles being moody and Yannis being old.'

'You're forgetting about Adonis.'

Christos's good-humoured face collapsed into a scowl. 'No,' he said vehemently, 'never do I forget about Adonis! He thinks too much of himself. He thinks that because of his good looks, he is God's gift to women. And because he thinks too much of himself, he is not a good worker. I think he should not come back next season. I think the team can very well do without him.'

Lewis's mouth twitched at the corners. Adonis was an excellent worker and he knew the only reason Christos would like to see the back of him was because he didn't like Adonis and Ella exchanging friendly banter. That Adonis had any serious designs on Ella and that, even if he had, Ella would be receptive to them was too ridiculous to be taken seriously, and as they neared the houses on the outskirts of Aroania his thoughts returned once again to Kate.

At the moment both she and Ella were safe remaining on Crete, but that situation would change the instant Germany declared war on Greece, and nothing was more certain than that Germany would do so and that it would do so sooner rather than later.

When that happened, Kate, Ella and baby Kostas Alfred would have to be evacuated to the safety of Cairo, along with all other British women and children on the island.

On paper, it was an arrangement that couldn't be argued with. What kept him awake at nights was the knowledge that neither Kate nor Ella would be happy to go along with it. Ella because she regarded herself as much of a Greek national as a British one, and Kate because all her loyalties were to the palace site at Kalamata, and to the villagers she had lived amongst for so long. To leave for a place of safety, when they couldn't, would be deeply abhorrent to her.

As he thought of how much he loved her, Lewis's heart tightened within his chest. In retrospect, he knew that ever since the tragedy that had robbed him of his parents and his sister he had been emotionally frozen. Nikoleta had made a dent in the icy wall he had erected around himself, but it had taken Kate – as ravishingly beautiful and sexy as she was intelligent – to thaw it out completely.

Knowing that she'd had no previous full-on love affairs, Kate's capacity for sexual enjoyment had both surprised and delighted him. Just thinking about her uninhibited responsiveness to him in bed sent a wild rush of blood to his groin. When it came to sex, Kate made him happier than any other woman he'd ever known. For the first time in his life he was in a relationship that seriously mattered to him; and tramping remote areas of Crete with Christos, sleeping at night in whatever modest accommodation could be found and which was, as often as not, a hay loft or bare boards was no compensation for being in his brass-headed feather bed with a gloriously naked Kate.

'There!' Christos pointed to a small whitewashed stone house standing a little higher than the other houses of the village. 'That is the ex-governor's house.'

The only way it stood out from other village houses was that its walls weren't sagging and its roof wasn't badly in need of repair.

Looking at it, Lewis hoped their trek up the valley was going to prove worthwhile. Many local chieftains he'd met were engaged in feuds with other local chieftains, sometimes in feuds that had gone on for generations, and the idea that if they wanted to be an effective fighting force they needed to work together and maintain close lines of communication with each other was alien to them.

As they entered a steep-stepped street, a pack of dogs hurtled towards them, barking aggressively. To protect his lower limbs from this kind of greeting he had taken to wearing thick Cretan *vraka* breeches tucked into high leather boots. So far it was protection that had served him well. He braced himself for the canine onslaught, fiercely hoping that his luck was going to continue.

Chapter Twenty-Seven

20 MAY 1941

Sholto was on his way from the British Vice-Consulate to a meeting with Brigadier Chappel of the 14th Infantry Brigade. A month ago Germany had launched a blitzkrieg attack on Greece, forcing the British, Australian, New Zealand and Greek forces who had been fighting the Italians into a retreat. Exhausted and battle-weary, they had been evacuated to Crete, adding to the large number of British troops already there.

Not long afterwards daylight air attacks on Suda Bay had begun, and now Heraklion was also on the receiving end of bombing raids. Yesterday evening the planned evacuation to Cairo of unnecessary personnel had taken place. The Squire had fought hard against being included under the heading of 'unnecessary personnel', but it was a battle with officialdom that he had lost. Together with his mother and a clutch of British women and children that had included Kate, Daphne, Caspian and Caspian's nanny, he had left from Heraklion harbour aboard a Royal Navy destroyer. That Daphne's friend Ella and her baby son hadn't left with them had been a huge disappointment to him, but both he and Lewis had failed to change her mind about staying behind.

'Of course I'm not leaving,' she had said defiantly, her eyes flashing fire. 'I'm married to a Cretan. Crete is my home – and Crete is where I'm staying.'

As he and Lewis had driven away from Archanes, Lewis had said, 'Her decision doesn't come as the slightest surprise, Sholto. It's a miracle to me that Kate agreed to leave. There was a hell of a row, before she saw reason.'

The natural affinity between the two men, coupled with the fact of Daphne and Kate's close friendship, had meant they had been on Christian-name terms with each other ever since the end of their first meeting.

As Sholto swerved at high speed out of the village and on to the road leading back to Heraklion, he'd said drily, 'I expected a similar tussle with Daphne, but because she had Caspian's safety to think of, and because I told her in no uncertain terms the kind of hell that would be unleashed when the invasion started, she saw sense for once, thank God.'

Now, no longer having to worry about his wife's safety, or his son's, Sholto's entire attention was focused on what Military Intelligence had told them was to be an almost immediate invasion by air.

Brigade Headquarters was a cave strategically placed between Heraklion and its aerodrome, and he entered it to find its gloomy interior thick with uniformed officers, all clustering around a table covered with a large-scale map of the city and the area around it.

'Glad you've made the meeting,' Chappel said to him. 'We need the consulate to be fully in the picture, with regard to troop strength and displacements.'

Room was made for Sholto at the table.

'Infantry is made up of five battalions, two of them Australian, plus two Greek regiments, the city garrison and a Royal Army Medical Corps field ambulance unit.' He gave a nod of recognition to a captain wearing the RAMC's distinctive blue beret. 'The Australians, 2nd Battalion Black Watch and 2nd Battalion Yorks and Lancs have been assigned the task of defending the aerodrome.' He tapped the map with a long cane. 'Of the two hills dominating the aerodrome area, the 2nd Battalion Leicesters are positioned on the hill immediately above the aerodrome, the 2nd Battalion Black Watch on the hill to the east of it.'

Sholto frowned. 'And Heraklion itself?'

'The Greek regiments and the Greek garrison will defend the city. Our main priority is the aerodrome. The entire defence of the region depends on our maintaining control of it.'

As he was speaking, Lewis and Christos entered the cave. Lewis was wearing his uniform of a captain in Military Intelligence and there was a pistol on his hip. It was Christos, though, who attracted Brigadier Chappel's – and everyone else's – attention.

His sweeping moustachios with their curly upturned ends were worthy of a demon king. Wide black *vraka* breeches were tucked into knee-high leather boots. A shabby black waistcoat was worn over an even shabbier black shirt; his thick mop of curly hair was constrained by a black tasselled headcloth; a deadly-looking Cretan knife was tucked through the folds of his waist sash; and a rifle was slung over his shoulder and ammunition bandoliers criss-crossed his chest.

'Captain Sinclair, SOE,' Lewis said briefly to Chappel. 'How can I and the guerrilla groups I've organized best be of help?'

'Ah, yes.' With difficulty Chappel dragged his eyes away from Christos. 'I was told to expect you. I was just putting Vice-Consul Hertford into the picture as to present troop displacements, which are that British and Australian battalions will defend the aerodrome and the hills overlooking it, and Greek troops will defend the city.'

Across the table Sholto's eyes met Lewis's. Both knew what the other was thinking. It wouldn't only be Greek troops defending the city. Heraklion's citizens knew the ground in a way troops from the mainland didn't. Coupled with the inbuilt Cretan instinct for banditry, and with every adult male possessing a hunting rifle, the entire city would be armed and fighting in its defence.

'The two Greek regiments are stationed on both sides of the town's city walls,' Brigadier Chappel continued, indicating on the map the wall's four huge bastions and three main entrance gates. 'It's with the Greek regiments, Captain Sinclair, that I think your groups can best be useful.'

He put his cane down, turning away from the table so that he was facing everyone. 'Our major difficulty is going to be lack of reliable communication with General Freyberg's HQ at Canea. Field telephones are proving erratic, due to wires being run too loosely, and so far today there has been no wireless communication as to what may or may not be happening in the Maleme airfield and Suda Bay region. One last thing: the Villa Ariadne, a large house situated inland three and a half miles away, has been commandeered as a field hospital.' He looked towards the RAMC officer. 'Captain Jowett, before you leave I'd like a word with you concerning the arrangements made there.'

'Yes, sir.' Sam flushed slightly at being so conspicuously singled out.

'Then that is all, gentlemen. Morale is high. Troop dispositions are in place. Twelve anti-aircraft guns are dug into pits around the airfield. Twelve field guns are ranged on it. Two tanks are in place at either end of it, and six light tanks are ready to move to wherever they might be needed. Our Prime Minister has promised the Greek government that Britain will look after Crete. It is a promise that will be kept.'

As the majority of the officers in the cave began making their way to its entrance, a motorcycle messenger hurried into it, making a beeline for Sholto, who was in deep conversation with Lewis.

'Excuse me, Lord Hertford. An urgent message, sir.'

The envelope he handed Sholto bore the distinctive crest of the consulate. Sholto ripped it open. A split second later, his face ashen, he thrust the message towards Lewis.

It was brief and to the point:

Lady Hertford and Miss Katherine Shelton not aboard when destroyer docked Alexandria.

'Christ Almighty!' Lewis felt as if he'd been hit by a sledgehammer. 'Then they're not in Cairo. So where the hell are they?'

It was a question born of deep shock. Even as he said it, he knew where they were. They were still on Crete.

Sholto said hoarsely, 'There's no mention of Caspian. *Where the hell is my son?*' And then, as it was a question Lewis couldn't possibly answer, he sprinted for his vehicle.

Lewis swung round on Christos. 'Are Kate and Daphne at Archanes with Ella?'

Christos vehemently shook his head.

Lewis ran towards his truck, Christos hard behind him. Daphne and Kate hadn't spent the night in Archanes and, as he had spent last night at Kalamata, he knew they hadn't spent the night there, either. So where were they?

As he jumped into the truck and Christos scrambled into the passenger seat, he was angrier than he had ever been before in his life. That Daphne was capable of deceiving Sholto into believing she had left aboard the destroyer didn't surprise him. He'd long ago realized Daphne was capable of anything. But that Kate could have been capable of such deception absolutely took his breath away. Daphne may have thought there would be other chances of evacuation, but Kate knew differently. Kate knew that anyone now on Crete would be on it until the battle was fought and won. Or until the island, bathed in blood, was lost.

He gunned the engine, swinging out on to the road leading into Heraklion. Presumably Kate would be facing him sometime during the day, to let him know she hadn't boarded the destroyer, but he was damned if he was going to wait for her to do so.

As Kate and Daphne hadn't spent the night at Archanes, the next most obvious place for them to have spent it was with Kostas and Eleni and, once in Heraklion, Lewis was going to drive straight out of it in the direction of Knossos. It was only when he was in Heraklion, heading for the Canea Gate that opened on to the Knossos road, that he realized shock and anger had addled his brain.

Kate may have spent the night at the Kourakis home at Knossos, but it was now late morning and she would be doing what she'd spent the last two days doing. She would be helping the Archaeological Museum staff transfer all its precious artefacts – including those found at Kalamata and the cave – into the cellars for safety.

Narrowly avoiding an open-sided lorry crammed with soldiers of the Black Watch, an army car flying a pennant – its passenger presumably Brigadier Chappel – and a donkey pulling a cart piled high with cabbages, he veered into Xanthoudidou Street and swerved to a halt outside the museum.

'Stay with the truck,' he said to Christos as he jumped from it, 'otherwise it will be commandeered.'

Grim-faced, Lewis sprinted into the museum. Frenzied

work was taking place, with cabinets being unlocked, emptied and their contents transferred into large straw-filled crates. As well known at the museum as if he was a member of staff, he wasn't given a second glance. He couldn't see Kate and headed for the steps leading to the building's cellars.

They were nearly as thronged with staff and volunteers as the upstairs rooms had been. He eased his way between people, looking for Kate's distinctive bob of sleek black hair. She was nowhere to be seen. He was just about to head off back to the truck when the member of staff who usually patrolled the Proto-palatial room paused in what he was doing, saying, 'If you're looking for Miss Shelton, she's in the far end cellar.'

Lewis nodded his thanks and, side-stepping several half-filled crates, made his way down a stone-floored passageway.

She was on her knees, packing boxes of sherds into a large steel container. To his great relief, he saw she was working without help. It meant there wouldn't be an audience to the ugly scene they were about to have.

He strode in on her, saying in white-hot fury, 'Why the *hell* are you still here, Kate?' Only with difficulty did he prevent himself from hauling her to her feet and shaking her until her teeth rattled. 'Sailors aboard that destroyer risked their lives in order to take you, Daphne, other British women and children and unnecessary personnel to safety – and you throw the risks they've taken in their faces! For absolutely no good reason you deceive everyone into thinking that you've boarded and . . .'

'We did board.'

'*You didn't bloody well sail!*'

He'd always had a temper, but was usually in control of it. This time he was filled with so much exasperation, and so much anxiety for her safety, that he felt like banging his head against the wall.

'I want an explanation,' he demanded savagely. 'And it had better be good!'

She rose to her feet, brushing packing straw from her skirt with an unsteady hand. 'Although you don't seem to think I can be of use, you're wrong, Lewis. I can. How many English Greek speakers are there on Crete? Barely any. Because I speak Greek, I can act as an army interpreter. When I've finished what I'm doing, I'm going to Brigade Headquarters.'

It was a response that failed to lower Lewis's anger level. 'And so, when we had our traumatic goodbye scene, you knew it was all a farce? When you boarded, you knew you were going to disembark almost immediately? It wasn't something Daphne talked you into at the last moment?'

'When we said goodbye, it wasn't a farce. I knew that once fighting on the island began, I might never see you again; that you might be killed.' Her voice wobbled. 'And it wasn't something Daphne talked me into. Our decisions to stay behind were arrived at separately.'

'And what was Daphne's reason?' he asked with sarcasm. 'Unlike you, she hasn't lived on Crete for years and doesn't have fluent Greek. What good is Oxford classical Greek going to be to the army?'

'She hasn't stayed behind because of her knowledge of classical Greek. She's stayed behind because she's a member of the St John Ambulance Brigade and she became a member so that, when the time came, she could do useful war work. And the time for her to be useful is here and now.'

Lewis breathed in hard. 'And where is she? *And where is Caspian?*'

'Daphne is at the Villa Ariadne. Caspian is in Cairo. He sailed in the care of his nanny and Mrs Hutchinson, and Mrs Hutchinson will by now have handed him into the care of

Lady Vanessa Dane. Lady Vanessa is a very good friend of Daphne's.'

Their eyes held; his so dark with anger and exasperation they were nearly black; hers unrepentant at the decision she had made, but full of growing panic at his reaction to it.

He said curtly, 'As Daphne didn't have the decency to make sure Sholto knew Caspian had sailed, I'm going to find him and put his mind at rest.'

He swung on his heel and she said urgently, appalled that he was leaving when he was still so angry with her, 'We didn't realize news would have got back to you so quickly about our not being aboard! I would have told you before today was over, and Daphne would have told Sholto.'

Without turning round, not trusting himself to do so in case, at the sight of her anguished face, he abandoned anger and took her in his arms, he said curtly, 'It wouldn't have altered the deceit, Kate. Or the reason for it.'

He strode out of the cellar, every line of his body taut with tension, and she fought the almost overwhelming desire to run after him and tell him she was sorry and that she wished she'd stayed aboard the destroyer.

She didn't, though, because it would have been a lie said in the hope of making things right between them and, much as she wanted to do that, she wasn't going to lie to do it. Staying behind to give what assistance she could to the army, however small that assistance might prove to be, had been the right thing to do. But her heart had never felt so heavy and she knew that if her action ended her relationship with Lewis, the heaviness would be so great her heart would break.

'I've been to Archanes!' Sholto said as Lewis strode into his office. 'They aren't with Ella. I've phoned every hotel in the damned city and they aren't in any of them.' From behind his desk he slammed a telephone receiver down on its rest.

'Kate is at the museum. Daphne is at the Villa Ariadne, and Caspian is in Cairo.'

'*On his own?*'

All Sholto's aristocratic sophistication abandoned him. He jackknifed to his feet, looking as if he was about to have a heart attack.

'Daphne gave him into Mrs Hutchinson's care and she will, by now, have handed him into the care of one of Daphne's friends, Vanessa Dane.'

As he spoke, mayhem broke out in nearby rooms and the door banged open with such force it nearly came off its hinges.

'The Jerries dropped paras in their thousands on Maleme airfield this morning,' a fresh-faced young man shouted. 'Christ knows why it's taken so long for us to get the message, but the invasion has started!'

The door slammed after him. Sholto said, 'I'm going to the Villa Ariadne.' He yanked a drawer open, snatching up a revolver. 'With luck I'll be back before the balloon goes up.'

Together they raced from the building, Lewis sprinting in the direction of the truck, Sholto in the direction of his car.

The streets were so jammed with soldiers and army trucks that getting out of Heraklion was a nightmare. The road to Knossos and the Villa was a little better, but not much. Sholto had never been a guest there, although he'd spent years hearing about it from Daphne.

Accustomed to living in a stately country house or a palatial town house, he'd imagined something more impressive than the flat-roofed Victorian mansion that finally met his eyes. Everywhere was a scene of organized chaos. Squaddies were running into the house carrying camp beds and Red Cross stores, and running out of it empty-handed so that they could take another load in.

Amongst army khaki he glimpsed an occasional flash of red cape and white starched headdress. Earlier that morning Brigadier Chappel had made no mention of there being army nurses on the island, although as it was reasonable to expect there would have been some on mainland Greece during the fighting, it was also reasonable to expect that when those troops had been evacuated to Crete, a handful of nurses had been amongst their number.

He strode through the mayhem in the direction of the stone steps fronting the house and then, at the foot of them, came to a sudden, shocked halt.

At the top of the steps a woman was in discussion with the blue-bereted RAMC officer he had seen earlier at the briefing. She was wearing a black, beautifully cut two-piece suit, white shirt, black tie, black stockings and black low-heeled shoes. Her hair was hidden by a black felt hat, a cockade in it indicating rank, and there were service epaulettes on her shoulders. She looked authoritative and, amid the hurly-burly, splendidly calm.

For a second Sholto didn't recognize her.

Then he realized the woman was Daphne.

He also realized that, in the present surroundings, they could hardly have the blistering marital row he was determined to have.

He took the steps two at time and as Daphne turned towards him, regarding him with an infuriating lack of surprise, he grasped hold of her arm, saying through gritted teeth to a startled Sam, 'Excuse me, Officer. I'd like a private word with my wife.'

Judging that anywhere in the house would give more privacy than the top of the steps, and without releasing his grip on her, he marched her into the entrance hall. It was just as thronged with people as the courtyard had been.

'The only empty room is the library,' Daphne said, finally succeeding in wrenching herself from his grasp. 'And you're behaving like an idiot, Sholto. You do realize that, don't you?'

Goaded beyond endurance, he would have made a physically angry response, but a Greek Orthodox nun was marching towards them, a pile of blankets in her arms.

Once in the library, he slammed the door behind them. 'How the *hell* did you have the nerve to needlessly abandon my son? He's only two years old . . .'

'Three in two months' time.'

'That's not being three now! He's *two*! You're not fit to be a mother. Or a wife.'

Daphne had been determined to hold on to her temper, but his last accusation was an accusation too far. She said explosively, 'That last remark is rich, coming from you. You're the one who is serially unfaithful. Not me. And I'm an excellent mother. Caspian is by now in the safe care of Vanessa . . .'

'Whom he doesn't know from Adam.'

'Of course he knows her. She's the closest friend I had in Cairo. Vanessa has spent time with Caspian on lots of occasions, but you wouldn't know that because you were never interested in the way I spent my time, were you? And that was probably because, if you'd asked, it would have led to my asking questions about how you were spending your time – and with whom!'

Sholto slapped her across the face.

She slapped him back.

Panting with anger, they glared at each other, a fraction away from a full-scale physical brawl.

He said tightly, 'This is the end, Daphne. Leaving our son in a foreign country without one of us being with him is something I will never forgive.'

'There's nothing *to* forgive! It's government policy to evacuate children. Thousands of them have been sent from London and other cities to Canada, Australia and New Zealand – a good many of them as young as Caspian, and all without a parent in tow.'

'*Their* mothers couldn't leave with them. *You* could.'

'And if I had,' she flashed back, 'what meaningful war work could I have done in Cairo? The Germans may be causing trouble in the desert south of Cairo, but they stand no chance of marching into Cairo. It's here that I'm needed. How many men in a battalion, Sholto? I've been told it's anything from five hundred to a thousand. And how many battalions are defending Heraklion? My information is that it's at least four, possibly five, and then there are a couple of Greek regiments and the city garrison. Do the maths. Think of the number of wounded there will be, and then take on board that for the troops defending Heraklion *this is the only field hospital*.'

For the first time he didn't immediately shout her down and she said in a different tone of voice, 'Of the Queen Alexandra's army nurses evacuated from the mainland, the vast majority are at Canea and only a small handful are here. Nuns from the local monastery have offered their help, but they are all elderly, and then there is me – and I've been thoroughly trained and I know what I'm doing.'

Looking at her, Sholto didn't doubt it.

His temper spent, wondering where the hell she'd got her devastatingly accurate facts and figures from, he said flatly, 'Hundreds of German paratroopers landed at Maleme and Canea earlier this morning. The news only came through as I was leaving to come here.'

Although the news meant an almost immediate attack on Heraklion, Daphne didn't show a glimmer of panic.

He felt a surge of admiration for her, and something else,

for in her figure-hugging suit and cockaded hat she looked provocatively seductive.

He reflected wryly that Daphne's habit of looking provocatively seductive was something he was just going to have to get over. When he had said that her not accompanying Caspian to Cairo was the last straw, as far as their marriage was concerned, he had meant it.

Because he had meant it, he didn't kiss her goodbye. He merely said, 'Keep safe for Caspian's sake, Daphs', opened the door and walked away.

Daphne stared after him, unable to believe that, with the Germans about to invade, he hadn't at least attempted to make things right between them.

Because of Sholto always having behaved as if he was still single, they'd had their fair share of fights in the past, and they had always followed the same pattern. Whenever she'd become aware of his faithlessness, she'd screamed at him that he was a bastard and he had yelled back that their shotgun marriage was a marriage he'd never wanted. Then, exhausted, they'd drunk whisky sours and gone to bed – and made love.

The scene that had just taken place between them – and his reaction to it – had been alarmingly different. For one thing, it hadn't been over another woman. It had been over an action of hers that had, as far as she was concerned, been totally reasonable. For another thing, there was no opportunity for them to go to bed and make up. They didn't even know when they would see each other again, or even *if* they would see each other again.

At the thought of the last possibility, Daphne began running after Sholto down the crowded corridor, but a group of nuns slowed her almost to a standstill and by the time she reached the top of the steps she could no longer see him. She ran down the steps and through Sir Arthur's Edwardian garden, weaving a way through the squaddies still coming and going between the house and the lodge gates, where the lorries – and presumably Sholto's car – were parked.

And then two things happened.

As she came within sight of the road, Sholto's car sped away in a cloud of dust, and as it did so there came the familiar drone of German planes. Within minutes the drone became a thunderous, almighty, earth-shaking roar. The air throbbed with the sound of engines and the sky became black with Junkers 52s, all homing in on Heraklion's airfield. They came in low and in columns that seemed endless.

In a massive understatement, a squaddie manning one of the lorries shouted, 'I don't like the look of that little lot!'

The first of the planes reached land and began shedding human loads. Above the toy-like figures of paratroopers, parachutes burst open. Not all the parachutes were white. Some were pink, some violet, some yellow. Like evil blossoms, they filled the sky and, dreadful as the sight was, a part of Daphne's brain registered that they were also obscenely, terrifyingly beautiful. Then, from defensive positions on the ground, there came the deafening sound of machine-gun, artillery and rifle fire.

Daphne turned and began running back towards the Villa, which would, she knew, soon be crammed full of wounded men needing emergency attention, and knowing that the hell Sholto had warned her about had started and that there was no telling when, or how, it would end.

Chapter Twenty-Eight

With an attempted invasion of the city imminent, Lewis and Christos had rounded up all the members of the Kalamata team save for Yanni, who still had to meet them in a bar near the harbour. Just as Yanni came trotting in, as heavily armed as the rest of them, there came the drone of approaching planes.

For days Heraklion had endured intermittent bombing raids, but this sound was like nothing previously experienced. Reverberations sent shelves of bottles and glasses crashing to the floor, heavy iron tables shuddered and rocked. The roar of engines was so ear-splitting it sounded as if the world was about to end.

Along with everyone else, Lewis sprinted out into the street and then stood transfixed, for it wasn't the usual squadron of bombers that were flying in over the sea. It was huge, lumbering air-transport planes and they were coming in tight formation, dropping stream after stream of many-coloured parachutes over the airfield, before wheeling away so that planes behind them could drop their loads.

'Holy Virgin!' Christos whispered devoutly as an army of paratroopers began swinging down to earth. 'There are thousands of them.'

As they watched, defensive ground fire opened up and, as well as shedding paratroopers over the airfield, some planes began shedding them to the west of the city.

'They'll try to enter by the Canea Gate!' Lewis shouted, and broke into a run in the direction of his parked truck.

Within seconds Christos and Nico were squeezing into the truck's cab with him, as Dimitri, Angelos, Pericles, Yanni and Adonis clambered into its rear.

The streets between the harbour and the Canea Gate were massed with citizens racing to the city's walls and carrying whatever weapon they'd been able to grab hold of: rifles, shotguns, ancient pistols, knives, rakes, spades, axes, even broom handles. It wasn't only men who had armed themselves; it was women and schoolchildren, too. Adding to the melee were trucks full of Greek soldiers, some of the trucks heading towards the docks, others to various city gates and bastions.

The Canea Gate was the west gate of the city and, when Lewis arrived at it, so did a couple of hundred men from the city garrison. Seeing Lewis's uniform, the officer in command made a beeline towards him. 'I've deployed two platoons into the areas they're dropping into,' he shouted over the deafening noise of planes and people. 'The more that can be killed before they reach the ground, or the gate, the easier defending the gate will be.' Another thought struck him and, despite the emergency of the moment, he paused long enough to add, before getting back to his men, 'Are you Greek?'

'Scottish.'

'You speak like a Greek and have the look of a Greek. No one would know differently.'

Which was all to the good, Lewis thought, considering the role he would be undertaking, if the attempted invasion succeeded and the island was occupied.

He turned to the team, saying succinctly, 'Follow me!'

The great medieval town gate had two enormous flanking buttresses through which ran two corridors, one to the left of the gate and one to the right. When the Venetians had built the gate in the sixteenth century, they had done so as a defence against the Turks and along the entire length of both buttresses there were positions from which now, four centuries later, bullets could be fired.

Heraklion's citizens were already surging down the corridors as the roar of Junkers 52s continued to thunder overhead.

Lewis ignored the corridors and, with his team at his heels, raced up narrow steps leading to the walkway that ran along the top of the town walls and all three of its massive entrance gates.

They weren't the first people to think it would be the best of all positions. Soldiers from the garrison were already up there, as well as a priest, rifle in hand, with a young boy by his side similarly armed.

'He is my son,' the priest said, as the team took up positions on either side of him and the boy. 'While I fire one rifle, he will reload the other. It will not be long, I think, before the first of those who have survived the landing will be upon us.'

Lewis looked down at his watch. It had been early afternoon when he'd left the museum and it was now just after six. By now Kate would be in the cave that was Brigade Headquarters and which was undoubtedly the safest place she could possibly be.

Although paratroopers were still being dropped and many of them were being killed before they reached the ground – even without field-glasses Lewis could see tiny black figures jumping and jerking as they were hit – there was also now the sound of answering ground fire, and some of the ground fire seemed to be coming from sub-machine guns, something Lewis knew the men of the garrison did not have.

He wondered which of the colour-coded parachutes were dropping heavy weapons and what else was being dropped. Even without sub-machine guns, the sheer difference of numbers – two platoons and civilians, against what he judged to be a thousand paratroopers trained to Germanic crack-perfection – was a mind-numbingly unequal fight. It wouldn't merely be unequal, it would be carnage: carnage that, with only garrison troops and civilians defending the gate, could soon be happening all around him.

Like everyone else, he was kneeling in position against the gate's parapet, with the stock of his rifle against his cheek. He'd never shot anyone and he doubted if any of his team had – apart perhaps from Yanni who, as a youth, had fought in the Balkan War. He looked towards twenty-three-year-old Nico, who was next to him. Every muscle of his body was tense with nervous expectation. Pericles, on the other side of Nico and fifteen years older, was chewing tobacco, his hawk-like face full of steely resolution.

Suddenly Lewis saw what he'd been expecting to see: civilians and garrison troops making a running retreat back towards the city walls.

At their rear, in terrifying numbers, were steel-helmeted, heavily armed Germans.

'Let them come,' the priest growled into his long white beard. 'In Venetian times these walls withstood a twenty-two-year siege by Turks. And what the Turks couldn't do, the Huns aren't going to do!'

Lewis's finger curled around the trigger of his rifle. Minutes later, as firing all along the city walls on the west side of the city broke out – and feeling unbelievably calm and focused – he fired and changed the clip, fired and changed the clip, fired and changed the clip until dusk fell and the Germans breached the gate, and the fighting in and on both sides of the gate turned into brutal hand-to-hand combat and he hurtled down the stairs to pitch himself into a battle that had become medieval.

*

Bush telegraph ensured that the villagers of Archanes had an almost blow-by blow account of what was happening in Heraklion. Christos was with Lewis, and Ella knew that now the invasion had started, there was no telling when she would see him again.

With Yorkshire optimism she was sure the city would be held, but with so many German paratroopers having been dropped in and around the city and the airfield, Archanes was no longer a safe place for Kostas Alfred to be.

By the following morning, when fighter planes replaced troop carriers over the city and bombing raid after bombing raid was carried out, Ella had decided the best place for Kostas Alfred was high up in the mountains at Kalamata.

For a long time Christos had had the use of one of the dig's small trucks. She made a travelling cot for Kostas Alfred by padding a wooden crate that had been used for transporting oranges. Then, with a bag packed with everything her baby could possibly need, she laid him in the crate and put it on the truck's bench-seat.

With Tinker riding shotgun, the journey to Kalamata took longer than usual, for she was constantly flagged down by people anxious for news of what was happening nearer to the coast. 'I know very little,' she said, time after time. 'Paratroopers have landed – many, many paratroopers – and so there must be hard fighting, but that is all I know.'

The ground steepened and was everywhere covered in pale-lilac sage; the lilac sage depicted in so many of the Palace of Minos frescoes, and on a fresco found at the Little Palace at Kalamata. What would happen to Minoan archaeological sites if the Germans succeeded in occupying the island? And what would happen to the Cretan people? Would they be treated as cruelly as the people of occupied Poland and Czechoslovakia were being treated?

In his orange box, Kostas Alfred had begun grizzling. Ella began singing to him and the grizzling turned to happy gurgling, but her throat hurt with the effort of singing, when in her head she was fervently praying, 'Please, Heavenly Father, don't let Christos be killed. Please, *please* don't let him be killed! I couldn't bear it if Christos was killed.'

As she took the winding road up the mountain to Kalamata, her knuckles were white on the wheel, not because the road was a poor one, with frequent perilous drops on one side of it – she had a good head for heights, and the road was one she knew like the back of her hand – but because her heart and mind were in the streets of Heraklion, where the Cretans she now so totally identified with were fighting for their freedom.

When she finally crested the lip of the plateau and saw the village in the distance she felt a spasm of relief. Kalamata wasn't Heraklion. There would be no slaughter in the streets here; no homes bombed to flaming ruins. By leaving Kostas Alfred in Andre and Agata's care, she need no longer fear for his safety and could return to Archanes, which was the most obvious place to hear news of Christos. She no longer had any need, either, of worrying about Kate and Daphne's safety, for by now, thank goodness, they were in Cairo.

She drove over the rough ground and through the narrow village streets and by the time she drew up outside the *cafeneion* there was not only the usual horde of children streaming after her, but every able-bodied villager as well.

'What news? What news?' Andre shouted, running to greet her before she had even turned off the truck's engine.

'Yesterday late afternoon, large planes dropped an army of paratroopers at Heraklion and now the city is being bombed. That is all the news I have, Andre.'

She jumped down from the truck and the women clustered around her.

'Why have the Germans fallen from the sky to fight us?' old Zenobia asked, wringing arthritic hands in agitation. 'Why? Why? Why?'

Other questions came from every side.

'What harm have we done to the Germans?'

'Why do they want Crete? Of what use is our island to them? All we have are olive trees and sheep and goats. Of what use are olive trees, sheep and goats to Germans?'

'Have you news of my daughter? She lives in Yiamalakis Street? She is lame and will not be able to run.'

'Will the Germans come here? Here will they come?'

'Dimitri,' Aminta Mamalakis said, her lustrous dark eyes full of anxiety. 'He is with Kyrie Sinclair. Have you news, Ella? Have you news?'

All the questions were unanswerable. Lifting the orange box from the truck, Ella said, 'Christos is also with Lewis, and I have no news, Aminta.'

Aminta gave a sound of anguish and Apollonia, tall for a Cretan and raw-boned, removed the orange box and its sleeping occupant from Ella's arms, saying, 'Have you come to leave the baby here, Ella? Are you going back to Archanes?'

'Yes. Agata will look after Kostas Alfred and Tinker for me, and at Archanes I will be near enough to the fighting to be useful.'

'Useful? In what way can you be useful?' Beneath her canary-coloured head-kerchief, Apollonia's long, bony face was doubtful. 'I could fight, but you are not built for fighting.'

As Agata finally succeeded in barrelling a way through the crush and proprietorially lifted Kostas Alfred into her arms, Ella said, 'No, I'm not, but I can do basic first aid and the news in Archanes is that the Villa Ariadne at Knossos is being turned into a hospital. I can be useful there – and maybe there I will hear news of Christos.'

'Then may I come with you? I am a very good nurse. Good I am. And I have no family to think about. Rhea will care for my goats. Being as bad-tempered as they are, she gets on well with them, and perhaps at Knossos I may hear news of Pericles.'

The little house at Archanes was exactly as Ella had left it. There was no note from Christos lying on the table. Archanes itself was crowded with people who had fled the bombing in Heraklion, and on both sides of the road from Archanes to Knossos were streams of people still heading for safety, bundles of possessions piled high on donkeys and mules.

There was so much frantic activity going on at the Villa Ariadne that Ella scarcely recognized it. The garden, once filled only with antique statuary, palms and large flowering shrubs in giant pots, was now crammed with wounded men.

Two men in the uniform of the Royal Army Medical Corps were carrying an unconscious Greek soldier on a stretcher into the house, and doing so at a run. Breaking into a trot to keep up with them, Ella said breathlessly, 'My friend and I are here to help with the nursing. Who do I need to speak to?'

'Anyone in nursing uniform,' one of the RAMC men said. 'A nun, a QA, the St John Ambulance woman. Absolutely anyone at all.'

With Apollonia close beside her, Ella was now in the house. It was even less recognizable than the garden had been. A nun, busy dressing an ashen-faced civilian's wound, pointed out a Queen Alexandra Corps nursing sister. 'Speak to her,' she said as the man she was treating coughed up a great spout of blood.

The QA sister, equally busy, said brusquely, 'The St John Ambulance woman will tell you who needs you most.'

When she was located, the St John Ambulance woman had her back to them and was in urgent conversation with an army surgeon, his gown heavily blood-stained, his operating mask pulled down from his face. She was wearing a bibbed apron over a short-sleeved white shirt and black skirt and, although Ella couldn't see the front of the apron, she knew it would have an eight-pointed Maltese Cross emblazoned on it. Beneath a nursing cap, the woman's hair was hidden.

The second her conversation with the surgeon had come to an end, Ella cleared her throat, about to ask what she and Apollonia could best be doing. Instead, as the woman turned towards her, Ella's jaw dropped. '*Daphne!* What on *earth* are you doing here? I thought you were with Kate in Cairo.'

'Well, I'm not in Cairo. And neither is Kate. I've had a message from Lewis, saying she's at Brigade Headquarters. Where is Kostas Alfred?'

'Kalamata, with Agata. Did Lewis have any news of Christos?'

'No. The message came via one of the walking wounded. There was no mention of Christos, and there would have been if anything had happened to him.'

As she was talking, she was rapidly taking sheets and red Queen Alexandra's Royal Army Nursing Corps blankets from a box of supplies. 'Other news we've had from men being brought in is that the Germans entered the town via the Canea Gate yesterday evening and that overnight they were driven back out – which is why the town is now being bombed. As they can't get in and take it, they're trying to destroy it. Here. Take these.'

She thrust sheets and blankets into Ella's and Apollonia's arms. 'Make up a giant Red Cross flag and put it on the roof. We need to indicate we're a field hospital and off-limits for mortar and air attacks, and when you've done that, go down to the basement. A couple of the bedrooms have been turned into an operating theatre, and other bedrooms are serving as a post-operative ward. You'll be able to be useful there.'

And with that Daphne – a totally different Daphne from the carefree, heedless Daphne whom Ella had known for the last ten years – marched off into the melee, to greet a new ambulance load of injured men and decide which should join the throngs of walking wounded and which needed immediate surgical help if their lives were to be saved.

'The flag has to be made up where it's going to be positioned,' Ella said to Apollonia and, thankful she knew where the stairs to the roof were, without having to waste time finding out, she led the way to them, her ears ringing with the cries and groans of the injured and her nose assaulted by the hideous smell of blood.

Up on the roof there was a clear view of a bombing raid in progress over Heraklion and of a plane breaking free from the pack and heading inland towards Knossos.

'Ignore it!' Ella shouted to Apollonia over the growing roar of its engine. 'Let's make up this flag, fast.'

Apollonia didn't waste time with speech, but, nodding her agreement, began stretching out sheets in a giant white square.

In happier days the roof had occasionally been used for sunbathing and there was a scattering of small terracotta tubs on it. As Ella began arranging red blankets in a giant cross on the sheeting, Apollonia anchored each corner of the sheeting with one of the tubs.

The plane came in so low above them that they both threw themselves flat, their hands over their ears.

There came the rat-tat-tat of machine-gun fire. It raked the roof, sending spits of concrete high into the air. As it rained down on them one of the pots was hit, exploding into smithereens.

The whole experience could only have lasted for seconds, but as the plane roared away, heading back out to sea, Ella felt as if those brief seconds had been hours.

As she shakily rose to her feet there came the sound of someone pelting up the stairs. 'Ella!' the person in question shouted. 'Ella! Are you okay?'

It was a voice very familiar to her.

A voice she hadn't heard in more than three years.

'Yes,' she said, as its owner erupted from the stairs onto the roof. 'I'm fine, Sam. And so is my friend.'

'Thank God!' His still-boyish face was ashen beneath his RAMC beret. 'I saw you on the roof, and then that plane came over and some bastard in it began machine-gunning . . .' He hugged her tight, his voice cracking and breaking. 'I thought I was going to find you and your friend dead. I've never been so scared in all my life, Ella love. Never, ever.'

Chapter Twenty-Nine

Five days after the landings both Heraklion and its airfield were at a stalemate. Since first gaining the town and then being driven from it, the Germans had made no attempt to retake it. They were only a few miles away, though, in fields and hills to the south and south-west. Along the coast road an entire parachute battalion had dug in at Perivolia, a small village a couple of miles east of Réthymnon, ensuring that Heraklion was completely cut off, not only from Réthymnon, but also from Canea, the next and final city along the coast road – as was all news from Suda Bay and the main airfield at Maleme.

For the last three days Lewis and Christos had been in the foothills of the mountains, coordinating already-formed bands of partisans in preparation for an all-out effort to help an Australian battalion dislodge the Germans. Leaving Christos to organize the partisan bands higher up in the mountains and avoiding several parties of paratroopers, Lewis was again in Heraklion. There were people he needed to speak to: Brigadier Chappel, for one; and Sholto, for another. He hadn't seen sight or sound of Sholto since the fighting had begun, and as Sholto hadn't made for the Canea Gate when the paratroopers had begun landing, Lewis could only assume that he'd headed to help defend the harbour, where fighting had also been prolonged and brutal.

The bombing that had taken place in his three days' absence

had left swathes of the town in ruins, but by a miracle the museum was still standing and the Morosini fountain was – although battered – still triumphantly intact.

When Lewis had left to meet the *Kapetans* of his resistance groups, Pericles and Adonis had been helping soldiers of the Black Watch guard hundreds of Germans who, during the street fighting, had been taken prisoner. The town's jail was totally inadequate for such numbers and they had been penned into a couple of sealed-off streets.

The officer in charge of the Black Watch guard gave Lewis a nod and allowed him into the street that Pericles and Adonis were helping to guard. Pericles, his rifle slung over his shoulder, a cigarette in his hand, strode across to him, Adonis in his wake.

'This is old men's work,' he said to Lewis bluntly. 'Both Adonis and I have had enough of it.'

'You won't be doing it for much longer. I need to make contact with Brigade Headquarters and with Sholto Hertford, if I can track him down. I'll take Adonis with me and come back for you, then we'll leave the city and join up with the resistance groups. Where are Dimitri, Angelos and Yanni?'

'They are helping to bury our dead. Earlier Yanni went out on the Knossos road to the Villa Ariadne. Ella is there, and her friend, Daphne. Yanni told Ella that Christos had left the city with you. Nikoleta and Apollonia are also at the Villa.'

'Apollonia?' Lewis raised an eyebrow questioningly. 'How on earth . . . ?'

'Ella took the baby to Kalamata and when she returned she had Apollonia with her.' He dropped his cigarette, grinding it out beneath a booted foot. 'The Villa is a field hospital and Apollonia is a good nurse.'

Lewis didn't doubt it. Despite Apollonia being at least fifteen years older than Pericles, he – like everyone else who knew them – was unsure what their relationship was. Was it still that of landlady and lodger? Was it friendship? Or was it something more? No one knew, and Pericles was obviously not about to clarify it now.

Lewis shifted his rifle a little more comfortably on his shoulder. 'If anyone by the name of Hertford comes looking for me, tell him I've gone to Brigade Headquarters and he's to leave word of where I can find him.'

Pericles nodded and, together with Adonis, Lewis strode back to where he'd left the truck, hoping the road to Brigade Headquarters was going to be as clear of Germans as the road to Knossos apparently was.

At the Villa Ariadne – and helped greatly by army nurses and Daphne – order had replaced chaos. Although there had been a couple of mortar attacks on the Villa, no serious damage had been caused and no lives lost and, thanks to the blanket and sheet flag on the roof, the Villa hadn't been strafed again and neither had it been bombed.

Daphne's gravest anxiety was that medical supplies – especially anaesthetics – were running dangerously low. It had been expected that by now the RAF would have been able to drop supplies, but the Luftwaffe still had mastery of the skies above Crete and supplies couldn't be obtained from the larger field hospitals at Réthymnon and Canea, because the only road west was cut off by the German battalion at Perivolia.

'We'll be down to pentothal sodium and Greek brandy before very long,' she'd said to Ella, as together they lifted a patient fresh from the Plaster Room onto his bed. 'What I don't understand is that if the Germans are at a standstill at Heraklion, how come it isn't the same situation at Réthymnon and Canea?'

'I reckon it *is* the same at Réthymnon,' their patient, a

private in the Yorks and Lancs, suddenly said. 'That's why there's such a large battalion of Huns holed up on this side of Réthymnon. Even if they'd taken the town, as they did here, they've been driven out, just as they have been at Heraklion; and just like here, they're on the outskirts, biding their time, waiting until they have access to at least one airfield – and as Maleme is the biggest airfield, my bet is that they're concentrating on taking Maleme. Once they've succeeded, they can then fly fresh troops and artillery in non-stop, around the clock. And once they can do that, the island is theirs.'

Across the plaster of Paris covering two-thirds of his body, Ella's and Daphne's eyes met in horrified understanding. It was simply that the Germans didn't choose to lose any more men in another attempt to take Heraklion when, once Maleme was taken, the battle for the island would be over.

Later, when she and Ella again had a few minutes together in which to talk, Daphne said, 'If our Yorks and Lancs private's opinion is right – and I have a horrible feeling it is – it means that a gigantic battle is still taking place in and around Maleme.' She fumbled beneath her apron for the pocket in her skirt and withdrew a packet of cigarettes, which were no longer Sobranies, but Woodbines given to her by a patient. Lighting up, she said in a voice fraught with anxiety, 'And there's still no news of Sholto. He knows I'm here. Surely, if he was all right, he would have got word to me saying so? And if he wasn't all right – if he'd been wounded – then he would have been brought here, wouldn't he? And as he hasn't been brought here . . .'

Before she could express her worst fear and say that perhaps he was dead, Ella said swiftly, 'I expect, like Christos, he's left the town. There's far more going on in the areas around it now than in it.'

'Even though Sam has never met Sholto, if their paths were

to cross, his name would ring a bell with him, wouldn't it? Especially as Sholto's now wearing Military Intelligence uniform. Next time you see Sam, ask him to ask around for me, Ella.' There was a break in her voice as she added, her eyes overly bright, 'Sholto can be a complete bastard at times, but he isn't so much of a bastard that I want him dead.'

'Of course I'll ask, but as things are running comparatively smoothly here and as the dressing station at the airfield is still inundated with wounded men – German as well as British, Australian and Greek – I've no idea when I'll see him again.'

As Daphne went off wearily to relieve a nun in the post-operative ward, Ella, who'd had as little sleep as Daphne over the last week, went back into a room that, once a basement bedroom, was now a frantically busy Plaster Room.

As she applied stockinette over the upper arm and shoulder of an officer who had been injured in the fight for the Canea Gate, her thoughts were on Sam. On the day he'd raced panic-stricken up to the roof, he'd been unable to stay with her long enough for them to have any meaningful conversation. That hadn't happened until two days later, when he'd had cause to be at the Villa again.

'I've half an hour,' he'd said. 'Where can we talk without being interrupted?'

'Nowhere here,' she'd said, 'but we could go to the palace.'

'The palace?' His face had been comically blank. 'What palace?'

'The Palace of Minos.' Her voice had been thick with amusement. 'You're at Knossos, Sam. One of the greatest archaeological discoveries in the world is merely a few hundred yards away.'

Ella had told the QA nurse she was working with that she wouldn't be available for half an hour and then had led the way out of the Villa and up the road, into the vast deserted remains of the palace Sir Arthur Evans had discovered nearly half a century ago.

'Crikey!' Sam had pushed his beret back on his head in astonishment. 'I'd no idea it covered such a huge area.'

'Six acres, all told,' she'd said. 'A good place for an overall view is from the Horns of Consecration, just to the left of the South Propylaeum.'

'Propylaeum? Sorry, Ella love. I'm a doctor, not an archaeologist. What in the name of Glory is a Propylaeum?'

'It's a grand entranceway.' She'd shot him a wide smile, amazed at how easy and natural it felt being with him again.

Companionably they had made their way along the reconstructed foundations of the West Porch and into the gypsum-paved Processional Corridor. As more and more of the labyrinthine remains of the palace – and of Sir Arthur Evans's reconstructions – came into view, Sam was as awed as she had hoped he would be.

When they stepped into the Central Court at the heart of the palace, he came to a sudden halt. 'Is this where Minoan youths leapt over the backs of charging bulls?'

'Yes.'

'And how does all that fit into the legend of Theseus and the Minotaur?'

'We don't know,' she'd said, 'not for sure. The present take on it is that the labyrinth the Minotaur was said to be kept in wasn't an underground labyrinth, but the labyrinth of the palace itself – and when you realize how many narrow, dark zigzagging corridors ended in dead ends, it's a theory that seems reasonable. As for the Minotaur, one theory is that in the sport of bull-leaping, a leaper, as he vaults the bull's horns, was seen as having become one with the bull and therefore half-man and half-bull; and you also have to take into account that in antiquity, worship of the Sacred Bull was common all around the eastern Mediterranean and bull-leaping may simply have had a religious connection.'

'You don't sound convinced.'

'Oh, I'm open to all sorts of theories,' she'd said, happy at having something else to talk about, other than the grim reality of maimed men suffering, with very little in the way of pain relief, 'but the one I like best is a Cretan legend my father-in-law told me.'

'Which is?' he'd asked as they'd reached the South Propylaeum and, to the right of it, the paved plinth on which Sir Arthur's giant granite reconstruction of a bull's horns rose in breathtaking beauty against a backdrop of a blazing blue sky.

'That Theseus came to Knossos to take part in funeral games.' For neatness's sake while nursing, Ella wore her hair in a long, thick braid. It had fallen over her shoulder and she lifted it back again, saying, 'King Minos had a wrestling champion named Taurus, who had never been beaten. Theseus threw him three times and claimed the championship and, in doing so, won the heart of King Minos's daughter, Ariadne – which explains how Ariadne came into the legend. As Taurus is the word for "bull" as well as being a person's name, the Minotaur – or Minotaurus – might simply have been a champion wrestler.'

'I think I prefer the better-known legend,' he'd said, 'that of a cannibalistic half-man, half-bull monster snorting and rampaging in a subterranean maze.'

Reaching into the breast-pocket of his army shirt, Sam had taken out a small photograph. From the creases in it, it was one that had been taken out and looked at many, many times.

'My wife Jenny,' he'd said simply, his voice thick with pride and love as he handed it to Ella, 'and Emma, our baby. I haven't held Emma yet. When she was born I'd already been posted overseas.'

The photograph showed a young woman who looked like every Sunday-school teacher Ella had ever known. She had a lovely smile, which saved her from plainness, and there was something impish in her eyes, which had told her that Jenny was someone who, if they were to meet, she would like very, very much.

She'd been so overcome with the relief that Sam was as happy in his marriage as she was in hers that a lump had formed in her throat.

'It's a beautiful photograph,' she'd said truthfully.

He'd slid it carefully back into his shirt pocket, saying, 'Things worked out grand for both of us, Ella, and now we can again be what we were – and that's best friends.'

'Yes, we'll always be that.' The words had come from her heart.

Now she was brought back to the present moment by the RAMC doctor she was working with in the Plaster Room saying, 'I'm ready for the bandages, Ella.'

She immersed the first of what would be several plaster-of-Paris bandages in a bowl of water and then, when the water had stopped bubbling, gently removed it, squeezing it from the ends to the centre. As she was pulling it back into shape before handing it over, the door opened and Nikoleta put her head around it, saying in hurried elation, 'Daphne's husband has just been brought in with a bullet lodged in his shoulder! I'm just going to get him ready for theatre.'

'Does Daphne know?'

'No, but as she's working in the operating theatre, she's soon going to find out.'

The door slammed shut and the doctor said with weary patience, 'The bandage, Ella, before it sets into a cast in your hands.'

*

346

The bullet had been in Sholto's shoulder for three days, and only when he'd begun to suspect that septicaemia was setting in had it occurred to him that he should do something about having it removed. His head was spinning, but that was because of the fever he now had and because the nurse looking after him wasn't a no-nonsense army nurse, or a nun. With flawless skin, dark-haired, dark-eyed and dazzling, she looked like Scarlett O'Hara in *Gone with the Wind*.

'If this bullet has been in your shoulder for three days, why did you not come in sooner?' she was saying scoldingly as, having removed his shirt, she began sponging the area of the wound with antiseptic.

'Because . . . because it didn't feel to be doing any great harm.' His voice seemed to be coming from a long distance away. It didn't surprise him. He knew his temperature was so high it had to be off the scale.

'And how would you know?' She was looking at him from beneath a sweep of soot-black lashes. 'You are not a doctor, are you?'

'No.' He wondered if she was real, or if he was hallucinating. He wanted her to be real. He could feel himself slipping into unconsciousness and fought against it. 'I was brought up with guns.' The words were mumbled, but it didn't matter. She was still there. Still the most beautiful creature he'd ever seen. Scarlett O'Hara and a dark-haired Madonna by Raphael, all rolled into one.

Nikoleta frowned. 'You are English. The English don't know about guns.'

He was about to try and explain the aristocratic pastime of pheasant-shooting and deer-stalking, but the effort was beyond him. Instead, as he slid into spiralling blackness, he said clearly, and meaning every word, 'One day . . . one day, Scarlett, I'm going to marry you.'

*

In Brigade Headquarters, Lewis was staring at one of Brigadier Chappel's colonels in stunned disbelief.

'What do you mean Miss Shelton isn't here? Goddamit, I *know* she's here. She's here acting as an interpreter.'

'Her skills weren't needed – and at a time like this, a woman amongst so many men was a distraction that was most certainly not needed. Immediately she arrived she was ordered to leave.'

Lewis's hands bunched into fists, and Adonis thought Lewis was going to deck the colonel. He didn't know much about acceptable and non-acceptable conduct in the British army, but was pretty sure that a Military Intelligence captain striking a colonel covered in stripes and pips would end up with the captain being court-martialled, and certainly with the captain in jail.

As Adonis held his breath, Lewis fought for control and said, white-lipped, 'She was ordered to leave here – when the battle had already begun?'

'Of course not unaccompanied, and the JU 52s hadn't yet come in.' There was angry spittle at the corners of the colonel's mouth. 'An officer, Lieutenant Illingworth, was detailed to escort her and they left by jeep.'

'And where is Lieutenant Illingworth now? I need to speak with him – and I need to do so fast!'

For the first time the colonel looked seriously discomposed. 'I'm afraid that's impossible. Lieutenant Illingworth is missing in action. And I have now given you as much of my time as I am able to give.'

With a sharp, decisive salute he stalked away.

Lewis's mind raced as he tried to think of the most likely place Kate would have asked to be escorted to.

An Australian who had been within earshot of his heated exchange with the colonel came up to him. 'Illingworth isn't MIA in quite the way Pickering indicated,' he said. 'He never returned, after he left on May the twentieth. He and the young woman with him either got caught in defensive ground-cover fire as the JU 52s flew in or were attacked by paras who landed in the first wave. I'm sorry, Captain. That's all I can tell you.'

'What does he mean, Lewis?' Adonis asked fearfully as the major moved away. 'Does he mean the lieutenant and Kate are dead?'

'He means it is thought they are. But Kate isn't dead. She can't be. If Kate had been killed five days ago, I would have known. She couldn't be dead and for me not to know. It isn't possible.'

With a pulse pounding at the corner of his jawline, he was already heading out of the cave, pushing his way through a mass of harassed army personnel.

'Then what are we going to do now?' Adonis's handsome face was etched with anxiety.

'What are we going to do?' Lewis rasped as they stepped out into the quarry. 'What we're going to do is find her!'

Once back in the truck, he revved the engine, fighting down panic as he struggled to think of where Kate would have asked Illingworth to take her. Kalamata was too far even to come into the equation. As the invasion had started within minutes of Illingworth and Kate leaving the quarry, where would they have headed? The only obvious place was the Villa Ariadne.

His hands tightened on the steering wheel. The only way to get to Knossos from where they were was to drive into Heraklion on the road they were now on, and then leave it by the Jesus Gate. And with Heraklion under attack, it wasn't reasonable to imagine Kate asking Illingworth to take her there. She simply wouldn't have put his life at risk in such a way. She would have wanted to be taken to the Villa – but not via Heraklion.

He said suddenly, 'Do any tracks run cross-country between here and Knossos?'

Adonis frowned. 'There is a dirt track over rough country to the small village of Stavria, and then a few steps from Stavria there is a slightly better track that leads eventually into the Knossos–Archanes road.'

Even before Adonis had finished speaking, Lewis had slammed the truck into gear.

'The track may not be wide enough to take the truck,' Adonis said apprehensively, 'and there are Germans every-where south of the town.'

Lewis made a non-committal sound in his throat, aware of the problems and heedless of them.

The road from Heraklion to the quarry had been grim enough, with German dead lying by the roadside unburied and with houses bombed into nothing but rubble, but the number of Germans who had been shot down in their para-chute harnesses in fields and vineyards was stupefying. At one point they passed a German major swinging lifelessly from a tree, his parachute enmeshed in the branches above him, a dangling monocle incongruously catching the light of the sun. Looking at him, Lewis wasn't remotely surprised that, where Heraklion was concerned, the Germans were now biding their time.

At the foot of a hill, a cottage some distance from the track came into view and Adonis said, 'It is not a cottage of Stavria. It is too soon for it to be already Stavria.'

They bucketed around a corner and came to a dead halt. In front of them, slewed half on and half off the track, was an abandoned jeep.

Lewis leapt from the truck, ashen-faced.

Bullet holes ran down one side of the jeep. There was blood on both the driver's and the passenger's seat and the track bore the imprints of four pairs of booted feet, a pair of smaller sandalled feet and then heel-marks, showing that someone had been dragged away in the direction of the cottage.

'Only four men at most,' Adonis said. 'Not a platoon. To take care of four of them will be no problem.'

Lewis shook his head. 'No. That's not the way to go about it. Even if you're right and it is only four men, if we open up with rifle fire, Kate and Illingworth are at risk of being caught in the crossfire or shot deliberately. Before I decide on a plan of action I want a rear-view of the cottage. A rear-view might give us more cover. Stay with the truck. I'll only be five minutes.'

Out of sight of the cottage and with five years' practice of climbing Cretan mountains, Lewis took the hill at a sprint. Once on top of it, and as he approached a vantage point giving a good view of the cottage, he dropped down, wriggling the last few yards on his belly.

The fenced-off rear of a garden was clearly visible, as was a small thicket of trees a little way beyond it. No soldiers were in the garden, but a Cretan girl was in one of them, feeding hens. She was wearing the usual black bodice and ankle-length skirt, her hair hidden by a black head-kerchief.

He'd seen all he needed to and turned his head away, about to wriggle back.

Then he stopped, turned his head and took another look.

She was too far away for him to see her face clearly, but he could see the way she walked and the way she moved, as she threw seed down for the hens.

Kate wasn't dead, and she wasn't wounded. He didn't have to wonder why she was so obviously making no effort to escape, when no one was standing over her with a gun. He instantly knew why. It was because she had no intention of abandoning an injured Lieutenant Illingworth. He wondered whose idea it had been that she would be safer, as they set off through country thick with Germans, if she was believed to be a Cretan. Whoever's idea it had been, it seemed to be working, but although the disguise had probably saved her from being shot, it wouldn't – and perhaps hadn't – saved her from being raped.

At the very thought, bile rose in his throat. Kate had to be got out of the cottage fast, as did Illingworth. But how? At the very least there were four armed Germans in it. No stealthy approach from the front could be made; the ground between the track and the cottage was far too open, and although there was a thicket of trees at the rear of the cottage, it wasn't near enough to the building to serve as good cover.

He thought of Kate with her fluent Greek, dressed as a Cretan and quite obviously passing for one.

He thought of his own very good German, honed to fluency by his long friendship with Helmut, and knew exactly how, with Adonis's help, he was going to remove Kate and Lieutenant Illingworth from the cottage – and how he was going to do it without a single shot being fired.

Chapter Thirty

Daphne's relief at the sight of Sholto was profound. She had become so convinced he had been killed in the fighting that she had spent hours worrying about how much he'd hate being buried on Crete, instead of in the Hertford family vault with the rest of his illustrious ancestors. A second huge wave of relief followed fast, for he wasn't suffering from septicaemia and therefore unlikely to die. Although severe, the infection in his wound was one that he was already beginning to recover from twenty-four hours later.

'Well, at least you're lucid again,' she'd said tartly, in no mood to forgive all the anxiety he'd put her through, now that she knew he could have sent word to her that he was still alive. 'I was beginning to think you were dead and, believe it or not, I really didn't want you to be dead.'

'Well, that's good, because I didn't want to be dead, either. I have to see the RAMC officer in charge, Daphne, and I have to do so immediately.'

'Stop being all-important, Sholto. It can wait until I've changed your dressing.'

'It bloody can't wait!' He struggled to his feet and for a shocked moment she thought he was about to hit her. 'Canea, Suda Bay and Maleme are all in German hands.' He'd swayed on his feet, looking as if he was about to faint. 'An evacuation of all troops is to begin tomorrow – or have I lost a day, and is tomorrow today? How many days have I been delirious? Get me to the officer in charge, Daphne, *and do it now!*'

The officer in charge that morning was Sam.

For a second he, like Daphne, wondered if Sholto was still delirious. He didn't think so for long.

'Communications have been established with General Freyberg in Canea,' Sholto said to Sam, still looking as if he could pass out at any moment, 'and the news is disastrous. Although both Heraklion and Réthymnon are holding out and are in control of their city's airfields, Canea, Suda Bay and Maleme are all in German hands and, with the Luftwaffe now flying hundreds of fresh troops and artillery into Maleme twenty-four hours a day, there's no way the island can be held. There is to be an evacuation.'

'Evacuation?' Sam struggled to comprehend it. A withdrawal he could have understood – withdrawal until a new assault could be mounted – but an evacuation, leaving Crete and the Cretans entirely in German hands? And after the fierce and bloody fight that had taken place in Heraklion, and when they had all been so confident that there had been similar successes as far as, and including, Canea, Suda Bay and Maleme?

He didn't have to ask what would happen to the wounded. The walking wounded would be amongst the thousands of troops to be evacuated; the others – the critically wounded – would be taken prisoner.

'The order hasn't been made official yet,' Sholto continued. 'When it is, it will be at the very last minute, as no risks can be run of the Germans getting wind of it. I'm giving you advance warning, so that you can have your walking wounded in full readiness for an immediate off into Heraklion, which is where, as we're still in possession of the harbour, the entire Heraklion sector is to be evacuated from.'

Sam nodded, deeply grateful for the advance information and fairly sure he knew one of the reasons he'd been given it. Sholto Hertford was determined that when the evacuation began, his wife, like Villa Ariadne's walking wounded, was going to be at the front of the queue, when it came to boarding a Royal Navy ship.

Minutes later, when they were on their own and Daphne was changing his dressing, Sholto said, 'This time there can be no acts of deceit, Daphne. When the evacuation from Heraklion begins, you have to leave as well.'

Daphne paused in what she was doing. 'There will still be wounded men needing nursing care.'

'The wounded who are not evacuated will be in prisoner-of-war camps, and the Villa will no longer be a field hospital. It will revert to being a private residence – and not the private residence of a curator of Knossos, but of whichever German general has command of this part of central Crete.'

Daphne put the lid back on a jar of sulfa powder and, when she could trust herself to speak, said, 'How can I leave Crete without knowing what's happened to Kate?'

He stared at her in stupefaction. 'What the devil are you talking about? According to Lewis, Kate was at the museum when the invasion started, and presumably – if she's not here at the Villa – then she's still at the museum.'

'She isn't. Yanni, a member of the Kalamata dig, has been there to check up on her. She left the museum shortly before the invasion started, and no one has had any news of her since.'

'What about Lewis?' He put his injured arm back into its sling. 'Surely he knows where she is?'

'The last news we had of Lewis – and again it was Yanni who gave us it – was that he left Heraklion with Adonis yesterday morning, saying he was going to Brigade Headquarters.'

Sholto said an ugly word beneath his breath. The one person

he needed to be in touch with, when the island was about to be handed into German hands, was Lewis.

They were standing facing each other, only inches apart, and as Daphne waited for him to make some belated gesture of marital affection, Sholto simply said, 'Whether or not you have news of Kate, you will be aboard a Royal Navy ship when the evacuation fleet sails for Egypt. Is that understood, Daphne?'

To his stunned amazement, she didn't defy him. Despite her anxiety about Kate, she'd known when Sholto had been telling Sam of how Allied troops were about to be taken off the island, and the island left in the hands of the Germans, that although Ella would most definitely stay behind – and that much as she herself wanted to stay behind with her – she couldn't do so. She had Caspian to think of.

When she had left Caspian in his nanny's and Mrs Hutchinson's care, she had done so confident that during the battle for the island her nursing skills would be desperately needed. She had truly believed that the battle would be over within a week, with the outcome proving to be a catastrophe for the Germans; and that, her conscience clear at having performed valuable war work, she could leave for Egypt and a reunion with Caspian.

The situation now was far different. If she stayed behind now, it could be years before she saw Caspian again – if, indeed, she ever saw him again. Sholto was quite right. This time she had to leave.

His relief at Daphne's response was obvious, but he didn't hug her fiercely with his one good arm, or kiss her passionately. It was as if between them all passion had been spent – except that it wasn't all spent, as far as she was concerned.

'What's the matter?' she asked, direct as always. 'You're not still mad at me, and trying to punish me for disembarking the evening before the invasion, are you?'

'For disembarking and leaving my two-year-old son in the care of an elderly lady and a nanny?' His sarcasm cut like a whip. 'For hoping – only hoping, mind you – that when the three of them reached Cairo, a friend of yours would then assume responsibility for him? For my not knowing for a certainty who the hell is looking after him, in a city that could still fall any day to Rommel and his Afrika Korps? No, I'm not still mad, Daphne. I'm appalled, disillusioned and as furious as hell – and if you think it's altered the relationship between us, then of course it has! How in the name of all that's holy could you expect it not to?'

The ground felt unsteady beneath her feet. She had anticipated Sholto's anger, when he first realized what it was she had done. What she hadn't anticipated was that it was anger that would endure – anger that would alter the very fabric of their marriage. Given the choice, though, even if she'd known the price to be paid, she knew she would still have acted as she had. For the last six days and nights her organizational and nursing skills had made the difference between life and death for countless numbers of badly injured men. For once in her life she had been truly needed, and for that she regretted nothing.

He said, 'I have to report back to Brigade Headquarters. I can give you a lift into Heraklion.'

'Thank you, but no. I'll leave here when everyone else who is to be evacuated leaves.'

He slid one arm into his jacket, leaving the other sleeve hanging empty. She was about to ask how he was going to manage to drive, and then remembered that he had driven himself to the Villa when he had not only been injured, but delirious.

'Will I not see you again until the war is over?' she said, aching for Sholto to pull her close to him and hold her tight.

He said, all anger and sarcasm gone, 'You know my orders,

Daphs. If Crete is occupied – and it's only hours away from being so – I must remain on the island to organize a resistance movement. What the outcome of that will be, I have no idea. It's possible I may find myself in Cairo before this bloody war is over, but whether I do, or don't, and no matter what the circumstances are, I expect Caspian to be your primary concern – and I want your solemn word that he will be.'

'He will.' Her throat felt very tight. Just the sight of Sholto in army uniform was bizarre enough, but the sight of him in an army uniform streaked with dried blood, a pistol at his hip, his hair rumpled and untidy, was so bizarre as to be surreal.

She sensed his thoughts were already elsewhere and that he was about to turn and leave her. Unable to bear the thought of him doing so without their having had physical contact, she closed the narrow gap between them, hugging him tight.

'Stay safe, darling,' she said thickly, his jacket rough against her cheek.

'And you, Daphs.' She felt him kiss her hair. 'It isn't likely to be an orderly evacuation. There are too many men to be boarded and too little time to do it in. You'll need to have your wits about you.'

'I always have.'

'That's true.' There was something approaching a wry chuckle in his voice and then he strode away from her – out of the room and out of the Villa.

For a few brief seconds she covered her face with her hands, struggling for composure. He had at least parted from her with affection, but it wasn't affection she wanted from him. She wanted deep passion and utter commitment – things he now seemed unable, or unwilling, to give her.

With a hurting heart she made her way back to a ward that might very soon be a ward no longer. The important thing now was to ensure that as many wounded men as possible reached Heraklion, and that any watching Germans remained oblivious as to the reason why.

Plaster Room shifts were always long and it was evening before Ella came off-duty, to the news that there was to be an evacuation of all Allied troops on the island.

'Sholto Hertford gave us the news unofficially several hours ago,' Sam said to her, grim-faced, 'and thanks to him, although news officially came through only minutes ago, all our walking wounded are already in the process of leaving. Navy ships will be coming in under cover of darkness at eleven-thirty tonight, and the departure deadline is two forty-five. Any later and the fleet will still be in the Aegean when the sun rises and Jerry bombers and Stukas are on the move. It means there's going to be very little time for upwards of three thousand men to embark.'

Ella stared at him dazedly, trying to take in the enormity of what he was telling her.

'Does this mean we've surrendered, Sam? But why? I thought the Germans were as good as beaten. We still have control of the airfield, don't we? And the harbour?'

'We do and, according to Sholto, so does Réthymnon, but Maleme and Canea have been overrun and the Jerries have gained control of Suda Bay.' His boyish, fresh-faced good looks were a thing of the past. His face was grey with weariness, disillusionment and, Ella realized, barely suppressed anger as well.

It was anger she understood.

The Allies had given a solemn promise to defend Crete, and it was a promise they had failed to keep. What would happen to the Cretans now? What would happen to Kostas and Eleni? To Andre and Agata and all her other friends in

Kalamata? Fear hit her stomach in a sheet of ice. What about her own little family? What about Christos and Kostas Alfred?

Sam said, 'As many of the other wounded who can be are about to be moved down to the harbour. Non-Cretan nursing staff, and that includes you and Daphne, will accompany them.'

'Of course.' That the men would need to be accompanied to the harbour with as many qualified and non-qualified nursing staff as possible made absolute sense.

Her easy acceptance that being evacuated would mean leaving her young son in the care of her Kalamata friends seemed more than a little odd and, not knowing quite what to make of it, he said reassuringly, 'You may not be separated from Kostas Alfred for too long, Ella love. And being in a mountain village far away from the coast and towns, he's bound to remain safe. I can't see Germans bothering to occupy some-where as hard to get to as Kalamata.'

She stared at him as if he'd taken leave of his senses. 'You can't possibly have imagined that I would leave with the wounded for Egypt?' At the utter disbelief in her voice, Sam's heart sank like a stone. 'How could I, when in the timeframe for the evacu-ation I couldn't possibly get to Kalamata and back in daylight, let alone in darkness, and that would be if I was doing so through a countryside free of Germans – which it isn't!'

'Daphne is happy to be evacuated . . .'

'Well, of course she is!' Ella was so exasperated with him that she could have boxed his ears. 'Daphne is going to be reunited with her child. She isn't going to be leaving him behind. Quite honestly, Sam Jowett, for an intelligent man you can be very stupid at times. Of *course* I'm not going to be evacuated.'

Sam hung on to his patience with difficulty. 'You're British, Ella. For how long do you think you're going to remain free, once the evacuation fleet has left? You'll be arrested and you won't be spending the war with Kostas Alfred. You'll be spending it in a prisoner-of-war camp.'

'No, I won't.' Her green cat-eyes flashed fire. 'I speak Greek and if I cover my hair – and every Cretan woman on the island, apart from Nikoleta, wears their hair covered – I can pass for a Greek.'

He gritted his teeth. 'I can see the impossibility of you being able to reach Kostas Alfred in time to be able to take him with you, but as he's being well cared for, surely your husband would prefer that you were evacuated, rather than constantly running the risk of being interned – and most likely, because of your sex, being interned not in Crete, but in a women's prisoner-of-war camp in Germany?'

'I won't be arrested and interned.'

He'd forgotten how infuriatingly obstinate she could be and, recognizing that nothing he could say or do would change her mind, and that he had urgent work to do in the next few hours, he said despairingly, 'Okay. So be it. From now on we're unlikely to get another chance to say a private goodbye, so it's best we say it now.' His voice was thick with emotion. 'Take care of yourself, Ella love. God bless.'

Only then did it dawn on her that, as an army medical officer, Sam, too, would be leaving with the rest of the troops. It was like being struck by a thunderbolt. Suddenly she realized just how much his dear familiarity and quiet strength had meant to her over the last stressful few days. She also thought of the high likelihood of the evacuation fleet coming under heavy enemy attack.

As if reading her mind – and not wanting to admit how much her concern for him meant to him – he said gently, 'Don't worry about the safety of the fleet. We'll be leaving, sailing and arriving in complete darkness.' And then he was gone, striding off to bring about whatever order was possible.

*

At nine-thirty the convoy that had been assembled moved off in the direction of Heraklion. Ella and Daphne were up front, in a truck that Ella was sure was the dig's much-loved Sally. The darkness had been too thick for her to know for certain and they were travelling without lights.

The officer from the Yorks and Lancs who was driving them said chattily, 'Don't worry, ladies. Embarking in Heraklion is going to be a piece of cake. We can think ourselves lucky we're not among the thousands of poor devils who were stationed in Canea, Maleme and Suda. They have to leave from a harbour on the south coast – and are having to make a route-march over the White Mountains to get to it. From what I've heard, it's a trek that will take days, and they'll most likely be under German air attack the whole way.'

Daphne's thoughts weren't on the defeated troops: they were on Kate.

'Where on earth can she be?' she whispered fiercely to Ella as the truck approached Heraklion's outskirts. 'I can't believe I'm going to be leaving without knowing where she is, and what's happened to her.'

'As Lewis is out of contact as well, perhaps the two of them are together.'

'Even if they are, it still doesn't answer the mystery as to why they haven't been seen or heard of for three days.' She left unsaid the terrible fear that perhaps they had been killed in one of the many reprisal air strikes the Germans had launched on the town since their failure to take it. What she couldn't leave unexpressed were her anxieties for Ella.

'You can't remain at the Villa Ariadne, hoping the Germans are going to run it as a field hospital for their own troops and that the Allied troops who couldn't be moved will continue to be treated, too. At a distance, you might pass as a Cretan if

362

you dress as one, but close day-to-day contact would find you out.'

'I know.' They were driving through the Jesus Gate. It had been fought for by Heraklion's citizens with as much desperate courage as had the Canea Gate. 'When things have settled down a bit, I shall make my way to Kalamata. Until then I'm going to stay with Kostas and Eleni and do my best to look, and act, as if I'm their biological daughter, not a British daughter-in-law.'

'Stay indoors. Don't even go outside to collect eggs.'

Ella didn't respond. Even though it was dark and there were few lights, the devastation wrought on the city by the bombing raids of the last few days was glaringly obvious. Ruined houses, their fronts blasted to smithereens, stood gauntly along streets running with polluted water from burst sewers. In some shattered buildings fires still smouldered. Occasionally she saw German dead in the streets, still waiting for burial. A dog was scavenging among the bodies, and in the eerie glow from the fires Ella was reminded of a medieval painting of hell.

On a quay littered with the wreckage of bombardment, a British sense of order had blessedly imposed itself. It may have been the congregating point for three and a half thousand men, but they weren't defeated men in the accepted sense. They had fought with grim tenacity and had held the ground they had been given to defend. If they were being evacuated due to failure elsewhere, that failure wasn't down to them. Two of the three companies who had defended the airfield, the Yorks and Lancs and the Leicesters, were already on the jetty, every man standing in full marching order as they waited for the ships to arrive.

At eleven thirty-two, cruisers accompanied by six destroyers arrived offshore.

'Where is Sam?' Ella asked urgently as, under a pale moon, two of the destroyers nosed into the harbour and up to the jetty. 'I can't see him.'

'Wounded aboard first!' a non-commissioned officer was shouting. 'Look lively there. We haven't got all night.'

Men of the Leicesters began efficiently decanting the wounded on stretchers from field ambulances and trucks. As they carried the stretchers aboard the nearest of the destroyers, men of the Yorks and Lancs began speedily boarding the second destroyer by scrambling up nets that had been thrown over the ship's side. Things were happening so fast that for the first time Ella felt something close to panic. Where, in the crush around her, was Sam? It was suddenly vitally important that she knew; that she at least had a last glimpse of him.

'Come along, Nurse. Aboard with your wounded!' an officer shouted at her.

'I'm not boarding,' she shouted back at him and then, with raw urgency to Daphne, 'Where's Sam, Daphne? Can you see him?'

'No – he probably boarded ahead of the first of the wounded so that he could count them all in. I have to go, Ella!' The exasperated officer had seized hold of Ella's arm. As he began firmly propelling her in the direction of the destroyer, Daphne shouted back over her shoulder, 'When Kate puts in an appearance, say goodbye to her for me. Tell her we'll all meet up again in Cairo. Or in a liberated Crete. Or anywhere. Even Oxford!'

And then she was gone; lost in darkness amongst a sea of heads as, with the wounded now all aboard, the Leicesters began their embarkation.

There was no longer any reason for Ella to stay on the jetty. Sam was quite obviously already aboard the destroyer and, if he wasn't, it was too dark to be able to pick him out amongst such a vast number of waiting men.

As she was about to turn and begin walking back to the quayside, the destroyer, now fully loaded, began sliding away from the jetty. Watching it head to the mouth of the harbour, she said to the officer standing nearest to her, 'The ship now leaving. Do you know its name?'

'HMS *Hotspur*,' he said succinctly, having far more important things on his mind than the names of the ships. They were already forty minutes down in time and there were still another four destroyers and two battleship cruisers to be loaded – and all before the Germans descended en masse. 'The destroyer following her out is HMS *Imperial*.'

Ella thanked him. Dizzy with fatigue, she began making her way to the quayside past seemingly endless columns of men. When would she see Daphne again? A realist, she knew that it could be years and, if the battle for North Africa now being waged by the Allies was unsuccessful and the Germans marched into Cairo, it might very well be never.

She comforted herself that at least she knew where, for the moment, Daphne was, which was more than she knew about other people she loved, like Kate and Christos. Neither did she know where Lewis and Sholto were. However, common sense told her Sam had to be aboard one or other of the destroyers that had now left the harbour.

Once on the quayside, she turned to look back at the frantic activity still taking place on the jetty. Two more destroyers from the evacuation fleet were now embarking men from the Leicesters and the Yorks and Lancs. For the first time she wondered where the distinctively kilted men of the Black Watch were – and then realization dawned. For the Leicesters and Yorks and Lancs to have been able to march from their defensive positions in and around the airfield to the harbour, their backs had had to be covered, and that task had clearly been allotted to the Scots. It meant the Black Watch would be the last to embark and that, when the time came for them to do so, they would have to make a very fast run for it – as, if she was to reach Kostas and Eleni's house safely, she was going to have to do.

The private who had driven them to Heraklion had given her the truck's keys, before standing in line with the rest of his company in order to embark. 'It's no use to me any more,' he'd said cheerily. 'No vehicles or heavy equipment are being taken on the ships. Orders are, when abandoning vehicles, to put sand in the sump and run the engine at full speed. As you're not hightailing it to Egypt with us and I don't want you on foot in the dark, the truck's yours. I just hope, Miss, that you get safely to wherever it is you're going.'

Ella clutched the key hard in her hand. Her only chance of reaching Knossos safely was for her to reach it before the Germans realized the island was now theirs, because once they did, there would be roadblocks everywhere. She was going to have to drive fast: faster than she'd ever driven in her life.

Chapter Thirty-One

It was a mild day, the sun warm and the sky showing no indication of the traditional October rain. The men tramped down the steep hillside towards the village, Lewis in deep conversation with Sholto, Tinker at his heels. Close behind them were Christos, Pericles and Dimitri Mamalakis. All of them were armed, Lewis and Sholto with pistols, the others with rifles slung over their shoulders. In the five months since the Allied surrender, no Germans had as yet reconnoitred as high as Kalamata, and as the small group left the holly oaks and cypresses behind them and entered Kalamata's steep-stepped streets, the village looked as it always had.

Scrawny hens pecked at anything they could find; old Zenobia grinned toothlessly at them from the doorway of her cavern-dark house; the usual horde of children rushed up to them, with the usual endless shouted questions.

Christos called out, 'I'm going to the *cafeneion*, Lewis, to see Ella and Kostas Alfred. Pericles is going to Apollonia's. Okay?'

'Okay.' Lewis hadn't expected anything else from either of them. For one thing, eight people in Dimitri's house would have been a squeeze; and for another, Christos never let the slightest opportunity go by without a visit to the *cafeneion*, which was where Ella was once again living.

As Christos and Pericles veered off down one of the village's narrow stony lanes, Sholto said, 'Now Illingworth is on his feet again, the sooner he's moved out of the Mamalakis home, the better. The Germans may not have reconnoitred Kalamata yet, but it won't be long before they do. And if the village is found to have been sheltering him, then people will be shot and the village may well be burned to the ground. It's an atrocity that's happened in my area. You don't want it happening here.'

Lewis's mouth tightened into a hard line. The present meeting between them was their first face-to-face meeting since the surrender, but bush telegraph had kept him up to date with the situation scores of miles to the west. Hundreds of troops from Canea, Suda Bay and Maleme who hadn't managed the crossing of the White Mountains in time to meet the evacuation deadline on the south coast had, rather than being rounded up into a POW camp, taken to the mountains – and in the mountains survival was only possible when the mountain villagers gave them shelter. Although the penalty for giving an Allied soldier shelter was death, the Cretans had given them shelter unhesitatingly, and many had already paid the price for doing so.

It wasn't a gamble Lewis intended taking in Kalamata.

As they neared his home, Dimitri strode ahead of them and Lewis said, 'When you return to your hideout on Mount Ida, I want you to take Illingworth with you. You don't have a problem with that, do you?'

'No. Not as long as he's up to the climb.'

The door of the Mamalakis house opened and a toddler uttering squeals of excitement came running out, to be immediately scooped up by Dimitri and seated upon his shoulders. Under normal circumstances Aminta would by now also have run joyously towards him, but Sholto was unknown to her and she stayed shyly in the doorway, blushing as he greeted her politely.

Once in the all-purpose room of the house, Illingworth was introduced to Sholto and they all gathered around the table, some of them sitting, and others – because Dimitri and Aminta didn't possess enough chairs for everyone to be able to sit – standing.

With relief, Sholto saw that Illingworth, despite the injuries he had received five months ago, now seemed able-bodied and fit. 'What I want to know,' he said to him, 'is the true story of how Lewis removed you and Kate from the cottage you were being held in. All I've been able to get from him is that he walked into the cottage with Adonis, and walked out with all three of you. There must have been more to it than that, but being an annoying bastard, he's not telling.'

Illingworth grinned, enjoying Sholto's bewilderment. 'To be honest, there's not much more to tell. It was just as he's said. He walked in with Adonis, and ten minutes later the four of us were in a truck heading for the mountains.'

'And Winston Churchill is my godfather.' Sholto turned round on his chair and looked over to where Lewis was leaning against the room's only window, one foot crossed over the other, his arms folded, 'Come on, Lewis. Joke over, or I get Kate to tell me. Spill the beans.'

'It's just as Illingworth said. I walked in with Adonis. What I didn't say was that I was wearing the uniform of a German major and that the uniform was embellished at the neck with a Knight's Cross – not the highest German award for bravery, but pretty impressive all the same.'

Still thinking he was having his leg pulled, Sholto said, 'A uniform you just happened to be travelling around the countryside with, in case it should prove useful?'

Lewis's tough, straight mouth twitched at the corners. 'No. On the drive from Brigade Headquarters we'd passed lots of dead paratroopers still in their parachute harnesses, one of them a major. I doubled back with Adonis to where he'd fallen and we relieved him of his uniform and identity papers.'

'And a rather natty monocle,' Kate interjected.

'And then what?' Sholto was riveted. 'How did you get away with the impersonation?'

Lewis shrugged. 'I'd already come to the assumption there were only going to be a small number of men to deal with. Boot marks around the jeep indicated it had been fired on by three – perhaps four – paratroopers at the most, and the cottage was too small for a platoon to be holed up in it. I'd also come to another assumption, which was that the paratroopers in question were deliberately keeping out of further action in a way that would, if a superior officer knew about it, have landed them in serious trouble.'

Illingworth said, 'When they saw Lewis striding towards the cottage, complete with Knight's Cross and monocle, they were like petrified rabbits.'

'As were we,' Kate said drily. 'Although once he was in the house and recognizable, it wasn't too bad for me. Poor Illingworth thought Lewis was the real thing – and, from Lewis's manic yelling and shouting, thought he was about to be dragged out of the cottage and shot.'

'And what exactly was it you were yelling and shouting, Lewis?'

'I was calling them some rather ugly words indicating they were cowards and a disgrace to their uniform; that they were to make their way north and join up immediately with other remaining members of their units; and that I was taking their prisoner somewhere he could be properly interrogated. I then ordered Kate to help Illingworth outside and into the truck, and three minutes later we were on our way. Whenever we ran into Germans after that I never stopped the truck, just hung out of it and shouted that I was taking a British officer to be interrogated. Once we reached the foothills of the mountains, the countryside was free of Germans and by evening we were in Kalamata.'

'Well, that's one mystery solved, but there's still another.' Sholto turned his attention to Illingworth. 'Why no Christian name? Your full name can't possibly be Illingworth Illingworth.'

'It isn't. My Christian name is Eustace. So if it's all the same to you . . .'

'It is.'

Lewis said, 'Now we've got that out of the way, it's time for me to share the latest news with Kate and Illingworth.'

Sholto, already in the know, straddled his chair, leaning folded arms on the back of it.

'An SOE officer has been brought in from Cairo by submarine, as has a wireless operator. They landed two nights ago on the south coast. First thing the officer in question did was send a Cretan ahead to let me know of their arrival. They are making their way here, but as avoiding Germans won't be easy, when hampered with a wireless transmitter, a heavy charging-engine and the batteries for it, it could be several days before they arrive.'

Illingworth fisted the air in satisfaction. If that kind of Royal Navy operation had been carried out once, it would most likely be carried out again and, when it was, his intention was to be on the landing beach when the submarine came in, and aboard it when it left.

Kate was equally elated at the news that they would finally be in touch with Cairo via wireless, but she was also puzzled. 'How did this new SOE officer know where to make contact with you?'

Across the small room their eyes met and the sexual tension she always felt when they were within touching distance of each other flooded through her.

'He probably didn't know for certain, Kate, but as Kalamata was my archaeological headquarters, it's the first place Cairo would have thought of when suggesting where I might be found.'

'And is that why you're here, Sholto?' Illingworth asked. 'Did the arriving SOE bloke send a runner to tell you of his arrival as well?'

'No. My being here is just happy coincidence, especially as Lewis feels the best place for the new man and his wireless operator isn't here, but with me on Mount Ida.'

Chairs scraped as everyone turned and looked questioningly towards Lewis.

He said, 'If the Germans discover Sholto's hideout on Mount Ida, there are more than a dozen escape routes that can be taken. The cave's position here is more difficult. Adonis has been acting as a runner between our headquarters for the last five months and now, when he does, he'll be taking with him whatever intelligence information from here needs sending to Cairo, and bringing back with him the latest information sent by Cairo.'

Sensing that all that needed to be told had been, Dimitri said, 'It is time for food. Aminta has made *fasolada* soup, *mizithra* pasties, *fava* salad and, especially for you and because they are Illingworth's favourite also, honey macaroons.'

Kate sprang to her feet to help Aminta with the food. Dimitri set a calabash of home-made wine on the table. Christos, Ella and baby Kostas Alfred arrived and, as the soup was being ladled out of a big pot, Pericles and Apollonia arrived.

It's a *glendi*!' Christos said ebulliently, throwing Kostas Alfred up into the air and catching him.

'A *glendi*?' Illingworth gave up his chair so that Apollonia could sit down.

'A party,' Ella said. 'Although for it to be a true party,

Christos and Pericles would be outside, firing off volley after volley of rifle shots.'

'Which Lewis will not let us do, for fear of it attracting unwelcome attention by those devils, the Germans.' Christos set Kostas Alfred back on his feet. 'Do you know where their divisional commander has set up his headquarters? He has done so in Archanes! Archanes, which is where Ella and I made our home – a home where, because the Germans are now everywhere in Archanes, Ella and Kostas Alfred can no longer live. And do you know where he has made his residence?' Christos's indignation was fast reaching boiling point. 'He has made his residence in the Villa Ariadne! In the Villa Ariadne he has made it, with no thought of the poor, badly wounded men who were there on his arrival and who were moved who knows where.'

Illingworth looked questioningly towards Ella and she said, 'Christos's sister, Nikoleta, was at the Villa when the wounded were moved out and the divisional commander moved in. No one would tell her where they were being taken.'

'And is Christos's sister still there? At the Villa?'

Ella nodded. Without sending word to Lewis or Christos of her intentions, Nikoleta had moved seamlessly from nursing duties at the Villa to domestic duties. It meant she was in an unrivalled position to eavesdrop and pry, and whenever she had information to pass on to Lewis, the Villa's delivery boy acted as courier. The risks the two of them were running were astronomical: torture to reveal the name and whereabouts of the person they were giving information to and then, whether they broke down under torture or didn't, execution. It was a situation that gave Ella endless nightmares.

From the street came the sound of children shouting excitedly and then there was a knock at the door. Knocks on doors in Kalamata were rare events, but the children's reactions to the caller indicated that it wouldn't be opened to someone in German uniform.

With Tinker at his heels, Dimitri swung the door open wide and then sucked in his breath, too stunned for speech.

'Good to see you again,' said a voice that everyone but Illingworth instantly recognized. 'I went to the *cafeneion* first, and Andre told me I'd find Lewis here.'

As he stepped into the house, followed by a fair-haired second man, Kate leapt to her feet. '*Kit!* Oh, my God, I don't believe it. I simply don't believe it!'

'You'd better believe it, Sis.'

She rushed towards him and he gave her a brotherly hug, as Kit struggled to recognize Lewis, who, now moustachioed and bearded and wearing a black shirt, black waistcoat and wide *vraka* trousers tucked into knee-high boots, was nearly indistinguishable from Christos and Pericles.

As he was enthusiastically back-slapped by everyone who knew him, Kit said over Kate's head, 'There are a couple of faces here that are new to me, Lewis – and Nick doesn't have a clue who anyone is, so introductions first, I think.'

'The Brits you don't know are Lieutenant Illingworth and Sholto Hertford, Daphne's husband. Illingworth isn't SOE. His jeep was shot up by a group of paras and he missed out on the evacuation. Sholto was seconded into Military Intelligence from the Foreign Office.'

Kit shook hands with them both and then, without waiting for Kit to introduce him, Kit's companion introduced himself. 'Nick Virtue,' he said, fair hair flopping low over his forehead. 'Signals sergeant. And as the wireless, charging-engine and batteries are outside on mules, perhaps we should get them under cover?'

Dimitri and Christos rushed outside to lead the mules from the front of the house round to the back of it, where the

Mamalakises' goats and donkey were stabled. 'We've never yet had Germans climb as high as our village,' Dimitri said to Nick, who'd had no intention of letting his precious equipment out of his sight. 'For tonight, hay will provide enough of a hiding place.'

Nick said that as long as it was only for one night, he was happy with the arrangement.

There were now a dozen people plus a toddler and Tinker squeezed into the small house. Kit shrugged himself out of his battledress jacket, saying, 'I see you and Sholto are in full Cretan rig, Lewis. Nick and I need similar duds, if we're not to stand out like two sore thumbs.'

'That's easily sorted. It's a miracle you travelled all the way from the south coast without being shot, dressed as you are. There's a lot you and Nick need to be filled in on, with regard to the situation here, but before we start on it – and as it will take some time – give us an update on any news we've had no way of receiving.'

There was a major shuffling of rush-bottomed chairs, with priority around the table now being given to Lewis, Christos, Sholto, Kit and Nick.

'A piece of news that wasn't even broadcast by the BBC, as it came under the category of being damaging to public morale, was that the evacuation fleet came under heavy air attack.'

The room was suddenly so silent that a pin could have been heard to drop.

'An hour and a half after the ships sailed, the steering gear on one of the destroyers jammed and the crew and soldiers were transferred to one of the other ships. It took time, and because it took time, the fleet was still in range of enemy bombers when the sun came up. All the ships came under heavy air attack, and by the time the ships limped into port at Alexandria, the death toll was close to five hundred and the number of wounded was even greater.'

Ella's face drained of blood.

Sholto looked as if he'd been slammed in the stomach by a baseball bat.

Seeing the effect his news had on him, Kit added hastily, 'Your wife arrived quite safely. I know Daphne, from when I was an archaeologist at Knossos and she visited Kate and Ella. A couple of weeks ago I saw her at Shepheard's Hotel having coffee with a woman friend.'

Sholto's relief that he hadn't been widowed without knowing about it was clearly obvious. Ella didn't feel any relief at all. Had Sam also survived the murderous crossing to Egypt? Chances were that if he'd been on HMS *Hotspur* with Daphne, he might have. But what if he hadn't been on the *Hotspur*? After all, she hadn't seen him board it. He could well have sailed aboard one of the other ships – one of the ships that had suffered a colossal loss of life. Kit might well know if there had been fatalities amongst the RAMC ranks, but if she asked about such fatalities, Christos would know it was Sam she was interested in, and her showing such concern for another man – especially as she would be doing so in front of so many people – would be an affront to his Cretan masculine pride. The question was one she would ask, but not until she could do so privately.

'Unless you've had access to the BBC, other war news you won't have had is that, in June, Hitler invaded Russia.'

The shouts of incredulity were so deafening that Tinker began barking as if the house was burning down. When Kit could again make himself heard he said, 'The most recent news is that although the Germans are at the gates of Leningrad and Moscow, neither city has been taken as yet.'

'And Egypt?' Sholto asked urgently, with Daphne and Caspian in mind. 'What is the state of play there?'

'We're holding our own. Rommel is no nearer to marching into Cairo than he was in May.'

The sense of relief in the room was profound.

Kit took a tobacco pouch, pipe and a box of matches from his jacket pocket and said, 'What is the situation here, Lewis? Is Kalamata your own and Sholto's joint headquarters?'

'No. Sholto's headquarters is a cave a few days' march to the west, on Mount Ida. My base is the sacred cave that Yanni found. From a security angle, it's ideal in that only members of my archaeological team know of its existence, and because its tunnel system is enormous. It's not ideal, though, in that there is only one way up and one way out of it. If it was to be found, escaping from it is virtually impossible. Which is why Sholto and I are both in agreement that his headquarters on Mount Ida would be a much better place for the wireless to be based.'

Kit tamped down the tobacco in his pipe. 'And approximately how many people are there in your resistance group, and how many men in Sholto's?'

'Twenty-five in mine. Thirty in Sholto's. The number of men we are able to call on is far bigger and impossible to head-count. In the mountains it's entire villages.'

'And you maintain contact with them via their local leaders?' The question came from Nick Virtue.

Lewis nodded. 'The Cretan name for a leader or a chieftain is a *Kapetan*. In this sector the most influential *Kapetan* is Antonio Tyrakis. Antonio is one hundred per cent pro-British and one of the biggest landowners in this part of Crete.'

Kit flashed a grin across at Nick. 'Sadly for you, you're not likely often to meet any colourful Cretan *Kapetans*. As a wireless operator, you'll be in a foxhole glued to your radio set twenty-four hours a day.'

Aware of that, Nick burst into rueful laughter.

That he and Kit were on easy, familiar terms with each other was obvious. Noticing it, Kate was pleased. Kit's natural reserve was something most people found difficult to crack, and as he and Nick Virtue would be spending mammoth amounts of time in each other's company, that they got on so well was a relief to her.

Kit said now to Lewis, 'What do you see as being a first SOE priority?'

'The men who were left behind when the evacuation fleet sailed. It's impossible to know the numbers, but there were certainly a couple of thousand, and probably double that figure. The bulk of them are now in POW camps, but hundreds avoided capture and are being sheltered and fed by mountain villagers who, when discovered doing it, pay with their lives. The sooner we can arrange with Cairo to get these men away by boat, the better. The other priority is straightforward intelligence-gathering. How many ships are entering the harbour at Heraklion and Réthymnon and then leaving fully loaded with equipment and men for North Africa. How many planes are flying into the airfields, carrying fresh troops from Germany. Which stretches of coastline are being mined, and which are still mine-free. Which landing places on the south coast are not yet patrolled by German units, and up-to-date lists of all those that are.'

'Do you have any Cretans placed in German garrisons where they can pick up and pass on information?'

'We do – and we also have someone in the Villa Ariadne, which is where the divisional commander has taken up residence.'

Kit was visibly impressed. 'Is this brave bloke someone I would know from my days at the Villa?'

Remembering Kit's past relationship with Nikoleta, Lewis hesitated and then said, 'It isn't a he, Kit. It's a she. It's Nikoleta.'

Kit choked over his pipe. When he could speak he said, deeply shocked, 'And you put a woman – *you put Nikoleta* – in a position where her activities could be discovered at any time? Where, if they were, she would pay with her life for them?'

'No one put her in that position, Kit. She acted on her own initiative.'

'Who,' Nick asked, deeply interested, 'is Nikoleta?'

'Nikoleta is my sister.' Christos rose to his feet. 'She is a great patriot.' He walked across to where, on the wall and below an icon of the Virgin Mary, there was a shelf with several photographs propped on it. 'See,' he said to Nick, picking up one of the photographs and walking back to the table with it. 'This photograph of her was taken on Dimitri and Aminta's son's baptism day.'

He handed Nick the photograph.

Sholto, who had never met Nikoleta, but who had heard about her from Daphne, held his hand out. After looking at the photograph and murmuring appropriate words of admiration, Nick passed it on to him.

It was of Scarlett O'Hara.

For Sholto, time halted.

Dizzyingly he thought he was delirious again, and then reality kicked in and the dizziness was replaced by euphoria. Scarlett hadn't been a product of his delirium. She was real. Not only was she real, but she was part of Lewis's resistance group. Somehow, some way, he was going to see her again. Determination flooded through him. He was going to see her again, if it was the last thing in life he ever did.

379

Chapter Thirty-Two

APRIL 1942

Despite her constant anxieties about Sholto, Ella and Kate –
and especially with regard to Kate – Daphne knew that by
living in Cairo she had scooped the jackpot. The unspeakable
horrors and misery that the rest of Europe were suffering were
not being inflicted on Cairo. In Cairo there were no food
shortages. Street-market stalls creaked under luscious-looking
oranges and lemons. Baskets of beans and maize fronted
grocery shops. There were vegetables in abundance: cabbages
and cauliflowers, leeks and asparagus. Groceries that were
nothing but a memory in war-torn Britain, such as butter and
sugar, were available everywhere, as were figs and dates and
cloudy green grapes.

The smallest, cheapest apartment came complete with a
houseboy and cook. The apartment Daphne was renting in
Garden City was neither small nor cheap, and came far more
lavishly staffed. To supervise it, she had persuaded Adjo to
leave her present employer and, as Caspian's nanny was still
with her, she had no domestic worries.

She was also one of a small, elite group, for there were very
few British women still living in Cairo, the army having evacuated military wives to South Africa more than a year ago. Only
women with clout and arrogant stubbornness, such as her

380

friend Vanessa, and those there officially, such as members of the Auxiliary Territorial Service, were still enjoying a city teeming with British, Australian, New Zealand and South African troops, all eager to party in a place that, thank to years of British colonialism, was made for partying.

Daphne who, through no fault of her own, had had no contact with Sholto for close on a year, partied – and often did so royally, for as Lady Hertford she automatically found herself on Egypt's royal family's guest list – something that, whenever she met up with him, amused Sam Jowett immensely.

Her friendship with Sam didn't amuse Vanessa, who never socialized beneath her class. 'Honestly, Daphne,' she'd said several times. 'Being seen having coffee at Groppi's with an RAMC officer is getting you talked about. Randolph thinks the two of you are having an affair.'

Randolph was Prime Minister Winston Churchill's son. Vanessa thought him as handsome as a film star, but Daphne didn't care for him and didn't give a fig what he thought.

'Sam,' she'd said to Vanessa for the umpteenth time, 'is a friend. Our shared experience in the depths of hell, when the *Hotspur* came under enemy attack, has bonded us for life.'

It was true. And the more coffee-morning meetings she and Sam had, like today, at Groppi's, the more convinced she was that Ella had made a great mistake in breaking off her engagement to him. If Sam also thought Ella had made a mistake, he never said so. He always spoke of her with deep affection, but what quickly became obvious was that Sam was that rare breed, a one-woman man – and now that he was married, the woman in question was his wife.

Their conversation nearly always revolved around whatever was going on in their very different lives. Sam was as intrigued about British Embassy garden parties and soirées at the Abdin Palace as she was about the city's red-light district – something

Sam unhappily knew a lot about, as several of the city's VD centres came under his medical supervision. Despite her hectic social life, Daphne still managed to devote time to the causes that had been close to her heart when she had previously lived in Cairo, mucking out stables at the Brooke Hospital for Horses and Donkeys like a Land Girl, only hours after coming home from a party at Princess Shevakier's; and raising money for the city's Anglican orphanage at every chance she got.

Sam was vastly interested in the latter and spent as many of his off-duty hours as possible at the orphanage, teaching the older boys how to play cricket. He was just as interested in Caspian, who, at nearly four years old, was as eager to learn how to hit a ball with a bat as the orphanage boys were.

Another shared subject of conversation was the Tetley family. Troops in Egypt were able to send and receive mail to and from England, and Sam wrote once a month to the Tetleys and always shared with Daphne the letters he received from them.

Always they talked about Crete and the people left behind there. Because she had left the island without knowing where Kate was, or what could possibly have happened to her, it was Kate that Daphne worried about most, but today she couldn't bring herself to speculate again as to why Kate had vanished off the face of the earth during the last days of the invasion. All such speculation was pointless. All she could do, where Kate was concerned, was pray she was still alive and, on an island under enemy occupation, safe.

'I wish I'd travelled to Crete before the war,' Sam said suddenly, breaking in on her thoughts. 'I did have the opportunity. When we were engaged, Ella suggested I visit her there. She wanted to show me Knossos and the dig she was working on, on the plateau above Kalamata.'

Daphne adjusted the seductive tilt of her straw hat so that

it gave her eyes more shade and said with her usual directness, 'Then why didn't you?'

'I'd just begun working at a medical practice in the Yorkshire Dales and taking time off so soon wouldn't have gone down well. And I'm ashamed to say that, in not going out to Crete, I was trying to pay Ella back in her own coin.'

'Meaning that she wasn't exactly returning to England every chance she got?'

He nodded, and then said with unexpected frankness, 'When Ella ended our engagement and told me she was going to marry Christos Kourakis, I was utterly shattered. I couldn't believe it. For months I thought my world had come to an end and that I'd never get over loving her, and then . . .'

'. . . and then you fell in love with Jenny.'

The tension that had been in his shoulders whilst he'd been speaking of Ella eased. 'Yes,' he said with a grin. 'I did . . . And I also realized that what had happened between me and Ella had happened for the best.'

He took a packet of Woodbines from the pocket of his khaki bush-shirt, offered her one and took one for himself.

When he had lit her cigarette, and his own, he went on, 'When the war is over, I'll be back to being a country GP. A lot is expected of a GP's wife. She's an unpaid secretary and receptionist. At home the phone is always ringing; messages always have to be taken. It's a full-time job and it isn't a role Ella – even if she'd given it her best shot – would have been happy in. Just as I'm a doctor and couldn't imagine being anything else, Ella is an archaeologist – and an archaeologist whose work will nearly always take her abroad. I don't know what kind of accommodation we would have come to, or what kind of marriage we might have had, but it wouldn't be anything like the marriage I have now with Jenny. Jenny's work has always been in a medical practice and she is as committed to my job as I am.'

They were seated at a table in Groppi's tree-shaded garden. A couple of New Zealand officers entered it and, although it was a quiet time of day and there were lots of tables empty, seated themselves at the one nearest to them.

Sam knew why they had done so. In a city where the ratio of men to women was hundreds to one, and where the majority of women were in the armed services and obliged to wear hideous lisle stockings, the sight of Daphne in a white crêpe-de-Chine shirtwaister, its skirt falling softly around shapely sheer-stockinged legs, was enough to make any red-blooded man position himself where he had the best possible view of them.

As long as their attention didn't annoy Daphne – which it very clearly didn't – Sam was happy to ignore them. Any hint of disrespect, though, and things would be different. Just because he was in the RAMC, and not a fighting regiment, that didn't mean he couldn't be intimidating. His broad shoulders had ensured that he'd played full-back in both his school's and his university's rugby teams, and the motto 'None Shall Pass' was burned into his psyche.

He'd surprised himself by suddenly talking about Ella so frankly, but now he'd begun being frank, he didn't see why he shouldn't continue in the same vein, although this time with Daphne, not Ella, as the subject matter.

Although Daphne chatted to him about the restaurants, clubs, charity events, polo matches, balls and functions at the Abdin Palace that she attended, she never named her escort or, as he strongly suspected, her many escorts. British women in Cairo – especially if they were as spectacularly beautiful as Daphne – were spoilt for choice when it came to men, and he was well aware how easily buttons came undone in Cairo, and what a blind eye the British turned to marital unfaithfulness when under a hot sun and far from home.

Normally he would have regarded Daphne's private life as being absolutely none of his business, but he'd met Sholto – albeit under the fraught circumstances of the imminent evacuation – and had liked him. If word got back to him of the racy life Daphne was living in Cairo, Sam didn't think their marriage would have much of a chance of surviving and thought that if it didn't, it could well be something Daphne would bitterly regret.

He said, 'Word is that Royal Navy submarines have dropped more SOE men and wireless operators on Crete; when they return, they're packed to the gunnels with some of the troops who, since missing out on the evacuation, have been living hand-to-mouth in the countryside.'

Daphne, whose eyes had slid in the direction of one of the two New Zealanders, smartly snapped her attention back to him. 'Does that mean it may be possible to send and receive mail?'

'I doubt it. What it does mean, though, is that new SOE officers going in will be meeting up with Sholto, and Cairene gossip is bound to get relayed.'

She frowned. 'What point are you trying to make, Sam?'

He said with a bluntness equal to her own, 'Three of the most talked-about women in Cairo high society are Brigadier Marriott's wife, Lady Vanessa Dane and yourself. And the subject most under discussion is who the three of you are having affairs with.'

Daphne stubbed her cigarette out. 'Well, Sam. That's a question easily answered. Momo Marriott is having an affair with Randolph Churchill. Vanessa is having an affair with Major-General Dalziel, who apparently isn't as boring in bed as Vanessa's husband. Who I sleep with, or don't sleep with, is a private matter. What I can tell you is that, unlike Momo and Vanessa, I don't indulge – and never have indulged – in full-on love affairs.'

Sam didn't know whether to be relieved or, at her indication of happy-go-lucky promiscuity, more shocked than ever.

'It's behaviour that could still lead to a divorce when your husband finds out – and he will find out.'

'I hope he does,' she flashed back spiritedly, 'because what you don't know, Sam, is that ever since we married, Sholto has been constantly unfaithful to me. I was pregnant with Caspian when we married. If we hadn't had to get married – and between his father and mine and the Foreign Office, Sholto didn't have much say in the matter – then I think things would be different. As it is, because our getting married was none of his choosing, he's taken the line that he doesn't owe me any faithfulness. And what you so obviously don't know about the British upper classes, Sam, is that adultery by both partners is quite often accepted as being nothing out of the norm; what isn't accepted is divorce. That being the case, there is no possible fear of one.'

It was a concept of marriage so alien to his own that Sam felt quite out of his depth. 'But what if you fall seriously in love with someone else; with someone who is too important to you to remain just an affair?'

'Oh, I shan't do that. It isn't possible.'

'Why not?'

'Why? Because I felt like that for someone once, and it isn't possible for me to feel like that again.'

He didn't ask her who the man had been, and she was glad. She'd known that she'd shocked his northern Methodist sensibilities enough, as it was. She didn't want to run the risk of losing Sam's friendship when she told him that the only man, other than her husband, that she'd ever fallen seriously, crazily in love with was a German – a German now fighting for Hitler in a field-grey uniform and jackboots. A German whose safety she prayed for daily, just as fervently as she prayed for Kate's and Ella's and Sholto's safety. A German that her heart ached for, and one she knew she had little hope of ever seeing again.

Hot needles stabbed behind her eyes and, so that Sam shouldn't see how close she was to tears, she turned her head swiftly, looking once again in the direction of the New Zealanders. This time she did so unseeingly, her thoughts full of Helmut: wondering where he was; what country he was fighting in; and if he was thinking of her with the same intense longing that she was thinking of him.

Chapter Thirty-Three

Helmut was in an agony of despair, both for his country and for himself. Hitler and his crazy anti-Semitism were a monster that had plunged Germany and the rest of Europe into a hell, the like of which the world had never known. The British were bombing German cities day and night. His grandparents' home city of Danzig had been pulverized. Düsseldorf had been reduced to rubble. Bremen had suffered more than a hundred raids. In North Africa, General Rommel had been halted at El Alamein. In Russia, thousands upon thousands of his fellow countrymen had died and were still dying, trying to bring Russia to her knees. And then nine months ago, with catastrophic failure staring him in the face in the east, Hitler had, for no reason anyone could think of, turned his attention to the west and declared war upon America, the mightiest industrial nation in the world.

It had been the act of a madman. Hitler needed assassinating and, much as he yearned to carry out the deed, he couldn't do so. Not when Hitler rarely left the Wolf's Lair, his headquarters in East Prussia, or the Berghof, his home in the Bavarian Alps, and he, Helmut, was in Crete.

He groaned, burying his head in his hands. How, in the name of all that was holy, had he ended up part of the occupying power in a country he loved – an enemy to people who had been his friends? It was the last thing on earth he had wanted. Even a winter in the frozen wastes of Russia and, at present, house-to-house fighting in Stalingrad would have been preferable.

He hadn't been part of the paramilitary invasion force of Crete, thank God. His battalion had been amongst the fresh troops sent in a year after the island's surrender. 'Let me be based somewhere there will be no Cretans I know,' he'd prayed in the noisy belly of the Junkers 52 as it flew over the Mediterranean. 'Let me be based in Canea, or if not in Canea, then in Réthymnon; anywhere – absolutely anywhere – but not Heraklion. Please, dear God, not Heraklion.'

Fate, of course, had kicked him in the teeth.

He had been stationed in Heraklion.

This time horrific bomb damage on a city he loved had been caused not by British bombers, but by German ones. When he walked the streets in the uniform of a German officer, a pistol at his hip, he no longer met the hospitable friendliness he had once met: instead, people looked at him with malevolent hatred.

It was hatred that was justified.

At the time of the invasion the Cretans had fought to defend their homes and island with every weapon they could lay their hands on – with axes and spades as well as knives – and consequently numberless paratroopers had not been killed by a bullet, but had been hacked or bludgeoned to death. After the surrender, when the island was in Nazi hands, reprisals on the civilian population who'd had the temerity to fight for what was theirs had been swift and savage. That he hadn't been on Crete then, left with no alternative but to take part in those reprisals, was something Helmut knew he would be eternally grateful for.

He lifted his head from his hands and looked around him. He was sitting on the steps of the Palace of Minos's South

Propylaeum. It wasn't long after dawn and the sky was still a soft rose-pink. He pushed his officer's cap to the back of his head, knowing that he shouldn't have come. For one thing, the memories were too raw, too painful; for another, the Korakis family home was far too near. There was a risk of running into Kostas or Eleni, and no way was he prepared for seeing hatred and contempt in their eyes. The Palace of Minos was also far too close to the Villa Ariadne where General Müller, the divisional commander of Crete, had taken up residence.

He had never been a regular guest at the Villa, as Lewis and Kit had been, but Helmut had several times had drinks there and once, on a day of strong Cretan sunlight, had partnered Lewis against Kit and the Squire in a tennis match. General Müller, a man known for his brutal attitude towards the Cretans and a man Helmut despised, was now in residence at the Villa. That was an obscenity he'd no wish to be reminded of.

As he watched a butterfly flutter over a clump of golden cinquefoil that had self-seeded at the foot of the steps, he wondered where Lewis, Kit and the Squire were now. Lewis, he knew, would be fighting, but where? He couldn't imagine Lewis being anywhere but under a hot sun, and his gut feeling was that he was with the Eighth Army in North Africa. He couldn't imagine Kit or the Squire in North Africa – or the Squire in anything other than a staff job behind a desk.

Wearily Helmut rose to his feet. Indulging in thoughts of the past, when Crete had been a very different place and all memories had been happy ones, was a waste of time. The days he had known then were not days that would ever return. He had to get to grips with the hideous reality, and the hideous reality was that he was due to lead the search of a village in the foothills of the mountains where an informant had said a wireless transmitter was being hidden.

He walked past the bronze bust of Sir Arthur Evans and on to the road where he'd left his motorcycle, hoping beyond hope that the search would prove to be void, for if it didn't, it would mean further searches in that area; searches higher up in the mountains; searches perilously close to Kalamata.

Ella was feeding the *cafeneion*'s hens. It was a task she enjoyed. Even though she was now pregnant again, Andre and Agata had refused to hear of her living anywhere else but with them. Apollonia, too, had a lodger again, this time a female one. Nikoleta's cover, and the cover of Villa Ariadne's delivery boy, had been blown. Both of them had been lucky to escape arrest and execution. The delivery boy had hightailed it to his grand-parents' village on the Lasithi Plain, and Nikoleta had hightailed it to Kalamata, bringing with her every last bit of information she had been able to glean from General Müller's desk.

If she had wanted to, she could have shared the former mayor's unused family house with Kate. When Nikoleta had arrived in Kalamata, it was something Kate had immediately suggested to her, but Nikoleta had politely declined the offer, saying she would prefer to share a room at the *cafeneion* with Ella and Kostas Alfred, who were, after all, family.

With the hens' food all scattered, Ella rested her hands on her tummy. The baby wasn't due for another six months, and as yet she hadn't begun to show. Christos, of course, was hoping for another boy. She didn't mind what sex the baby was, as long as it was healthy and had the right number of fingers and toes. If it was a girl, though, she was going to name her Alice, after her mother.

It was early morning and the light was a soft, shimmering mother-of-pearl. She never got tired of how jewelled the light at Kalamata always was. At dusk it would be the colour of amethysts – and this evening would be the second evening running that Christos would spend with her.

Sometimes, for weeks on end, she didn't know where he was. The network of partisan groups that Lewis constantly kept in touch with covered a huge region, all of it mountainous, all of which had to be traversed on foot; and, as his second-in-command, Christos invariably travelled with him. Evenings when he and Lewis were in Kalamata were red-letter evenings.

She'd once asked Lewis why it was so necessary that, once a group was organized, he had to keep in such regular contact with it.

'I wish to God I didn't,' he'd said with deep feeling, 'but you have to understand the social system in the mountains, Ella. It's very like the social system in the Highlands of Scotland – and, being a Scot, I understand it.'

'You mean that it's a clan system?'

He'd nodded. 'And it comes with all the advantages and disadvantages of a clan system. On the plus side, it means family loyalty and honour are paramount, and that no member of a clan whose chief is a resistance leader will ever betray it. Another plus is that where the chief gives his loyalty, the clan automatically follows. The downside is that for centuries clans have rustled each other's cattle, abducted each other's womenfolk and pursued feuds and vendettas that have sometimes lasted for generations. Working together in trusting cooperation – something that is now essential – is as foreign to them as flying to the moon.'

Something that Lewis hadn't said was that sometimes Cretans took risks that could bring danger to their villages. Word had come late yesterday evening that a small group of partisans had travelled from the Messara Plain in order to attend a family wedding at Leskla, a village in the foothills of the mountain chain that hid Kalamata. The Germans rarely ventured into the high mountains, but the foothills were different – and if an enemy patrol found partisans in the village, the entire village would suffer.

Lewis, Christos, Yanni and Nico had set off for Leskla just before dawn, in order to speak with the partisans and emphasize to them the danger they were bringing to Leskla and other nearby villages. By tomorrow, Lewis and Christos would be off on another long trek, shepherding Illingworth and other servicemen who had missed out on the evacuation to the south coast, where they would rendezvous with a Royal Navy submarine and be taken to Egypt to be reunited with their units.

What – and where – Christos's next assignment might be was anyone's guess. All Ella knew was that he was going to be spending tonight with her, and that knowledge was enough to quicken her pulses and make her day a golden one.

They didn't take the usual track down the mountain from Kalamata's plateau. Instead, with Tinker at their heels, they left from the opposite edge of the plateau, cutting across the mountain's flank in the direction of the pass that linked it to the next mountain, in the chain of mountains that extended all the way to Mount Ida and beyond.

It was a perfect September day, the sun hot, but – unlike high summer – pleasantly so. After a couple of hours, white rocky escarpments and ravines were left behind them and they entered chestnut woods, Christos, Yanni and Nico carrying their rifles across their shoulders like yokes, the way the shepherds carried their crooks.

The way led still steeply downhill and then, with surprising suddenness, the woods petered out and the men were on the edge of open hillside. At its foot was a narrow belt of trees, and beyond the trees there was a distant glimpse of Leskla village.

An elderly shepherd eyed them with interest. 'Are you going to Leskla?' he asked them.

'Yes,' Lewis said easily. 'We have come for the wedding.'

'Then you may be in time for the wedding, but you have missed all the fun.'

'And what fun was that?'

'The Germans.' He spat, as if to clear his mouth out after saying the word. 'The devils have been, and the devils have gone.'

'And did they find what they were looking for?'

The shepherd's eyes narrowed. 'They found nothing. What would there be for them to find?' He adjusted the rifle, which he would no more have been without than he would his crook, adding slyly, 'And if you and your friends don't continue into Leskla, you will be late for the wedding ceremony.'

It was Yanni who first saw the German step out of the belt of trees at the bottom of the hill.

He laid a hand on Lewis's arm, giving a nod of his head in the German's direction.

'I thought you said they had all left the area,' Lewis said to the shepherd, as they all swiftly stepped back under cover of the trees.

'I said they had all left the village,' the old man responded. 'And he is on his own. Earlier there were at least thirty of them.'

The German – wearing the peaked cap of an officer – certainly appeared to be on his own, which was odd, for even in Heraklion no German ever walked anywhere alone. Even odder was the manner in which he was making his way up the lower slopes of the hill. Every now and again he came to a halt, shading his eyes from the sun and looking upwards, not to where they were standing, but way over to the east and high, very high.

Christos, Yanni and Nico swung their rifles from their shoulders and Lewis stretched a hand towards them restrainingly. 'He isn't a threat – and no harm has apparently been done to any villagers.'

He reached into his *sakouli* for his binoculars.

As he lifted them to his eyes, the shepherd, a step behind him and a yard to his left, raised his rifle.

In the split second that Lewis focused the glasses and uttered a disbelieving 'Jesus God!', the shepherd fired. Lewis spun round, knocking the rifle out of his hands, shouting as he did so, 'Don't let him fire again!' And then he was sprinting down the seemingly endless hillside to where Helmut lay inert, his blood staining the grass an ugly crimson.

Chapter Thirty-Four

With Christos, Yanni, Nico and the shepherd hard on his heels, Lewis half fell to the ground beside Helmut. The bullet had entered the right side of Helmut's chest and he was semi-conscious with pain and shock. Seeing only what appeared to be Leskla villagers surrounding him and, he thought, about to deliver the *coup de grâce*, Helmut struggled vainly for his pistol.

The shepherd was trying to wrench his rifle out of Nico's possession, dancing up and down in demented fury, shouting, 'Hun-lovers, traitors and collaborators! Pigs and dogs! Let me get at him and I'll show you how we deal with Germans in Leskla.'

With warning pressure, Lewis grasped hold of one of Helmut's wrists and, whipping his head round to the shepherd, snarled, 'Shut up, you fool! He's not a German. He's a British Liaison officer, as I am. We came here to meet him. It's why he was behaving as he was. He was waiting for us and looking for us.'

Praying that Helmut would say and do nothing that would ruin the cover he was giving him, Lewis began ripping off his shirt, saying urgently to Christos, 'Your shirt as well, Christos. And yours, Nico. We have to staunch the blood. Yanni, go into the village and bring back a mule.' To Helmut he said fiercely in English, 'Only speak English. Do you understand?'

Helmut's response was a feeble, dazed nod.

The shepherd, terrified that if Helmut died he would be held responsible for the death of a brave Greek ally, said pathetically, 'I didn't mean it, *Kyrie*. How was I to know? I thought you were a Cretan. You look like a Cretan and speak like a Cretan, and you said you were here for the wedding. How was I to know differently?'

Lewis didn't answer him. He was too busy helping Christos try to stem the blood seeping from Helmut's chest.

'What are we to do with him, Lewis?' Christos asked urgently. 'We can't leave him in Leskla. When his absence is realized, Leskla is the first place that will be searched and when he's found – and when it's known he was shot by a Leskla shepherd – reprisal executions will follow.'

'We take him back with us.'

'But his transport? Whatever his reason for doubling back here alone after this morning's search, he can't have walked here. He must either have arrived on a motorbike or in a car. And whichever it was, when a search is mounted for him, it will be found and innocent villagers will die because of it.'

It was then that, for the first time, Helmut showed that he was taking in what was being said.

'Motorbike,' he whispered, adding so faintly and with such difficulty he could scarcely be heard, 'Réthymnon. Expected there.'

The shirts they were using as pressure compresses were already wet with blood, their hands slippery with it. Now Nico's shirt was added to the padding and Lewis used his waist-sash to bind it in place. For how much longer Helmut could survive was doubtful to all three of them, but with Helmut registering what was being said, no one put their fear into words.

Lewis, aware that a search centred on Réthymnon would buy enough time for the men of Leskla to deal with the bike, said to the shepherd, 'The motorbike this British officer came on from Heraklion must be found and hidden. The Germans will not look here first, but when they don't find this officer elsewhere, they will return – and there must be no trace this officer was ever here. Do you understand?'

The shepherd nodded vigorously, more than eager to see that no trace of a British officer was found in his village.

There came the sound of Yanni leading a mule through the belt of trees at a brisk trot.

'Thanks be to the Holy Virgin and all the Saints,' Christos said devoutly. 'Now all we have to do is to get him on the animal's back.'

When it came to doing so, Helmut was in so much pain that he lost consciousness completely. If Lewis could have thought of any other course of action other than the one they were taking, he would have opted for it – but without bringing death and destruction down on Leskla, there wasn't one.

The shepherd gave them his bed roll to help prop Helmut in the wooden saddle and then Christos began leading the animal up the hill in the direction of the chestnut trees, with Yanni and Nico walking at either side of the mule ready to catch Helmut if, in either direction, he slid off it.

Lewis hesitated before following in their wake. He was standing in the spot Helmut had been standing in when he'd been shot. He looked in the direction Helmut had been looking, curious to see what it was that had so held his attention; and whether it would give a clue as to why he'd returned alone to Leskla and, once there, had stood at the foot of the hill, gazing at the view as if in another world.

It was certainly a stunning view, with mountain peak after mountain peak cresting away into the far distance. But the peak that held his attention was one Lewis knew well; one he knew like the back of his hand. It was the peak above Kalamata.

With his throat tight with emotion, he began striding up the hill in the wake of the mule. Helmut's last thoughts before being shot had been of Kalamata and, with every fibre of his being, he hoped Helmut would live to reach it – and, if he did, that he wouldn't die there.

Over the years Lewis had walked hundreds of miles of Crete's perilously rugged mountain landscape, first as an archaeologist and then in his military capacity. With members of what had once been his archaeological team, he had fought his way out of confrontations with German patrols; had shepherded many parties of what were referred to as 'stragglers' – men like Illingworth – across the nail-biting heights of the White Mountains to the south coast, where caiques or submarines had been waiting for them; had travelled the length and breadth of the island, liaising with its clan chieftains. On no journey he had ever undertaken had he been as fraught with tension as on the reasonably straightforward journey from Leskla to Kalamata.

Helmut's deep groans ended only when he intermittently lapsed into unconsciousness. At first Lewis had been colossally thankful for those periods of time, but as the stretches of unconsciousness became longer and longer, they only increased his fear that Helmut wasn't going to survive.

When he finally felt Kalamata's village plateau beneath his feet and saw its white-sailed windmills in the distance, relief washed over him in crashing waves.

'Run and tell Kate what's happened,' he said to Nico, 'tell her I need boiled water, raki, clean linen and towelling. If she isn't at home – if she's gone up to the dig – get Ella to go to the house and get things ready. And Nikoleta nursed with Ella at Villa Ariadne. Find her as well.'

Their entry into the village was sombre. The children who rushed noisily to greet them came to a bewildered, silent halt the minute they saw Helmut's unrecognizable bloody figure slumped on the mule. Old Zenobia, who was seated in her doorway spinning, crossed herself, heaved herself to her feet and retreated into her ramshackle cottage. Other women had a different reaction, watching the sight of a wounded German being taken through their streets with deep apprehension.

Andre was standing outside the *cafeneion*, arms folded. So far no trouble had come to Kalamata, but he knew executions had taken place elsewhere, when men of a village had been held responsible for the death of a German soldier; ten Cretans for one soldier seemed to be the going rate, but he had heard rumours of far higher numbers of men and boys having been executed in reprisal for a German death.

'Nico has been for Ella,' he said to Lewis as the little procession drew level with him. 'I know who is on the mule. God willing, he'll survive and be gone before he brings trouble here.'

Lewis nodded wholehearted agreement, grateful that when Helmut had been on the Kalamata dig he had been popular among the villagers. Another thing he was grateful for was his certainty that there were no collaborators in Kalamata; that no one would run to the nearest German garrison with information as to where Helmut could be found.

'Kate is at the dig!' Ella's words came out in a rush of shock and disbelief as he and Christos lifted Helmut from the back of the mule. 'Nikoleta is here, and I have sent word to Apollonia.'

Helped by Yanni and Nico, Lewis and Christos carried the unconscious Helmut into the house and laid him on a bed that Ella had protected with an old blanket. Together, as gently as they could, they began easing him out of his jacket.

'What happened?' Nikoleta demanded, putting a bucket by Lewis's side for the bloodied shirts. 'Who shot him?'

'A Leskla shepherd.' Lewis handed Helmut's jacket to Ella, saying, 'Have you got a fresh compress ready?'

'Yes, and a sash for bandaging.'

As Lewis tentatively lifted the last blood-saturated shirt from Helmut's chest, Kate hurtled into the room. At the sight that met her eyes she came to a stunned halt, whispering devoutly, 'Oh, my God!'

She wasn't the only person in the room to be inexpressibly shocked at the sight that met her eyes. Ella and Nikoleta had both had plenty of experience of bullet wounds when nursing at the Villa Ariadne and it was immediately obvious to them, as it was to Lewis, that Helmut's life couldn't be saved by them. That it could only be saved by a surgeon in an operating theatre.

Fresh blood began seeping through the coagulated blood, and Lewis worked as swiftly as he could, swabbing the wound with cooled boiled water and then, in the hope that it would act as an antiseptic and ignoring Helmut's cries of agony, with raki.

With the blood beginning to flow faster, Ella handed Lewis a compress of thick towelling. Grim-faced and helped by Christos, Lewis bound it in place with the clean sash.

'He has to be got back to his garrison.' Kate's face was chalk-white. 'His only chance of survival is for him to be flown to a German army hospital.'

Christos rounded on her. 'How in the name of the Holy Virgin is that possible? The nearest garrison is in Heraklion and there are a dozen military posts between here and Heraklion. And even if by a miracle I were to reach Heraklion and drive into the garrison with him, I would never drive out alive. I would either be accused of being the person who shot him, or tortured to reveal who it was that had shot him. The same goes for Lewis and for Yanni and Nico.'

'The person taking him wouldn't have to reach the garrison gates, or Heraklion. All they would have to do is take him to the nearest military post. From there on, the Germans would see that Helmut reached the garrison in double-quick time – and though none of you may be able to get away with taking him to a military post, a woman could get away with it. My Greek is good enough for a German not to suspect that I'm British. I could take him.' Before Lewis could angrily reject the idea, Kate said urgently, 'Unless he is taken to a military post – and taken there quickly – not only will he die, but as a reprisal for his disappearance, innocent Cretans will also die.'

To Kate's surprise, it was Nikoleta who backed her up. 'She speaks the truth,' she said, 'but although she may deceive a German if he should stop and question her in the street, she would never deceive one under torture. Not,' she added with rare generosity, 'because Kate would give way under torture, but at a time like that would she scream out in Greek, not English? I do not think so. I do not think it is humanly possible that she would do so. And so I will be the one to take him.'

She held Lewis's eyes defiantly, knowing that if he rejected her proposal he would both have to watch Helmut die and know himself responsible, when news filtered back to him of reprisal executions in Leskla.

It was Helmut – whom they had thought to be unconscious – who broke the silence, saying faintly and with great difficulty, 'It will work, Lewis. I will say I was questioning a Cretan – that he fired at me and that before I collapsed, I fired back and killed him. That way no village or villager will be involved. Nikoleta found me and is to be thanked for bringing me to a military post.'

A pulse throbbed at the corner of Lewis's jaw. 'You would have to be taken in on a donkey cart – you'd never survive another journey on the back of a mule – and if Nikoleta is to do this, she runs the risk of being recognized as the young woman who passed information to the resistance when she was part of General Müller's household staff. And that would result in arrest and execution.'

Nikoleta shrugged the risk away. 'Only colonels and brigadiers and major-generals came and went when I was a maid for General Müller. There will be no colonels and brigadiers and major-generals at the military post – and who, in their right mind, would expect a woman with a price on her head to be driving a wounded German officer to a military post?'

Aware that he was between a rock and a hard place, Lewis said to Nico, 'Bring Zenobia's donkey and cart to the house – and bring plenty of straw with it. He'll need to be hidden until the last moment. Any Cretan seeing him will immediately finish him off – and probably shoot Nikoleta, too.'

Nico headed for the door and Lewis said to Christos, 'Round up the rest of the team. We'll shadow Nikoleta as far as it's possible to shadow her – and if it looks as if she's meeting with trouble, we're going to get her out of it, no matter what the cost.'

A brief half-hour later, as Lewis, Christos and Yanni were carrying Helmut out to the donkey cart, Ella picked up Helmut's jacket. Manhandling him back into it had been out of the question, and yet it was important when he arrived at the military post that his jacket and cap were in clear view, making his rank instantly obvious. As she walked out of the house with it she felt something small and sharp in one of the breast-pockets. Curious, she unbuttoned the pocket's flap. The object was a silver crucifix on a chain. With it was a photograph.

And the photograph was of Daphne.

It had been taken at Knossos. Wearing a white halter-necked

sundress and a white wide-brimmed sun hat, Daphne was sitting on one of the steps leading to the South Propylaeum. Her arms were clasped around her knees and she was laughing, brimming with happiness.

It was a photograph of a woman in love with the person taking the photograph and, certain that person had been Helmut, Ella replaced it in his jacket pocket and carefully rebuttoned the pocket's flap, tears pricking the backs of her eyes at the realization of how much Daphne had meant to him – and of how much she still meant.

With Helmut laid in the back of the cart and covered by straw, Nikoleta at the reins and, until the foothills of the mountain were reached, a heavily armed Lewis and an equally heavily armed team following on foot close behind, the grim little convoy set off for the nearest military post.

In the gathering dusk, Kate, Ella, Aminta and Apollonia watched them go, each with their own anxieties. Kate's anxiety was that Helmut would again be unconscious when they reached their destination and, being unconscious, would not be able to give Nikoleta the cover story she so desperately needed. Ella's was that Christos, always hot-headed, would open up with gunfire before it was necessary, thereby precipitating a calamity. Aminta's were all for her husband, for if it became necessary for the team to come to Nikoleta's aid, she could envisage no other outcome but his death. Apollonia couldn't imagine death for Pericles, but she could easily imagine Nikoleta's death – and the manner of it.

As the donkey cart and men faded from view, the women returned sombrely to the house to do what women in their situation had done from time immemorial: to wait and take comfort and strength from each other.

Chapter Thirty-Five

JULY 1943

Striding up a ravine on the eastern slopes of Mount Ida, Kate couldn't remember when she had last felt so happy and carefree. She was with Lewis, Christos, Nikoleta and the hard-core team of Dimitri, Angelos, Pericles, Nico, Adonis and Yanni. In North Africa, Rommel and his Afrika Korps had been utterly routed. Cairo was no longer under threat. Daphne and Caspian were safe.

In Britain, the fear of invasion had long since vanished and so her parents in Canterbury and Ella's family in Wilsden were also safe. The icing on the cake had been the news transmitted to Nick Virtue that the Allies had landed on Sicily. 'Which is a clever ruse of Mr Churchill's to make Hitler believe that our invasion of Europe is going to begin on Sicily, not Crete,' Christos had said to her in high satisfaction, 'and Hitler will be unprepared for it, which is a very clever idea, is it not?'

Everyone – Lewis, Sholto, Kit and the other SOE officers who had now been landed on the island – was as convinced as Christos that Crete had long been intended as the jumping-off point for an Allied invasion; an invasion that, driving up through Greece and the Balkans into the heart of Hitler's stronghold, would bring an Allied victory and an end to the war. To aid such an invasion was what, for the last two years, they had been preparing for. Their present trek to meet up with Sholto and his thirty-strong band of partisans on Mount Ida was another in a long line of indications that Crete was to be the invasion's springboard, for a large arms-drop on Ida was due that night and, when they returned to Kalamata, they would be doing so with a string of mules carrying cases of handguns, rifles, sub-machine guns and ammunition.

The way the war was now going and the imminent arms drop weren't the only causes for Kate's sense of well-being. Four months ago Ella had given birth to a healthy baby girl that she and Christos had named Alice Ariadne. Although it was now ten months since Nikoleta had risked her life in taking the gravely injured Helmut to a German military post, the relief that she had done so successfully still lingered; and, for some reason Kate didn't understand but was grateful for, Nikoleta's attitude towards her had changed since then. Although not the bosom friend she was with Ella, Nikoleta was now on amiable terms with her and, as they neared the head of the ravine, was walking only yards away from her.

'It's going to be something of a family reunion for Christos, Nikoleta and Georgio,' Lewis had said, as they had set off. 'Since Georgio joined Sholto's resistance group, Christos has met up with him several times, but this will be the first time Nikoleta has seen Georgio in over a year.'

As well as now being friendly towards her, Nikoleta had changed in other ways. Ever since she had returned from Athens she had stopped dressing in a citified way. Today she was dressed like Kate, in a shirt, trousers that were tucked into knee-high boots and a bobble-fringed *sariki*. Both of them had rifles slung over their shoulders. Even Ella always had a rifle to hand now and was familiar with how to use it.

'It is necessary,' Christos had said to her, 'and it is also necessary that you learn how to use it – and how to use it with accuracy.'

Long before they reached the cave that was their destination, members of Sholto's band came running and leaping down the steep scree towards them, shouting greetings.

Moments later Nikoleta was being hugged by her tousled-haired younger brother, and all around Kate other enthusiastic greetings were taking place. Dimitri and Angelos were exuberantly meeting up with a couple of their cousins; Yanni was meeting up with a nephew and Nico with a god-brother. Only she, Adonis and Pericles were left out of the loop – Adonis because, as the runner between Sholto and Lewis, he was so often with the partisans now swarming around them as to be counted as one of their number, and Pericles because he was a mainland Greek with no relatives or god-brothers on Crete, and because there was something about him that made even Cretans keep a respectful distance.

She wasn't left out of the loop for long, because Sholto, in full heroic rig, his light-brown hair hidden by a black tasselled *sariki* and let down only by a moustache and beard that were too close to being blond to be Cretan, came striding towards her.

'Welcome to Mount Ida, Kate!' He gave her a bear-hug. 'Does Kit know you're roaming Crete armed with a rifle?'

'Probably not – and I'm living in hope that I never have to use it. Is Kit here? I don't see him.'

The noisy melee of those greeting and being greeted was now making its way up the steep scree to the mouth of the cave.

'Kit is down in the Amari valley, meeting up with Xan Fielding, the SOE officer responsible for western Crete; and Nick is in the cave, huddled over his wireless transmitter in case there are any alterations to the timing of tonight's drop.'

As he was talking to her and they were climbing the scree, in the wake of everyone else, his eyes were on Nikoleta as, sandwiched tightly between her brothers, she headed towards the cave.

Seeing what she took to be natural curiosity, Kate said, 'You haven't met Nikoleta yet, have you, Sholto? I'll introduce the two of you properly when we reach the cave.'

'As if the three of us were at a Canterbury tea party?' There was vast amusement in his voice. 'There's no need, Kate. I met Scarlett when she was part of the nursing staff at the Villa Ariadne and I was there with a bullet buried in my shoulder.'

'Her name is Nikoleta, Sholto. Not Scarlett.'

'Not to me it isn't,' he said, with such intensity in his voice that Kate wondered if his troglodyte existence was beginning to get him down.

When they finally reached the cave she was interested to see that it was almost as big as the one at Kalamata – and that it had been made almost as comfortable, with blanket-covered beds of deep brushwood all around the sides. A fire was burning, on which meat was roasting, and in the glowing ashes, potatoes were baking. As always, there was an abundance of locally made raki and, mindful of the trek that would soon have to be made to the dropping zone, Kate resolved to treat it with caution. After their meal, as dusk deepened into night, the singing of *mantinádes* began.

Mantinádes fascinated Kate. They were rhyming couplets sung to musical accompaniment. Each *mantináda* was complete in itself, but it was usual for a verse to receive a verse in response, and this would lead to another verse, and then another. When she had asked Christos why the framework of the couplets was so inflexible, he'd said simply, 'Because it has always been so, Kate. Even since the fifteenth century and the time of the Venetians it has been so. Never will it be changed.'

Now, seated with Lewis in the flickering firelight on blanket-covered, sweet-smelling thyme and juniper brushwood, she waited expectantly as Angelos Mamalakis began playing a lyre and Georgio stood up to sing.

He sang about his love for his country; for the brotherhood he shared with those he had broken bread with; how, if he died, he would not want his mother told and made sad, but would rather she was told that he had married and was living in a far-distant part of Greece. And as he sang it was quite obvious that, singing, he no longer felt shy.

Other *mantinádes* followed, some sung by other members of Sholto's resistance group and some by members of their own group, with Adonis and Yannis carrying away the honours. Afterwards the traditional *maleviziotis* was danced by the men, with much twirling and leaping and clicking together of booted heels, and then there was another men-only dance; and then, finally, dances that she and Nikoleta could enthusiastically join in.

By the time it came for setting out in deep darkness for the drop site, Kate was having such an exhilarating time dancing shoulder-to-shoulder between Lewis and Christos that she'd almost forgotten why they were all there.

For security's sake, the drop site was a good distance from the cave. 'And so even if those billy-goats, the Germans, are alerted to the drop, they will not find Kyrie Sholto's headquarters,' Georgio said, no longer quite as shy with Kate, 'and as the site is high and flat, it is also where I graze my sheep.'

'Is that where the meat we ate tonight came from?'

'Yes. It was good meat. Good meat it was. Without my sheep, our diet in the cave would not be so good. The billy-goats are always on the lookout for high plateaus where sheep are grazed. When they first seized our island they supplemented their rations with livestock stolen from villages and, now that the villages have no livestock left, they go further afield to steal a sheep.'

Negotiating a mountainside in the dark – and with a string of mules – wasn't easy and Kate breathed a huge sigh of relief when they reached their destination. Immediately brushwood was unloaded from the backs of the mules and signal fires were built.

'But don't anticipate the plane coming in at the arranged time,' Lewis said to her as he stacked juniper branches into a pyre, 'or even appearing at all. Three months ago Sholto and his men came up here nine nights running, before the drop took place.'

Kate looked across to where, in the darkness, Sholto was talking with Nikoleta. They appeared to be getting on extremely well. As Nikoleta had given him medical treatment for a bullet wound, it was no surprise that they had something to talk about, but knowing from Daphne Sholto's reputation with women, Kate hoped he wasn't making a nuisance of himself.

The thought had barely flashed through her mind when Nikoleta gave a smothered laugh. In a moment of déjà vu, Kate was once again on Villa Ariadne's terrace, listening to the sound of Nikoleta's smothered laughter as, in darkness seven years ago, she met Lewis in the Villa's Edwardian garden.

There came the unmistakable drone of an aircraft and, as men ran to light the fires, Kate knew one thing with certainty: if Sholto was again in Lothario-mode, Nikoleta was not finding it objectionable.

The plane flew in low, waggled its wing tips in greeting and, as it passed overhead, disgorged a stream of parachutes. As heavy packages and canisters landed, Kate sprinted with everyone else to retrieve them. The plane circled and came in again, streaming more parachutes in its wake, and then did a third run before, with another friendly waggle of its wing tips, it turned south, flying off in darkness towards British-held Egypt.

It was a most successful drop. As arms and ammunition were borne triumphantly back to the Mount Ida cave on the backs of the mules, Lewis slid an arm around Kate's shoulders and hugged her tight. 'Only two 'chutes missed the site,' he said as Nico and Adonis, striding close behind them, began singing a rude song about Hitler. 'They fell into a ravine. Georgio and Christos are coming back in the morning to retrieve them.'

Pericles came up to them. 'Are we dividing the drop between our two groups immediately we get back to the cave, Lewis? Or are we doing it in the morning?'

'In the morning. By the time we get back to the cave we're going to be in need of a few hours' sleep.'

'And once we get our share of the drop back to Kalamata, who is going to be in charge of distributing some of it to Kapetan Tyrakis?'

'I am – and I'll be doing it with you and Christos.'

Pericles nodded, happy that a *Kapetan* like Antonio Tyrakis would be aware of how important a part he played in Lewis's group.

As Pericles settled into an easy stride beside them, Kate knew that her one-to-one conversation with Lewis had come to an abrupt end. For Cretans, conversation was always communal – and usually noisily so. That two people might enjoy talking to each other without anyone else taking part in what they were saying was something that simply never occurred to them.

For two people deeply in love, other kinds of privacy were just as hard to come by, especially under the conditions in which she and Lewis were living. Lewis was absent from Kalamata far more often than he was in his hideout high above the village. Even though there were now a handful of other SOE officers on the island, keeping in touch with resistance groups under the leadership of local *Kapetans* – and, more importantly, control of them – was becoming an increasingly full-time occupation. The Cretans wanted to hit back at the Germans in any and every way they could; but actions such as ambushing a German patrol and slaughtering it, something the Cretans were extremely good at, led without exception to horrifically bloody reprisals, and it was the innocent who suffered. Men and boys who had not taken part in the ambush were rounded up and executed in front of wives and mothers; villages were burned to the ground. The satisfaction that a handful of German deaths gave was not, in Lewis and Sholto's judgement – and that of Xan and other SOE officers – worth the price that had to be paid. It was intelligence that was important, and worthwhile sabotage, such as fixing limpet mines to German ships in Suda Bay or blowing up aircraft on the new airfield the Germans had built at Tymbaki.

Even when Lewis was in his headquarters in the sacred cave, nights couldn't be spent together, for the team and other members of his resistance group were always there as well. Neither, if he was to retain a shred of respect with his men, was it possible for him to spend the night with Kate in the house they had lived in together before the occupation – and where she still lived.

A wry smile touched the corners of Kate's mouth. However much Sholto might want to make headway in his relationship with Nikoleta, the chances of his doing so were slim. He was going to have to live in agonized frustration, as she and Lewis were living. In Sholto's case, it would be a frustration that was all to the good, for although in Cretan society Nikoleta had got away with having her name linked to Lewis's, she certainly wouldn't get away with having it linked to Sholto's. And

Daphne's reaction, if word was to reach her that Nikoleta was Sholto's latest fling, would not be nice. It would not be nice at all.

That night she and Nikoleta shared a blanketed brushwood bed several yards away from the men's beds and it gave Kate an opportunity for reminding Nikoleta of her friend Daphne's existence. 'She must miss Sholto,' she said, 'and I expect Sholto would like to be recalled to Cairo, so that he and Daphne can be together again.'

Nikoleta was lying on her back, her arms behind her head. 'Sholto is a *pallikari*,' she said dismissively. 'A *pallikari* is a brave and fearless freedom-fighter. In medieval days they fought the Turks and freed Crete from Turkish enslavement. Now *pallikariá* like Sholto fight to free Crete from Nazi enslavement and, as such, they do not have time for thoughts of wives and children.' And with that she rolled over and away from Kate, the subject determinedly closed.

When Kate woke next morning, Georgio and Christos had already left to retrieve the parachutes and canisters that had fallen in the ravine. Nick Virtue was making porridge and, not having any oats to make it with, was doing so out of a concoction of spelt flour and sheep's milk.

'We're not heading straight back to Kalamata, Kate,' Lewis said to her, sticking a long Cretan knife down the folds of his waist sash. 'Kit is due back this morning from his meeting with Xan, and I'm going to hang on until he can give me a first-hand report about it. Meanwhile I'm going to divvy up last night's haul with Sholto.'

It was a task that was going to take some time and, with Nikoleta nowhere to be seen and as she was beginning to find the cave claustrophobic, Kate went outside and found herself a convenient-sized boulder to sit on. The sun was already sizzling hot and she raised her face to it, closing her eyes, her happiness in her personal life – and in her certainty that an Allied invasion was imminent – bone-deep.

It was a moment that would be seared in her memory forever.

It was the Cretans, with their finely attuned sense of hearing, who first heard the long, painful cries. Yanni, who had been reloading a mule a few feet away from Kate, stopped what he was doing. 'Holy Virgin!' he said, eyes widening. 'What is that?'

Angelos, Dimitri, Adonis and Nico all ran out of the cave, with Lewis, Sholto and Pericles hard on their heels. Kate rose to her feet, filled with a nameless dread as, shielding her eyes from the sun, she looked across the scree in the direction that the cries were coming from. It was the direction they had taken the previous evening when going to the drop zone; the direction that Christos and Georgiou had taken earlier that morning – and that at any moment they were expected to be returning from.

The scree was still bare, but it was skirted by a thick belt of cypress and pine and, as the anguished cries grew louder and nearer, the entire team, including Lewis, began sprinting in the direction of the trees.

Sholto and his partisans stood tensely at the cave entrance, rifles at the ready.

As Lewis and the team neared the trees, Kate clenched her hands into fists, terrified as to what was going to emerge from them.

Howling with grief, Georgio appeared, leading one of the two mules he and Christos had set off with just hours earlier – and the load on the mule's back wasn't rifles or ammunition.

It was Christos.

Chapter Thirty-Six

Ella was in the *cafeneion*'s kitchen, baking *Christopsomo* bread, just as she had baked it every Christmas Eve for the last seven years. This time, though, she wasn't baking with a heart full of joy and happy anticipation. This time, as she kneaded the dough, she was doing so with a heart so broken she couldn't even begin to envisage the day when it might begin to heal.

She had been in the kitchen baking, on the day Kate had told her that the love of her life was dead. Until that moment it had been just an ordinary day. In anticipation of Christos returning from Mount Ida with Lewis's share of the arms drop, Ella had been baking his favourite *kourabiedes* cakes.

Kostas Alfred had been rolling tablespoons of dough into small balls with the heel of a hand when the presentiment of something being very, very wrong had overwhelmed her. Even before she'd heard the *cafeneion*'s outside door open, she'd known that bad news was about to come; and the instant Kate had stepped into the kitchen and Ella had seen the expression on her face, she had known what the bad news was.

She had screamed, terrifying Kostas Alfred, who had been making a dimple in one of the dough balls; and sending Tinker, who had been beneath the table, into a frenzy of barking.

'Where is he?' she had demanded hysterically, trying to push past Kate to the door. 'What happened, Kate? WHAT HAPPENED?'

Agata had hurtled into the room, scooped up a shrieking Kostas Alfred and, shooing the still-barking Tinker in front of her and sensing the news about to be broken, had left it with the same speed with which she'd entered.

And, holding Ella in her arms, Kate had told her.

She'd told her of how Christos and Georgio had returned to the drop site and retrieved two parachute loads that had fallen into a ravine. She'd told her of how, just as they were about to set off back to the cave with their loaded mule, Georgio had seen a cluster of his sheep heading towards the corrie at the far end of the ravine, and of how Georgio had gone back into the ravine in order to herd them back on to the plateau.

'And then,' Kate had said unsteadily, 'Christos saw a small party of Germans making their way towards the corrie. It was obvious they were intent on stealing the sheep and hadn't yet seen Georgio. Christos knew that when they did see him, he would be cornered, so he began firing towards them and leading them off away from the mule and the guns; away from Georgio.'

Later, Georgio had told Kate of how, on hearing the firing, he had raced out of the corrie to come to Christos's aid; of how his additional firing had convinced the Germans there were more Cretans in the ravine than they could deal with and how they'd speedily exited it; and of how he had found Christos dying from gunshot wounds.

'And the last words he spoke,' Georgio had said, his face contorted with grief, his voice thick with it, was, 'Tell my little Yorkshire girl she must be brave and strong. Tell her I love her. That I've always loved her, and that I die loving her.'

Ella stared down at the *Christopsomo* bread she had been kneading, tears falling in a flood she couldn't stop. How could it be Christmas and Christos not spending it with her? How could he not be about to breeze in through the door and whirl her around in his arms and throw Alice Ariadne high in the air, making her squeal with delight, and tell Kostas Alfred what a big strong boy he was? How could the loving, laughter-filled, tempestuous, so-very-satisfying life they had lived together be so finally and irrevocably over?

Numbly she put the dough to one side to rise.

For the sake of Kostas Alfred and Alice Ariadne, she had to live through each and every day, but it was hard; so hard that if it hadn't been for Kate she didn't know where the strength she was finding would have come from.

Lewis, too, had been exquisitely kind and supportive to her. From the moment she had arrived at Kalamata as a member of the dig-team, they'd had a good working relationship; a relationship that had quickly turned into friendship. Now he talked with her about the way the war was going and how it was affecting Crete, with the same frankness with which he talked with Kate – and had once talked with Christos.

In the few days between Christmas and New Year he called in to see her at the *cafeneion* en route to a meeting with a Réthymnon *Kapetan*. After he'd had a game of ball with Kostas Alfred and had agreed with her that Alice Ariadne's hair – which was as red as her own – showed little signs of ever turning dark, they'd sat outside in the pale winter sunshine and he'd said grimly, 'The war may be going well for the Allies in general, Ella, but that we've invaded Europe via Sicily is having a disastrous effect on the unity of resistance groups here in Crete.'

It was something Ella already knew from village gossip, but hearing Lewis admit it was infinitely more dispiriting. She warmed her hands around a mug of dandelion tea – the only kind still available. 'It's understandable that people would be both disappointed and angry, Lewis. Everything pointed to the landing taking place here. The entire island was ready to rise up in wholehearted support of it. The realization that instead Crete was being used as a decoy to deceive Hitler has come as a betrayal. Even to *me* it has come as a betrayal.'

Lewis sighed heavily and ran a hand through his hair. 'Trust me, Ella, when I tell you that every British officer on Crete was similarly deceived. That it was Sicily used for the landing came as a huge surprise. And the problem we have now is in keeping powerful chieftains who, before the occupation, were always at each other's throats from being at each other's throats again.'

'Because of politics? Because of so many *Kapetans* being Communists?'

He nodded. Politics and Cretans were indivisible. He'd never yet met one Cretan who wasn't a passionate supporter of one party or another. That some of his *Kapetans* – and the men they led – were Communist had never been a problem. And then had come the realization that Allied troops were not going to use Crete as a springboard for the invasion of Europe and, in doing so, liberate Crete. And from then on, the problems had been massive.

'If the Allies will not liberate us, then they must give us the weapons for us to liberate ourselves,' Antonio Tyrakis had said to him angrily. 'And that means far more weapons than we have so far received.'

The same kind of reaction had come from every other *Kapetan* that Lewis had dealings with, both Communist and non-Communist. It was a major problem, but it wasn't the greatest one. The greatest problem was that although Communist and non-Communist resistance groups had previously worked well together, now, with liberation no longer a possibility until the war finally ended, they no longer did so.

The meeting he was en route to at Réthymnon was to try and make a powerful *Kapetan* who was a member of ELAS – the Communist National Liberation Front – and another equally powerful *Kapetan* who was a member of EOK – the non-Communist National Organization of Crete – bury their differences and continue working together. Unless they and others like them did so, Crete's resistance movement would fall apart in bloody infighting.

He voiced his thoughts to Ella and her pale skin paled even further. She pushed her mug of tea away, rose to her feet and went indoors for two glasses of raki. When she came out with the raki, she said, 'Infighting is a possibility too ghastly to even think about, Lewis. There must be some way the Communists can be persuaded to work in harmony with everyone else.'

'I and every other SOE officer on Crete are struggling to find it. What you have to realize, Ella, is that the Communists have an agenda over and above freeing Crete from Nazi occupation. They're looking to when the war has been won and, when it is, they want Crete – and the rest of Greece – Communist; not royalist and democratic. Xan Fielding has managed to set up a non-aggression pact between EOK and ELAS *Kapetans* in the western half of the island, and so far it's holding. Here, however, Antonio Tyrakis is not only demanding more arms than I'm able to give him; he's refusing to accept my suggestions as to how he should distribute and use them. The same goes for the *Kapetan* I'm going to meet in Réthymnon. Trying to reason with hot-headed Cretan chieftains, who think nothing of carrying out vendettas that last for generations, isn't easy.'

Ella, knowing how hot-headed Christos had been, could well believe it. Changing the subject, she said, 'Do you see much of Kit and Nick Virtue, now they're no longer with Sholto?'

'I don't see as much of Kit. The White Mountains are Xan Fielding's area and I don't have much call to be there. Nick didn't move with him, as there is already a Signals sergeant at Nipos; and so, yes, whenever I meet up with Sholto, I also get a few words with Nick.'

Ella hesitated for a moment and then said cautiously, 'It's a shame the Nipos operator couldn't have moved to Mount Ida.'

Lewis quirked an eyebrow, 'You mean so that Nick could have gone with Kit?'

She held his eyes steadily. 'Yes. It must be so frustrating for them to be separated, when it would have been so easy for the new operator to have taken over at Mount Ida and for Nick to have gone with Kit to Nipos.'

Lewis's mouth crooked into a smile. 'You're very sharp, Ella. When did you guess?'

'When I saw how relaxed and happy they were in each other's company. When I saw the difference that being with Nick had made to Kit. I find it's always easy to tell when two people are in love, no matter how hard they try to hide it.'

'No condemnation then?'

'No – and there's none from you either, is there?'

'Not really. But I wouldn't want anyone else to pick up on it, in the way you have. If Cairo caught a whiff of it, one or other of them would probably be recalled. And homosexuality may have been an accepted norm in ancient Greece, but wartime Crete isn't ancient Greece. If word got about, there's no telling how Kit's band of partisans would react. They may very well be fine with it, but on the other hand, they may not. And without the confidence and trust of the men he leads, an SOE officer can't function.' He drained his glass of raki and said, 'You haven't said anything to anyone else, have you, Ella?'

'No. Not even to Kate. I think it's something Kit will want to tell her himself – when the time is right and when he both wants to and has the opportunity.'

Kostas Alfred, who had been rolling his ball against the *cafeneion* wall, hopeful of Lewis throwing it to him again, finally gave up all hope and, with the ball in both hands, ran up to Ella. 'Can I see if Orestes wants to play ball with me, Mummy?

'Yes, sweetheart, but remember you are three and a half, and Orestes isn't three until Easter. Don't throw the ball at him too hard.'

'Would that be Orestes Mamalakis?' Lewis asked, as Kostas Alfred raced off on sturdy fat legs, 'Angelo's youngest?'

'Yes. In Kalamata there are plenty of children his age to play with. Dimitri's two boys are three and four years old, and Zenobia's granddaughter is four.'

As he saw Pericles enter the far side of the square, Lewis rose to his feet and slung his *sakouli* over his shoulder. 'Just before I go, what do the women of Kalamata think about Nikoleta having moved in with Nico's mother at Réthymnon?'

Ella tilted her head a little to one side. 'They think that she and Nico are preparing to marry. And because they know Nikoleta is wanted for spying, they are relieved that she is no longer living at the *cafeneion* where, if a stranger were to come and recognize her, they might betray her and bring the Germans down on the village. Instead of which . . . ?'

Lewis was waving towards Pericles and entirely missed the odd inflection in Ella's voice.

'Instead of which,' he said, 'she is in Réthymnon, where no one knows she is wanted for spying and where she is constantly picking up information and passing it on to Sholto who, on the eastern slopes of Mount Ida, is not too far from Réthymnon.' He grinned. 'You never know, Ella. Nikoleta and Nico make a very good-looking couple and perhaps Kalamata's gossips are right. Perhaps she and Nico will marry.' And with that, he kissed her on the cheek and set off across the square towards Pericles.

Ella watched him go. That Nikoleta had moved to Réthymnon

so that she could continue being active in the resistance and, in the bargain, see more of Nico was certainly not Kate's reading of why Nikoleta had gone there. However, as Kate had obviously not shared her thoughts with Lewis, she had no intention of doing so. In her opinion, when it came to her sister-in-law Nikoleta, it was best to let sleeping dogs lie.

Chapter Thirty-Seven

Nikoleta and Sholto were sitting in a small, dark bar in one of the warren of narrow streets that huddled around Réthymnon's harbour. For Sholto, time unaccompanied by any of his partisans, *Kapetans* or another SOE officer was time hard won and he was hoping to make the most of it. For both of them, passing through the checkpoints before the city could be accessed and walking through the German-sentried streets of Réthymnon was an adrenalin-powered buzz that, reckless by nature, they both got a kick out of.

For Nikoleta, lodging with Nico's mother near the Church of Our Lady of the Angels, brushing past German soldiers in the streets was something she did on a daily basis and, because she did, she dressed unobtrusively in black and with a black head-kerchief covering her hair. When in Réthymnon, Sholto also dressed plainly in shabby breeches and a many-buttoned shiny-with-wear waistcoat, his give-away light-brown hair hidden by a black head-cloth. False identity papers ensured they had no trouble at checkpoints, and Sholto was unarmed – a necessity when a checkpoint had to be passed. That he was unarmed only added to the thrill of danger that he felt.

He'd come into Réthymnon for a meeting with the town's mayor, nearly giving the mayor a heart attack when, almost cheek-by-jowl with a German officer, Sholto entered the mayor's office.

Now, seated across a zinc-topped table from Nikoleta, he took hold of her hands and imprisoned them in his, saying fiercely, 'The Allies are going to win this war, Scarlett, and when they do, I'll no longer be on Crete and an SOE officer. Life will get back to normal, and when it does I want you to be with me.'

Her almond-shaped eyes, like the eyes in a Minoan fresco, flashed fire. 'How can I be with you when we are not married? And how can we be married, when you are already married?'

It was, he had to admit, a question that needed some kind of an answer.

He said fiercely, 'Daphne and I will be divorcing when the war is over.'

'Divorce? I do not know this word. What is it? And does Daphne know she will be getting one of these and will then not be married to you any more?'

Sholto thought of being reunited in Cairo with Daphne and of then almost immediately announcing that not only did he want a divorce, but that he wanted one as quickly as possible; and that, no matter how much she protested, he was going to get one.

He thought of the grounds on which he could get one.

Adultery was the most straightforward, but also the most messy. His career at the Foreign Office would go down the pan. Did he care? Yes, passionately; but not as passionately as he wanted to tie Scarlett to him forever. Five years' separation was also grounds for divorce, but wartime separation wouldn't count and, on the grounds of separation, it was Daphne who would have to bring the divorce action – something she was very unlikely to do.

Nikoleta's eyes were still flashing fire and holding his.

He remembered the last time he and Daphne had been together. It had been in the Villa Ariadne, minutes before the sky over Heraklion had blackened with invading Nazi para-troopers. He also remembered his parting words to her. He hadn't yet become enslaved by Scarlett, but what he had said had, nevertheless, been very specific.

He had told Daphne he would never forgive her for not accompanying Caspian to Cairo and that it was all over between them. And if that didn't mean she knew he wanted a divorce, he didn't know what did.

Now he said with deep passion, 'Three years ago I told Daphne it was all over between us. She knows that when the war is over, our marriage will end in divorce.'

'Truly?'

'Truly.' His voice was low with sincerity.

'And when this happens, you will marry me?'

He wanted to reach across the table and drag Nikoleta into his arms, but it would be behaviour in public so un-Cretan-like it would draw unwelcome attention from a bartender, who could, for all he knew, be a collaborationist. He had to content himself with clasping her hands even more tightly, and saying thickly, 'Yes, Scarlett my darling. I promise you on all that is sacred that I will marry you. What I want to know is, will you marry me?'

'If I marry you, will we live in London and will I be able to have tea with King George and Queen Elizabeth and the little princesses?'

'Yes, we'll live in London,' he said, dealing with the easiest part of the question first. He thought of the damage a divorce and remarriage to a Cretan girl was going to do to his career and swiftly amended what he'd said. 'And if we don't live in London, we will always have a home in London that we can visit.'

'But why . . . ?' she began, a frown pulling her sleek, dark eyebrows together.

'Why is it possible we wouldn't be living in our London house? Because I might very well be working in Washington.'

It was true. In America he might, God willing, still have a career in the world of diplomacy and, in America, Nikoleta wouldn't be socially cold-shouldered. As Lady Hertford, she would be regarded as an exotic knockout.

'And the King and Queen and little princesses?'

It was a question he couldn't answer as she wanted him to. As a man who had been divorced, he wouldn't stand a hope in hell of socializing with the royal family again, but he knew what Nikoleta's reaction would be if he said so. He said instead, 'When we marry, you will be a viscountess and at grand events will wear a tiara.'

'A tiara?'

'A tiara is a type of crown.'

Nikoleta let out a deep sigh of satisfaction. Being a viscountess and wearing a tiara were not things Lewis, or Kit, had ever promised.

Sholto had clinched it, and he knew it. 'I have to make love to you,' he said urgently. 'If I don't make love to you soon, I shall explode.'

They had both been leaning over the table towards each other, but now, although her hands were still imprisoned in his, she drew back a little, her navy-dark eyes cautious. 'That is not the custom in Crete. Not until after marriage. Lewis never asked such a thing of me, and neither did Kit.'

It was something Sholto found hard to believe of Lewis, but quite easy to believe of Kit.

He said, 'Lewis and Kit didn't love you as I do. They didn't want to have you with them always, as I do. They didn't know how very, very special you are, Scarlett.'

'That is true.' There was complacency in her voice. 'I *am* special. Always I have known it. Ever since the great Sir Arthur said I was like a god-daughter to him, I have known it. I was different because Sir Arthur had me taught English and gave me English books to read: *Alice in Wonderland*; *Peter Pan*; *The Secret Garden*; *The Children's Homer*; *The Golden Treasury of Children's Poems*; *The Kings and Queens of England*. And I grew up spending time with Palace of Minos archaeologists. I was always different from other village children. I never fit in. Not even when I was small. And because when I was seventeen Lewis took such an interest in me, no Cretan man ever thought of asking me to marry him.'

Laughter bubbled up in her throat. 'And I did not mind, because I did not want a Cretan man, all smelling of sheep and wanting a wife who would bring water in from the pump, and dry laundry on boulders and milk the goats and look after the hens. And now I never will have, because I will be a viscountess and wear a tiara!'

Her delight at the prospect of her future with him was so infectious that Sholto cracked with laughter. The insane thing he'd now committed himself to – divorcing Daphne in order to marry a Cretan village girl – was something he'd never felt more sure of in his life. Unlike with Daphne, this time he wasn't being pressured into anything. This time the decision he'd come to was his, and his alone, and he was so goddamn sure of it that, uncaring of the bartender – and anyone else – he let out a whoop and punched the air.

Kit wasn't feeling similarly exuberant. He was sixty miles distant from Nick and, because of the mountainous terrain of those sixty miles, might just as well have been six hundred miles distant. Logically he knew he shouldn't be feeling so lack-lustre and dejected about their separation. It wasn't as if his love affair with Nick was over. He knew with utter confidence that was never going to happen; that he and Nick were going to be together forever. They were only divided by the circumstances of war – as was half the world – and the war had turned in the Allies' favour, which was cause for massive relief, not dejection. Two weeks ago Allied troops in Italy had liberated Rome, and only two days later news had come from Cairo that the Allies had stormed ashore in Normandy. Hitler's Fortress Europe had been breached. Victory was now a certainty, and was only a matter of time.

The Signals sergeant he was working with, Jimmy McKay, was a good-humoured Scot.

'I didn't know there was such a thing as a jovial Scot,' he'd said to Jimmy not long after their introduction, thinking it an amusing thing to say and knowing that, no matter how much he wished it was Nick and not Jimmy who was with him, he and Jimmy needed to get on well together.

'Oh, aye,' Jimmy had responded with a grin. 'We're nae all maungy buggers.'

So things could be worse, for he and Jimmy did get on, but Kit was careful not to give Jimmy a clue as to his sexuality. Living as they did in such close proximity to each other, he was fairly sure it was something Jimmy would be more comfortable not knowing about.

The information that was collected in and sent out from Nipos was nearly all to do with the German fleet anchored in Suda Bay and with the German planes flying in and out of Maleme airfield. Before the Allied landings in Sicily, it was the kind of information that had been vital; now, a measure of its importance had been lost, but the indication such information gave of German troop strengths in the eastern Mediterranean was still of major interest to Cairo – and was not gathered without men risking their lives.

Unlike Lewis and Sholto, Kit didn't live cheek-by-jowl with a hard core of the men he led, and his and Jimmy's hideout wasn't a cave, but one of the circular stone huts above Nipos that the shepherds used for shelter and for making cheese. They were built like igloos and the cramped conditions meant he spent as little time in it as possible, unlike Jimmy, who only left his wireless transmitting set for calls of nature.

'Lucky sod,' Jimmy had said to him that morning as, rifle over his shoulder, Kit had left the cheese-hut for a climb to a spot a few miles away that gave an excellent view of the only serviceable motor road the island possessed – the road that clung to the coast and ran from Heraklion via Réthymnon to Canea.

Canea, situated between Suda Bay and Maleme, had been German central headquarters from the first days of the island's occupation and was the most heavily garrisoned part of the island. Because of German security, it was a town difficult to get information out of, but his partisans did so, bringing to Nipos the information they garnered, which Jimmy then promptly passed on by wireless to Cairo. The latest information had indicated that something unusual was taking place in Canea, and Kit wanted to check the traffic travelling towards it.

As Kit headed northwards over rough mountainous terrain, his thoughts were no longer on what might, or might not, be happening in Canea. They were on Nick. Nick had transformed his life. He had enabled Kit to accept his sexuality without any feelings of guilt or shame. And he had done so in such a matter-of-fact, easy manner that Kit blessed him for it.

It had happened when they had been sitting by the side of a waterfall pool, high on the eastern side of Mount Ida. It had been a hot day and, in mutual accord, they'd pulled their boots off and plunged their feet into the deliciously icy water.

Nick had pulled a packet of cigarettes from his shirt pocket and, when they had both lit up, he'd said casually, 'I hadn't realized, when Christos showed us the photograph of his sister, that you and she had had a romance.'

All his feelings of relaxation had fled. Kit didn't like talking about Nikoleta – and he didn't want Nick thinking badly of him, for the way he had treated her.

'It wasn't exactly a romance,' he'd said as laconically as he could manage.

Nick had blown a plume of acrid blue smoke into the air and said, 'Even though she is stunningly beautiful?'

'No.' He'd avoided looking towards Nick. 'It was just a friendship that became misunderstood.' Nick hadn't said anything, and Kit had continued, prompted by an impulse he couldn't restrain, 'Is Nikoleta the sort of woman you go for, Nick?'

'Me?' There had been affectionate amusement in Nick's voice. 'No, Kit. I like women – back home I have lots of women friends – but I don't "go" for them, as you put it. Women don't affect me that way.'

Kit had felt as if his heart had ceased to beat. He'd spun his head round and said, not even pretending to misunderstand him, 'And you're at *ease* with it? You're *happy* to be thought queer?'

Nick had given Kit his slow smile and said, 'Yes. Because of the attitude towards homosexuality, it isn't always easy, but acknowledging what you are is far more comfortable than an emotional sham of a life, don't you think?'

Their eyes had held. The noise of the waterfall had thundered in Kit's ears. 'Yes,' he'd heard himself say, and then, 'You know, don't you?'

'Yes.' Nick's smile had deepened. 'I knew the minute I first shook your hand.'

Dry-mouthed, he'd said, 'And you know how I feel about you?'

And Nick had said, 'Of course. It's exactly how I feel about you.'

Feeling as if he was about to step off a precipice into infinite space and plucking up all the courage he possessed, Kit had said, 'And now what do we do?'

Nick had put his arm around his shoulder and said, 'What we do now is strip off and dive into the pool, buck-naked.'

'And after?' he'd said.

Nick's eyes had met his, dark with heat. 'And after I'll show you what making love without shame or pretence is like.'

As Kit sat on his mountain perch now, simply remembering that day sent desire flooding through him. It had been his Rubicon. It had been the day his life had changed forever. The day there would never be any going back from.

A movement on the road caught his attention and he focused his binoculars a little more sharply. A convoy of trucks was coming in from the east. As the convoy drew nearer, he saw that every truck was packed tight with German soldiers. The convoy skirted the long nine-mile arm of Suda Bay and entered the outer limits of Canea.

Thoughtful, he lit up a Woodbine.

By the end of the day two more separate convoys of troop-laden trucks had travelled westwards into Canea and very little traffic had travelled eastwards. One thing was for certain. His informants in Canea were right: something very odd was happening there.

He set off for the hike back to Nipos, ninety-nine per cent certain that, with the war turning against them, the Germans were beginning to withdraw troops from outlying areas into

Canea, which might mean that sentry posts and blockhouses at remote crossroads were being abandoned.

It was something that needed checking out.

And it was something Jimmy would be informing Cairo about, before the day was over.

Chapter Thirty-Eight

The realization that over the last few months troop numbers in outlying areas had substantially decreased, together with a rumour that the Germans were beginning to send their nurses home, had had a profound impact at Kalamata. Everyone was certain that the end of the occupation was in sight and, despite the conflict of interests taking place between Communist-led and non-Communist-led resistance groups, spirits were high. Lewis and the team had always carefully rationed their visits to the village, not because they were fearful for their own safety, but because if they were to be found there, it was the village and the villagers that would suffer.

Now such caution was relaxed, and Lewis and the team were enjoying the comforts of Andre and Agata's *cafeneion*. Aminta and Rhea Mamalakis and their children were also there, as were Apollonia and old Zenobia and her grand-daughter. All in all, it was quite a *glendi*, with children rushing around everywhere, raki glasses clinking and gales of laughter rising to the ceiling.

Only Kate was aware of how agonizingly difficult Ella was finding it, having all the team together in riotous high spirits, and Christos – who had always been the centre of any such gathering – no longer the heart and soul of it.

'Auntie Kate! Auntie Kate! Come outside and play catch

with me,' Kostas Alfred shouted, rushing up to her and throwing his arms around her legs.

Because she was in the village and not on a mountainside, a rifle over her shoulder, Kate wasn't wearing knee-high boots and breeches. Instead, wearing a black skirt, black blouse and a black bolero, she was indistinguishable from all the other women of the village. With her skirt swinging a couple of inches below her knees, she headed out of the *cafeneion* and into the square, with Kostas Alfred trotting happily by her side.

Although it was now September and Kalamata was high in the mountains, the sun was still hot and, in retrospect, it was a miracle the *glendi* hadn't been taking place out of doors, for even before she and Kostas Alfred had begun playing, she heard the unmistakable sound of approaching German jeeps.

The flat-roofed, higgledy-piggledy whitewashed stone houses on the other side of the square blocked any view of the plateau, but from the sound of their engines, the jeeps had already crested it – and would be sweeping into the village square within minutes.

Yanking Kostas Alfred off his feet, Kate sprinted with him back into the *cafeneion*, shouting, 'There are jeeps approaching!'

Every man grabbed the rifle that was never far from him, and Lewis rasped, 'Everyone but Andre upstairs! We can't shoot our way out, with women and children in the room. Andre, keep your head. Kate, if they make a move towards the stairs, get the children out, whatever the cost!'

As the team took the stairs two and three steps at a time, the jeeps could be heard entering the square. Kate said to Ella, 'Cover your hair. Keep in the background. Zenobia, start cleaning the bar. Rhea, grab a bowl. Look as if you're preparing food. Aminta, be brushing the floor. Apollonia, play a noisy game with the children.' While giving instructions she was tying a head-kerchief over her hair. 'Let them walk in on a scene of normal activity. Agata, be ready with raki.'

As the jeeps drew up outside the *cafeneion*, her thoughts were racing. What if Kostas Alfred started chattering in English? What if Orestes Mamalakis said his daddy was upstairs? What if . . . ?

There came the sound of men jumping from the jeeps and she shut her mind to her fears and, her heart pumping like a piston, waited for the *cafeneion*'s door to burst open.

It didn't do so. Instead, seemingly in no hurry, a German major opened the door and strolled into the room, six of his men with him.

'Soldiers!' Kostas Alfred squealed excitedly in Greek. 'Soldiers!'

The major came to a halt and scanned the room.

Kate felt her heartbeat steady. He wasn't carrying a bullwhip. And he hadn't come in with all his men, for as there had been the sound of more than one jeep pulling up, it meant there were more soldiers still outside. He didn't look as if he was on a brutal reprisal or search mission.

'Would you and your soldiers like wine, Major?' she asked.

'No, thank you. Where are your men?'

Fiercely hoping the major would be ignorant as to the months in which sheep were sheared, and with a carelessness she was far from feeling, she said, 'Our men are all out on the high pastures, shearing sheep. We have local-made raki, Major. And cheese pasties. I made the cheese pasties myself. They are very good.'

'I'm not interested in pasties and raki.' He looked towards Andre. 'Rumour has it that a Minoan palace has been found on your plateau. I would like to see it.'

Agata dropped one of the glasses she was carrying.

From the other side of the ceiling there came the sound of a movement, quickly stilled.

Andre, at a loss as to how to reply, said, 'Speak to the girl. She has to do with such things.'

'The palace?' Kate was alarmed at how good the major's Greek was. It meant that any thoughtless words would be immediately understood. 'You would like to see it? Then of course I will show it to you. It is on the far side of the plateau. A fifteen-minute walk. Your men, I think, would like to see it as well? It is of great interest.'

Even to Zenobia it was obvious that the 'palace' she was going to show him was the relatively unimportant villa Lewis had excavated eight years ago.

As she followed the major out of the *cafeneion*, Kate said to Aminta, aware that the soldiers who hadn't yet entered the *cafeneion* might still do so, 'Don't forget the priest is expecting the older children for their weekly lesson. You'd best take them now or they'll be late.'

Aminta's relief at being able to unsuspiciously shepherd the three- and four-year-olds out of harm's way was vast, and Kate's relief was just as great – especially as Kalamata didn't have a priest, and Zenobia hadn't bewilderedly and loudly pointed this out.

As she led the way across the plateau, passing the village fields and then Kalamata's canvas-sailed windmills, the major and a lieutenant conversed in German.

Kate's German wasn't fluent, but she had studied it to school level, plus what she'd picked up over years of friendship with Helmut.

'With a withdrawal to Canea, this is my last chance to see if the rumour is true' was a sentence she heard that explained the laid-back attitude of the major and his men. They were leaving central Crete for good and no longer gave a fig for policing and brutalizing its population.

She also picked up enough to know that the major wasn't idly interested in Minoan palaces, but had an academic knowledge of them. The German words for Proto-palatial and Neo-palatial were unmistakable. As he was a classicist, it explained his ability to speak Greek, and she thought he was probably more than just a classicist. The more she listened to him, the more certain she became that he was a classicist who was also an archaeologist.

As the windmills were left behind them and they approached the site of the villa, she reminded herself that whatever was said when they reached it, she couldn't allow herself to sound any more knowledgeable than an ordinary village girl. The present German indifference wouldn't stretch to remaining indifferent, if they suspected she wasn't what she appeared to be – and the consequences of that would be a thorough search of the *cafeneion*. At the thought of the Germans storming up the narrow stairs and Lewis and the team storming down them, and of the bloodshed and deaths that would result, her stomach churned.

'Ah! We are there,' the major said suddenly. 'I see the remains!'

Minutes later he said to his lieutenant, 'The paving we are now standing on is over three thousand years old. It would have been a small courtyard, I think. An entrance courtyard. See these round bases in the ground? Columns would once have stood on them and here . . . yes . . . here would have been the entrance vestibule.'

He frowned suddenly, looking around him. 'It is very small.'

It was very small. Within a few strides he had crossed into the area where the main hall of the villa had once stood.

'Ha! A bigger entrance porch,' the major said in German

that Kate was still able to understand. 'See how there would have been three exits here?'

Despite all her anxieties as to what was taking place back at the *cafeneion*, and how the major was going to accept his disappointment when he realized the archaeological remains were not going to indicate a great central courtyard and a king's megaron, she couldn't help but be impressed at his speedy understanding of what he was seeing.

'These flooring remains are limestone,' he was saying now. 'See how they are different from the gypsum in the footings, indicating passageways?'

The ever-dutiful lieutenant nodded his head and feigned deep interest.

Seconds later came the moment Kate had been waiting for.

Standing at the central axis of the villa, the major said, 'Is this it? Traces of a vestibule, a hall, a central room, passageways and a series of rooms only big enough to be storerooms?'

'Yes,' she said guilelessly, adding in typical Cretan idiom, 'It is wonderful, is it not? Wonderful it is.'

The major, who was probably Lewis's age and verged on being good-looking, breathed in hard, his nostrils whitening. 'Not to me, it isn't!' he said explosively. 'This is a Minoan country house, not a palace. Are you sure there are no other remains nearby?'

'No. Here is the palace. Here it is. Why should there be another one?'

The major swore. Then, barking an order towards the soldiers who hadn't accompanied him on his inspection of the site, and with his lieutenant at his side, he swung on his heel, striding off at a furious pace back to the village.

What Kate had hoped she would find when they arrived was a *cafeneion* empty of all children old enough to chatter and let slip that fathers, godfathers and uncles were only a ceiling space away. She had also hoped to find the *cafeneion* as empty of soldiers as when they had left. Instead, although the older children were thankfully no longer there, all the soldiers who had previously been sitting in the jeeps were now in the *cafeneion* and were hard at work having a good time.

Drink was flowing. Andre was playing his fiddle and looking so unhappy about it, it was obvious he'd been forced into doing so. A couple of the soldiers, arms around each other's shoulders, were attempting to dance a Cretan *maleviziotis*. Rhea was being whirled around the floor by an inebriated corporal. Ella was sitting on the lap of a bull-necked sergeant. Apollonia had a gurgling Alice Ariadne on her knee, and Zenobia, finding herself at a *glendi* with the enemy, was rocking backwards and forwards in bewildered anguish.

Kate gave Rhea, Ella and Apollonia full marks for having staved off a search of the upper rooms by distracting the soldiers as they had, but for how long could it go on? What if the corporal and the sergeant thought it a good idea to take Rhea and Ella upstairs and get to know them better? Counting the major, there were eighteen Germans in the *cafeneion*. What chance would seven men armed with rifles have against eighteen men armed with pistols – especially when the seven would be desperately trying to avoid hitting six women and a baby in the crossfire.

'*Achtung!*' The major shouted. '*Raus!*'

The dancing stopped instantly. The sergeant leapt to his feet so swiftly that Ella tumbled to the floor. Apprehensively, not knowing what was going to come next, Andre lowered his fiddle and his bow. Unhappy at the sudden cessation of noise, Alice Ariadne began howling.

The major noticed her for the first time. 'Why does that child have red hair?' he demanded, as all the soldiers except

439

for the lieutenant beat a hasty retreat from the room. 'Cretan children have black hair.'

'Not when they have Venetian heritage, Major,' Kate said swiftly.

'Is that so?' Ice-blue eyes held hers.

The lieutenant said conversationally, 'I believe many northern Italian women are blondes, Major.'

Not acknowledging the remark, and still holding her eyes, the major said with deep feeling, 'And according to this young woman, many Minoan palaces are only villas!'

With that, he broke eye contact with her and looked thoughtfully up at the ceiling.

Kate's heart banged so hard against her ribs that she felt as if she was about to have heart failure. As Ella shot her an agonized glance, the major, one hand on the pistol at his hip, began walking towards the stairs.

Struggling to keep the terror she was feeling from showing in her voice, Kate said, 'Allow me to come with you, Major.'

As he began climbing the wooden stairs, she climbed them behind him, saying, 'My young sister is up here. She has mumps. It is why our menfolk have gone to shear sheep. They are frightened of catching it and becoming sterile.'

The major came to an abrupt halt.

On both floors of the *cafeneion* a pin could have been heard to drop.

After a pause that seemed to go on forever, he swung round on her, saying brusquely, 'If the child is sick, I shall not disturb her.' And then he pushed past her and stormed out of the *cafeneion*, furious at being seen to be no different from a Cretan shepherd, when it came to the fear of catching mumps, and furious at being led on a wild goose chase where a supposed Minoan palace was concerned.

Later, as Angelos Mamalakis teasingly demanded to know

what kind of a wife he had, who danced with Germans, and as, for the first time in public, Pericles put his arm around Apollonia's shoulders and hugged her hard against him, Ella said, weak-kneed with relief, 'Thank God Nikoleta wasn't here. The major might have recognized her from the Villa Ariadne, or from "Wanted" posters.'

'And then we would have all been in the soup,' Adonis said cheerfully. 'And if you're happy to sit on a billy-goat's knee Ella, why won't you sit on mine?'

Nikoleta was in a mountain village of strong resistance sympathies seventy-eight miles away. It nestled beneath a gigantic limestone crag, and beyond the crag, as the slopes steepened, were thick woods of pine and cypress. Somewhere in the higher reaches of the woods Sholto and the men of the village were having a meeting with a Communist *Kapetan* and, as the *Kapetan* in question would have taken great exception to a woman being at the meeting, she had stayed in the village, sitting on the steps of its tiny church, eating preserved cherries given to her by one of the village women.

The door behind her creaked open and an altar-boy stepped out of the church into the searing sunshine.

He regarded her with interest and she held out the pot of sticky, syrupy fruit.

He dipped a finger into it, sucked the crimson preserve from it, as Nikoleta had been doing, and then said, 'My village grows the best preserving cherries in all of Crete.'

Whatever a village produced, it was always fiercely deemed to be better than that produced by any other village. In this case, Nikoleta thought the altar-boy was speaking the truth. The preserved cherries were the most delicious she had ever tasted.

'You speak truly,' she said, and was rewarded by a gratified smile.

Encouraged, he said, 'My name is Heracles. I am a man of this village.'

He didn't look a day over ten years old, but Cretan male dignity began early.

'It is a fine village,' she said of the handful of sagging-roofed houses that spread haphazardly away from the open space of bare earth they were facing. 'My name is Nikoleta. My village is Knossos. It is far away in central Crete.'

Heracles, who had clearly never heard of Knossos, was unimpressed. He said, 'My father has gone with the other men and the British man to meet with the Communists. I know where they are meeting. It is on the higher slopes and not too far away.'

A handful of women had now gathered around, eager for a gossip and an exchange of news. Before it could be embarked upon, Nikoleta heard the same sound Kate had heard two hours earlier in Kalamata: the sound of approaching engines that could only be German.

She thrust the pot of preserved cherries towards Heracles, made a grab for her rifle and sprang to her feet.

'No, *Kyria*!' the woman who had given her the pot of preserved cherries said instantly. 'If the Germans see you are armed, it will bring trouble down on us, and we have had no trouble since a month ago when the villages in the Amari were torched.'

Another woman said with great force, 'Since the withdrawal to Canea, the billy-goats come here for vegetables and fruit. We are a resistance village that has never come under suspicion. You must not bring catastrophe down on us now, *Kyria*! Hide your rifle in the church.'

Heracles slid his hand into hers. 'It's true,' he said, his brown eyes urgent. 'Do nothing or we will all be punished.'

Nikoleta held his eyes for a moment and then, aware there was little option, she turned and did as they asked.

Inside, the church was as dark as a cave and she stuffed the rifle into the most obscure corner of it that she could find. If everything was as the women said, then the Germans hadn't come because they'd been tipped off about the EOK and ELAS meeting. Sholto wasn't in danger and, as she was at the opposite end of the island from Knossos and the Villa Ariadne, there was little chance of being recognized as the woman who had infiltrated General Müller's headquarters and passed on information to the resistance.

Soft footsteps approached from behind her and she whirled around and found herself facing an elderly, white-bearded, black-cassocked priest. Even though it was obvious he had seen what she had just done, she instinctively greeted him in the proper manner, saying with right hand over left and palms upwards, 'Father, bless me.'

'May the Lord bless you,' he responded, making the Sign of the Cross and then placing his right hand on hers.

She kissed it and said, speaking fast, 'I am a partisan, Father. Germans have arrived and I had no time to hide my rifle elsewhere.'

'It will be safe, daughter,' he said complacently. 'Many rifles have been hidden in this church. Always when the Germans come I step outside so that, if they should wish to speak to me, God's house is not polluted by them. It is my advice to you also.'

Together they made their way through the gloom to the church door and stepped out into the brilliant sunlight.

A small flatbed truck and three jeeps were parked in the square, and the square was a hive of activity, with a dozen soldiers watching eagle-eyed as the village women ran to and fro, loading the back of the truck with hard-worked-for produce.

The last remnants of Nikoleta's tension vanished. All she

had been told was true. The Germans had no suspicion at all that they were in a resistance village.

'*Mehr Pflaumen! Mehr Pflaumen!*' one of the soldiers called out, and a woman as old and wizened as Zenobia hobbled with difficulty across the square with another giant bag of plums.

Another soldier came out of one of the houses with a cageful of complaining hens. As the cage was thrown on top of the fruit and vegetables, Heracles joined Nikoleta and the priest in front of the church.

'There is nothing we have that they do not take,' he said fiercely. 'All our sheep they have taken and our goats. Now they take hens, and soon there will be no hens left. Thieves, the Germans are. Thieves and devils.'

The priest adjusted his black soft-sided cap and did not disagree with him.

Only when the women had parted with all their produce did the hurried toing and froing across the square come to an end.

'Do not worry, Kyria Nikoleta,' Heracles whispered. 'The rest of our fruit and vegetables are in an underground pit outside of the village, where they can't be found.'

The relief was palpable, as two of the Germans climbed into the cab of the truck and the rest, apart from the officer in command, vaulted into the jeeps. As engines were revved, the officer paused, one foot on a running board.

Because of the visor on his peaked cap, Nikoleta couldn't see his face clearly, much less the expression in his eyes, but he was obviously looking in the direction of her and the priest and Heracles.

Suddenly he took his foot off the running board and began striding purposefully towards them.

'Do not worry,' the priest said, sensing Nikoleta's alarm. 'It is me he will wish to speak with.'

But Nikoleta, the pupils of her eyes huge in a face that was stark white, knew differently. Now that he was nearer and the visor was no longer the same handicap, she recognized him, for, when she had been one of General Müller's maids, he had been one of the general's staff officers.

'*Sie!*' he spat, pulling his pistol from its holder and halting in front of her. And then, shouting to his men, '*Dies ist die Villa Ariadne Spion!*'

There was no escape. There hadn't been even before the barrel of his pistol was jammed into the centre of her forehead.

As the men sprinted to surround her, Nikoleta could hear Heracles shouting distraughtly, '*No! No! No!*', although she couldn't see him.

She couldn't see the priest.

All she could see, her arms now wrenched behind her back, her head yanked at an impossible angle, was a sea of grey uniforms and a dozen pair of eyes as hard as splintered slate.

'*Was machen wir mit ihr?*' one of the soldiers asked. '*Nehmen Sie das Mädchen zu Ayia?*'

Nikoleta didn't speak or understand German, but Ayia was the name of the notorious Nazi jail in Canea, where hundreds of Cretans had been tortured and executed, and she knew what the soldier was asking. He was asking what they were going to do with her. Were they going to take her to Ayia jail?

'*Nein! Wir töten sie hier. Und wir lehren das Dorf eine Lektion. Bringen Sie mir ein Dutzend Frauen und den Priester.*'

As half a dozen of the soldiers began rounding up screaming women at gunpoint, Nikoleta didn't need to understand what he was saying to know what was about to happen. She was going to be executed – and, because of her, so were totally innocent wives and mothers. And the tally didn't end there, for with gut-wrenching horror she saw that the priest also had a pistol jammed against his head.

Desperately she tried to see where Heracles was, terrified that as he, too, had been standing next to her, he, like the priest, was about to be shot alongside her. There was no sign of him, and hope sprang into life. If he was no longer in the square, did it mean he was now sprinting up into the woods to tell Sholto and his father, and the rest of the men of the village, what was happening? And if he was, was it possible he would reach them and that help could come, before she and the others were shot?

Her wrists had been bound tightly behind her back, but she was able to dig her nails into her palms and as she prayed, she dug them deep; so deep she drew blood.

Sholto and the men he had gone to the meeting with were already trudging down through steep woodland on their way back to the village when they heard Heracles crashing upwards towards them, shouting, 'Papa! Papa! The billy-goats are going to shoot people. Papa! PAPA!'

He burst breathlessly into view, tears streaming down his face, the robe he wore as an altar-boy torn and filthy, from where he'd had to scramble on hands and knees.

'They're going to shoot Kyria Nikoleta, the British officer's friend,' he gasped as his father ran to catch hold of him. 'They say she is a spy. And they are going to shoot Father Skoulos and . . .'

Sholto didn't wait to hear who else was about to be shot. He broke into a run, haring down through the wooded mountainside, running with fear in his heart, and running as he had never run before in his life. He had no idea how many Germans he was going to be faced with when he reached the village, and he didn't care. All he cared about was reaching it before Nikoleta died in a hail of gunfire.

Ahead of him the trees began thinning out. He was nearly at the point where the crag butted out of the slope of the mountain to overshadow the church and village square. It was a point that, on the climb up, he and everyone else had circumnavigated, and it was one to be circumnavigated again on the way down. Sholto didn't circumnavigate it, though. Instead, as the men from the village continued a furious downhill charge, he peeled away towards it, knowing the risk he was taking.

If, from the crag, he didn't have a clear shot into the square, then he would have added minutes to the time it was now going to take him to reach the square. If the executions weren't going to take place in the square, then the same thing applied. And even if the executions were about to take place in the square and he had a clear line of sight from the crag, would he be near enough to get the vital shots? And if he was too late . . . ? If Nikoleta was already dead . . . ?

He scrambled up and on to the crag, his heart slamming in his chest, sweat streaming into his eyes.

From the top of the crag he could see the church; he could see the square. A machine gun had been set up in it on a tripod. Facing it, hands tied behind their backs and their backs against the blazingly white church wall, were Nikoleta, a priest and a dozen terrified women.

With the blood pounding in his ears, he judged the time and distance. The men of the village could now only be five minutes or less away from bursting on the scene, but they were going to arrive too late – as he would have, if he had continued with them.

What he had to do from the crag was shoot the commanding officer and whoever was manning the machine gun. By the time he had done so, the remaining ten men would be too busy firing back in his direction to give a thought to finishing the job of executing thirteen women and an elderly priest.

But could he make the necessary two shots from the distance he was? He'd gone out with the guns on his father's Highland estate since he was a child. He could judge distances and knew how far he could shoot for the shot still to be deadly accurate. The longest distance, under ideal conditions, was three hundred and fifty yards. He estimated the village square to be quarter of a mile away, and a quarter of a mile was four hundred and forty yards.

It was a gamble – the biggest of his life.

With the officer by his side, a soldier knelt in a firing position at the machine gun.

Knowing he had only seconds left, Sholto flung himself full-length on the rock, rammed the butt of his rifle into his shoulder and curled his finger around the trigger.

One of the women screamed and fell to her knees. Nikoleta crossed herself and raised her already proudly held head a fraction higher.

The machine-gunner set his sights, preparatory to firing.

Sholto took careful aim and then, as the machine-gunner made another movement, about to let loose a fusillade of bullets that would mow down all those in front of him, Sholto pulled back the trigger – and did so long and smoothly, and with ice-cold steadiness.

Blood and brains spattered the officer's grey-uniformed chest.

Before the officer had time to register the direction from which the shot had come, Sholto re-aimed and fired again.

As the officer fell lifeless in the dirt and dust of the square, blood oozing from his nose and ears, his men reacted as Sholto had judged they would. No one ran to take their comrade's place at the machine gun. There was instant panic as to where the shots had come from and, in the panic, and no longer held at gunpoint, the village women began fleeing down the little lanes leading away from the square and, as they did so, their menfolk burst into it, rifles firing.

It was too much for the ten remaining Germans. They raced for their truck and their jeeps. Sholto didn't wait to see the outcome, from his viewpoint on the crag. All that mattered to him was that Nikoleta wasn't dead; that he and she still had a roller-coaster of a life in front of them – and he was sprinting with the speed of an Olympic athlete to crush her in his arms and tell her so.

Chapter Thirty-Nine

MAY 1945

Daphne was in Cairo, and in a city wild with British relief and celebration. Although no formal announcement had yet been made, the war in Europe was over. A week ago had come the news that, in Milan, Mussolini and his mistress had been shot dead and strung up by their heels in a garage forecourt. Two days later had come the news that in Berlin Hitler had committed suicide. On the second of May all German troops in Italy and Austria had surrendered; two days later all German troops in Holland, North Germany and Denmark had surrendered; and a day after that, on the fifth of May, all German troops in Norway had surrendered.

On mainland Greece, British troops were maintaining order between the Communist-led factions that were jockeying for power, now that peace had finally come, and the non-Communist-led factions. British troops were also back on Crete, and news from the British Embassy was that a British general was occupying the Villa Ariadne.

A formal unconditional surrender still needed to be announced, but even before it was announced, celebrations were rife.

Thanks to her friend, Sir Miles Lampson, Daphne also had other news to celebrate.

'Sholto has been recalled,' Sir Miles had said to her earlier that morning over the telephone. 'He's on his way back to Cairo as we speak.'

Daphne had let out such a cry of elation that Adjo, usually so imperturbable, had come running, and Caspian had looked up from the *Boys' Book of Adventures* that he was reading and said, 'What's the excitement, Mummy? Has Mr Churchill declared the war over?'

'No, sweetheart,' she'd said, fizzing with expectation. 'That announcement will probably come later today, or tomorrow. But the absolutely *brilliant* news is that Daddy is on his way here.'

He'd frowned and said, 'What if I don't recognize him?'

It had been something she hadn't thought of, and it had punctured her elation a little. It had been four years. The last time Caspian had seen Sholto, he'd been three. Now he was just two months from being seven.

She thought of that time-lapse. Four years. It was a long time – and when she and Sholto had parted, it hadn't been on the best of terms. Together with his wireless operator, Nick Virtue, Kit had been recalled to Cairo a month ago, and when she had prodded Kit for news of Sholto, he had been uncomfortably evasive, except for saying that Sholto was fit and well.

She knew what the evasiveness had been about. It meant that her habitually unfaithful husband was still being unfaithful, even though there were no British women on Crete for him to be unfaithful with, and even though his domestic quarters were either a cave in the summer or a cheese-hut in the winter.

The knowledge neither disturbed nor distressed Daphne.

It was – had been – wartime, and wartime faithlessness was in a category all its own. Quite simply, it didn't matter. It was something that, not having been a paragon of virtue herself over the last four years, she was quite sure of. What mattered now was the future.

She thought about the future as she waited for a taxi to draw up outside her Garden City apartment. Sholto would resume his life as a diplomat, and she would resume hers as a diplomat's wife. Caspian would soon, at seven, be going off as a boarder to the same preparatory school that Sholto had gone to. It wasn't something she liked the thought of, but it was the kind of thing Sholto would be adamant about, and Caspian was a self-confident, gregarious little boy who would no doubt enjoy every minute of boarding with lots of other boys his age.

She walked out on to a balcony that gave a corner view of the British Embassy. She was thirty-one. Was thirty-one too old to be thinking about having another baby? She didn't think so, but wasn't too sure what Sholto might think. Perhaps it might be best to say nothing and just let events take their course. Thinking about events taking their course led her to thinking about bed.

They had always been good together in bed, even when Sholto had been involved with someone else. The only man who had ever surpassed Sholto, when it came to giving her pleasure in bed, was Helmut, and she had schooled herself never to think of Helmut. Thinking about Helmut was too disturbing; too unsettling. Where Helmut was concerned, the most she would allow herself was to pray that he was still alive.

A taxi sped into the street and swerved to a halt outside her apartment block. Without waiting to see who was going to step from it, knowing who was going to step from it, she ran from the balcony and into the bedroom. The big double bed, always crisply made, was even more crisply made than usual – and Daphne had not left it for a maid to make. She had made it herself. There was champagne chilling and she had given her household staff, including Adjo, the afternoon off. Caspian was at Vanessa Dane's house on Zamalek, enjoying pony rides in a garden that shelved down to the Nile. She and Sholto were going to have all the privacy they could wish for.

The entrance bell rang. She checked her ivory-pale hair in the triple glass of her dressing table, gave herself an extra spray of Shalimar and, with her heart in her mouth, ran into the hall and pressed the button that would let him into the apartment block.

Once in, he didn't take the lift.

She could hear him running up the stairs, taking them two at a time.

He didn't knock on the door, either. He simply opened it, let it slam shut behind him and strode towards her.

For a few dizzying seconds she didn't recognize him.

It wasn't that he was still dressed as a Cretan, because he wasn't. He was wearing a shirt, flannels and sandals – though a shirt, flannels and sandals that he had obviously been issued with. Anything Sholto had bought for himself would have been distinctively handmade.

What had disorientated her wasn't so much his clothes as the sheer unexpectedness of his physical appearance.

From years of near-permanent exposure to a scorching sun, his skin was burned a deep bronze. His hair, always longer than society deemed proper for a diplomat, was now below his shirt collar and he had a full-on beard and moustache. The Foreign Secretary, Sir Anthony Eden, also wore a moustache, but his was a pin-neat, pencil-thin line. Sholto's moustache was luxuriant and untamed.

There was something else about him that was far different from the sophisticated, reckless bohemian who had parted from her in anger four years ago. There was a raw toughness about him that even a dockside brawler would have been instinctively wary of.

For a second the shock checked her rush towards him, and

453

then she was over it, hurtling towards him and throwing her arms around his neck. Sholto didn't give her the long, deep kiss she had been expecting, but with his head buried in her neck, he did embrace her in a hug so long and tight she could scarcely breathe.

When he finally raised his head and relaxed his hold of her a little, he said emotionally, 'It's good to see you looking so well, Daphs. Where's Caspian? He's here, isn't he?'

Laughter bubbled in her throat. 'If you mean living here, of course he is – but he's not here at this precise moment, he's pony-riding and, as I've given the staff the rest of the day off, it means we're going to be able to have a *wonderful* reunion, completely undisturbed!'

She clasped hold of his hand. 'The bedroom is this way. I've got champagne on ice and . . .'

'There's something I need to say to you, Daphne.'

The tone of his voice and his use of her full name represented the moment when she realized things weren't quite as they should have been. Her instant assumption was that Sholto was crushed with disappointment at Caspian not being there to greet him, and that he'd been expecting Caspian to come sprinting towards him and to throw himself into Sholto's arms. As Caspian had indicated that he was going to need time to adjust to having a daddy back in his life, Daphne decided it was best to tell Sholto this now. Once that was out of the way, the two of them could begin the long-awaited task of getting into the swing of married life again.

She said, 'There's something I should have warned you about, darling. Caspian . . .'

'Me first, Daphs.' His voice was tense. 'Have you any whisky in the apartment? I'd prefer it to champagne. Under the circumstances.'

All the elation she had been feeling fled. Certain he had

454

seriously bad news for her, and that the bad news had to do with Kate, or Ella, or Lewis, she headed straight for the drawing room and the cocktail cabinet and poured two generous measures of Laphroaig single malt into whisky tumblers.

'Tell me,' she said unsteadily. 'Is someone I love dead? Is it Kate? Ella?'

'God, no!' He was appalled at what she had been imagining. 'Both Kate and Ella are as fit as fleas.' He took a deep swallow of whisky and then said, 'The thing is, Daphs, over the last couple of years there's been someone else . . .'

She cut him off, dizzy with relief. 'Oh, for goodness sake! Is that all? I thought someone had died! I haven't been living these last four years believing you've been faithful, Sholto. Come to that, *I* haven't been a hundred per cent faithful, although I've only been unfaithful occasionally and I've never got involved in anything meaningful. The last four years have been four years of war and hell, and life being completely topsy-turvy and nothing normal, and the kind of stress I hope none of us ever have to live through again.' She put her glass of whisky down and slid her arms around his waist. 'Wartime unfaithfulness can stay where it belongs, in the war – and the war, thank God, is over. What matters, darling Sholto, is the here and now – and the future.'

He said gently, 'There isn't going to be a future for us, Daphs. At least not together. I've met someone I want to marry, and I want a divorce.'

For the briefest of seconds she didn't believe him – couldn't believe him – and then, as she saw the expression in his eyes and on his face, she said incredulously, 'But you can't divorce me and marry again. You're a diplomat! Your career would be ruined. You would be ruined socially. No Hertford has ever divorced – they may have lived apart from their wives for a lifetime, but they've never divorced. And who on earth is it that you want to marry? A Cretan girl who barely speaks English? A girl who has never travelled outside Crete? A girl who hasn't the faintest clue as to the kind of life you live, when you're not living in a cave or a cheese-hut?'

He said, 'I want to marry Nikoleta. I'm in love with her. I've told her I'm going to marry her – and I am. I want a divorce on the grounds of my adultery. It will be quicker than desertion.'

Daphne gaped at him, too stupefied for speech.

He picked up her glass of untouched whisky and pushed it into her hands. Hating the hurt he was causing, but having no second thoughts about causing it, he went on, 'There are no ifs and buts, Daphs. Even if I hadn't fallen in love with Nikoleta, I would still want a divorce. I made it plain it was all over between us, the last time we were together.'

'But that was just a silly row over my staying on in Crete, when Caspian was evacuated from it.'

'It wasn't a silly row to me. It was the moment things finally ended between us. And now, four years later, I want a divorce so that I can marry Nikoleta.'

All she could think of was that once again Sholto had been unfaithful to her with someone she had counted a friend. In that, at least, he had been consistent. But that the friend in question should have been Nikoleta? Nikoleta who, for a time, had ensnared both Lewis and Kit? Nikoleta, for whom she had always had time and been kind towards?

She swallowed the whisky and said, the breath so tight in her chest that she had to fight for it, 'Nikoleta isn't going to marry you because she loves you! You do know that, don't you? She's marrying you for the same reason she would have married Lewis, or Kit, if they had been insane enough to ask her. She's marrying you so that she can get away from Crete.

So that she can live out her fantasy of being an English lady who meets royalty.'

'You may be right,' he said, and in his bronzed face white lines showed around his mouth. 'But you know what, Daphne? I don't care why she wants to marry me! I just want her to marry me.'

Daphne felt as if the floor was shelving beneath her feet. Never in a hundred years could she imagine Sholto reacting like that over her – or of any of the women he'd had affairs with in the past – and in that moment she knew that she had lost him; that there was no point in continuing to fight for their marriage; that it was a fight she wasn't going to win.

Unsteadily she walked away from him and out on to the balcony. In the hazy light of late afternoon she gripped its iron railing. She had married Sholto because she had been crazily in love with him, but he had never loved her in quite the same way. If he had, he would never have indulged in so many careless affairs and flings. And now he had indulged in an affair that wasn't careless; in an affair that, by the passionate way he had spoken of it, had been life-changing for him.

He stepped out onto the balcony behind her and put an arm around her shoulders. 'I'd like for us to be loving friends, Daphs,' he said thickly.

She didn't answer him, because she couldn't. She had never wanted to be loving friends with him. What she had wanted to be, always, was his wife and lover.

Accepting that was now never going to happen, she said bleakly, 'I shall want full custody of Caspian.'

His response was the final nail in the coffin of their tempestuous marriage.

'Yes,' he said. 'There'll be no problem about that.'

*

457

In Heraklion, Kate and Lewis were waiting for the announcement that the war was officially over. They were also waiting for something else. In a small chapel at British Army Headquarters, and accompanied by Ella and Pericles, they were waiting for the arrival of the army chaplain who was to marry them.

Kate was wearing a sky-blue dress that several years ago had been her best 'dining at the Villa Ariadne' dress. Her white straw hat was decorated with a wild red rose and she was holding a posy of roses mixed with honeysuckle.

'Daphne is never going to forgive me for not waiting until she could be with us today,' she said, more nervous than she could have believed possible.

'Of course she will.' There wasn't a shadow of doubt in Ella's voice. 'She forgave me for getting married without her being there.'

Lewis, in SOE officer's uniform, said reasonably, 'And as I'm not being recalled to Cairo, but to London, this is the only possible arrangement. This way, at least Ella is with us.'

Behind them the chapel door opened and swung shut and the chaplain, also in uniform, hurried towards them, saying in high elation, 'The BBC have just announced that there is shortly to be a special announcement! We none of us want to miss it, do we? Are these your witnesses, and have you got all your paperwork with you? You have? Jolly good. Then let's begin.'

Eager to get back to a radio, he raced through the service at high speed. Neither Lewis nor Kate minded. The words were the words of the Anglican prayer book, and speed couldn't mar the beauty or the solemnity of them.

When Lewis took the ring from the breast-pocket of his jacket and slid it on the fourth finger of Kate's left hand, saying, 'With this ring I thee wed, with my body I thee worship and with all my worldly goods I thee endow', tears blurred Ella's eyes. It was a moment in which Christos had never seemed so near and, at the same time, so far from her.

'Those whom God hath joined together, let no man put asunder,' the chaplain said.

From outside the chapel there erupted a thunderous storm of cheering, whistling, foot-stamping and triumphant shouting.

Aware that he was missing the historic announcement of a lifetime, the chaplain added in great hurry, 'I now pronounce you man and wife!' and set off at a run down the aisle, heading for the nearest radio.

Lewis took Kate in his arms and gave her a long, lingering, first married kiss.

Ella blinked her tears away and, at the chaplain's undignified exit, began laughing.

Pericles said decisively, 'This has made my mind up. I'm going to ask Apollonia to marry me.'

When, moments later, the four of them stepped out of the chapel into hot sunshine, every church bell in Heraklion was ringing and the air was thick with the deafening sound of volley after volley of celebratory Cretan into-the-sky rifle shots.

'And to think,' Lewis said lovingly to his wife, 'that I thought our wedding was going to be a quiet one!'

Chapter Forty

It was early morning and Ella was in the kitchen of her little house in Archanes finishing baking for a very special event. It was the sixth anniversary of Christos's death and, as it was coinciding with Daphne's first visit back to Crete since she had left it during the British and Allied troop evacuation of 1941, it had seemed an ideal time to hold a memorial service for him. It was a day both Georgio and Adonis had always spent with her, and they would be doing so again. Even more importantly, so would Kate and Lewis – and the last time she, Kate and Daphne had all been together had been eight years ago, in the days immediately preceding the German invasion. All of which meant that, as well as celebrating Christos's life, there were other things to celebrate as well – and not all of them were to do with personal friendships.

When Germany had unconditionally surrendered on the seventh of May 1945 and the rest of Europe had begun rebuilding shattered lives and bomb-blasted cities, war hadn't ended in Greece. Greece had simply exchanged war against a foreign enemy for a civil war between those who wanted Greece to be Communist and those who did not – and, thanks in part to the amount of American aid now pouring into Greece, those who did not were clearly in the ascendancy and the end of the war was at last within sight.

It was not, Ella thought with relief as she gave the last cake a sprinkling of icing sugar, a civil war that had affected Crete in the same horrific way it had affected the mainland. Cretans had always thought themselves different from those in the rest of Greece, just as Yorkshire folk thought they were different from people in the rest of England; and if overall the island was anything politically, it was ardently republican.

The civil war had, though, meant that travelling abroad over the last few years hadn't been easy, and when she'd taken Kostas Alfred and Alice Ariadne to meet their Yorkshire grandma, grandpa and great-grandpa, Ella had travelled the Heraklion–London part of the journey by cargo boat.

It had been a wonderful trip. Her mum had cried over the children and said what wonderfully curly hair they both had, and how Alice Ariadne was the image of Ella when Ella had been her age; her dad had initiated Kostas Albert into the art of pigeon-racing; and her granddad, whom she'd been relieved to find in fine fettle, had taken Kostas Albert and Alice Ariadne tramping over the nearby moor, fishing for sticklebacks in the beck that ran close to the house and, in the evenings and amid gales of laughter, playing card games such as Snap and Old Maid with them.

Although she had been a little nervous about doing so, she had contacted Sam.

'Hello, Sam. It's me, Ella,' she had said tentatively when he had answered his home telephone. 'I'm home for a few weeks and I wondered – if Jenny doesn't mind – if we could all meet up?'

'Ella?' he'd said, dumbfounded. '*Ella?* I don't believe it!' And then, speaking away from the phone, 'It's Ella, Jenny! And she's in Wilsden and wants to meet up.'

As she had no transport, Sam had insisted that, together with Jenny and their two children, he would drive down to Wilsden.

'It's nearly a year since Emma and Edward last saw your mum and dad and Jos,' he'd said. 'This is going to be a real treat for them – and I can't begin to tell you how much of a treat seeing you is going to be, for Jenny and me.'

Ella's mother had gone to town on the Yorkshire high tea that she had laid on, and it had become obvious to Ella that, as far as her mum, dad and granddad were concerned, Sam and Jenny and their children were family.

She, too, felt as if they were family. Jenny's delight at finally meeting her was so sincere she'd known immediately that Jenny had no qualms about her husband meeting up with his ex-fiancée; that she was in a marriage far too strong and loving for such insecurity.

As for herself, very little had changed in the way she felt about Sam. Her feelings for him had always, at bottom, been sisterly, and they still were. He was the brother she'd never had; the person she could always turn to, in the safe knowledge that he would never let her down.

That evening when, in their little Morris Minor, the Jowett family had been lovingly waved off on their way back to their happy family life in Scooby, and when her mother was washing up the tea things and she was drying them, her mother had paused in what she was doing and said, 'Do you have any regrets, Ella love? It could so easily have been you married to Sam and . . .'

'No, Mum,' she'd said gently, but firmly. 'I have no regrets. Not one.'

It was true.

As she'd lain that night in the little single bed of her child-hood, she'd known that nothing in the world would make her regret even a day of her marriage to Christos; that he would be a part of her for always.

Her return journey to Crete had also been by cargo boat – and she doubted that anyone had previously been taken to the dock it sailed from in a Rolls-Royce.

'You can't mean it,' she'd said disbelievingly, when Kate had met her and the children off the Leeds–Bradford train at King's Cross Station. 'We're going to drive to the Port of London in a Rolls-Royce?'

'Lewis's godfather insists, and not only that, but before you leave for the dock he's also insisting that you and the children have tea with him at Claridge's.'

She'd already known, from Kate's letters to her, that Lewis's godfather, Nathaniel Golding, was a South African who was rich as Croesus, and that it had been Nathaniel's money that had funded the Kalamata Little Palace dig. What she hadn't expected, though, was that she would ever meet him.

After the years of wartime occupation, stepping into Claridge's for afternoon tea had been surreal.

'Is this Fairyland?' Alice Ariadne had whispered, round-eyed with wonder as, beneath glittering chandeliers, she sank up to her ankles in thick, deep carpet.

'It's Uncle Nathaniel's kind of Fairyland,' Kate had whispered back to her.

Despite the sea of haute-couture dresses and carelessly draped fur stoles at other tables, and despite having married a man who had turned out to be the laird of a considerable estate in Sutherland, Kate was dressed as she had always preferred to be dressed, in a sweater and skirt; the only difference being that her skirt was made of beautiful tweed and her sweater was cashmere.

In a bizarre kind of way, Nathaniel had reminded Ella of her grandfather. He was a little gnome of a man, who obviously had a great appetite for life and who, like her grandfather, took people as he found them.

'And so, Ella, have Lewis and Kate given you the good news about the Little Palace dig?' he'd asked, as Kostas Albert and Alice Ariadne had happily set about choosing cakes from a dizzying array.

Her eyes had immediately widened.

'No,' she'd said, her heart beating fast and light. 'What is it?'

Nathaniel had leaned forward in his chair, hands clasped between his knees. 'You have no doubt been worrying that, where Greek archaeological digs are concerned, things are now going to be different from what they were pre-war?'

She'd nodded, knowing that the only digs he, Lewis, Kate and herself had concerns about were the still-unfinished Little Palace and Sacred Cave digs.

'I'm afraid the kind of agreement for permission to dig that I had with the former Greek government no longer stands. I regret it, but there it is.' He paused. 'However, as I said, there is good news. Both the Kalamata and Sacred Cave digs will now operate under the aegis of the British School of Archaeology in Athens, just as Knossos has, ever since Sir Arthur Evans transferred ownership of it to the British School in 1926. And the British School has agreed that Lewis will, as before, direct both digs.'

'That means,' Kate added, 'that Lewis and I will be living at Kalamata again, and that you will be able to rattle between Archanes and Kalamata in the Sally. We may even get Daphne aboard – she's somewhere in the South of France at the moment and we haven't been able to contact her yet.'

'And Kit?' she'd said. 'Will Kit be aboard as well?'

Lewis had said, 'Kit and Nick are on a dig in the Sudan, but when it comes to an end there will be a place for Kit on the dig at Kalamata – and Nick, too. A professional photographer is something the team has always been short of.'

'It's going to leave you light-handed, as far as qualified archaeologists are concerned, Lewis. There's going to be just you, Kate, Ella and possibly the delightful-sounding Lady Daphne.' Nathaniel had given Lewis a long, shrewd look and then said, 'Unless, of course, you have a contact number for Helmut?'

'I don't.' Lewis's handsome face had become suddenly sombre. 'I wish I did. I've contacted the German State Archaeologists' Association and all they were able to tell me was that, at the end of the war, Helmut had gone to live in Switzerland.'

Later, in the rear seat of the Rolls-Royce with Kostas Albert, Alice Ariadne and Kate, Ella had said musingly, 'Wasn't it strange how Sholto and Nikoleta's names never came up in the conversation?'

'Not really.' There had been wry amusement in Kate's voice. 'But if you want the latest update, they are married and living in Washington, where, by all accounts, the new Lady Hertford is a huge social success. A friend of Lewis's was there recently and he says the general belief is that there was never a first Lady Hertford, and that Sholto met Nikoleta in Crete when he was a dashing British Liaison officer and she was a glamorous rifle-toting heroine, risking her life for her country. Daphne, I'm happy to say, is indifferent to being written out of Sholto's history, but is tickled to death at Nikoleta's apparent indignation that, although Daphne is divorced from Sholto, the only difference in their titles is that instead of being "Lady Hertford", she is now "Daphne, Lady Hertford". It's something Nikoleta can't get her head around.'

Ella hadn't been able to get her head around it, either, but then aristocratic titles had never been her forte.

Now she slid the icing-sugared cake onto a pretty dish and

looked across to where a photograph of Christos hung on the wall, where she could always see it. She had taken the photograph when they had been together on the Little Palace dig. He was leaning on a spade, wearing his habitual black shirt, breeches, waistcoat and cummerbund, his thick black curls falling chaotically low over his forehead.

From the photograph, his dark eyes, full of mischievous high spirits, met hers and love welled up inside her in an overwhelming torrent. Over the last few years Adonis had asked her several times if she would marry him, and every time he had asked, Ella's answer had been the same: that she wasn't ready to marry again; that although she was a widow, she felt herself to be a married widow.

'Then I will wait,' he had said each time. 'In the Bible, Jacob had to wait seven years before he could marry Rachel. Maybe, *agápi mou*, when you have been seven years a widow, you will no longer feel a married one and will be ready to marry me?'

The house, which would so soon be full of the friends and family who would walk with her to the church for the memorial service, was very still and quiet. Not moving, Ella thought about the quietness that had permeated the site of the Little Palace all through the years since work on it had ended. Soon it would be a hive of activity again, for under Lewis's direction work on the site was to begin within days – and when it did, they would no longer be referring to the site as the Little Palace, but as the Dower House.

'For that is what it is,' she had said to Lewis within hours of his arrival. 'Where else would a priestess-queen go, when widowed?"

His mouth had tugged into a smile. 'It's a nice theory, Ella,' he'd said gently, 'but nothing we know about the Minoans indicates a society sophisticated enough to be housing a widowed priestess-queen in the equivalent of a medieval dower house.'

It had been the response she had expected and she had set her jaw stubbornly and said, 'We know so little about Minoan society, Lewis, that anything is possible. And once the idea had occurred to me, I set about trying to find something amongst the artefacts we've found at the site and the Sacred Cave, to back it up.'

He'd quirked an eyebrow. 'And did you?'

'Oh, yes,' she'd said, like a cat with the cream. 'The museum authorities gave me full access to all the finds from the Kalamata dig and, amongst those common to all sacred caves, there was a type of offering I've been unable to trace amongst any other collection.'

'And?' he'd said.

'And we didn't take any notice of it, probably because we thought it all of a piece with other small clay figurines, purposely missing a body part to indicate where the person making the offering was injured, and where he, or she, needed supernatural help in order to be healed.'

Lewis had frowned and she'd known he was thinking back to the Sacred Cave dig. It hadn't been carried out under his direction, for he had been far too involved with the Little Palace dig. Helmut had overseen the Sacred Cave site, but before any finds from it had been packed and taken into storage for later, more detailed study, he – Lewis – had examined them carefully. Or at least he'd thought he had.

He'd said slowly, 'Votive clay figures missing body parts are so commonplace a find in a sacred cave that I might well have not examined all of them with the care I should have and, for the same reason, Helmut may well have thought my doing so unnecessary. So tell me what it is, among our Sacred Cave artefacts, that you've been unable to trace in other collections of cave findings.'

'This,' she'd said, laying a photograph in front of him.

It was a photograph of a clay figurine, but whereas all the other clay figurines had been no more than asexual stick-figures with a hand, foot, leg or arm intentionally missing, the figurine in the photograph was quite clearly of a woman. The outline of an open-bodiced, ankle-length gown had been etched into the clay. Her arms were raised in an act of supplication, her breasts were bare, and directly beneath the fullness of her left breast her body was pierced by a long, vicious-looking metal pin.

'The figurine is of a widowed priestess-queen,' Ella had said, with quiet confidence. 'The pin through her heart is an arrow indicating the way grief has pierced and broken it. I know, because I know how grief feels.'

He hadn't argued with her. Instead, with barely controlled excitement in his voice, he'd said, 'You could be right, Ella, and if you are . . .'

He hadn't finished his sentence, because he'd had no need to. If she was right, it would open up fresh thought as to the way Minoan society had functioned, but for that to happen there had to be other finds to back up her theory. As their eyes held, both had known what the other was thinking. It was that when they again began excavating on the Little Palace and Sacred Cave sites, their sense of hope and expectation would be ratcheted to almost unbearable levels.

Her house door was open and the sound of people turning into her cobbled street brought Ella back to the present.

Ever since Christos's death there had been a void in her heart: an aching emptiness she had been certain nothing would ever fill. Now, suddenly and wonderingly, she knew she was on the brink of change; that although she had never intended for Christos's memorial service to bring closure, it was about to do so. Unlike the priestess-queen, the rest of her life was not going to be defined by her grievous loss. Nothing would ever remove Christos from the memory of her heart, but she was ready to love again.

With an aged Tinker at her heels, she went to the doorway in order to greet the friends and family who were about to accompany her to church.

As it was traditional for women to wear black at Greek Orthodox memorial services, Daphne was wearing a black sheath-dress topped by a tiny fitted black jacket. A wide-brimmed black hat covered her hair, and her black court shoes were, as always, perilously high-heeled. It was a look that wouldn't have attracted a second glance in Bond Street or the Champs-Elysées, but it looked positively bizarre in a small Cretan hilltop town, especially as she was walking arm-in-arm with Eleni, who was a foot shorter than she was and whose black dress and shawl were so shapeless it was hard to know where one left off and the other began.

Kostas said, 'I have taken the *koliva* to the church, Ella. Eleni was up all night making it, and her tears have watered it. Every spoonful have her tears watered.'

Koliva was a dish with great ritual significance and it was obligatory at Greek Orthodox funeral and memorial services. Made from boiled wheat, flour, raisins, cinnamon, sugar, walnuts, almonds and pomegranate seeds, it was a dish Eleni had insisted on making and, as she was doing so for the memorial service of her son, Ella could well believe that Eleni had shed some tears while making it. That her tears had watered every spoonful was, she hoped, typical Cretan male exaggeration.

'Remind me later that, in a letter I've just received from Nathaniel, there was a separate note addressed to you,' Lewis said to Ella as, knowing the drill when it came to following a widow to church, he made no attempt to enter the house.

'If you're going to change into your best black, Ella, it's time you did so,' Kate said. 'I know Cretans aren't sticklers for time-keeping, but even so, we should by now be en route to the church.'

Ella hesitated, watching as Pericles and Apollonia turned into the street accompanied by Adonis. The three of them were Alice Ariadne's favourite people and she squeezed past Ella's legs, hurtling down over the cobbles to greet them.

'I'm serious about the time, Ella.' Kate glanced anxiously at her watch.

Ella ignored her, waiting for the moment she knew would come; the moment when Adonis would lift a squealing Alice Ariadne up onto his shoulders and, with her hands clutching at his hair, would begin carrying her the rest of the way to the house.

When he'd done so, she turned and, smiling, went inside to change her dress and pin her waist-length braid of hair into a heavy circlet on top of her head. Then, covering her hair with a black lace scarf, she blew a kiss to Christos's photograph and stepped into the street where, together with Kostas, Eleni and Georgio, she led Kate, Lewis, Daphne, Dimitri and Aminta and their children, Angelos and Rhea and their children, Pericles, Apollonia, Yanni, Nico, Adonis, Andre and Agata to the little white-walled church in the town square.

The service was very different from Kate and Daphne's experience of memorial services in England. During it, everyone held white flickering candles as, amid clouds of heavy incense, psalms, litanies and prayers were said and hymns sung. The *koliva* Eleni had made was in full view on a table that also held a crucifix and candelabra.

'Afterwards,' Pericles whispered to Kate, 'it will be taken to the refectory and we will all be given a small pot of it. The wheat in it symbolizes the circle of death and rebirth.'

It was two hours before Ella, Kostas, Eleni and Georgio led everyone back to the little house with a cypress tree in its courtyard for a traditional *glendi*.

By late afternoon the *glendi* was as noisy and as riotous as a wedding-party *glendi*. 'Which is,' Ella said to Kate as, led by Lewis and Georgio, the entire team began a foot-stamping *maleviziotis*, 'just as Christos would have wanted it. However, I'm ready for a little reflective peace and quiet. I'd like for you, me and Daphne to have a little time on our own. And I'd like us to have it in the Palace of Minos.'

Whenever the three of them had been together, it had always been Kate who had driven the Sally and she drove it now, bowling down the hill, across the valley floor and up the narrow road that led to Knossos.

The light was smoking to dusk as they arrived and, apart from rabbits enjoying the last light of the day, the three-thousand year-old ruins of what had once been the mightiest palace in the western hemisphere were deserted.

They walked past the bust of Sir Arthur and the line of jacaranda trees that led across the paved west entrance court, instinctively making their way to the South Propylaeum, where the gigantic gypsum Horns of Consecration rose spectacularly against the flushed early-evening sky.

The plinth that fronted the horns was the same plinth Ella had once sat on with Sam, when they had so unexpectedly met up while the battle for the island had been raging; and it was where, on a very special afternoon before the war, Helmut had once take a photograph of Daphne.

She said now, sitting down on the plinth and hugging her

knees, 'This palace has played such a large part in all our lives, hasn't it? Without it, and without Kit being an archaeologist on the nearby tomb site, you would never have come to Crete, Kate. You would never have met Lewis and become a member of his team and, if you hadn't done so, Ella would never have come out to Crete to join you on the Kalamata Little Palace dig and would never have met and fallen in love with Christos – and it would never have become so much a part of my life, because although Sholto was posted here as a vice-consul, I wouldn't have come out here and joined him, if it hadn't been that you were both already here.'

'And now that we are all here again together, the way we once saw our future is finally about to happen.' The satisfaction in Ella's voice was immense.

Kate quirked a mystified eyebrow and Ella said, 'When the Little Palace dig starts again, Daphne is going to be a member of the team. It's what we always dreamed of, isn't it? The three of us working together – although, when we dreamed of it, we could never have imagined we would be working on a dig of such great importance.'

The sky had now spangled into dusk, and from somewhere close by an owl hooted.

Kate said, 'I think it's time you read the note Nathaniel sent to you, care of Lewis, Ella. That is, if you've got it on you.'

'Yes, I have. I didn't want to read it amid all the noise of the *glendi*.' She took it out of her jacket pocket. 'It won't be bad news, because if it had been, Lewis would have forewarned me.'

'No,' Kate said, betraying that she already knew what the news was. 'It isn't bad news.'

Daphne looked across at her with raised eyebrows.

Kate shot her a wide grin and waited for Ella's stunned reaction.

It came barely a heartbeat later.

'Oh!' she gasped, 'Oh, how *wonderful*! How absolutely un-believable!' The note dropped to her lap as she pressed both hands against her cheeks in stunned disbelief. 'Nathaniel has had correspondence with the director of the Archaeological Museum in Heraklion, and the director has agreed that from now on there will be a card on the cabinet of the necklace that Christos found, naming Christos as the finder and the year in which he found it. Oh, isn't that amazing of Nathaniel – and isn't it incredible that I should get the news today, of all days?'

Tears of gratitude and joy streamed down her cheeks.

'We should have brought champagne,' Daphne said, 'because news that deserves champagne doesn't end with yours, Ella.'

She was seated between Kate and Ella and, as they both swivelled to look at her, she said, her face radiant, 'I received a letter the week before I left London. Someone wants to see me. It means my being away for a week or two, but when I return I'll not only be in the throes of a scorching grand passion, I'll also be bringing a highly qualified team member back with me.'

Kate's eyes widened.

Ella's jaw dropped.

Kate said, hardly able to believe it, 'You're going to Switz-erland?'

Ella said, 'And bringing Helmut back with you?'

'Yes,' Daphne said, 'and if that news doesn't deserve cham-pagne, then I don't know what does!'

Acknowledgements

Huge thanks are due to my wonderful publisher, Wayne Brookes, and to my always supportive editor, Catherine Richards. Thanks are also due to the rest of the formidable Pan Macmillan team, especially to copy editor Mandy Greenfield, editorial manager Kate Tolley and proofreader Eugenie Woodhouse. At Curtis Brown I owe thanks to my agent, Sheila Crowley, who has always been there when needed, and to Abbie Greaves. Other people I am indebted to are Janet Kidd, Polly Pemberton, Philippa Stamatakis and Jeffrey Vernes. Last, but by no means least, I could have had no better companion when trekking the remoter parts of Crete's mountainous hinterland than my husband, Mike.

Select Bibliography

Antony Beevor, *Crete: The Battle and the Resistance*
Alan Clark, *The Fall of Crete*
Artemis Cooper, *Cairo in the War: 1939–45*
Murray Elliott, *Vasili: The Lion of Crete*
Joan Evans, *Time and Chance*
Xan Fielding, *Hide & Seek*
Richard G. Geldard, *The Traveller's Key to Ancient Greece*
J. W. Graham, *The Palaces of Crete*
Anna Michailidou, *Knossos: A Complete Guide to the Palace of Minos*
Dilys Powell, *An Affair of the Heart*
Dilys Powell, *The Villa Ariadne*
George Psychoundakis, *The Cretan Runner*